Royal Di-lemma
By: Mike Rollin

"ROYAL DI-LEMMA" is a work of fiction. This novel is a product of the author's imagination. The characters, incidents and dialogues, organisations and events portrayed here are not to be construed as real.

Credits:
Publisher: MRL Productions, LLC
Cover Photo: Gate at Buckingham Palace by Radiusimages
Author Photo: Tiffany Studio
Publishing Advisor: Gerard Theurin
British/English Edit: Professional Editing Services & Sandra Grierson
Partner: Gary L. Marvel

ISBN   978-0-9797677-0-8

For information on other mystery novels by Mike Rollin, visit the web site: **mrlproductions.net**

Royal Di-lemma

FROM THE AUTHOR

Most Artists, composers, writers, or designers, are often called gifted. But really they are slaves, at the mercy of that intangible and unpredictable spirit called inspiration.

He who pays his visits spasmodically and at the most inopportune moments. He shoots the seeds of ideas that translate into visions, music and words, for posterity.

This writer is no stranger to the rule and Royal Di-Lemma like all enjoyable journeys or operas will start slowly, introducing you to the characters, take your time, don't be in a hurry.

It will then pick up the pace and build into a crescendo, that will make you feel part of the cast.

Then as you read further it will bring you back down to earth again, at the finish leaving an indelible question mark on your heart.

I hope that you enjoy the experience, as much as I have enjoyed putting these visits of inspiration into my own words.

Preface

This Royal Family has always been an institution. Generally they've been well respected, apart from a few glitches, such as the odd abdication, along with a trio of divorces and a number of scandalous rumors, some proven, others not.

They are what they are: a group of foreign imports who dismissed their given name then adopted the name of one of England's finest historic castles.

Over the decades they have continued to prosper and are recognised as one of the richest families in the world. Until recently they'd paid no taxes whatsoever.

Lately their image has become somewhat tarnished, resulting from three divorces of their current generation: three sons and one daughter. Their dirty linen has been washed openly in public for all to see.

Of the current vintage, the first son and heir to the throne married the daughter of a nobleman, in what seemed a fairy tale marriage watched by the whole world, but this marriage seemed doomed from the outset. However, his princess was not as easily dismissed as the two from the family's other failed marriages. Although harshly stripped of her royal title, her image and popularity grew beyond that of the dynasty. She was the most popular and loved of all the 'royals' worldwide until her tragic death where she died alongside her lover, the son of an Arab multi-millionaire.

This horrific event stunned the whole world. She died a sad, horrible death in the back of a wrecked car down a darkened Paris underpass.

WAS SHE PUSHED OR DID SHE FALL? Was this tragic death an accident or was she murdered?

Royal Di-lemma

Inspector Hank Marlin had been Princess Anna's personal bodyguard at the palace since her inclusion in the Royal Family. He was a highly trained member of the Royalty Protection Squad, or A1 as it was also known. Hank suspected it was murder. So did Michael Meadows, Private Secretary to the princess.

Both men became determined to get to the bottom of their princess's death, whatever the cost. They followed a trail of intrigue, treachery, murder and terror. They battled with massive odds coming at them from all directions, emanating from three different factions:

The Palace Mafia: Determined to put a stop to the princess's run of overwhelming popularity, which now overshadowed the whole family and endangered its continuance. They were prepared to try anything — maybe even to the point of employing foreign assassins. This was a contract of paramount importance. The aim: put an end to her relationship with her Arab lover at any cost.

Government Agencies: Instructed to bring an end to her frivolous relationship. They were informed that she intended to marry and could even be pregnant by a Muslim.

Her ex-husband John is the current heir to the throne. If crowned king, he would also become head of the Church of England. Anna's eldest son, George, is also a future king. Some say the monarch could abdicate, step over John and name George as king.

In either event, any offspring, male or female, would be a half brother/sister to this future King of England. **The aim: succeed in stopping her, whatever the cost.**

The Arab Mafia: A paid team of experts whose job was to ensure that nothing got in the way of this blossoming relationship. The paymaster was her lover's father, who can already see himself moving in royal circles. Money was no object. The aim: succeed whatever the cost.

With the addition of the mixed interests of the CIA and Mossad lending a hand to British government agencies, Hank and Michael's lives eventually became worthless.

The Royals were fighting for their very existence.

Could the Royal Dynasty crumble and fall? Why not?
The Great British Empire did!

Introduction

The Majestic Palace Hotel, Paris 1997

The black Mercedes stood in the shadows at the rear of the Paris hotel, engine purring quietly, lights extinguished, awaiting its celebrity passengers.

At the front of the hotel the black Bentley Turbo was parked, glistening in the bright hotel lights. It was almost totally surrounded by unpopular members of the tabloid press: hoards of ugly, vulture-like specimens of humanity haggling, arguing and squabbling for position — the dreaded paparazzi were there in force.

A chauffeur sat in the driver's seat with a blank expression on his face, knowing full well that these ugly parasites were going to be disappointed. They continued to shout and argue, almost engulfing the car, just like a flock of seagulls scrambling around a few crumbs of bread. There was a crescendo of noise from the 'seagulls' as a group moved quickly from the front entrance of the hotel.

The heavy bodyguards surrounding a couple pushed and glared at the frantic crowd, as cameras and shutters clattered in unison. The woman had a shawl pulled over her head; the man had completely covered his with a copy of a newspaper as they scurried with their protectors toward the waiting limousine. The mob closed in around them like the waters of an ebbing tide around a doomed sand castle.

At that precise moment the revolving doors at the rear of the hotel began to spin noiselessly. Paul Gastard, the French driver, emerged from the hotel followed by Gavin Jones, a bodyguard, whose trained eyes searched the darkness, his ears alert for any sounds of the press.

Close behind him a couple came out through the doors holding hands. The woman's head was covered with a headscarf, her collar was pulled up high around her face touching her dark sunglasses. The man too, was camouflaged under a large-brimmed hat. The bodyguard never once took his eyes off the street; he heard the final thuds behind him as the rear doors closed confirming to him that his valuable passengers had entered the vehicle. Gavin Jones then slid effortlessly into the front passenger seat, closing the door behind him, but not before he heard the sound of heavy footsteps coming out of the darkness accompanied by loud voices.

"Move it, lets go!" he yelled at the driver, as a group of photographers emerged from the shadows sprinting towards the car. They stopped in their tracks thwarted; only exhaust fumes remained as the big car sprang forward into the darkness, its tyres squealing. An acrid stench of burning rubber hung in the still night air; the car's bright red rear lights reflecting on their angry faces as the focus of their attention, and livelihood, roared off into the Paris night.

One solitary motorcycle followed in pursuit.

Buckingham Palace: The Offices of Her Majesty the Queen, 1992

Her Majesty the Queen sat at her desk drumming her fingers irritably as she read a newspaper. She became more furious by the minute, suddenly grabbing the publication and screwing it up into a tight ball then flinging it the length of the room. Once again the headlines showed her daughter-in-law on the front page in the company of a popular male tennis star.

The Queen's knuckles began to whiten as she gripped the arms of her chair, which promptly went spinning as she jumped to her feet shouting for her secretary, Sir Geoffrey Bowles, who appeared in the doorway to the office looking very concerned.

"Your Majesty?" the aide asked.

"This sister-in-law of yours is testing our patience to the limit!" She slapped the palm of her hand uncharacteristically on the desk as she spoke.

"Have you seen the latest escapade today?" she snapped.

"Yes, your Majesty, I'm afraid I have."

"Get her secretary on the phone right now!" She paced across the room hands clasped behind her back, lips pursed. He'd never seen her in such a rage.

"And make an appointment for Princess Anna to see me as soon as possible." She spun round quickly on her toes. "No, never mind! I'll damn-well do it myself."

"But your Majesty, I think it would be better..."

"Get her secretary on the phone right now! Do it this minute. Do you hear me damn it?" Her voice was now raised to a shout.

Kengsington Palace, 1997

"Come in!" Princess Anna shouted as Michael Meadows, her private secretary, stood in the doorway to her room.

"Good morning Ma'am, and what a lovely morning it is too. Here's your mail."

"What kind of a day are we to have today?" she asked.

"A pretty quiet one it seems Ma'am; no real highlights, nothing especially exciting." Michael left the princess to her mail and coffee.

No real highlights nothing especially exciting, if only he knew, she thought as her attention strayed from the opened letters in front of her. She sat staring into space, deep in thought, her mind working overtime. During the last conversation with her current lover, she'd agreed, rightly or wrongly, that he should make arrangements for her to visit his family doctor in Cairo, Egypt.

They had jointly agreed that Anna's suspected, but not yet confirmed, pregnancy would tragically have to be terminated right away, otherwise the knock-on effect would be disastrous to her sons, the Royal Family and, indeed, to the country.

This visit was planned for early next week. Anna was scheduled to make a trip to the Bosnian mine fields and would divert secretly to Cairo en-route back to London. He would be there to meet her.

This was one journey that Anna didn't relish in the least. She would be more than pleased when it was all over. *How on earth did I get myself into this situation?* She wondered, as she felt the pressures building up on her.

She'd thought at long last that her life was becoming more enjoyable and relaxed, those awful dreary days at the palace had begun to fade into distant, bad memories. She had begun to feel free, and now this. *Why is it that things never seem to go right for me?* She thought to herself. She was just about to reach for her pill box as the phone rang.

"Here's a pleasant surprise for you; it's Hank Marlin on the phone Ma'am," said Michael, the pleasure of the unexpected call reflecting in his voice.

"Get his number; I'll call him right back," She was learning from Gavin Jones, her boyfriend Raffi's bodyguard.

"Use the mobile when you can," he'd said.

"Ma'am, how are you?" Inspector Marlin exclaimed as he answered his cell phone. "Thanks for coming back so quickly. Life has become quite boring since they took me off your detail, Ma'am."

After the usual pleasantries had been exchanged the princess said:

"So what's the problem, Hank — what can I do for you?"

"It's really what I can do for you, Ma'am," he replied hesitantly. "Do you think we could meet very soon? There are a couple of things I feel that you should really know about."

"Why, certainly Hank. It all sounds a bit hush, hush. Where are you now?"

"I'm just leaving the rear of Kensington Palace. We've just finished an escort detail with the Queen Mum."

"Come up right away, I don't have any appointments for the rest of the day," she said pausing, looking for Michael's confirmation, as he walked into the room. He nodded in agreement.

"Are you sure that's going to be alright, Ma'am?"

"I'm absolutely positive. Come right up, Hank."

"Get the Granada ready Michael, will you please?" said Anna, "I'm going to have an hour or two out with the inspector."

"That will be great for you. It's been such a long time since you saw Hank. I know how much you've missed his company." Michael had a genuine look of pleasure on his face. For the last few days he'd felt that all was not right with the princess; something seemed to be bothering her, she was beginning to look pale and nervy, like she was during her palace days.

"I want you to come along too, Michael; there are some things that I need to talk with you both about, in absolute secrecy. You two are the closest confidants that I have. Off you go and get into some casual gear," the princess said with an exaggerated bossy smile, her hands on her hips. "I'm going to do the same. Call Hank back on his mobile and tell him to log in with security that he's doing a further a duty with the Queen's Mum. I'll explain why when he gets here."

When Anna entered the room Hank and Michael were both waiting for her. Michael had changed into casual clothes and had also loaned a sweater and jacket to Hank.

"Morning, Hank. How nice to see you again," Anna said very sincerely as she walked over and shook Hank's hand warmly. "How has life been treating you?"

"Fine Ma'am, but it hasn't been anywhere near as interesting since I came off your detail."

"Did you organise the car, Michael?"

"Well sort of, Ma'am. I thought we might take mine. It will be less conspicuous and no one in the car pool will know that you're out."

"Damn good thinking, Michael," said Anna grinning from ear to ear. She pulled a rather masculine tweed flat cap over her eyes and turned to the others.

"What are we waiting for? Let's go then." she spoke eagerly with the excitement of an ordinary young girl about to be taken on a special trip to the seaside.

Michael and Hank left by the rear exit, walked across the car parking area and climbed into Michael's BMW 5 series then drove back to the staff entrance where Hank spoke with the security man, purposely detracting his attention while Anna jumped lithely into the rear seat.

"Would you mind just keeping down on the seat until we are clear Ma'am?" Hank asked Anna. "There's always someone from the press lurking around outside here. If you would just cover yourself up with the travel rug, we can be absolutely sure of not arousing any suspicion," he added.

The gate security policeman was already out of his kiosk as their car drew up. The officer saw Michael.

"Mornin' Mr Meadows," he said, looking across to the front passenger seat. He saluted again. "Mornin' inspector. You're becoming quite the regular today, sir," he said to Hank as the car moved on. They drove off down the road and were soon coasting along the Thames embankment before crossing the river and heading south.

"You can come out now, Ma'am," said Hank as Anna surfaced, shaking her blonde locks and replacing her cap.

"Where are we?" she said in that excited schoolgirl tone, anticipating an adventure.

"We're just about to cross Battersea Bridge Ma'am. I thought we might hit the A23 then shoot down to Brighton. We can sit and talk on my boat there without any fear of interference. The traffic doesn't look too bad, so we should be there in an hour and a half."

"Splendid idea, Michael. How are you off for time, Hank?" asked the princess.

"I'll need to check in. I was on very early this morning, so I will sign off for the rest of the day. I could use a good day out; I can't remember when I last took a day off."

"Well that's settled that," said Anna, slapping the palms of her hands on her knees in conclusion, and pushing her head back into the restraint.

The trip to the coast was uneventful; Hank had called in on his cell phone, clearing his absence officially.

"How did we ever get on without those things?" asked Anna, referring to the cell phone. "Raffi's bodyguard says we must use them all of the time to avoid tapping."

"I'm afraid that's not quite correct," Hank interjected.

"There are scanners now that make eavesdropping easy. I think your man needs to get up to date. Admittedly, the mobile phone is easier to move around and has to be re-found by the listener each time, but if they know your location, it's a piece of cake. If you really have to use them make sure to talk in code and don't use names. Sorry to disillusion you, Ma'am."

As they entered the rural outskirts of Brighton, Michael turned from the main road into a small village. He pulled up outside a thatch-roofed store on the well manicured, oak tree lined village green. He got out of the car and walked a couple of paces then turned and beckoned the other two to follow.

"Are you sure?" said Hank through the open window.

"Yes, come on; bring Anna too. This is my aunt's store. She's half blind and won't recognise her anyway!"

Anna followed the other two into the quaint little shop. A metal bell tinkled noisily as they opened the door.

"Watch this," whispered Michael, with a roughish grin on his face.

"Good morning young man," the old woman said from behind the counter as she squinted through a pair of very thick prescription lenses that were more akin to opera glasses.

"Morning missus. Got any Beluga caviar please?" She leaned across the counter, peering quizzically through the thick magnification.

"Belug.... Michael that's you isn't it?" She said, a smile breaking across her lined face.

"You almost had me going then, you bad boy! What a pleasant surprise though; how nice to see you."

"Aunt Mary, these are two friends of mine, Anna and Hank. We are going down to the boat for the day and we need a few supplies."

"Well help yourself; you know where they are. I'll go and make us all a nice cup of tea."

Hank followed her through to the back whilst Anna helped her secretary with the shopping. It reminded her of those special times skiing in Switzerland with her sons, during the rare après ski raids on the local delicatessen. She had just selected a packet of her favourite chocolate digestive biscuits when the doorbell began to tinkle as someone entered the store. Anna instinctively went out back to find Hank while Michael stayed behind the shelves.

A hefty, tall man walked up to the counter. He waited for about thirty seconds then rapped his knuckles on the wood surface.

"Hello, anybody home?" he shouted.

Michael's aunt appeared in the doorway behind the counter.

"Yes young man, what can I get for you today?"

"I'm trying to find my way to the Brighton boat marina," the man said. "Could you kindly direct me there?" He looked around the store as he spoke. Michael noticed particularly that he seemed to be checking the whole building, rather than perusing the goods. Aunt Mary gave him directions. He thanked her and went out of the store.

Michael went towards the window, saw the man pause and look at the BMW, and then bend down on one knee to fasten his shoelace, stumbling against Michael's car and almost falling over. Hank came to his side.

"That face looks a little familiar to me," said Hank, watching the man wipe the dust from his knees then climb into his car and drive off. Hank made a mental note of the registration number.

They thanked Aunt Mary for the tea, Michael paid for the supplies and they left for the boat.

The marina was a hive of industry, as most are. Michael maneuvered the car as close as possible to the boat.

"She's the forty-four Jeannue over there, called Royal Blue. Here are the keys, Hank. Take the princess straight below; I'll be there as soon as I've parked the car."

They were soon sitting below in the boat's salon.

"Well, this is a pleasant change," said Anna, as she stretched out on one of the comfortable sofas. She threw her hat onto the table and comfortably placed her hands behind her head.

"I'll take a look around up top," Hank said as he climbed the steep stairway to the cockpit. He walked along the deck to the bow of the boat, enjoying a stiff breeze that came off the ocean. He noticed that the boat next to Michael's was unoccupied. Everything on it was tied down and there were locks on the doors and hatches. He saw that there were two empty berths on the other side. Across the far side of the marina on the opposite wall, one boat seemed to be preparing to sail, then Hank caught a reflection coming from under the forward hatch on her deck.

The hatch was partially open. He caught a glimpse of binocular lenses just before the hatch was slowly closed down. He noticed the dish half-way up the mast. *It could be satellite navigation, or television, but it could well be a listening device. It's difficult to tell in this fast moving hi-tech world,* Hank thought to himself. He went below again.

"Would it pose much of a problem if we took the boat out for an hour?" Hank asked Michael.

"Well no, not really," answered Michael,

"In fact it's a really good day for a sail; the wind is just right."

"What do you say Ma'am?" Michael said to his boss.

"It's fine with me, I could think of nothing better right now."

"Then that's settled. Let's get things moving."

The two men moved to go topside, followed by the princess.

"If you don't mind, Ma'am, I think you ought to stay down here until we clear the harbour," Hank said. The princess looked somewhat disappointed, but didn't voice her feelings.

"Sorry, but it's better that way," said Michael with a shrug.

"That's what they're always saying to me," Anna replied, leaning heavily against the galley stove, her arms folded and a petulant expression on her face. They began to prepare the boat.

Michael was impressed by Hank's apparent knowledge.

"You've done this before haven't you?" Michael asked of the policeman.

"Yes. My father had a boat at Hamble for years. We used to race at Cowes every year. You could say it's in my blood," he replied.

"I'll start the engine; it needs a good run anyway," said Michael. Hank let go the aft ropes, then the forrard. Royal Blue slipped gracefully out of her mooring, all canvass still stowed.

Hank paid attention to the boat opposite. As Michael turned the boat to port the stern slewed around very close to the moored boat. Hank saw two men that he didn't recognise, and then they left the marina for the choppier waters of the sea.

Princess Anna's head popped up from the hatchway. She had found a knitted woollen cap that she was wearing along with a bright yellow anorak, and sporting a pair of oversize reflective sunglasses.

"How's that for the master of disguise?" she said with a broad grin as she sat down next to Michael in the cockpit, stretching her arms above, inhaling deeply.

"This is the life: no press, no snoopers, no eavesdroppers." As the princess spoke, Hank looked back towards the harbour. He saw the mast then the bow of a sailboat slipping out to sea. He noticed it was the boat that had been moored on the opposite wall of the harbour.

"Maybe we can discuss what we planned now," Anna said. "This conversation is for your ears only and must not be discussed with anyone. I mean absolutely nobody," She opened her eyes to their full extent to emphasise her point. She went on to tell them all that had happened over the last few months, of her involvement with her current beau Raffi Sahaed, her increasing fondness for him, then finally the news of her suspected pregnancy. Both men sat listening in stunned silence. Hank's face registered his appreciation of the seriousness of what the princess had just told them. He, above all, clearly understood the ramifications. He wondered deep down if Anna truly understood the dangers she faced. A shudder went through his frame as the princess continued.

"The trouble now is that we are being followed everywhere we go. Raffi has some good security people, especially one very good and devoted personal bodyguard, who also takes extra care of me."

"When you say you are being followed, do you see the people? Do you know who they are?" Hank asked.

"No, not exactly. Wherever we go, when the rooms are swept electronically for devices, invariably bugs are found. These people are most certainly not press," said Anna.

"You can bet your bottom dollar on that," Hank said, looking around suspiciously at the sailboat behind them.

"Ma'am, what you've just said petrifies me. I really don't like the sound of this at all. When we get back to town I'm going to get my ear to the ground, see what I can pick up from the palace mafia. I've heard nothing that would concern me so far, but then, they wouldn't tell me anything. They know where my allegiance lies, but believe me Ma'am…"

"Please call me Anna will you Hank; I would much prefer it that way."

"Of course Anna," said Hank, and continued: "This matter is extremely serious and could have some very grave consequences. There must be a number of conflicting interests at work here. What you have to do is try and figure out which ones are which."

"What do you mean by 'conflicting interest'?" Anna asked.

Hank looked astern as the other boat was now less than half a mile behind them.

"Do you think you can cut the engine and let us drift for a while?" Hank asked Michael. "At the risk of seeming mysterious would you mind just going below for a minute or two Anna?"

"Is something the matter?" she asked.

"Please do as I ask Ma'am. Sorry, I mean Anna."

The princess went below.

"The boat behind has been following us since we left the marina," he whispered to Michael. "I want to see what they will do now that we have stopped."

They sat; Hank talking about one of his Cowes races as the boat rolled and pitched uncontrollably in the water. The sea was not rough, just a good, regular swell.

"I hope Anna doesn't suffer from sea sickness; this is a healthy roll here" said Michael, as he hung on to the edge of the seat.

"I hadn't thought about that," said Hank, putting his head down the hatchway and asking Anna if she was alright.

"Seems fine," he said to Michael. Looking back they both saw the other boat turn off at right angles. They watched until it had gone a good three or four miles away.

"You can come up now, Anna," Hank shouted to the princess. A very white and drawn face appeared at the hatchway.

"I don't think I could have coped with another minute of that," she said, forcing a smile as she wildly gulped the fresh air down into her lungs, trying desperately to swallow continually in defiance of her stomach's obvious intentions!

Anna sat down between Michael and Hank. As they enjoyed the peace and quiet and solitude it wasn't long before the colour slowly began to return to Anna's cheeks.

"There is just one other thing that I haven't told you," Anna said as she looked down at her feet and splashed the small puddle of seawater with the toe of her canvas shoe. Her voice and lips began to wobble as she spoke.

"If the pregnancy is confirmed, I'm going into a clinic in Cairo next week, to have a termination." She broke down and began to sob uncontrollably. Hank put his arm around her shoulder as her emotions took over completely.

He looked shocked and was very concerned. He turned to look again for the other boat, which was coming back in their direction, but was still a few miles off; too far distant to eavesdrop, he assumed.

Anna slowly began to compose herself, sitting between her two close friends.

"Anna, you must try understand that the forces at work here have different motives. Let's start with the only one that can be thrilled about this whole affair, Raffi's father, Anwar Sahaed. I'm sure you're aware of his many failed attempts to obtain British citizenship and the reasons why he continues to fail. Does he know of the possible pregnancy?" Hank asked.

"Not that I'm aware," the princess replied.

"Don't be too sure about that. You most certainly must not underestimate that man. If you go to their family doctor in Cairo for the diagnosis, you can bet that Sahaed will find out. To him that will be the best news he's heard since he last talked with Allah.

"I imagine the other interested parties are the British Government and most certainly the palace mafia. In which case, it's in both of their interests to have this relationship brought to an end as speedily and efficiently as possible. Of course, there is no way that those two factions will work together on this.

"In a nutshell, for Government, read MI6. Their instructions will be to stop a potential marriage between the mother of a future King of England and a Muslim. As any resultant offspring would be half brothers or sisters to the future British monarch, a marriage of this sort is absolutely unconscionable to them and must be stopped at any costs.

"On the other hand, while the palace mafia will imagine the same scenario, they will also see this as a direct threat to the very continuance of the monarchy. That means that they will regard both you and Raffi as a direct threat. In either case you cannot win; you are in extreme danger.

"If you ever needed security you are going to need it right now, Anna. I would suggest that you suspend all public engagements for a while and keep away from any contact with Raffi, or for that matter, any member of the Sahaed family. In the meantime, I will find out whatever I can about activities at the palace." They all sat in complete silence for what seemed an age as the implications sunk in.

Hank looked around a full 380 degrees and seeing that the other boat had disappeared he assumed it had gone back to the marina.

The sea had now flattened considerably and the wind was picking up slightly.

"Hey, let's get some canvas out; the conditions are perfect!" Michael said, breaking the silence. He'd not said a word throughout the whole conversation between the other two.

"An excellent idea," replied Hank. Anna sat back in the cockpit watching the two experts as they put up the sails. At first slack, the canvas flapped and chattered noisily before the wind, then as ratchets began to whir ropes were tightened and set, the sailboat lurched gently and silently into action heeling over as she gathered speed. Hank let the spinnaker out as the sailboat picked up further momentum. "We'll tack along the beach for an hour or so. Mind your head when the boom comes round as we turn, Anna.

"Fancy a sandwich anybody?" Michael asked as two heads nodded enthusiastically in unison.

They were now nearly four miles offshore; they had sailed for a couple of hours and were just about to negotiate their final turn opposite Hove, a town west of Brighton. As usual the unpredictable English weather had started to blow up.

Michael and Hank knew only too well how quickly that sea could change, and change it had. The wind from the west was blowing up even more. Directly behind them the sky had darkened, even blackened, as very heavy rain began to drive at them, which was quickly turning to hail. Within minutes, hailstones half the size of golf balls clattered and banged noisily on the boat's deck. Hank and Michael had donned foul weather gear. Anna was by now standing halfway down the partially closed hatchway, which sheltered her somewhat from the worsening conditions.

"We've got too much canvas up for this wind," Michael shouted at the top of his voice as the wind began to howl, pointing aloft at the same time. Hank had read Michael's lips as he tied on a safety harness. He clipped it to the steel cable rails, then slowly inched forward along the dangerously shifting deck. He had to bring down the main sail and quickly. He knew from experience that in such conditions it was the right thing to do and then they could either revert to the engine, or just sit out the storm.

He struggled against the movement of the sailboat as the deck kept on coming up to meet him. They were, at that very moment, going into a head sea. Enormous waves were coming directly over the bow, and had twice put him smartly onto his back. As he struggled to his knees for the second time he decided to crawl along for the remainder of the way. Then above the noise of the storm he thought he'd heard the sound of an engine. He dismissed it as a figment of his imagination, or the howling of the wind, but then he definitely heard it again just as another massive mound of freezing cold water hit him full in the face.

He hung on for dear life and cleared the stinging seawater from his eyes just in time to catch a glimpse of a large white hull powering down directly at the bow of Royal Blue. He saw by the wake that the powerboat was moving at very high speed.

Michael also saw the powerboat at the same time. He knew that the sails were still set so he was sailing very close to the wind. Nevertheless, he threw the wheel hard to starboard. Being so close to the wind, the bow came round in an instant, the boom flew across faster than he'd anticipated, hitting him heavily on the side of the temple, opening up a massive gash and knocking him down onto the floor of the cockpit - unconscious.

At that same instant the wind howled through the cloth as the sailboat jibed, making a complete about-turn somehow, amazingly staying upright. The thwarted powerboat, was now presented with only a partial view of the port side and rear of the sailboat. She smashed powerfully into the dinghy hanging from the stern of Royal Blue, ripping it and the davits from the boat and at the same time tearing away most of the starboard rear quarter of the Royal Blue, as gallons of water rushed into her hull. The damaged powerboat's bow shot skywards, almost becoming airborne as it screamed off disappearing into the storm.

Anna struggled to help her secretary as his seemingly lifeless body was being thrown like a soaked rag doll around the floor of the cockpit. The blood that was now pouring from the wound was diluted by the constant flood of seawater. Anna became aware of Hank's voice; he was standing next to her holding the ships radio mike in hand.

"Mayday, mayday, mayday! This is the sailing yacht Royal Blue. We have been holed in the rear and are taking on water fast. We are sinking and require emergency rescue. Mayday, mayday, mayday," then Anna heard the explosion of a distress rocket pistol as Hank fired it, the red flare tailing heavenwards lighting up the darkened sky.

"Royal Blue, Royal Blue, this is the Shoreham Lifeboat Station. We read you loud and clear. We will launch the boat immediately, do you read, Royal Blue, come back?"

"Roger, Shoreham Lifeboat Station. My position is approximately ten miles south, southeast, of Hove. I repeat ten miles south southeast of Hove; we are in heavy seas and taking on water fast; we have lost our dinghy, do you read me Shoreham, come back?"

"Royal Blue, Royal Blue, we read you. We are under way; we should be with you in approximately ten minutes. Are there any casualties Royal Blue, come back?"

"We have one man hurt with serious head injuries, losing blood heavily. He's unconscious." Another voice broke into the transmission.

"Shoreham rescue, this is Royal Air Force air sea rescue chopper A.R.5. We have the damaged craft in view. We will go in and take the injured man off, do you read, Shoreham?"

"Roger, loud and clear A.R.5, will rendezvous at the boat. Shoreham Rescue out, and standing by on channel sixteen."

"Royal Blue R.A.F. air sea rescue, come in Royal Blue."

"Go ahead R.A.F. A.R.5."

The rear end of the sailboat began to fall noticeably below the water-line, while the bow began to rise. The lifeboat came into view at the same time as the scream of the helicopter hovered above. Hank heard the conversation between the two rescue craft. They had jointly agreed that it would be better to transfer everyone to the lifeboat, get away from the doomed sailboat, and then transfer Michael to the chopper.

The lifeboat had made two unsuccessful attempts to come alongside. On the third attempt Hank had caught a rope and held on knowing that tying off to a sinking boat is not the cleverest of ideas. As Royal Blue was sinking, she tended to move around in the water less than before, but it was obvious that they could not get Michael to the lifeboat.

One of the chopper's crew came down sitting astride the gurney. After an amazing piece of handling, the gurney and its passenger were put safely into the half-submerged cockpit. The white and still lifeless form of Michael was strapped in and quickly taken aloft, followed by the crewman. Then the helicopter rushed off toward the shore.

After a few attempts Hank and the princess were taken aboard the lifeboat. As it sped away towards the shore and safety, they saw the bow of Royal Blue raise perpendicular, and then slide dramatically beneath the surface of the angry waves.

Anna and Hank sat outside a private room at Brighton's General Hospital. Anna still wore her woollen hat. She had the collar of the yellow anorak pulled up so that only her eyes were visible. As yet she had not been recognised. She was in the habit of carrying a fictitious ID.

The police and rescue had required full details, which Hank had given, showing his own police ID and managing to skillfully sidetrack any serious questioning of Anna. Michael had just come out of the operating theatre with a hairline fracture to his skull and with some serious lacerations to the side of his head, which required stitches. There was no brain damage, but he was said to be badly concussed. The sailboat had sunk, and at this stage it was too deep to consider re-floating her. Hank and the princess eventually left the hospital by taxi to go back to the marina; luckily the hospital staff had located Michael's car keys amongst his clothing. They sat silently for a few moments in his car, both with the same question on their minds.

Was it an accident? They would like to have thought so, but each knew better. All that expanse of water, miles and miles of it, and a powerboat had to hit them by accident. The odds were phenomenal!

Hank moved out of the parking space, then drove off toward the road. He stopped suddenly, turning the car around and heading back to the parking entrance.

"Where are we going?" Anna asked.

"I want to take a very quick look around the marina. If the other boat came from there, and it was put back, it's bound to look a bit of a mess. It can't possibly still be out at sea in that storm."

They drove up to the barrier. Hank pulled the ticket from the machine, the arm was raised, and they drove into the marina once more, this time much closer to the mooring.

Anna followed Hank around to the opposite side from Michael's mooring. The sailboat that had initially followed them was there, tied up and unoccupied.

Hank didn't want to spend too much time with Princess Anna out in the open, but he had thought it better to bring her than leave her unattended in the car. It was then that they both saw the commotion across in the empty spaces next to Michael's vacant berth.

There were about twenty people, including a number of police officers, standing around a boat that had obviously sunk at the mooring. Hank and Anna rushed across the footbridge and came up to the scene. A man, seemingly the owner of the stricken boat, was rushing around waving his arms in the air frantically.

"I purposely don't hide keys aboard like many others do. How the hell did they get the bloody thing started?" he asked a nearby policeman. "Look they've ripped out the whole of the back end from my boat I've only had the damn thing for two weeks," the owner said, looking down with anger at the half submerged wreck surrounded by the floating debris of personal belongings.

"There was a collision earlier out there, sir; a sailboat was sunk. We can safely assume that your boat was the other vessel in the collision," said the policemen.

Hank was searching the faces in the crowd. He looked for any signs of reaction or potential trouble that could harm Anna. Then he saw the face of a man that he recognised. It was the man he'd seen earlier that day at the village store. He glanced at Anna then looked back again, but the man was gone.

. "Come on Anna, we've seen all that we need to see here," he said to the princess. They turned to walk back to the car.

"Excuse me, sir, just one moment before you leave." Hank turned to see one of the uniformed policemen walking towards them.

"Do you mind if I ask you both a couple of questions before you depart?"

"I don't think there's anything we can help you with officer, we only just arrived," Hank said irritably to the constable.

"Just a few quick questions, sir."

"Officer, here's my parking ticket, look it's timed only five minutes ago," Hank said passing the timed, dated parking ticket to the constable.

"That's fine, sir, sorry to bother you. Carry on."

The ride back to London was somewhat of an anti-climax for the two of them. They traveled the first few miles in complete silence, both reflecting on their almost early invite to their after life.

"Things are getting very serious, Hank," said Anna. "I'm scared," she added in a whisper.

"You'd better believe it Ma'am, sorry, Anna; your life is in real danger. There's absolutely no point in asking for protection from the palace and by the same token you can hardly go to the police.

"If you are going to continue your relationship with this young man, and knowing you Anna, I suspect that you will, your security has to be beefed up considerably. Maybe I should meet with this new bodyguard of yours — off the record. Let me at least check him out and at the same time see what he's made of, and how good he really would be if the chips were down."

"I wish that you were around now Hank," she said, turning to the inspector.

"So do I Ma'am, sorry, I mean Anna. Damn! I'll never get used to using your Christian name Ma'am. It's no good, you are my princess and that's what you will always be to me Ma'am," said Hank, smiling. "I would give anything to be taking care of you now. This whole business scares the living daylights out of me."

Hank drove up to the entrance of Kensington Palace. They were stopped by security, the princess now sitting openly in the front passenger seat. Hank parked Michael's car next to his own. Before he left the car Hank turned to Anna and said; "I'll see what I can find out from the grape vine I'll also meet with your man as agreed. Please Ma'am, I beg of you, consider my suggestions and cut your public appearances, give your relationship a break, if only until the dust settles a bit."

"I can't. No, won't do either of those things, Hank. You above all people know the life I've had to live for the past few years. Now that I've met someone at last who means something to me, someone who cares about me, not for my position or for what I'm worth, I'll be damned if I'll let the bloody Royal Family mess this one up!"

"Well then, that being the case Ma'am, please take a lesson from today. There is no doubt: someone actually tried to kill us all. Not my imagination Ma'am, but fact. Be assured, they will try again, not pie in the sky, a certainty. I want you to promise me that you will contact me at any time for any reason, however silly it may sometimes seem to you.

"Please listen to your bodyguard at all times. Don't use the phone when you don't want to be overheard, remember what I told you about cell phones. Wherever you are, on or off a phone, one device or another can find you and overhear you when you speak. Finally you are up against very clever highly trained professionals, perhaps some of the best in the world. To stay ahead, your people have to be better than them. Get Raffi's father to put some real money into keeping you both alive. God alone knows he's got plenty of that."

They both left the car, shaking hands. I'll be in touch soon," Anna held onto his hand. Hank, once again, without you around today, I would be dead. Inspector Hank, my dear friend, I thank you from the bottom of my heart."

She leaned forward and kissed him tenderly on the cheek, then walked off towards the Palace. He stood for a while watching with a heavy heart, as the princess entered the building, he climbed into his car shaking his head pensively. Anna turned as Hank drove off, knowing in her heart of hearts his fears were justified and he was right in what he had said to her. Back in her apartments, she called the hospital, checking on Michael's condition.

Kensington Palace 1992

Anna began to go back over the events leading up to her divorce and eventual dismissal from the ranks of the Royal Family, but not before being stripped of the title 'Her Royal Highness'.

She clearly remembered that gloomy morning back in 1992 at her apartments inside Buckingham Palace. She'd awakened with a start as her personal maid knocked on the door and then entered the room. Her mind was in turmoil as a result of a realistic and dramatic dream. She couldn't remember all of it, though what she could recall sent a shudder through her body. Her maid began to pull back the heavy drapes, allowing the daylight to burst into the room.

"I trust you slept well, it's another drab day, Your Royal Highness," she said as yet another maid entered the adjacent room pushing a breakfast trolley, who then turned and curtsied through the open door towards Anna who'd nodded in recognition.

She slipped her arms robotically into the robe held out by the first maid, and walked on through to her rooms.

"It looks like another busy day, Ma'am," said the maid as she prepared the breakfast table, carefully laying out the usual array of newspapers for the princess's perusal.

As Anna sat alone in the silence and solitude of the room, she stared at the fork in her hand that pushed scrambled eggs aimlessly around the plate, as though by another's hand. Taking one token nibble from the corner of a piece of toast, she threw her napkin down in disgust, kicked the chair away, and picked up the collection of newspapers.

Walking slowly toward her sitting room, she paused briefly to look down at the empty bed, then moved on quickly thinking of happier times.

It seemed a hundred years ago since she'd ridden in the historic fairy tale coach along the streets of London. Her Prince Charming by her side; the whole world seemed to rejoice.

Through the tumultuous shouts and roars of the largest gathering in history, even the peeling bells of St Paul's Cathedral were almost silenced by the sounds of her adoring public. This beautiful young woman had, just minutes before, become the future Queen. She shrugged her shoulders as she stared down at the newspapers, and wondered how things had deteriorated to the current state of affairs

Anna opened the first of the daily papers, seeing that yet again, the press had her in headlines across the front page. **'Princess Anna was seen leaving nightclub with tennis star.'** She felt like a damn goldfish in a glass bowl. Her fist screwed the edge of the pages as she clenched her teeth in a grimace of anger. Anna hated the press with a fierce passion. What did they want from her? Would she ever have a life of her own?

She reached across the coffee table and opened a small silver container, shaking it irritably as a number of small pills tumbled into the palm of her hand. Taking two, she threw them into the back of her mouth and swallowed emphatically. The princess was becoming dependent on these small pieces of chemistry: without her tranquilisers, and her uppers she doubted she'd get through the day.

A loud rapping on the door took her attention away from the newspaper; her maid entered the room.

"Your private secretary is here to see your Royal Highness. He says that the matter is most important."

"Show him in will you, and please throw these disgusting newspapers away."

Michael Meadows entered the room, looking a little harassed.

"Good morning to you Ma'am," bowing his head as he walked towards his princess.

"I er, suppose that you have already seen the newspapers this morning," he added hesitantly.

"Yes I have, is that why you wished to see me Michael?" The secretary shook his head.

"Ma'am, Her Majesty wishes to see you at your earliest possible convenience. She has asked me to get right back to Your Royal Highness, she sounded most put out, and as angry as I have heard her for some time. She actually called and spoke to me personally."

"You had better re-schedule my appointments then Michael; we mustn't keep the Queen waiting, now must we?"

"Her Majesty wishes to see you at 3:30 this afternoon Ma'am," said Meadows.

"Where am I to meet her?"

"Sir Geoffrey said he would give you those details over lunch, Ma'am."

"Thank you Michael," she replied as he left the room, and returned to the double spaced draft of a boring speech to the Women's Guild of Floral Decorators. Taking her pen, she promptly scored out a good fifty percent of the convoluted and meandering verbiage contained there, adding some humorous narratives, smiling inwardly as she envisaged the reaction of the strait laced, somber faced critics at such un-royal behaviour.

Later, she called a friend and arranged to meet at the weekend for a game of tennis at her club. Though it was one of the most exclusive in the south of England, she knew she couldn't expect a quiet game. Somehow the press would be there in force, with their clicking cameras and flashing lights, along with a myriad of personal gabbling comments and questions. *Why won't they leave me alone just once?* She thought but she knew better than that.

Prince John sat in his rooms staring down pensively at his hands, fiddling unconsciously with the seal ring on his little finger. He, too, had received the royal summons and was due to meet with his Mother in the next few minutes. He hadn't liked the tone of the summons one little bit. She sounded as angry as he'd heard her for many a year.

Number 10 Downing Street, 1992

The Prime Minister sat in his office. For the first time that day he relaxed back into the firm leather seat, his fingers interlocked across his stomach, the most recent cabinet meeting just over. Earlier, after the main agenda had been painstakingly covered to the full, the separate and important subject of the royal marriage was tabled.

Earlier in the House of Commons questions had been asked about recent Royal marital calamities, along with concerns of rumours regarding Prince John and Princess Anna.

At today's meeting, the foreign secretary described the situation as "a potential matrimonial disaster of national importance." Not only were questions being asked in the house, but also across the country. In fact questions were emanating from around the wide world.

"It is high time that these, and other questions, were put to the Royal Family," the Home Secretary had said tersely.

"For many years the Royals have been our best ambassadors. They are now in danger of becoming a laughing stock. Something needs to be done to repair this tarnished image," the Minister of Transport had added.

John Mannors sat upright in his chair as his deputy walked into the study of Number 10.

"What is the best way to broach the subject with Her Majesty?" The Prime Minister asked.

"Direct and to the point," was the swift reply. The Prime Minister picked up the phone to his Private Secretary.

"Get onto the palace. I want an audience with Her Majesty as soon as possible please."

John Mannors and his deputy then sat discussing the outcome of the recent meeting over a cup of tea, when the shrill ring of the phone brought the conversation to a sudden end.

"It's Sir Geoffrey Bowles for you Prime Minister."

"Sir Geoffrey. Thank you for returning my call so promptly."

"The pleasure is entirely mine Prime Minister. Her Majesty will see you tomorrow at 10:15am. Would you care to let me have the subject matter Prime Minister?"

"That is a little delicate; I would rather keep the matter to myself until I meet with The Queen."

"Prime Minister, you know how Her Majesty dislikes meeting without an agenda."

"Indeed I do, Sir Geoffrey, but this is one occasion when she will not be apprised of the subject matter. My visit pertains directly to the Royal Family and their private affairs, so I'm afraid that is my last word on the matter. I bid you good day, Sir Geoffrey," concluded the PM as he put the phone down. "Pompous twit! They still live in the dark ages!" he said as he stomped out of his office. He paused at the door. "I have real bad vibes about this affair, you know. I feel that serious trouble is brewing."

He left his office to go through to his private apartments, not really looking forward to his next meeting with the Queen.

London's West End 1992

Anwar Sahaed, resplendent in his sumptuous suite of offices looked around with pride and satisfaction. He strutted like a turkey cock across the thick Persian carpet. He looked down at busy Knightsbridge from a window of the most prestigious department store in the whole world, Harrobys. Not just a store, but also a British institution, known the world over.

"And I own it all," he said out loud, as he stood legs astride, his hands on his hips, a broad grin across his dark Arabic features. It had been an uphill battle over a long period of time, but he had eventually reigned supreme in the conquest to own the London megastore. Every possible hurdle that could be found had been placed in his way; eventually he had come through victoriously, but not without some significant financial assistance; the source of which continued to be a mystery to most financial pundits, and members of the Government. Since owning the store he had earned the reputation as a hard and somewhat tyrannical boss, who was as ruthless in his running of the business as he had been in the buying of it. This latest acquisition, along with his other prizes across the world, meant that he could continually feed his addiction, his favourite sensation in the whole world: the feeling of control, of immense power. London, Paris, Rome, Dubai. The world was his kingdom now.

The only thorn in his side, the one thing that had eluded him absolutely, was the refusal of the British Government to grant him a passport, or more importantly, British citizenship. As his attempts became more prolific, the refusals became more adamant.

"He may have bought Harrobys, but he certainly won't buy British citizenship," one senior Home Office official was heard to say.

Anwar Sahaed was to continue his quest that very day. He had a meeting with a member of parliament. In fact no ordinary member: he was The Right Honourable Lawrence Goodfellow MP and Under Secretary of State.

The Prime Minister's Office — Houses of Parliament

"Prime Minister, your next appointment is here: the Right Honourable Lawrence Goodfellow," the aide said, as the Under Secretary entered and walked across the room.

"Lawrence, my dear boy, do take a seat," said the PM shaking the other man warmly by the hand and gesturing towards an empty chair.

"The world treating you well of late?" he asked rhetorically, as he sat down behind his desk, picked up one of his phones and gave terse instructions to his Private Secretary. "No interruptions for the next few minutes. Hold all my calls, barring emergencies."

"Now, Lawrence, I believe that you want to bring up the subject, once more, of that irritating man, Anwar Sahaed."

"Yes John, the matter of his application for citizenship continues to be an ongoing irritant to us all. It's starting to become a running sore in my department. I would like to have some plausible explanation I can give him for the constant refusals of his repeated applications. Quite frankly, we're running short of excuses at the Home Office."

The PM looked down at the papers on his desk then looked up quizzically, pushing his spectacles up the bridge of his nose habitually as he spoke. John Mannors dropped his chin staring emphatically over the rims of his glasses.

"Lawrence, I don't ever want to hear any of my ministers or senior members, telling me that they are incapable of doing their job." He stabbed his forefinger down hard on the desk blotter as he spoke forcefully, and then went on. "Lawrence, we have investigated this man from every standpoint. We just cannot get an angle on the true source of his wealth; it continues to remain a complete mystery. There are some who believe that he is funded from unacceptable sources and while this shadow hangs over him there will be no change in the attitude of the Government, on this subject."

"John, you do, of course, appreciate that he's intimating substantial funds could be donated to the Tory party coffers, which as you know are badly in need of a boost prior to the oncoming general election."

Mannors stood up with an adamant posture and looked Lawrence directly in the eyes.

"That's even more reason to refuse the bloody man. He may have succeeded in the ownership of Harrobys, but while I control this Government, he most certainly won't buy us. I do hope and pray that you are not suggesting for one moment that..."

"I most certainly am not, Prime Minister. I only wanted to have a better understanding of the Government's reasons, before speaking to Mr Sahaed again. Are you aware of the meetings held between Sahaed and the Leader of the Opposition? The most recent was held last week. We are reliably informed that our friend is about to change his political allegiances. The matter of his citizenship has become the greatest issue of his life. He is becoming quite fanatical on the whole matter." The PM sat down heavily.

"You have my opinion, and my decision. Until such information is forthcoming to change things, the matter will rest." As Goodfellow walked towards the door, the Prime Minister said, "Do give my best wishes to Mary and the family, Lawrence." Goodfellow turned.

"Thanks John, I will. I don't suppose that you want to tell me the suspected source of Mr Sahaed's funds?"

"Afraid not old chap. That's really top secret; known only to the people at MI6 and of course, myself."

"Thanks for your time, John." Lawrence left the office none the wiser. John Manners then picked up his private phone and tapped out a number, which was answered after the first ring.

"Lawrence Goodfellow just left my office. He's been approached by Sahaed, who he says is offering incentives to him. Evidently Sahaed has already met with the opposition and one would assume he has made similar approaches to them. I wasn't sure whether you knew about his meetings. You most certainly couldn't know their content, that is, unless you have this and other offices bugged." When he had finished his brief conversation, the PM put the phone down to the chief of MI6. *I wouldn't put it past that lot to actually bug this office,* he thought as he took off his glasses with his left hand, pinching the bridge of his nose with the thumb and forefinger of his right, his eyes closed in thought.

Simpson's Restaurant the Strand London

The Rolls Royce drew silently up to the curb outside the restaurant. A chauffeur opened the rear door of the car and the diminutive figure of Anwar Sahaed stepped onto the pavement. Without looking round he strode briskly into the restaurant and climbed the stairs.

"Good afternoon, sir. I have your usual corner table. If you would care to come this way... your guest has arrived," the head waiter said as he walked off in front of Sahaed.

"Mr Sahaed," said his guest, standing up as his host neared the table.

"Please sit down," Sahaed said to the other man almost irritably, taking a seat as the waiter pulled back the chair subserviently.

"I am so glad you could make it today, and at such short notice too," he said to the Member of Parliament sitting opposite him.

"It's my pleasure entirely Mr Sahaed. I got your message at the last minute, so I had to switch a few appointments, but nevertheless here we are."

"May I get you something from the bar Mr Sahaed?" asked the waiter.

"Just a glass of mineral water," he replied, noting that his guest already had an alcoholic beverage in front of him.

The waiter quickly returned with the drink and took the order for lunch. The MP ordered the roast beef carved at the table, a dish that had made this establishment famous throughout the world. As a practicing Muslim, the host ordered a fish dish and salad.

"What is it that I can do for you?" asked the honourable MP. Sahaed did not answer immediately. He chewed noisily on his lettuce while carefully studying the other man's face, then looked directly into his eyes. His own intense beady eyes seemed to bore right through to the back of the politician's head. Dabbing his lips rapidly with his napkin, he moved over the table closer to him, saying very quietly and most deliberately:

"I want to achieve British citizenship, and I am prepared to pay any price to get it." His eyes had widened to twice their size, as he had leaned on the words 'any price.'

Sitting at the next table, the tall blonde-haired man, fiddled with his hearing aid then picked up the last fork full of roast beef, dipping it into the horseradish sauce.

"May I get you some more beef, sir?" the waiter asked the man. He got no reaction, so he tapped him lightly on the shoulder. "Would you care for some more beef, sir?" he spoke louder repeating his question.

"What? Oh, no. Thank you, no," the blonde man answered pointing his index finger to the hearing aid protruding from his ear. "Sorry, I didn't hear you the first time," he explained loudly and apologetically.

Anwar Sahaed had turned round looking slightly irked as the waiter's raised vocal interruption had cut across his own conversation, at such an important point too, noticing the deaf man he raised his eyes toward the ceiling. Then repeated his last words: "Any price. You hear me? I don't want you to commit yourself right away," Sahaed said to his guest, lowering voice considerably.

"I am prepared to make some very substantial donations to the party. I will make sure that you yourself receive sufficient reward for your efforts." His dark piercing gaze switched rapidly back and forth between the other man's eyeballs, watching for any reaction, almost as though he saw right down into his very soul. He sat back in his chair, his wrists resting loosely on the edge of the table. Any apparent tension had left his posture, as he dabbed at his mouth delicately with a napkin as though his lips were fine bone china. "Of course that can be done in any form that you may wish, from cash to property, a Swiss account, whatever you desire, it's entirely up to you."

The blonde MI6 agent at the next table adjusted his listening device as he heard...

"I don't want you to commit yourself right away I am prepared to wai...."

The blonde man looked up angrily as the conversation was suddenly cut off. A waiter had stood between him and the Arab, as he'd positioned the carvery trolley, blocking the remainder of the conversation.

"Damn!" the man whispered the oath, as he tried to move sideways, aiming his wrist microphone towards the next table.

"It's entirely up to you," he heard as the waiter moved away, then his eardrum was nearly burst open at the magnified tone, as the MP's beeper went off.

"If you'll excuse me Mr Sahaed, I must use the phone." The MP got up and went across the room. He returned in a few short minutes.

"I am afraid I have to rush off," he said apologetically to his host. "I will bear in mind what you've said and will most certainly be in touch soon."

"Here are a number of details that may help you in your research," said the Arab. He stood up and passed a rather stout envelope to the MP then shook his hand.

Shortly afterwards the Arab called for his bill, scribbled hurriedly across the bottom, threw down the pen, then got up and left the room. He visited the men's room then went down the stairs and out into the busy bustling Strand. He had hardly reached the curbside before his Rolls swept up to a halt.

"Take me to the club," he snapped at the driver, then sat back and tapped out a number on his cell phone.

"You are back then, Raffi," he said to his son, pressing forcefully on the button beside him as the darkly tinted and soundproofed glass divider closed off the rear of the car from the front.

"I want you to get the yacht ready for some guests next week. You will be host to a number of Government dignitaries that I will be inviting. I want the boat in Nice, ready to cruise and standing by from next Wednesday onwards.

Raffi, my son, I don't care what plans you have made, just cancel them. I don't want to hear another word on the matter, just see to it. I will be at the house tomorrow night."

Sahaed closed up the cell phone and pressed the intercom.

"Were there any calls for me during lunch?" he asked.

"None at all, sir," the chauffeur replied.

The car drew up outside a Mayfair club. The tall doorman strode purposefully across and opened the car door.

"Good afternoon Mr Sahaed, how nice to see you today," he said, as he discreetly palmed the five-pound note passed to him, without as much as dropping his eyes.

The Arab beckoned and as the taller man stooped, Sahaed whispered into his ear. The doorman replied:

"Yes sir, Lord Boothroyd is here; he was only just asking after you, sir."

The Arab strutted off into the club with a look of a determined terrier on his face. The hostess took his coat as he entered the reception area, then he walked across towards the bar and took an empty seat next to a portly man who sat staring blankly into space.

"Lord Boothroyd, how are you?" he asked the overweight peer. "You were miles away there."

"Anwar old boy, I was hoping I'd find you here. I seem to be having a bit of a problem since we last met."

"A problem, what kind of a problem is that George?" the Arab asked, looking apparently genuinely concerned.

"You remember the last time we talked you asked me if I could put some weight behind that application of yours? I think I may have been a little hasty when I refused to be of assistance. May I get you a drink?" the peer asked, a sad doleful look on his face

"I'll just have a soda water with ice, please George. Let's go and find a quiet table where we can talk in privacy." They retired to the far corner of the room, which was, as yet, unoccupied, and sat down at a table.

"Now tell me what's bothering you," Sahaed said to the peer.

"Well, it is a little difficult. I think you know what's going on Anwar. I have recently received a threat. In fact, I think that someone is trying to blackmail me!"

"Really, George, and what makes you think that? Surely someone is either blackmailing you or they're not." the Arab said with a look of complete sincerity and innocence on his face. As he read the expression on the face of the other man he could detect the worry and fear emanating from the man's very pores as he mopped his sweaty forehead and dried his clammy hands with a club napkin. The Arab began to experience his favourite sensation as the feeling of power coursed through his body.

"I received some photographs in the mail shortly after we last met. They were pictures of me in situations that could cost me my reputation and the directorships that I hold on numerous company boards, one of which, of course, is Harrobys."

Anwar Sahaed knew quite well what the pictures were all about. The noble Lord was a raging homosexual, and had a penchant for young boys. Somehow he had managed to keep this from the public at large, and from the House of Lords, but now, clearly, he feared that his secret was about to be released.

"What exactly are the... err... the blackmailers asking for?"

"They remain anonymous, suggesting that if I don't comply with a recent request made by one of their friends, then the cat will be let out of the bag, pictures will be sent to the press, to the House of Lords, and to my family. This is your doing, Anwar. There is no point in you denying the fact." The other man showed no reaction to the tale of woe, nor indeed to the blatant accusation.

"Granted, I do have some very powerful and determined friends throughout the world. But in my world, friends will do almost anything to prove true loyalty, George. That's what friends are for."

"So what am I to do?" asked the shaking pathetic Peer of the Realm.

"If I were in your shoes I would bend to their wishes. I don't see what other choices there are. Do you? Here, let me get you another drink,

George. It's not the end of the world you know. Your secret is safe with me. Why not do as these people ask? If you're successful in your attempts, maybe you'll never have another problem for as long as you live." Sahaed ordered a bottle of Bollinger, gave fifty pounds to the waiter, and then stood to leave the premises.

"George, as usual, it has been so nice to see you again. Please give my best wishes to your dear mother and to the rest of the family, and don't forget what I said: look after your friends and they will help you."
Sahaed looked menacingly at the snivelling man then walked out of the club with the gait of a surviving fighting cock, completely ignoring the farewell comments of the doorman.

Back in the club, the man with the blonde hair and the hearing aid walked across to Lord Boothroyd who continued staring into his champagne as the bubbles spilled over the top of his glass and down his stubby fingers onto the polished surface of the table. He sat down opposite the peer who hadn't seemed to notice his arrival. Tears were streaming down the peer's swollen cheeks.

"Having problems Lord Boothroyd?" asked the man from MI6. The tearful Lord looked up and noticed the stranger for the first time.

"Nothing that a glass or two of this bubbly won't cure. Why don't you join me? Let me get you a glass."

"I don't mind if I do. It seems such a great shame to watch a man drown his sorrows alone."

"I haven't seen you in here before, have I?" the peer asked, now looking directly and interestingly at the big good-looking man.

"No, it's my first time in here," the agent replied, "It's quite a nice place though."
The peer looked the man up and down, then his eyes hardened and a scowl puckered his brow.

"How did you know my name?" he asked.

"I've seen your face in the press and on the TV. You're quite a celebrity," he said, flattering his Lordship.

"I didn't quite catch your name," he said brushing his hand against the agents arm.

"David's my name. I'll go and get that other glass," he said, changing the subject quickly. He got up from the seat and moved across towards the bar. Lord Boothroyd admired the physique of the big man and the way his powerful frame seemed to slide catlike across the surface of the rich carpet.

Harrobys later that Afternoon, 1997

"Get me Paris!" The voice of Sahaed pierced the comparative silence of his secretary's office. She jumped at the sudden intrusion from the intercom.

"Right away, sir," she replied, in her usual unruffled diction.

Within a couple of minutes the phone on his desk rang. Sahaed flipped the speaker switch nonchalantly, and then sat back in his chair.

"Majestic Palace Hotel, may we help you?"

"Sahaed here. Get me the manager."

"Yes Mr Sahaed, sir. Right away, sir. Putting you through to his office now."

"I don't want his office, I want him! Get him to call me back and be quick about it!" he snapped viciously.

The door to his office opened and in walked a handsome young Arabic man, wearing a very expensive Armani suit and stylish shoes. His sleek black hair shone under the crystal chandeliers. The large diamond on his finger outshone the magnificent crystal light fittings above. He had the same deep dark eyes as his father. He was in trim shape. He walked around the desk and embraced his father on both cheeks.

"How many times must I tell you not to walk straight into this office without seeing my secretary first?" Sahaed said to his son.

Raffi smiled and threw his coat on an adjacent couch, then sat on the corner of the massive desk as though he hadn't heard his father's comment.

"Hello my son, and how nice to see you again," Sahaed said sarcastically.

"It's so nice to see you again, father," Raffi replied emphatically and facetiously, a roguish look on his face: the look of a young man who knows he's the apple of his father's eye.

His father smiled. "And where has my licentious son and heir been for the last two weeks?" he asked.

"If you must know, I've been to a party with your friend, the Sheik's son, in Dubai. He is an awful bore. I think he is going to end up gay, you know!" he smirked as he sank into a chair by his father's desk. He threw his leg over the padded arm as he spoke.

"I did as you asked; the yacht will be ready as and when you wanted. Your dutiful son will be there to serve, Oh Master." He stood, sweeping his hand across his front and bowed irreverently, grinning as he picked up his coat and walked across the room. He embraced his father then left the office just as the phone rang.

"Sahaed," he grunted into the instrument.

"I have Monsieur Le Clare for you Mr Sahaed," a woman's voice announced with a strong French accent. There was a pause, then;

"Where were you when I called and why has it taken so long for you to return my call?"

"I was with Monsieur Le President of the hotel, sir. We had a meeting about the banquet for the engagement party for the daughter of the President of Michelin, the tyre giants."

"I don't much care if you were with the Queen of England. May I remind you that the president of the hotel works for me and for that matter, so do you! If you wish both of those situations to remain constant then answer me when I call, is that clear?" he shouted at the manager.

"Yes, sir, it is abundantly clear."

"I want the two royal suites prepared and ready for tomorrow night. The premier suite is for my brother-in-law, Mr Agnin Armimi, and the other for me."

There was a long pause at the other end, then a nervous cough, and an attempt to clear a throat.

"We have a slight problem with your request, sir. Both suites have been booked by a delegation from the Chinese Republic."

"*We* don't have a problem, *you* do. I expect to see those suites prepared and ready as ordered." He threw the switch on the speakerphone, disconnecting the line, then immediately buzzed for his secretary. The door opened as she came in, notepad and pencil at the ready.

"I want my plane ready in the morning to get me to Paris in time for lunch. Make an appointment with the keeper of the royal polo ponies one day next week. I would also like an invitation to the Duke of Cornwall's Ball. I wish to be seated at the Duke's table. I also want to see the Prime Minister on my return." He rattled off his instructions with the rapidity of an automatic weapon in nervous hands, and then dismissed her with a wave of his hand without looking once in her direction.

Buckingham Palace, 1992

Princess Anna made her way towards the part of the palace that was occupied by the Queen. She had been summoned to a meeting in the Queen's private suite. The tone of the request itself was to set the tenor of the meeting; she had no doubt as to the subject matter.

"Good morning, Your Royal Highness," said the Queen's secretary to Anna, his sister-in-law.

"Good morning, Geoffrey. Is there any need to be so formal and stuffy?" she asked.

"The Queen will see you straight away," the secretary replied, ignoring her comment.

"Sir Geoffrey, did you hear my question, or are you perhaps going a little deaf in your dotage?" the princess asked.

"Yes Ma'am, I did hear the question, and no, my sense of hearing is perfectly fine, thank you."

"Good, then do have the damn good manners and decency to answer the question. I was always convinced that Mannors and respect were low on your agenda," she walked towards the enormous double doors that led into the Queen's chambers. The secretary scurried past the princess, knocking on the big doors. He opened both, and then announced Anna to Her Majesty, The Queen.

The Queen was not sitting behind her desk as Anna had anticipated, but on a large couch. The top of her two-piece was undone and her right arm was stretched in a relaxed manner along the back of the couch. A similar seat was opposite. She beckoned for Anna to approach.

"Take a seat," she said, gesturing toward the opposite couch.

"Thank you, Ma'am," she said, sitting down.

"I will get right to the point, Anna." There was a knock at the door, her aide entered the room

"Sir Geoffrey, you have my instructions." the Queen said.

"Begging your pardon Ma'am, but it's the Prime Minister for you."

"I don't care who it is, I am not to be disturbed under any circumstances, is that quite clear?"

"Yes Ma'am." The Queen turned to the princess, her hands resting in her lap.

"We are sure that you have a good idea as to why we want to see you today, Anna."

"Not exactly, Ma'am, though I must confess the way that John and I live must be of great concern to you, as indeed it is to me."

"You're damn right it is of great concern to us, and, it seems, to half the civilized world," the Queen roared. Her face coloured as she tried to grip her emotions and remain calm. "The time has come when some serious action needs to be taken or the whole of the monarchy will be endangered. We had a long discussion with John. According to his version, it seems that the marriage is irretrievable. Firstly, we want to hear that from you. We don't expect that decision to be made without a lot of serious thinking on the part of you both, having in mind the possible consequences on the whole of the monarchy. And let us not forget your two sons, George and Edward, and the effect that such a rift could have on their young lives."

"I have given this matter some very serious consideration, Ma'am, having every concern for the monarchy, and being cognizant of my role therein. I feel like a complete stranger here. Everyone seems to want to make my life difficult and painful. On top of which, my husband carries on an affair with another woman right under my nose."

"Do you think that bringing this sort of attention to yourself helps the situation?" asked the Queen, slapping the back of her hand demonstratively onto the front page of the newspaper, then leaning across and tossing it into Anna's lap. The front page showed Anna with the tennis celebrity.

"This sort of behavior has to stop and we mean immediately! Between the both of you, untold and irreparable damage is being done to us all. The matter is receiving attention on a worldwide basis. We have a meeting later today with the Prime Minister, called at his behest, I might add. We wish you to go away and lend some serious thought to this farce of a marriage. We have asked your husband to do likewise and we will call a joint meeting within the next few days. Anna, we want this matter resolved, very quickly and as painlessly as possible.

"As you know, there is to be a royal visit to Africa. We think that maybe this should be carried out by the two of you, using the royal yacht, which will take the heat off things here, giving you both the chance to talk things over in a private setting. That trip, by the way, is not a point for discussion.

"You may leave now, Anna. We are most displeased and there is nothing more to say on the matter." Princess Anna stood and bowed her head.

"Thank you, Ma'am. I will, as instructed, prepare myself for the next meeting." The door opened as though by an electronic sensor. Sir Geoffrey stood there, a facetious smirk on his face. The Queen spoke again.

"Oh, and do try to be a little more tolerant of the palace staff. After all, they are here to help, you know."

"Yes Ma'am," she replied, as she went through the doorway. She turned and looked at Sir Geoffrey. She stood for a good twenty seconds in silence, staring at her brother-in-law.

"Is there a problem, Anna?" he asked.

"Yes. I am still awaiting a reply to my earlier question, from this helpful member of the palace staff. You may also wish to preface your answer with 'Your Royal Highness,' if you don't mind, Sir Geoffrey!"

Charles De Gaulle Airport, Paris

The Gulf Stream jet purred on its second and final circuit of the holding pattern, coming in on final approach to Charles De Gaulle airport. The tyres screeched as the pilot flared the plane's nose up, putting the main wheels firmly onto the runway, then the nose wheel. The engines screamed in protest as the pilot applied the brakes and reversed the thrust, rapidly slowing the aircraft down as it scurried toward the private jet terminal.

"Your car is waiting on the apron, sir," said the captain over the PA system. The plane came to a halt and the door containing the built in stairway was lowered. A steward came down first, closely followed by the diminutive figure of Anwar Sahaed, carrying only a small attaché case. There were two vehicles standing by: one a French customs car, the other a black 500 series Mercedes limousine. The customs officer saluted Sahaed, glanced at the small piece of hand baggage, and then waved him on into the open door of the Mercedes, which seconds later swept off along the tarmac, towards the centre of Paris.

As the car drew away Anwar Sahaed saw the massive sleek Boeing 767 in the all black livery of his relative, Agnin Armimi, one of the wealthiest men on the planet. Once out on the main highway, the traffic began to thicken until, as usual in rush hour, it ground to a halt. *Just like most other major cities in the world, but Paris always seems worse*, the Arab thought to himself.

"Phone ahead and tell them we are delayed in this usual French stupidity."

"Oui, Monsieur," replied the French driver as he reached for the telephone.

Buckingham Palace

The princess had returned to her apartments after her meeting with the Queen, feeling like a schoolgirl chastised by her form teacher and given 500 lines. She knew that this state of affairs could not be allowed to continue for very much longer. The thought of a State visit to Africa was unattractive to her. She felt equally sure that Prince John would feel the same. She wondered why everyone thought it was as simple as waking up one morning, and saying to oneself, ok, that's enough of this, let's fall in love again and stop all the gossip and have things as the world would like to see them. *Fairy tales are for storybooks* she thought to herself.

She knew that she was no longer in love with the prince; in fact she had begun to loathe the pompous man. She had listened to his telephone conversations with that awful woman, Caroline Hunter Parks. She had known right from the start that there was an ongoing affair between them. Anna had even seen the furtive look on Hunter Parks' face in the congregation as she'd walked down the aisle in St Paul's Cathedral on the day of their wedding. It was a look of loss, and defeat. Anna had thought in her naivety that she could make a difference, but it was not to be.

There were three of them in this marriage, as she had said to her husband, after she heard him talking to Caroline on his mobile phone from the bathroom. She had overheard him asking her, above all people, for advice on their marriage. When she had taxed him on the matter a frightful argument had ensued. Anna sighed, opened her little silver box and tossed a couple of pills onto the back of her tongue.

Westminster the Houses of Parliament

The Leader of the Opposition party, Tony Blain, sat in his office. Due to the untimely death of his predecessor, there had been a party election in which he had successfully defeated all-comers in somewhat of a landslide victory. He was very young for such a position — in fact the youngest in Opposition in history, a pleasant looking young man, sartorially well suited with a boyish grin and a stylish eloquence that came from his training as a lawyer. He had a half-way accent, best described as educated northern. His burning ambition was to become the youngest Prime Minister, or at least the youngest Socialist Leader. The late Tory, William Pitt the younger, still held that distinction.

Tony Blain had the smell of Number 10 Downing Street in his nostrils. He knew that nothing could stop him now. The tide was turning: the conservative government under the leadership of John Mannors had gone downhill since the defeat of the previous female incumbent, the first woman Prime Minister, *and hopefully the last*, Blain thought to himself.

"I want to hear about any subject or bandwagon that can put us in a good light. Emotion is what wins elections. Tell the people what they want to hear, show them what they want to see. The days of broken empty promises are gone," he had said at a Members' meeting recently. "This is New Labour." Tony Blain smiled his famous chipped tooth schoolboy grin as his secretary walked into the room.

"Your next appointment has arrived Mr Blain. Mr Sahaed is waiting in the outer office."

"Then show him in. Did you get the details I asked for?"

"They are in the file on your desk, along with the minutes from your meeting at Whitehall. Incidentally, talking of Whitehall, that MI6 agent called earlier whilst you were in the House."

"Keep Mr Sahaed waiting for a while. I want to speak with the agent first. I'll get him on my direct line."

Tony Blain stood up as the Arab walked into his office.

"Mr Sahaed, how nice to meet you again. Let me see, the last time was at Princess Anna's Feed the Children charity dinner, was it not, at The Dorchester, as memory serves?"

"This is quite correct," replied the owner of Harrobys, "Three months ago," he concluded.

"What can we do for you today?" the Labour Leader asked, smiling as he sat down behind his desk.

"I think that it is more, what I can do for you Mr Blain," said the Arab, smirking.

"What exactly do you mean Mr Sahaed?" he replied with a roguish smile.

"It's obvious to me, as it is to many others, that you are heading towards a victory in the next election. I have never been known for backing losers, Mr Blain. I also appreciate that such large-scale victories are not achieved purely on personalities and dreams, but rather on funding and support. I want to offer such support in this matter. In the past, I have always been a staunch supporter of the Tory Party, but like you, and I suspect the majority of sensible people, I believe that this country is due for a change, not just in its leadership, but more so in its direction."

"Bravo! Bravo!" said Blain clapping his hands as he spoke. "I, for one, have to agree with your sentiments entirely. Sounds like an election speech written especially for me," he said to the Arab.

"How do you intend to demonstrate the effects of your new found fervour, Mr Sahaed?" asked the Leader of the Opposition, "And what do you seek in return for your support, and err… um… funding. It has been my experience that successful and mega-rich people such as yourself, rarely, if ever, make magnanimous gestures without having an ulterior motive, wouldn't you say?"

"Would you think that a million pounds into your election campaign fund would assist the turn of the tide Mr Blain?" Anwar Sahaed looked directly into the other man's eyes as he spoke.

"Of that there is no doubt whatsoever Mr Sahaed, but will you please answer my question. The use of rhetoric is a practice that I abhor. I like to see a direct question answered by an equally direct retort, sir," Blain snapped, banging the flat of his hand hard on the surface of the desk, returning the Arab's stare with a frankness and ferocity that left the other man in no doubt as to his attitude.

The Arab paused as though not quite sure of what to say. He too was an accomplished manipulator, his command of the English language was commendable, and as a verbal tactician he had few equals. Now, it seemed, he had met one here.

"I want very little in return, other than the satisfaction of knowing that my input was partially responsible for the success of the operation."

"In that case, Mr Sahaed, there being no strings attached, I will be delighted to put you together with our party finance committee chairman, and take you up on your generous offer. I assume that you wish your donation to be published, and made general knowledge?"

"No, no; quite the contrary. I would rather it remained anonymous and a secret, or that at least it was not made public, if you don't mind."

"That will be no problem, sir. Anonymous donations are quite commonplace, though normally not as err... generous as yours. Well, if that's all Mr Sahaed, I have a few more meetings to get through before the day is over." Tony Blain stood and offered his hand to the Arab.

"There is... just one other subject that I would like to mention briefly, and please, call me Anwar. I've been having great problems with immigration..."

The Majestic Palace Hotel, Paris

The doorman rushed forward as he saw the Mercedes pull up in front of the hotel. He opened the door and touched the peak of his cap as Anwar Sahaed, followed by his secretary, stepped out into the Paris air.

"Good day, sir," he said to his boss, who nodded in recognition, then strode off into the hotel. The President of the Establishment, his senior employee and a shareholder, met him at the door. They went into the office that Sahaed used during his visits to Paris. His secretary was already glancing through the file of things that needed the attention of her boss, though she had either been apprised of them already, or they had been previously faxed to her London office. There was nothing of sufficient import to require the attention of her boss.

"Is Mr Armimi in his suite?" he asked of the Hotel President.

"Yes, Mr Sahaed. Monsieur Armimi arrived about two hours ago. He asked us to call him on your arrival."

Sahaed picked up the phone and tapped out a number. He spoke in Arabic. As the phone was answered his posture seemed a little more subservient than normal.

"My brother, how are you. Yes, I landed a good hour ago; the traffic from the airport was appalling. I will see you in your suite in thirty minutes. Please give me time to wash up," he said. He put the receiver down and began to thumb through the file in front of him. "Check with London and see if there's been any contact from Lord George Booth-royd," he said to his secretary.

"I spoke to the London office as soon as we arrived from the airport, sir. There were no messages, other than confirmation of your invitation to The Duke of Cornwall's Ball, and your meeting with the Master of the Royal Stables."

Later Anwar Sahaed stood surrounded by genuine heavy gold leaf-framed Louis XIV mirrors, as one of the most expensively decorated elevators in Paris ascended silently towards the royal suite at the top of the building. The attendant stood opposite, smartly attired; his white-gloved hands by his sides as the luxuriant box stopped at the twentieth floor. The attendant inserted a gold card into a slot behind a previously locked panel, and then the car continued its ascent until it came to a halt. The doors slid silently aside opening onto a scene of decadent opulence.

Sahaed stepped onto the specially made Persian rugs, fitted wall to wall, and at least one and a half inches thick. Turning right he walked along the hallway under a cascade of brilliant light from hundreds of bulbs reflecting the thousands of angles in the cut crystal on the magnificent chandeliers, as they sparkled in the cut glass mirrors along the walls.

Even he marvelled at the beauty and never ceased to be amazed by the sheer art and craftsmanship on display. He loved rare and expensive things, but best of all he liked to possess them. His whole life had become a crusade, setting out to own the unobtainable.

As he approached the big man standing in front of the massive carved doors, their solid gold fittings reflected the brilliant lights. He nodded at the man, and then smiled to himself. *With the continued help of my brother-in-law I could own the whole world. Not bad for the grandson of an Egyptian tailor*, he thought to himself, as the bodyguard turned and pushed open the doors to the royal suite.

"Mr Anwar Sahaed is here, sir," he announced.

A most attractive blonde woman got up from the couch and assisted the old man. He was wearing a loose fitting Arabic caftan. As he got to his feet he raised both hands aloft, a warm smile of welcome on his lined face.

"Anwar, my special brother! What a pleasure it is to see you." They embraced in true Arabic fashion: cheek against cheek, then the old man stood back, arms outstretched, gripping both shoulders of his in-law and cohort.

"Let me look at you, Anwar. I think perhaps you look a little tired. First we relax, then we have much to talk about." The old man clapped his hands as two Arabic females entered the room. "Take care of my brother," he said with a salutary wave of his hand. Anwar was led off into another room. He returned within minutes, dressed in loose fitting Arabic garb. He was directed to a seat opposite the old man, who clapped his hands. As he gestured, the blonde woman, along with the two Arabic women, quietly left the room.

Speaking in his native tongue the older man beckoned for Sahaed to sit next to him.

"We have much to discuss my brother." Armimi was one of the richest men on earth, who had originally started out at the end of the Second World War as an arms dealer. He had become the largest Mr Fix-It in the world today. Nowadays he bought leaders and even countries. Euphemistically he was an armaments negotiator, rather than 'gun runner.' Early on in his life he had chosen wealth rather than popularity, and had succeeded beyond his wildest dreams on both counts, possibly becoming one of the most unpopular men in the world.

"Tell me, how are you progressing with your application for British citizenship Anwar?"

"I am drawing a blank at every attempt. I have tried every conceivable approach I can think of. It seems that a complete embargo has been drawn up. Some Indian from Bombay can stroll into the country and get a passport and social benefits at the drop of a hat, yet I can't even get a hearing." He raised his hands in a gesture of defeat. If I was Jamaican and came floating up the River Thames on a rubber tyre, then perhaps I would have a better a chance. You would think that the amount of money that has been put into the country from our purchase of Harrobys alone would give me VIP status," said Sahaed, becoming noticeably more agitated and angry as he spoke. The old man held up a manicured hand, shaking it from side to side.

"Getting annoyed is not the way to carry on. It's a waste of energy and time — two most valuable commodities. Getting even is a totally different matter," he chastened the younger man. "Remember what the ancient Persian philosopher Omar Khiam had to say: 'The Moving Finger writes; and, having writ, Moves on: nor all thy Piety nor Wit shall lure it back to cancel half a Line, Nor all thy Tears wash out a word of it.' What is done, is done, what is gone, is gone. We have to try other avenues and we will succeed eventually. You see my brother, in this life everything has a price, everything! It's just that sometimes the price is too great to pay." He stared down at his hands in silence, as though in prayer. After what seemed an age, he reached across and took a drink from a glass of water and went on to say:

"I understand the Conservative party is expected to fare badly in the forthcoming election; that it should not be too long before such an election is called. If this is the case, should we not be turning our attentions to this splendid area of opportunity? I am reliably informed that the new leader of the opposition party is a very ambitious young man. Such ambition requires sustenance and support, does it not? The situation is sent to us from Allah." He looked heavenwards with hands outstretched; his facial expression a mixture of greed and anticipation.

"Such burning ambitions can sometimes fog a man's vision and distort his values. That creates weakness, which in turn becomes our strength. My reliable informants also tell me that a breakup is expected at any moment in the marriage between Prince John and the unfortunate Princess Anna. I will talk to you a little later on that subject. It could present us with opportunities beyond any of our wildest dreams." The old man smirked with a look of relish in his eyes almost salivating and licking his tight lips as he spoke, and then his countenance changed he began to look more serious.

"In the meantime please continue along the same lines as before. Don't forget what I told you. Everything has a price. In obtaining your citizenship, money is no object. If we cannot buy what we desire, then we must steal it. Look for weaknesses in people, they are always there, then make an offer that cannot be refused. Make the alternative too great for them to pay, but remember always that a price too costly can work both ways.

"This matter is taking far too long to conclude. If you do not succeed soon I shall have to take a hand in the matter," As the older man spoke Sahaed noticed the severe and vicious look in the older man's eyes, the immaculate hands now balled up into fists, knuckles white, shaking very slightly. Sahaed was reminded of his late father's words. *'Woe betide anyone who ever crosses the path of your brother-in-law. He has adopted a God-like attitude. He would even fight with Allah himself if the stakes were high enough!'*

"Go now, Anwar, I am tired after a long day's travelling. Remember that there is a solution to every riddle. Sometimes the answer lies in the eyes of your opponent, at other times it stares you right in the face with its absolute simplicity. Go with Allah and may you be victorious." Agnin Armimi got up on his feet, touched his forehead with the tips of his manicured fingers, rolling his hand down in a clockwise motion, resting them above his heart, his head bowed. Sahaed copied the motion then left the room. He walked back along the ornate corridor to the second suite at the other end of the floor.

Outside the hotel, members of MI6 sat in a van, surrounded by a mass of complicated electronic devices. This time, the blonde man was not wearing a hearing aid, but was listening through a lightweight headset. Outside, the directional sound sensor lifted and turned like a submarine periscope.

"It's bloody incredible!" agent David Steel said to one of the techs. "They seem to be able to block us completely. I can't pick up a damn thing. Mind you, I suppose as Armimi sells the damn stuff, he's obviously one up on all of us." The headset clattered noisily as he threw it down in disgust, pushing his fingers through his thick mop of unkempt hair.

"I'm going to take a look around. By the way, do you know if our boys got the bugs installed in both aircraft today?"

"They were successful with the Gulf Stream, but security on the 767 is too tight to break."

"Then get customs or airport security to board the plane. The French are right behind us on this one," Steel said confidently. He banged the door as he left the van. This case was beginning to irritate him. Ever since his return from East Germany, David Steel had found life particularly dull and lacking the ability to get his adrenalin flowing. With the Cold War over now there was little action within the department, other than dreary diplomatic stuff, much backside kissing, people jockeying for promotions; not the scene for a man of action.

He headed towards the bar behind the hotel on the opposite side of the street. Inside, the air hung thick with second-hand cigarette smoke that you could cut with a knife; this was the favourite haunt of many of the hotel staff. He sat at the bar and ordered a well-earned whisky and soda, irritated by the slow pace of his own progress in this case.

After his eyes became more accustomed to the dark, he looked around the room recognising not one face. He gave a cursory glance towards the television and then he did a quick retake as he saw a view of the House of Lords in London, followed by a still picture of his latest acquaintance, Lord Geoffrey Boothroyd. From his slight grasp of the French language, and hampered by the noise in the bar, he understood that the noble Lord had committed suicide earlier that day. He was found dead after a suspected overdose; by his side an empty pillbox and a half empty bottle of Bollinger champagne.

"I trust it was vintage M' Lord," he said aloud, raising his glass toward the TV set.

"Monsieur?" said a bemused barman looking quizzically at the agent, but received no reply and then looking heavenwards.

The innocent young boys of England can rest a little easier tonight, good riddance, the MI6 agent thought to himself.

Steel remained sitting at the bar for another few minutes. He had lost track of time. He thought about the unfortunate peer. He knew full well why the sad and pathetic apology for a man had taken his own life. *At least that makes one weirdo less in the world*, he thought *and more importantly, one less avenue for Anwar Sahaed to continue his pointless pursuit of British citizenship*. A sardonic smile crossed his lips at the thought. *When will he realise that he'll never achieve his goal, and that the more he tries the harder it will become. I wonder who'll be his next victim.* He raised his eyebrows at that thought.

All that Steel had to do was to lead the Arab into a trap where he would break the law, then as a non-resident, he would simply be expelled or deported from the country.

His ownership of Harrobys had no bearing on the Government's attitude: the famous store would still be there whoever owned it; it would also continue to employ the same number of British people.

Steel knew, though unfortunately not everyone shared the same opinion, that there were people who would happily take incentives from the Arab, making promises that they could not hope to keep. Such people could be putting their careers and indeed their lives in jeopardy. The agent knew only too well that the likes of this Arab played for keeps.

"Another whisky, Monsieur?' the bartender asked.

"Yes please, but go easy on the soda this time. In fact, make it a double will you?"

"Oui, Monsieur."

As he sipped at the decidedly stronger drink, another man sat down on the stool next to him wearing the uniform of the Majestic Palace Hotel (some kind of a bellboy, he guessed). The new arrival spoke in French to the bartender, ordering a Pernod and water with ice. Steel had often wondered why people order water and ice, as the ice melts in the heated air forming more water. *What a waste.*

The man turned towards Steel.

"Good evening, sir," he said in perfect English. "I couldn't help overhearing that you're an Englishman."

"Your English is very good," the agent replied.

"My parents sent me to school in your country; my father was English. Unfortunately they split up some years ago when my mother came back to France. I say, I don't suppose you play darts do you?" he asked smiling enthusiastically. "They have an English board in the other room."

"I suppose so. Why the hell not?" Steel replied, following the other man as he bounded across the floor. The Frenchman went towards the dartboard on the opposite wall of the unoccupied room.

"So what went wrong?" said Steel to the Frenchman.

"Nothing. I placed the bugs as instructed. What's the problem?" he replied, throwing a dart into the board.

"I'll tell you what the problem is. Either you didn't activate the devices, or they found them," said Steel irritably, totally missing the board, his dart clattering noisily on the tiled floor.

"That's not possible, I checked them after their men swept the room. They were still in place ten minutes before Armimi arrived, switched on and working."

"That's odd," said Steel. The other man paused with his arm in the air, took aim and threw his darts; the second and third going into the bull's eye.

"There is a securely locked room on the same floor as the royal suites. I saw the door open yesterday, it was packed with electronics," said the other MI6 man. "Maybe they have some silent kind of scrambler set up. I'll try and take a look tomorrow."

"We're getting absolutely nothing, not a peep. You may have to put a recorder in the room. We really do need to hear what they're up to," said Steel.

"Fancy a proper game?" said the other man.

"No thanks. You're too rich for my blood. Where the hell did you learn to play darts like that?"

"In prison, of course! Where else?"

"What?" said Steel in a surprised tone.

"Yes, I did three months in Brixton undercover. Remember the Welsh-man selling our secrets to the Chinese last year? Very good practice for the darts, and cards!" he said with a wide grin on his face as he left the room. Steel walked back into the bar and sat down where he had been before.

"Whisky, Monsieur? The bartender asked.

Buckingham Palace the following day

"Your Royal Highness, that speech was an absolute knockout. It's not every day that you receive a standing ovation. Who gives a damn what the palace PR people think. So you changed most of the verbiage in their draft – what of it? If they had any sense they would shut up and take credit for the reaction, which is certain to receive good press tomorrow. Those women were delighted. I know, because as I walked around I heard nothing but praise. You could have heard a pin drop as you spoke. I was proud of you, Ma'am."

"Thank you kind sir," the princess said, curtseying to her secretary. "You had quite some input too, you know. I have to ready myself for this afternoon's meeting with Her Majesty. I fear that this one will be the meeting of all meetings, Michael. Pass my pills will you, there's a good chap."

Michael had been secretary to the princess since she joined the Royal Family so he knew Anna's every mood. He alone appreciated the extent of the pressure placed on the princess, both by her position, and by those who wanted to see her fall flat on her face. Because of his own station the palace staff hierarchy disliked him equally. As secretary to the princess he was avoided, left uninvited to the meetings and gatherings periodically held by other secretaries and senior members of the palace staff. He was loyal and therefore did not mind too much. His only regret was that he missed all of the gossip that would, in turn, have been of use to the princess. Somewhat of a catch twenty-two situation, as that was more than likely the reason for his not being invited in the first place.

He worried as he watched his princess become more dependent on her pills as each day passed. Today was going to be a big day. He could feel the atmosphere around the palace; he had uncomfortable, bad feelings — the kind of feeling that you have when in an office where everyone but the victim knows he's going to be fired shortly.

The Houses of Parliament — Prime Minister's Question Time

The Prime Minister, John Mannors, had been on his feet for the best part of an hour undergoing the usual barrage of questions from both the Opposition and from members of the Conservative party. Those from the other side were more often than not, flippant, giving a few minutes of exposure to lesser members of the opposition, who enjoyed trying to bait the Government leader, and at the same time showing their constituents that they were still alive, if not kicking. All sittings of the House were now televised making a distinct improvement in the general sartorial elegance of the members, which seemed to be the only benefit there, but even then there was no accounting for taste. Earlier, the not-so-surprising announcement made by the Prime Minister, had put an end to national and indeed international speculation.

"It was announced from Buckingham Palace today, that Princess Anna and Prince John have decided to separate, on the grounds of irreconcilable differences. There has been no mention of divorce; the royal couple will continue to carry out their civic duties. I am sure that we all share a feeling of sadness at this decision," said a sombre John Mannors. There followed much shouting and jeering from both sides of the house.

"Order, order!" followed by the loud banging of the Speaker's gavel.

"Order! I will have order in this house!" Silence fell as the voice of Madame Speaker echoed around the ancient building.

"There being no further questions, Madame Speaker, I propose that we take a recess for lunch," said the Prime Minister.

Sahaed's Office, Harrobys, Knightsbridge, London

"Mr Sahaed, I have Mr Armimi on line one, sir," said the voice of his secretary. "He sounds a little irritated if I may say so, sir."

"Put him through."

"Anwar, I want to meet you as soon as possible. I am more than a little disappointed at your handling of the British peer. I want to be sure that there can be no connection to us in this matter. By the way did you hear the announcement in Parliament a few minutes ago?"

"Which announcement was that?"

"The Prime Minister has just issued a statement on the official separation of the royal couple, John and Anna."

Sahaed hated it when his brother-in-law was able to inform him on subjects that he should be aware of first.

"No I had not heard, but it comes as no surprise," he said to Armimi.

"I am in the plane at the moment en-route from Bermuda. We have changed our flight plan and will be at London Gatwick in two hours. Book a private dining room at the Gatwick Hilton and have a car collect me. I will see you then," replied Armimi.

"It will be as you say."

"Anwar, I want chapter and verse on your meetings with the late Lord." The phone went dead. Sahaed roared at his secretary, "Get into this office immediately!"

Buckingham Palace — the same day

The princess had been back from a meeting with Her Majesty The Queen, the Duke and her husband, John. It seemed that most decisions were already made and that a separation was to take place from the end of the meeting. Eventually divorce would be allowed after a so-called 'respectable period of time,' as yet unspecified, at which time a financial settlement would be made. The size and nature of the settlement would depend entirely on the behaviour of the princess in the meantime.

The princess was to move out of the palace and take up residence in Kensington Palace, where she would be afforded apartments and staff befitting her position.

Princess Anna sat with her secretary and her personal maid and was not sure whether she felt happy and relieved, or sad and defeated. Her only question during the audience was regarding her sons. She had told the Queen that she would fight to her last breath for them. Their only concern seemed to hinge around the image of the royal family. Anna just wished from the bottom of her heart that the boys could be spared all of this. She vowed that she would do all in her power to make sure that they did not grow up like these unfeeling, uncaring zombies, whose only concern was trying to be something that they were not. In some respects a great load had been taken from her mind. They still had not beaten her down, not yet, not ever.

"Better start packing," Anna said to her trusty aides.

Kensington Palace

The divorce was over, the whole messy affair was done, and neither the prince nor Anna had attended court. The settlement had been quite generous: the princess had been given twenty-one million pounds. She was to continue living at Kensington Palace; she had full access to her sons George and Edward; the title of 'Her Royal Highness' was to be dropped; she would be addressed as Princess Anna.

Over the past couple of years the princess had carried out a punishing schedule. She had opened more events, shaken even more hands and started a large number of charities, which were particularly special to her. Her popularity had increased beyond the belief of most onlookers, and to the detriment and annoyance of the Royal Family.

The Queen was so annoyed with the general public's reaction to some of Anna's recent performances that she'd forbidden the use of her name within the royal household — a somewhat churlish reaction, but those who knew of it thought it was par for the course.

The princess was earning such titles as 'The People's princess,' and 'The princess of Kindness.' She was seen touching AIDS patients and lepers; small sick children were cheered after sitting on her knee and receiving encouragement. While the Royal Family continued to bury their heads in the sand Princess Anna was beginning to enjoy her life at last. She had been romantically linked with a number of different men, none of them taken too seriously.

This week she was invited to a party at the Savoy Hotel, thrown by Anwar Sahaed, the wealthy Arab owner of Harrobys. Michael Meadows had accepted the invitation on behalf of the princess. She raised no objection to attending the function. The Arab was known for his generosity, the lavish parties that he threw, and the glittering array of celebrities who attended each function, though he always had some ulterior motive or other.

He also had an extremely charming, suave and attractive son, as Michael had been quick to point out to the princess. There was no new romance in the wind as Princess Anna had not stopped working for the last couple of months. In fact, she was currently in Bosnia where she had been supporting one of her dearest causes, the abolition of the use of anti-personnel land mines.

One ongoing situation that never seemed to change was the constant and continued harassment by the world press. They had published private pictures, taken with the latest high tech super powered lenses from distances so far that it became impossible to relax at all.

"They will soon have x-ray cameras that take pictures through a solid wall," the princess had said as she spoke at a fund raising dinner, much to the amusement of the guests. Though beneath the humour, she was deadly serious in her comments. Nevertheless, pictures appeared world-wide, making her the most photographed person in the world. Her pictures appeared in the tabloid press from America to New Zealand.

Sometimes her photographs appeared on the same front page as those of her ex-husband, His Royal Highness, The Prince of Wales. His relationship with Caroline Hunter Parks seemed more open to the public after his surprisingly candid interview on British TV where he had managed to kill off any last vestiges of support or respect after he'd said that he had never loved the princess.

Aboard an Airliner Somewhere Over the Atlantic

Agnin Armimi slouched on the sumptuous couch in the rear salon of his Boeing 767 as he spoke to Sahaed. He slurped noisily from a glass, due to an excess of ice cubes containing his favourite cocktail. Looking across at his brother-in-law, who sat erect in a more formal chair, he continued:

"What long term plans have been made to instigate and perpetuate this new relationship?"

Purposely ignoring the question and then titivating the older man's vanity and ego, he replied after an overt pause...

"I have to say that your idea, Agnin, of making the worldwide banning of land mines a new cause for the princess, is catching on and receiving much acclaim. It is especially amusing that such a clever scheme should come from one of the largest arms dealers in the world today," he replied with a sly satisfying grin. "In answer to your question, I have a lavish party arranged at the Savoy Hotel this coming week, where the first introduction will take place, as instructed by you. Raffi himself has no idea that we have any involvement in setting up such a meeting. He is aware that the princess will be in attendance, but beyond that, she, nor any other person outside we two, has any inkling of an organised meeting," Sahaed said, as he sat back in his seat slapping his knees with the palms of his hands, a look of smug satisfaction on his face.

"That is good. It is of paramount importance that this meeting appears pre-ordained, as though by Allah himself. Though it is wrong, as the English say, to count one's chickens before they hatch, such a union could give us so much power in Britain and Europe that the issue of your citizenship would pale into insignificance against such a prize."

"I am very pleased with you, Anwar. When we chose you, we made a good choice of husband for my worthless sister," he said, rattling the ice around the empty Waterford tumbler in his hand. A female attendant appeared at the sound.

Sahaed almost purred with satisfaction at the comments from his financier and mentor.

"Champagne. We need to celebrate, before we go to dine," he said as he clapped his hands in the direction of the woman, who promptly disappeared into the rear galley.

British MI6 Secret Intelligence Service Headquarters

"Yes, Prime Minister, we have undeniable evidence that there is such a plot afoot. That is precisely why I took the unprecedented step of inviting you here today, knowing you had already scheduled another meeting here at Vauxhall Cross."

"How did you know that?"

"Prime Minister! We are one of the top intelligence agencies in the world. We know everything that goes on in our own back yard; in particular your back yard, sir," said the MI6 chief.

"Yes, I suppose that was rather a silly question," said the PM.

As with all intelligence chiefs, whether they are British, American, Russian, or whatever, they have the driving seat in most conversations or meetings involving civil servants and parliamentarians. This case was to be no exception.

"Prime Minister, we have kept close tabs on Sahaed, and to a lesser degree, on his brother-in-law Armimi. Sahaed's quest for citizenship has remained relentless. We know that he recently invested vast sums of money into the Opposition party's coffers, and that along the way, at least three people have died as a result of obstructing his efforts — unproven of course." The MI6 chief paused to take a drink from his coffee cup, then stood and walked to the window. "In fact, Prime Minister, you are just about to have one of your assistant under secretaries exposed in the press by Sahaed's system, for accepting... err, shall we say, incentives, and not coming up with the goods. It will appear in the Guardian tomorrow.

"I will give you that name before the end of this meeting, though I imagine you will have your own suspicions already." The Prime Minister passed no comment.

"Let's get back to the point at issue."

"Fine," said the MI6 chief. "I would like you to hear excerpts from some recently obtained tapes. Of course, I will not disclose their location or origin, and naturally you never heard them here Prime Minister."

John Mannors had listened with interest and intrigue to the fuzzy, barely distinguishable voices on the recordings. However, he understood clearly the topic being discussed, and to some degree, the plans being laid. He found it incredulous that people, foreigners, were actually plotting to have one of their family marry a member of the British Royal Family, even more importantly, the mother of a future King of England. It was unprecedented!

The PM sat in silence. After the short tapes were played, the Head of MI6, Sir Martin Fields, sat at the other side of his desk with a cocky, 'cat that got the cream' expression on his face.

"Needless to say, this is for your ears only, and must not be mentioned outside these four walls. Any leak would jeopardize not only our operations, but maybe the lives of other people," said Sir Martin, a stern look on an otherwise expressionless face.

"What's to be done?" asked the PM. "This cannot be allowed to happen."

"Precisely sir, what's to be done? that's the question," said Sir Martin." I think it would be wise if you were to dismiss the thought from your mind, sir. I will keep you abreast of things as they progress. To ask you for a decision now would be a little premature to say the least. I just wanted to bring you up to date and have you know that we are right on top of it. It's called covering my backside, Prime Minister."

The two men shook hands and parted company. Sir Martin knew that the PM had his work cut out in the weeks leading up to the forthcoming general election. Sir Martin also knew that he could well be talking to a different PM in the not-too-distant future, maybe even of a different political persuasion. Politicians changed with monotonous regularity. *Only the civil servants remained constant and reliable, though not even the royals seemed permanent any more*, he thought as the door closed behind the British Premier.

The PM was now convinced that the princess was becoming one hell of a loose cannon, her behaviour over the last year was unacceptable in her open relationships and cavalier affairs. *This just cannot be allowed to happen! It must be avoided at all costs, but how the hell can I get involved?* he thought to himself.

The Savoy Hotel, The Strand, London

The cul-de-sac-style entrance off The Strand to the London Savoy shared with the famous Savoy Theatre was extra busy this evening. The theatre goers opposite had settled in their seats. Now the street was filled with an ever-moving parade of magnificent limousines, Rolls Royces, Bentleys, stretched Mercedes, Daimlers and Jaguars, dropping off their celebrity passengers, from film stars to multi-millionaire producers, to prominent authors and politicians. It was rumoured that tonight royalty, but not just any royalty: none other than the people's princess, Princess Anna herself, was to attend.

A dark blue Jaguar pulled up to the edge of the red carpet. The uniformed attendant opened the rear door as the princess climbed out to a tumultuous roar from the large crowd who had collected there. At the same time a barrage of lights turned night into day, as a hundred cameras flashed simultaneously.

"Who is the latest love in your life?" "Who are you here to see tonight?" along with a myriad of other questions. The princess tried to fight her way through the crowds. The police attempted unsuccessfully to hold back the combination of adoring fans and determined members of the press.

At the same time as Princess Anna's divorce two years ago when her title of 'Her Royal Highness' had been dropped, her official bodyguard courtesy of Buck House had also been discontinued. The removal of her title had absolutely no effect on her increased popularity. In fact, it was quite to the contrary. She had to admit she missed her protection man, Inspector Hank Marlin, badly. She had employed a number of her own replacements, none of whom came up to Marlin's high standards.

The princess was greeted in the foyer by management and then she crossed the hall to the ballroom where she was welcomed at the door by her host, Mr Anwar Sahaed, and his son Raffi who bowed his head as he was presented to the princess.

Though she had heard a lot about Raffi Sahaed, Anna was taken aback by his natural good looks and his deep dark eyes. There was instant chemistry there as he lifted her hand and brushed his lips across the back of it, through the material of her evening gloves. She sensed an instant tingle of emotional electricity between this Middle Eastern playboy, but then so did many other women.

"Princess Anna, I took the liberty of asking my son to be your escort for the evening. I trust that this is acceptable to Your Highness?"

"I'm honoured and delighted to accept," Anna replied. Raffi moved to her right side as they stood talking for a while, and then Raffi excused himself for a few moments.

Just then her secretary, Michael Meadows, came to her side holding a glass of champagne as the function began to get underway.

"He seems like a pleasant character, Ma'am?" he said to the princess, referring to Raffi, as he walked across towards where his father stood.

"I'm bound to agree with you, Michael and he's damn handsome to boot. On this occasion there's not the slightest distortion in your judgement," said the princess bowing her head.

"As though there ever is, Your Highness," he replied, smiling.

"Since my life at the palace, I have to admit it's on occasions like this that I miss Hank Marlin, you know, Michael," the princess said, a pensive look on her face. "However, he's about all that I do miss," she said as an afterthought. The handsome Raffi returned smiling warmly.

"Who was that?" he asked the princess as Michael walked away.

"That's Michael, my private secretary. He is the one trusted aide in my life," the princess said as they walked towards the banqueting room.

They took their places at the table. As they sat, ate and talked, the princess felt an uncommon warmness towards her host; a different feeling than was normal in such circumstances. He was more relaxed than most other men would be in the same situation. She was used to an initial atmosphere of tension, which she would normally have to dispel, but not on this occasion. She too felt relaxed in this intriguing man's company.

After dinner and a few speeches, none from her this time, for a change, they left the table and went onto the dance floor. She began to enjoy the closeness of his body, the touch of his hands. By the end of the evening she was totally enraptured by Raffi. He too, was a little more than attracted to his guest, a most strange feeling, which he attributed to being in the presence of such a celebrity. The People's princess, the idol of the nation and maybe the world. But Raffi knew this was not the case. He was not an impressionable young man; he was an intelligent and sophisticated man who knew himself far better than most men of his age. He knew that this night was the start of something very different in his life.

After her departure at the end of the evening he had made up his mind to see more of her. She too, was of the same mind, though neither of them had expressed their feelings to the other. Raffi accompanied the princess to the foyer of the hotel after she had said goodnight to his father. After a special squeeze of his hand she said goodnight and left the hotel. A crowd of disappointed press watched as she got into her car without him.

As the car carrying the princess and her secretary turned left onto the Strand heading towards Trafalgar Square, a small white car followed. As it drove towards Kensington Palace, the Jaguar pulled up to the entrance. The princess got out of the car and disappeared inside.

The small white car waited for ten minutes or so, long enough to see a little black Mini Metro leave the rear of Kensington Palace, driven away by a man wearing a grey deerstalker hat. As the driver had left the staff entrance, the two men in the white car could have assumed that the he was indeed a member of the Kensington Palace staff, but the two occupants were too well trained to assume.

The car pulled up to the security office, one man got out, then the white car followed the black Mini Metro as it sped off towards west London, eventually parking outside a house in Hounslow where the dresser to the princess went into her home.

Back at Kensington Palace, the other occupant of the car showed his ID to the security police on the door. He didn't see the red Rover car leave the rear of the palace, nor did he see the smile on the face of the princess as she pulled the flat cap down over her noble eyes, a broad grin on her face as she looked into the rear view mirror. Not a car in sight; the night was just about to begin. It was 1:30 in the morning as the vehicle disappeared into the great metropolis, just another ordinary car amongst many others.

The Mediterranean: Aboard the Sahaed Yacht

Raffi stretched out on the sundeck of his father's yacht. The gentle swell of the Mediterranean rocked the big boat as it swayed in unison with the sea, the motion sending him into a mild sleep. The smell of the sea and the distant call of gulls added to his sense of peace and serenity.

He was awakened from his sleep by the sound of voices and the clink of glasses. A steward put down a tray of iced drinks on the low table next to where he lay on the lounger as he said;

"Princess Anna, here's a tequila sunrise for you and a Bacardi coke for Master Raffi."

"Absolutely splendid," he heard the princess reply as she reached across to pick up her drink, chinking the ice noisily around the glass.

"Ah, you're awake my dear," the princess nodded to the awakened sleeper.

"You seemed so fast asleep it was a shame to disturb you."

"We were a little late to bed last night after the flight and all that subterfuge. Having to fly to Scotland first in order to put the press off our scent added another half day to an otherwise two-hour trip," replied Raffi, smiling as he clinked his glass against that of his very special guest.

Apart from the crew, they had the magnificent yacht totally to themselves. The princess lay back on the luxurious sun lounger, her hands behind her head as she looked up at the clear blue sky, a sigh of pleasure crossing her lips.

"This is the life for me: no hassle, no press, no pressure of work, no general public, no security guards hovering."

"Er...um," interrupted Raffi as he nodded in the direction of the broad shouldered, white shirted back of one of the two body guards who always attended him wherever he went.

"Well, you know what I mean," Anna replied.

The yacht was some ten miles off the southern coast of the Mediterranean island of Cyprus where they were headed and would be docking later that evening. Although Raffi had instructed the captain to stay offshore and cruise as long as possible and maybe even anchor offshore, he too was now becoming super sensitive towards the interminable press and its tenacious photographers.

The chief of Anwar Sahaed's security still had the words of his master ringing in his ears. "I want the couple to have complete and absolute privacy. As usual, if one hair on their heads were to be harmed, suicide would be your only option. If a member of the gutter press should get near, you know what to do. Hurt them badly, shoot the bastards if you have to," he had said quietly as an after thought with a look of absolute hatred in his eyes.

"I will not have this trash interfere with my life or any of my plans, you understand?" he'd added as he had stormed off.

The security man, now acting as first mate on board the yacht, looked down from the bridge at his two important charges as they stretched out in the warm Mediterranean sun. He shuddered physically as the words of his master still rang in his ears. He knew that he hadn't been given instructions to kill, but he also knew his master well. When he spoke this way there was something afoot, something so important, that if he or his team of experts had to assist someone from this world to the next, it would not be the end of his own world. Neither would it be for the first time, nor indeed assumed, the last.

Looking down at the two people on deck, in particular the princess, he began to realise the magnitude of the responsibility that he carried on his shoulders.

Princess Anna heard the unmistakable throb of a distant helicopter; the sky had clouded over above the island of Cyprus. She shielded her eyes with her hands but couldn't see the aircraft.

"I do hope that this is not the blasted press coming to pry," she said to Raffi. At the same moment the small radio by the side of the coffee table crackled.

"Mr Raffi, we have a chopper approaching from the north, coming from the direction of Cyprus. Maybe it would be wise to go below for a short while until we identify the aircraft. As yet they are not responding to our communications. We've had them on the radar since they left the island. They went around the other side first."

"OK captain," replied Raffi. Anna had heard the message as she picked up her drink.

"Looks like I spoke too soon," she said to Raffi.

"Let's go below for a while. I suppose the captain's right."

They both went into the saloon, just as the sound of the approaching chopper became louder. It came into view from behind the clouds. The mate looked at the machine through binoculars. He could see no Greek Cypriot military, or police markings or the more rare Turkish Cypriot insignia.

After many years of continued fighting, the Turks now occupied the northern part of the once beautiful island of Cyprus, around the city of Famagusta, once called the golden sands paradise and now quite the opposite. The Greeks still occupied the southern territory, the dividing line from east to west, level with and including the original capital of the island, the old City of Nicosia.

The Greek Cypriots had again rebuilt the southern part into a tourist paradise, the main city and airport now being Limassol. The Royal Air Force still retained a presence in the Greek sector.

The aircraft took its second pass over the yacht, this time hovering at around three hundred feet. The mate came out onto the foredeck, opened a tripod and placed a hand held Russian infantry rocket launcher onto the teak surface, capable of bringing about the demise of the average artillery tank. He crouched behind the weapon and methodically proceeded adjusting the sights. The helicopter instantly banked steeply, disappearing towards the island at a great rate of knots.

The mate went back to the bridge, a big smile covering his face, as the captain gave him the thumbs up, his face alight with laughter.

Anna and Raffi had tears running down their faces. Anna had never laughed so much for many a year. When the laughter had subsided, Raffi took Anna in his arms, kissing her tenderly on the lips.

"I don't think I can remember a time when I felt so happy and so relaxed," she said to him as he led her by the hand through the saloon and down the stairway to the master state room.

Afterwards they lay in each other's arms relaxing to the gentle roll of the yacht. The harsh ringing of the phone by the bedside broke their peace.

"You take it darling, please, it's the internal phone," said Anna.

Raffi picked up the receiver.

"Captain here, sir,"

"Yes, captain."

"I was thinking, sir, though we are cleared to enter the port, in view of our visitors earlier today, maybe we should head further out of the Med, towards Rhodes or Crete perhaps. Though the mate's little ruse had the desired effect, we did draw attention to ourselves. Assuming that the press was using the chopper, it was still a Greek Cypriot charter. The pilot will no doubt have filed a report."

"Quite right, captain, no point in asking for trouble. We are in no hurry. Come to think of it, I haven't ever been to the island of Crete. It would make a nice change. Thank you, captain. Just a moment," said Raffi, turning to Anna.

"What time would you like to eat, darling?"

She turned. "Right now," she said, biting his right nipple hard.

"Ouch!" exclaimed Raffi. "We'll get a snack later, thank you, captain," he said, smiling as he replaced the phone.

They felt the motion of the boat change as the captain brought her around and lifted the engines up to cruising speed. Anna turned and looked into the deep dark eyes of Raffi Sahaed.

"You must be the most gorgeous man that I ever met. I thank God for the day that your father invited me to the Savoy Hotel. I have a feeling that you are about to change the whole of my life." Raffi could not believe what he was hearing. Here he was with the most eligible woman in the whole world. He was falling in love with her.

Sometime earlier, Steel had sat in the waiting room of the small Greek Cypriot helicopter charter company. He had been kept waiting now for a full hour and a quarter. He spoke almost no Greek — he could count to five, that was about it. The receptionist spoke little English and kept on repeating:

"Working on the machine," by which Steel assumed that she meant working on the engine of the chopper. If so, the longer it took the less he fancied the idea of flying in the damn thing. Just as he was about to cancel the whole idea, a young Cypriot walked into the room, his face full of smiles.

"Well that's fine," he said to the agent. "We can go when you are ready, sir." He spoke in perfect English. With the paperwork completed and the charter fee paid, they left the building, walked across the apron and climbed into the Bell Jet Ranger. Steel took the seat beside the pilot, as instructed and the rotors began to turn. He strapped himself into the harness. The pilot wound up the revs, pointed to his earphones indicating that the agent should turn on his headset and flicked the switch on the side of his microphone. There was an audible click, and then he heard the pilot's voice.

"OK, sir, here we go," he said as the aircraft lifted vertically for twenty feet or so, sweeping off sideways, then nose down gathering speed forward and upwards.

"Now, sir I understand that we are looking for a large private yacht. Do you have any information as to the location of the craft or maybe the name?"

"No, I don't happen to have either. I don't want you to make any radio contact or any visual signs of our recognition of them," Steel replied, adjusting the headset as he spoke.

"Do you happen to know what flag they may be flying then?"

"No, I do not," the agent replied, "but I'd like to take a look at the northern side of the island first."

"That could present a problem, sir. We can run into trouble going over Turkish territory at low altitude. I'll have to get clearance, and they will insist on a high ceiling," the pilot said, not sounding very happy about the prospect.

"See what you can do."

After much conversation backwards and forwards to the ground, all spoken in Greek, the pilot turned to Steel.

"We're being allowed to fly over the northern part of the coast, not the island, and we have to maintain an altitude of fifteen hundred feet, staying three miles off shore. Here we go then," said the young man as the Jet Ranger gathered speed and altitude.

They climbed through a thousand feet then began to hit cloud, sporadic at first, then solid below and above.

"I will need to climb higher, sir," the pilot said in the usual matter of fact pilot tone.

They went through two thousand feet as the sky above became clear and blue, the whole of the northern side of the island was out of view. "Shall I take her south, sir?" asked the pilot.

"Yes I suppose you'd better," replied the disgruntled secret service agent, who had hoped to kill two birds with one stone and take a look at a particular building of interest in the northern sector.

The helicopter eventually began to descend into the cloud. The agent wondered if the pilot felt as uncomfortable as he did, not being able to see anything, above, below or around them.

Then the cloud began to break up, a little at first then disappearing totally. Steel saw over in the distance a large sleek white yacht, only the slightest wake coming from her bows, and even less from behind.

"Do you think that's her, sir?" asked the pilot.

"Possibly," said Steel, "possibly." He spoke slowly, taking a closer look through the high-powered binoculars, pulling on the extra zoom.

"Do you want me to make a pass first, sir, or do you want to hover directly above the boat?" The young aviator asked, this time looking at the agent as he spoke.

"You'd better make a couple of passes first. If it is the right boat then we can take a closer look."

"Roger, sir, you're the boss," he said giving a mock salute with his left hand.

They were approaching the yacht within minutes. The pilot told the agent that the boat was about three miles away.

"Three point seven five to be precise," he had said.

The first pass was too high. At the agent's request the pilot turned to make a second, when the radio crackled then a loud voice rasped into the agent's ears.

"This is private motor yacht Lady Saqqquuuuushshshs," the name disappearing in heavy squelch.

"Helicopter Charlie Tango Bravo three zero, please identify yourself, come back."

"Don't answer that," the agent said to the pilot.

"But, sir!"

"You heard what I said, now pass over one more time please."

The radio came back again, crystal clear and asking for identification but this time not volunteering the name of the boat. The agent could not see a name on the vessel.

"Go in lower, and hover please, young man," the agent muttered peering intently through the powerful binoculars.

The pilot did as he was asked. He came in at about one hundred feet, just in time to see a uniformed man carrying a dark object across the brilliant white surface of the forward deck, and then set it down on top of a raised hatch cover.

"What is that?" asked the pilot.

"Jesus! Get the hell out of here; move, get this bloody helicopter out of here, do it now! For Christ's sake move your ass!"

"What was all that about?" asked a bemused pilot as they sped towards Cyprus.

"That young man, was a hand held rocket launcher, that pierces the armour plate of a military tank, or ship, and certainly the delicate skin of a whirlybird like this," said the slightly perturbed secret service agent as he looked behind wondering whether they had sent one after them. A cold shiver went down his spine, and knowing a lot about the owner of the boat that he was looking for, he felt sure the boat he had just left was one and the same. That was exactly the kind of ruthless act to be expected of Mr Sahaed. *Not so much an act, more a gesture or threat,* he thought to himself as he climbed down from the helicopter.

"Round one to you, Sahaed," he said aloud as he walked towards his rental car.

Labour Party Headquarters, London

The general election was well under way. To all intents and purposes the Socialists had it in the bag. According to the opinion polls the electorate's decision was all over bar the shouting of such phrases as 'Landslide victory, walkover, whitewash,' that were appearing in the press. The Labour Party had put together one of the finest election campaigns in recent history. Their leader, the Right Honourable Tony Blain, had, without doubt, run a personal PR campaign, the like of which had never been seen in the history of British political electioneering.

The Labour party campaign was more akin to an American Presidential performance, coupled with the fact that the image of the Tory party was already at an all time low. The recently resigned outgoing Prime Minister had been unable to control his party, they had argued and squabbled themselves into oblivion in front of the whole world. One columnist said:

'To achieve a victory over such a watered down ineffective bunch of old women who couldn't even agree amongst themselves, let alone on government policy, whose thinking and policies were still back in the dark ages, should not really be regarded as a great feat, more a happy release.'

Another one of the more vicious and verbally colourful journalists had put it: 'Like seeing a favourite aunt struck down with a terminal disease, suffering untold agony for months, then the happy release of death.'

Actual polling was to take place in three days' time. As in the last election, anticipation was high on both sides. Last time the Tories had crept in with a fine margin, a last minute turn around.

'The quality of the Labour party campaign must have cost a fortune,' said a well-known middle-of-the-road reporter. A leading public relations company had been retained by the Socialists, and had built Tony Blain into a most marketable political commodity.

'A victory for Labour would be a vote for a personality and not a party,' said a headline in a leading national newspaper, known for its Tory affiliations.

Anwar Sahaed sat in his apartment above Harrobys, feeling like the king of the castle. Everything was going to plan. He listened with a permanent grin on his face as television procrastinators continued to forecast the demise of the Tory party. Members of the public were interviewed on the streets. The same answer came back with monotonous regularity.

"It's time for us to cast off the old and bring on the new." Sahaed caught the smell of change in the air. He also knew that he had made significant input into the scenario.

"I will take the look of arrogance from the face of that pompous John Mannors," he had said after a meeting with the Prime Minister, who had chided him for his muted offers of funds.

"Mr Sahaed, if I understand your intimations correctly, and the more pointed ones made to other colleagues recently, let me leave you in no doubt whatsoever, that Her Majesty's Government is not for sale. If you should wish to make a donation to the party, then you must do it through the proper channels, with no strings attached," Mannors had said, in a gesture that ended the meeting. Sahaed watched a television interviewer talking to Mannors.

"You will pay now, Mr. Big Shot. You will see that nobody messes with Anwar Sahaed," he said, raising a glass to his portrait on the wall, a look of supreme arrogance emblazoned across his face.

The Sahaed Residence, Cairo, Egypt

Princess Anna sat in the ornate surroundings of the Sahaed mansion. By Cairo standards it was more a palace than a mansion and in fact the building used to be the palace of Egyptian royalty many hundreds of years before.   Raffi came into the room dressed in traditional Arabic attire. He looked relaxed, his darker skin and jet black hair against the gold edged white gave him the look of a king from biblical times, The whole setting gave an aura of times long ago, though looking out into the courtyard she saw Rolls Royces and helicopters, rather than horse drawn chariots.

Walking from the room together, Anna half expected to see a steel helmeted guard with shield and spear, rather than the well suited body-guard who stood there instead. They walked along the terrace, which was covered by grape vines, fig trees and fan palms. They sat at a table where a servant poured them iced drinks, and then left as Raffi waved him away.

"There's something I have to tell you, my darling," she said, taking the hand of the Arab in hers. Raffi took on a stern look at the serious note in her voice.

"What is it my dear?" he asked. She paused and took a sip of her citrus juice.

"You are the first person I have discussed this matter with," she said to Raffi, dropping her eyes to the glass in her hand. "Raffi I think I'm pregnant. I am carrying your child."

Raffi could not hide the shock of her statement, his eyes opened wide. He instantly understood the ramifications of what she had just said. She too knew the problems involved and the dangers that would ensue. Though she was relatively free from the royal constraints, the spin off from this could be catastrophic.

General Election Countdown London

It was one o'clock in the morning following the day of polling. There had been an overwhelming defeat for the Conservative party, as constituencies fell one after another to the Labour Party. The full count would not be known until much later in the day, but victory was assured. Tony Blain was the new occupant of Number 10 Downing Street, the youngest-ever Socialist incumbent, and one of the youngest Prime Ministers in history.

The scene was set for change. The Tory party was in disarray, and would be licking its wounds, re-grouping, and electing new leadership for the future. They looked like being in opposition for a long time to come. The Labour party was far different from the old working class only party of the past. Maybe the country was in for some drastic changes. The general opinion of most, including many staunch Tories was, 'maybe it's a good thing, let's wait and see.' This was not a marginal affair. The British public had made its voice felt in no uncertain manner.

Princess Anna sat in her apartments in Kensington Palace watching the events on television as they unfolded. She had met Tony Blain on a number of occasions recently, and held him in high esteem. This was a younger man with whom the princess could more easily relate.

Anna was to see her sons later. She was to have lunch with Edward who was in London for the day. Eton school was on vacation. Then she was to go to the theatre with both he and George in the evening. She could not get Raffi out of her mind, or the ever-increasing problems that her pregnancy was sure to bring.

Cairo, Egypt

The cocktail bar at the Cairo Hilton was crowded, as usual, during happy hour. It had become the 'in' place; the meeting place for many of the business people and professionals enjoying a cocktail en-route home to dinner. In fact, if you wanted to drink in the company of the largest cross-section in the city, this was the watering hole. Likewise, if you were desirous of catching up on the gossip of the city or picking up information on most topics, this was the place to be.

Steel was booked into the Hilton for one night. He sat drinking alone, and paying rapt attention to a number of the more interesting discourses taking place. *Thank God, but why is it that all conversations in a bar are carried out at twice the decibel level of any other type of meeting*, he thought to himself.

The majority of the customers spoke either English or one of the European languages, which made listening a little easier. The agent was just about to start on his second cocktail when he received a hearty slap on the back followed by another loud voice, this time American.

"Well, I'll be a son of a gun, if it's not the one and only big David. What brings you to these parts, my old friend?" He looked into the face of Kevin Reilly, the resident CIA station boss on the Arab desk.

"Well, fancy seeing you here my friend, and not so much of the old if you don't mind." They took their drinks and went across to an empty table in a slightly quieter part of the room.

"I got your message only a half hour ago, buddy. What's up; what's the big panic? Somebody shot the Queen?" asked the American, smiling sarcastically as he spoke.

"No, not quite, but the problem I have is nearly as serious," the MI6 man said, keeping his voice down and looking casually around the bar as he spoke.

"Well, come on, give. Are you going to tell me, or what?" snapped the American.

"I wish I could, Kev, I wish I could. This matter is so hush, hush that I don't have the complete facts. Nevertheless, I still need some help from you. I want to take a look at a local man, Dr Hasseem Nasser, evidently a quack of some eminence in these parts."

"You can say that again. He is the equivalent of our presidential physician, or your doctor to the Royal Household," the American agent said.

"Where does he practice? Does he spend time at the big hospitals here?"

"Hey, slow down with the questions," said the American. "He has extensive consulting rooms and research facilities in the professional quarter of the city. He is prominent in most of the larger hospitals and he specialises in internal medicine. He is also as popular with the ex-pats as he is with the local population. Needless to say, he is an extremely wealthy man. He recently flew to London to carry out an operation at a private clinic, on the stomach of none other than Anwar Sahaed," the CIA man paused, raising his eyebrows with a knowing smirk. When Steel had gleaned all of the information possible on the good doctor, he bought the American a meal at a small local restaurant, and then took a cab back to his Hotel.

The Professional Quarter of Cairo

The figure of a man moved quickly into the shadow of the shop doorway, then slid out and disappeared down a side alley. He was wearing a black knitted ski cap and a tight fitting black exercise suit. He heaved himself effortlessly onto the top of a dumpster filled with trash. Swinging up onto a higher wall he ran swiftly along its length with agility of a circus high wire expert, and then began to climb lithely up the water down pipe on the side of the building. He swung across to the third storey window ledge, lost his handgrip and narrowly missed a fatal fall. Hanging onto the ledge with one hand, he deftly forced the window with the other. As it popped open with a loud resounding crack the man looked down, but could see no movement below. He hoped that the noise had not been heard by anyone inside the building.

From across the other side of the street, a man in his car looked through his infrared night sight binoculars. He watched the trespasser slide effortlessly into the building.

The man made short work of the fire exit door, which, as he had assumed, was not connected to an alarm system. Inside, the building was in complete darkness. He stood at the top of the inside fire escape stairway listening for the slightest sound, but the pumping of his own blood was all that he heard hissing in his ears. He began to search the whole floor thoroughly, until he found the office of the doctor. Here the emergency door lights gave sufficient glow for him to read the plate on the door: **Dr Hasseem Nasser MD, Consulting Rooms and Research Institute.**

Leading off from the door were the consulting rooms and clinic. He went into an administration area equipped with a patient record cards system covering a whole wall. He went through the area of names that were of interest to him, but could not find what he needed. He shone the thin quartz flashlight around the room, which settled on the computer. He sat down and began to search the records system. Every time he hit a patient name, especially one of those he had gleaned from the American agent, the computer called for a password to enter the secret patient record files.

He knew this was going to be a long night as he dialled the mini-mobile phone he had taken from his pocket. Anywhere in the world one could buy a computer hacker; Cairo was certainly no exception to that rule.

After searching the computer for three hours, trying every conceivable combination and at the same time being coached by a pro geek on the phone, he found what he wanted.

"Bingo!" shouted the masked hacker. "That's it! You did it you crazy young bugger, you did it. I owe you one," he said, lifting off the ski mask and revealing the face of David Steel. He got into the file quickly.

"Got it, Jesus, it's all here," he said quietly. *Jesus Christ, now the shit really hits the fan*, he thought to himself. As he pressed file/print the paper began to emerge from the printer. He had taken the whole file of VIP patients for good measure. He folded the document, stuffing it into his inside pocket.

He left the building, this time going down the inside fire stairway, exiting by the ground floor fire door. As it opened the electronic alarm began to screech. He was just about to leave the alleyway when a car squealed to a halt. A familiar voice shouted through the open passenger window.

"Get in, you noisy son of a bitch. What you trying to do? Wake up the pharaohs and the Sphinx?" It was the voice of Kevin Reilly.

"Now, do you want to tell me what's going on, or shall I drop you off at the local precinct?"

"OK, you Yank bum, but when I tell you that this is top secret, I mean, top secret," the British agent replied. Another police car flew screaming past them as they drove along the road. The rear bumper on the American's car carried diplomatic plates.

They arrived back at the Hilton Hotel, called the night porter and ordered coffee and a large cognac each. The MI6 man brought the CIA man up to date, after a sworn oath of secrecy, on peril of death, from The Company man SSA (Senior Supervising Agent) Reilly.

The following morning Steel arrived at the airport very early. He was to meet an agency jet that had been re-routed on its way to London from Africa. He had met a man from the British Embassy in Cairo, who was not at all pleased having to come to the airport at 4:30am just to clear the departure of some secret agent. The British Lear Jet took off from Cairo at 6am.

The aircraft in front of Steel had just received clearance to take off as the captain of the Gulf Stream jet pushed forward on the throttles. The sleek plane shot into the air, its only passenger and owner sat back in his seat, a look of total satisfaction on his face. *Things are really going above my expectations*, Anwar Sahaed thought.

The Dorchester Hotel, Hyde Park, London

Raffi sat in the magnificent royal suite at the Dorchester. His father usually had one of the suites booked permanently to accommodate any visiting VIPs. He had told his father that he wanted to stay in London and that he would be entertaining Princess Anna. He had insisted Raffi take the royal suite.

"Nothing else will suffice," he had said to his son with a magnanimous gesture of his arms.

The noise of a phone warbling brought him from the depth of his thoughts. He picked up the receiver.

"Oh, Anna darling, how nice of you to call. I was just thinking of you — you must be telepathic. Sounds great to me, what time will you be over?" There was a pause as the conversation continued. "That's great. I'll see you here. Yes I'll send one of my men down to the car park under the hotel at seven o'clock precisely. A white Ford Granada you said? That will be no problem my love."

Raffi sat down with a sigh, perhaps of relief, perhaps of concern. He wondered what his father would have to say when he told him of the pregnancy. The affair was moving ahead far too quickly. What had started as a wild fling with a romantic princess was now getting well out of hand. As he sat staring into space, he was startled as the telephone gave half a ring then went silent again.

Raffi picked up the walkie-talkie, and spoke to his bodyguard in the special security room just along the corridor.

"Did you try to call me just then? Somebody did, it only rang a half ring, just a tinkle. Yes, check it out will you please." he was becoming paranoid of the security measures since meeting Princess Anna.

He answered a knock at the door of the suite and one of his bodyguards walked into the room.

"I want you to go down to the car park at seven o'clock. Princess Anna will arrive there in a white Ford Granada. She will be driving, and wearing a tweed flat cap. What was the problem with the phone?" he asked him.

"I spoke with the desk and they did not try to put a call through. All calls have to go through them, as you know. They are all vetted and logged — every one. That is a standing instruction from your father. Anyhow, they are sending someone up to check the system at this end. We already swept the place, there are no devices here, of that you can be sure," said the big man.

There was another knock at the door. The bodyguard went across and spoke, then opened the door. Standing there was another of his security men, along with a man carrying electronic meters, and a belt full of tools who was wearing hotel ID. The first bodyguard frisked the man, made him take the tool belt off, and went through it thoroughly. He then made the man empty his pockets totally.

"This is all a bit much guv, isn't it? I've heard of the third degree, but this is bloody ridiculous."

"That's as may be and if you don't like it you can always bugger off," said the guard, with a strong Welsh accent, as he frisked the man once again, this time considerably more enthusiastically.

"Well don't just stand there, get on with it," said the second bodyguard to the workman.

The man proceeded to check each of the five telephone extensions, finally going over the main junction box. Apart from one time when Raffi asked him a question, the bodyguard never took his eyes away. He watched every move made by the telephone technician.

Across the road from the Dorchester Hotel, a van of the Royal Parks Department stood in the trees on the edge of Hyde Park.

"There it goes, he's done it," exclaimed one of the men in the back of the van.

"Don't ask me how, but he has. I can't hear any sounds directly from the room, but we are certainly connected to the phone line. There are only four rooms in the suite: bedroom, bathroom, kitchenette and sitting room. If he could only put one in, it could be in any of those rooms," said the eavesdropping expert to the other man in the back of the Parks van.

"I hope it's not the bathroom," said Steel. "Knowing my luck I'll bet it is," he said to the man wearing the headset.

The man held up his hand.

"You're wrong. I can hear the chink of a glass so it's either the kitchen or the sitting room," replied the other man, smiling as he spoke. He passed another set of headphones to the agent, who took a seat, making himself as comfortable as was possible in the confined space.

"I'll take it for a while, if you want to go and stretch your legs and have a smoke and take a pee," the agent said.

"Thanks," said the other man as he threw down the headset and left the van.

"I will get back along the corridor now, sir. Seven o'clock you said the princess would arrive, I assume she will park near the elevator. I'll be off then."

Steel had heard every word clearly. He looked at his watch it was just four thirty.

"As I said, it's going to be a long day, old lad," he said to himself, sighing. At least he seemed to be getting somewhere at last. There was a knocking on the side door of the van.

"Anybody in there,"

"It's the police here. Is there anyone in there?" Steel opened the door.

"Good evening, officer," he said, showing the constable a Metropolitan Police Flying Squad ID of a Chief Inspector.

"Sorry to bother you, sir," said the policeman. "Anything interesting, sir?" he asked.

"Just a spot of ear wigging," replied the agent. "I'll swap you jobs anytime. I hate pulling these duties," he said to the constable.

"No thanks, sir, I'm doing just fine," replied the younger man as he went on his way.

"Bloody cops," he said aloud climbing back into the van.

Kensington Palace

Princess Anna left by the rear door wearing blue jeans, a loose fitting workout sweater, Nike sneakers and an old tweed flat cap on her head. She walked casually across to the white Ford Granada, climbed in and drove off. With the windows tinted, she felt totally invisible as she melted into the evening traffic, *just another face in another Ford*, she thought.

She had failed to notice the motorcycle that pulled in behind her as she went around the traffic island at Hyde Park Corner. She passed the building with the most unique address in the world, 'Number 1, London,' the home of a former a Prime Minister of England, Benjamin Disraeli, back in 1868.

Anna turned to drive along Hyde Park and caught sight of the bike out of the corner of her eye. The rider was wearing the reflective vest of a courier service, its name emblazoned front and back. Unlike most motorcycle couriers in the city, this one was not in the usual hurry, weaving in and out of the traffic at high speeds as though on a vital mission of mercy. This one kept alongside the princess's car with his head continually turning to the left trying to see past the heavily tinted glass.

Anna instantly recognised the style of the press, or paparazzi, as they had recently been christened. She drove on past the Dorchester. As she approached Marble Arch, she saw a larger crowd than usual gathered at Speakers Corner, the famous area for free speaking orators of all callings. She really wanted to shake this human parasite, but was not sure which way to go, straight on up the Edgware Road, or right towards busy Oxford Street. She waited until the very last minute then threw the wheel violently to the right, then back to the left; with an almighty screech of tyres, the front of the Granada narrowly missing the big Kawasaki bike. As its rider struggled admirably to stay upright, he eventually lost the battle, and hit the curbside, smashing into a pedestrian barrier. He lay sprawled on the road, his machine was in the centre of the road ten feet ahead, the front wheel still spinning freely as fuel gushed out onto the road surface. Anna had continued straight across into the Edgware Road, just another car amidst the noise and confusion of yet another London accident.

The princess smiled as she looked into her rear view mirror. The traffic behind had come to a complete standstill as an ambulance tried in vain to reach the immobilised, upturned invader of her valuable privacy.

Serves the cretin right, Anna thought to herself as she turned into a side street in preparation of retracing her tracks, which was not going to be simple, through the system of one way streets that seemed to change by the day, sometimes seemingly by the hour.

The Dorchester Hotel

Gavin Jones stood in the shadows of the concrete pillars in the underground car park, opposite the entrance to the hotel elevator. He looked at his watch. It was 7:20pm. The earpiece crackled slightly.

"What's going on Gavin, any signs yet?" He lifted his right hand and scratched his nose.

"Nothing yet," he whispered into the microphone clipped to his wristwatch strap.

"Gavin, the princess just called on the mobile, she'll be there in a couple of minutes," said the voice in his ear.

"Roger," he whispered in reply. All the time Gavin had been speaking, he had not taken his eyes off a Ford Sierra parked diagonally across from the elevator entrance. There was a man sitting in the car. He went behind the pillar next to him, bent down to waist height, and then moved quickly behind a row of parked cars. He moved in a complete circle. Coming up cautiously behind the Ford Sierra, he lifted up sufficiently to see into the car. The vehicle was unoccupied.

He looked around, and then dropped to the ground on his stomach. Looking across the ground a full ninety degrees, in search of a pair of feet, he saw nothing but the wheels of the white Granada as it pulled up opposite the entrance. Gavin sprang to his feet, and was at the door of the car in a trice. He opened the driver's door.

"Good evening, Ma'am. Please move over. I would like to take the car from here."

"What's up, Gavin?"

"Just routine Ma'am. Nothing to worry about. Can't be too careful these days," the bodyguard said as he took the car around the underground car park one more time. When he returned to the elevator entrance he noticed that the Sierra had gone.

"I have the goods, and will be home in about five minutes," he said into the hand mike.

"Roger, I'll be down with the elevator now," came the reply. Jones drove the car into the coned off space next to the elevator, pushing the red rubber cone along with the front of the car.

"Ready when you are, Princess Anna, Ma'am," he said with the open door in his hand. They both moved quickly through the door into the elevator lobby. The doors slid silently open.

"Good evening, Your Highness," said a second security man from inside the elevator. "An uneventful evening I trust," as the doors slid shut.

"Not exactly," the princess replied,"but then that's par for the course."

Jones had opened the 'not to be opened' panel on the wall of the elevator, and turned the indicator switch to non-stop. The car went all the way up to the royal suite.

Across the other side of the road, Steel pulled up behind the Royal Parks van in the Ford Sierra. He locked the car, walked across and gave four short taps on the side of the van. The side door slid open.

"She's in there," he said to the man wearing the headset.

"Those security men are quite good. Let's not underestimate them," he said as an afterthought.

The princess went into the royal suite. Gavin Jones nodded to his colleague who stayed outside the door of his boss's rooms. Jones walked towards the specially prepared security room that was now a standard feature of most VIP suites throughout the world. He went inside, kicked off his shoes, undid his tie, and sat in an easy chair. He looked at the bank of four television monitors. The one showing inside the suite went blank, the others showing the car park, the hotel reception and the entrance to the suite, all showed their pictures. The earpiece crackled into life again.

"You get some shut-eye Gav. I'll call you in a couple of hours," came the voice on the other end. Jones was not keen on sleeping while on duty, so he continued to watch the screens out of the corner of his eye while he read a book. Gavin enjoyed his job nearly as much as he had enjoyed the love of his life, rugby. He was born in the Welsh valleys, where he had initially worked down the coal mine. He had always been a big lad and took to the game of rugby like a duck to water. He had played for his home town and then later for Cardiff, and eventually had played for his country.

Like a lot of the boys from the valleys, the call of the outside world became overpowering. Gavin had followed his mates and joined the British Paratroop Regiment. He had seen active service in the desert during the Iraqi Desert Storm war. Then he passed the stringent tests and transferred to the world's top military special service, the Twenty-Second Regiment, better known as 22 or the SAS. Afterwards, the prospect of going back to the peace of the Welsh valleys was not for him, so he joined the London Metropolitan Police force. After three years of boredom and shift work, the internal bureaucracy became too much, so he went to a private security school, where one of the instructors was an ex-22 sergeant. His choice later was to either join a bunch of mercenaries or find some protection work.

He worked for a year as a bodyguard for the infamous Colonel Gadaffi, then a year with one of the Dubai Sheiks. He then joined up with Sahaed two years ago, and enjoyed every minute of his job.

Jones put down his book with a start; a sudden thought came to his mind. *Who the hell was the man in the Sierra? He certainly wasn't the press, he'd been too smart and slippery for that. He was either from Brit security or palace security - either way his appearance there was not accidental.*

He put on his shoes; straightened his tie, turned up the volume control of his microphone.

"Everything quiet there?" he said to his colleague.

"Yeah Guv, not a murmur. What's up chum? Something bugging you?"

"Yes, as it happens, there is. I'm coming out there now."   Meanwhile, in the van across the road, the eavesdroppers sat glued to their headsets.

"You were right. Our man was able to place only the one bug and it was in the sitting room," said Steel to the other man. "Evidently that big Welshman doesn't miss a trick." Then they heard through the speakers:

"Let me pour you a drink, darling," Raffi said to Princess Anna, "you look a little harassed."

"Thanks, I don't mind if I do. I had a bit of a problem with those damned press people on the way here. That's why I was a little late. Bloody man followed me on a motorbike. I knocked him off it, actually," the princess said with a broad grin.

"You did what?"

"I turned the wheel at him and he fell off the bike," said Anna.

"Was he hurt?" asked Raffi.

"I don't think so, but I'll bet he wasn't too damn happy. Thanks darling, that's fine," she said as he passed her a glass. "We are really going to have to address this situation of ours, my darling," said Anna. "The only real solution is a termination, and soon. I know it sounds a bit drastic, but everything considered, it's the only thing to do. But where could it be done in total secrecy?"

"We have a family doct..."

The ringing of the room telephone interrupted the conversation. "Yes Gavin.... well I suppose so.... but is that really necessary? Alright then, you had better get on with it," said Raffi, putting the phone down.

"What was that all about?" asked Anna.

Raffi put his finger to her lips, and shook his open hand in a gesture for her not to speak.

There was a knock on the door. Jones and his number two came into the room. The bodyguard was carrying an electronic device. He went into the bedroom, then seconds later he went into the kitchen, then went to a phone point on the baseboard in the sitting room. He bent down put the device to the little plastic box. His head shot back as his face lit up when a green light began to flash rapidly. He took off the cover of the junction box and with a pair of pliers pulled out a small object, the size of a penny.

"There you are, I was right," he beamed as he held up the tiny electronic bug.

"I don't know how they got that sodding thing in there, if you'll pardon the vernacular, Ma'am," he said turning to the princess.

"Somebody is determined to watch and listen to you both, sir, and I'm not quite sure who, but I intend to find out. I am going to reconnect this device in a minute. When I do, turn on the television. Please don't speak, we will double sweep the bedroom, then you can go in there and speak freely. Then I'll go and find the eavesdroppers," Jones said to the couple.

Raffi went into the bathroom. Anna lay on the bed, her hands behind her head.

"Well that's the first time we've been ordered to the bed chamber," said Raffi, as he rolled over on the bed towards Anna.

Across the road in the van the bug had gone dead, then somehow miraculously come to life again. All they could hear were television adverts, then the introduction of the soap, Eastenders.

"We can pack up and go home now, young man," the agent said to the other man in the van.

"Why, what's up?" he asked Steel.

"They found the bug. That security man of theirs, the Welshman, he's good. I'm going to enjoy doing further battle with him," said the agent, throwing the headset down onto the surface of the workbench. "He's very good; he's damn good, in fact." He moved to the door with a semi-embarrassed grin on his face like the boxer who knew he'd just lost the last round, but savoured the prospect of the next.

"I'll see you later," he added, and then opened the sliding door, disappearing into the night.

MI6 Offices: Vauxhall Cross, London

David Steel sat in the office of his boss Sir Martin Fields. They had discussed the royal affair in great detail. Steel was well and truly debriefed. Now that he was fully up to date, Sir Martin sat and looked at the agent for a full twenty seconds without speaking, then stood and walked towards the window, pulling back the heavy drapes, looking out on busy Vauxhall.

"This can't be allowed to continue," he said, referring to the latest reports from his agent.

"You do realise the ramifications here, don't you, Steel?" The chief turned and looked the agent square in the eyes as he spoke, the force of his comment being emphasised by his action.

"Yes, I suppose that I do, sir. The princess is sowing her wild oats, and seems have gotten herself into the family way. But she is divorced and over twenty-one, sir!"

"You don't seem to have grasped the seriousness of the situati…"

"Of course I damn well appreciate the seriousness, I'd even say the severity. Are you trying to insult my intelligence, sir?" said the agent who'd jumped to his feet as he'd cut across his pompous boss. "My flippancy was in answer to your perceived insult, sir," he replied, facetiously.

Sir Martin sat down in his chair with a loud bang and a resigned sigh. He continued, totally ignoring the outburst from his subordinate.

"This all adds up to a definite no-no, then add to those facts, pressure from the Prime Minister's office and you don't have to be a genius to work out who is pressuring the PM. You have a situation that just has to be stopped. The questions are quite simply, how and by whom?"

David Steel did not like the look on his boss's face as he spoke glaring emphatically into the agent's eyes.

"It is on that note, Mr Steel that I'll close the subject for now, and let you go away and reflect on those questions. We have to answer them and carry out the conclusions, and quickly, before the matter gets completely out of hand." He waved his hand, dismissing the agent.

Sir Martin picked up the phone as it rang. The agent remained sitting in the chair opposite his boss.

"You may leave now, Steel," he said irritably, waving his hand in a gesture of dismissal once more.

"Call me back tomorrow with your solutions to the situation. Sorry about that Prime Minister… Yes, I was just discussing the matter with one of my senior operatives... yes I agree that the matter is reaching serious proportions. I understand, sir. If you will leave the matter in our hands, we'll find a solution, rest assured."

Sir Martin Fields, chief of MI6, hated outside interference from any source, and in particular from Number 10 Downing Street. The new tenant had only been there for a couple of days, and here he was already trying to take over the Secret Service.

"Leave the brainwork to the professionals, for Christ's sake," he said out loud, banging his fist down hard on his blotter. "Bloody politicians," he muttered to himself, as he got up and walked out of his office.

Sitting in the rear seat of the Jaguar with traffic already starting to build up to the rush hour crescendo, he had to agree with the PM's sentiments. This matter was out of hand and had to be stopped. Sir Martin knew that the new Premier had already got onto MI5, the other branch of Government security, which was looked upon as being second in line to his agency, and that he'd instituted plans with them to discredit the princess in the eyes of the public. Their section F specialised in subversive tactics, such as discrediting people and organisations. Much like the USA, where the FBI operates within the country and the CIA overseas, MI5 operates mainly in Great Britain and MI6 abroad, though the defining lines are not quite so clear cut. The offices of both secret intelligence services are a short distance from the other, separated only by Old Father Thames.

Harrobys, Knightsbridge, London

Anwar Sahaed had just received final confirmation from his friend and cohort, Dr Hasseem Nasser, that Princess Anna was indeed pregnant. The second confirmation had arrived that very day. Sahaed was beside himself with joy. His wildest dreams were just around the corner. *A marriage, then I will have a member of the British Royal Family as a daughter-in-law. In future years, the mother of my grandchild would be the mother of the King of England. If my grandchild were a boy, then he would be half brother to the King of England. Not only would they have to give me British citizenship then, they may even give me a title*, he thought with a smile.

He took both lapels of his jacket in the palms of his hands. Standing in front of the mirrored wall of the office, he lifted his head inclining it to one side. "The Duke of Knightsbridge is here to see you your Highness!" Sahaed said out loud. He swept his right arm across his waist, and bowed his head in a regal gesture.

He was jolted back to reality by the ringing of the phone. He walked across to his desk and flipped the speaker switch. "Yes," he snapped.

"I have Mr Armimi on the line for you, sir,"

He moved quickly around his desk, picking up the receiver. "Put him through please," he said in a more friendly tone then normal. "Agnin, how are you my brother-in-law?"

"I'm fine," came the curt reply in Arabic.

"I shall be in London tomorrow. Arrange accommodation for me at the Savoy for two nights. There are some very important things that we have to discuss. I have talked with Hasseem Nasser today. On the one hand, the news is good, but it could also herald much trouble. Evidently his offices in Egypt were broken into. The computer, where top security medical records like yours and mine are kept, was violated.

"In future we will keep telephone conversations to a minimum, and then only in our own tongue. Anything pertaining to this subject will from now on be discussed only face to face," said Agnin Armimi. The phone went dead.

Anwar Sahaed hung up then picked up the phone again, tapped out a London number, drumming his fingers on his desk. The phone rang too many times for his liking.

"Yes, Sahaed here, I want to talk to Jones," he said to a member of his security team. Gavin Jones came to the phone

"I want you to get round to my office right away, drop whatever you're doing, cover yourself first. Be here in twenty minutes at the latest."

"Yes sir, I'll be there right away,"

Jones reorganised his morning. He had put other people onto work that he would normally have been doing himself. Once he was fully covered, he was in his car and speeding across the West End towards Harrobys.

It was exactly fifteen minutes to the second since his boss had called when he pulled into the private part of the underground parking area, beneath the famous store. He parked between a Rolls Royce and a Maserati Mistral.

"How's it going, Gavin?" said a voice from behind a Bentley Turbo. He looked across to see the cheerful face of the boss's chauffeur, as he polished away at the gleaming car.

"Fine thanks, boyo, and you?"

"Plenty to keep me busy here," replied the driver.

"Mr Jones is here to see you, sir," said the voice of Sahaed's secretary over the intercom.

"He says he has an appointment, but I didn't make one for you, sir."

"That's alright, send him through. I made the arrangement myself a few minutes ago, but forgot to tell you."

"Take a seat, Jones," the Arab said to the bodyguard. Jones looked around him ogling the opulent surroundings as he had never seen a room such as this before, let alone an office. "There are a few potential problems coming our way," Sahaed continued, "I want you and the rest of the security staff fully prepared for all contingencies. You're already fully aware that Mr Raffi has been watched around the clock since he became friendly with the princess."

"That's right, sir," Jones replied. "I was going to talk to you on that very subject. Their room was bugged at the Dorchester last week. I also spotted someone sitting in a car in the underground car park that same evening sir. I did some research, the car used that night was a Hertz rental, led me to a dead end, sir," he said to his boss.

"Do you have any idea who these people are?" asked Sahaed.

"No sir, but I am sure there are at least three different groups involved, none of which is connected. I think that one of the groups is the press. They are clumsy and very obvious — amateur, when it comes to subtle operations, sir," the security man said with a smile. "Don't get me wrong though, sir, they're still very dangerous as they're a new breed and very tenacious. The media have christened them the paparazzi. They will stop at nothing to get their pictures, sir. Both of the other groups are extremely professional. In fact sir, I think that we have at least one of the 'M' branches on our tails." A very serious look came across Jones' face.

Sahaed held up his hand.

"There are other happenings that are of equal concern. Princess Anna went for a medical check up at our family doctor's surgery back in Cairo last week. Shortly afterwards, those offices were broken into. Nothing was taken, but the private patient files in the computer were entered, and prints were made, including the files of my son. Such a break-in is beyond the wiles of the paparazzi, I am sure. Also, during my son's last Mediterranean cruise with Princess Anna, they were buzzed by a helicopter off Cyprus. We must tighten up our security. I want you to let me know what increases in manpower are necessary. I, like you, am convinced that there are forces following us who will stop at nothing to end this relationship between Raffi and the princess, and who would at the same time like to discredit the Sahaed name."

The scene in the private underground garage at Harrobys was one of much activity amongst the ten or so garage hands who were working there. One was part of the security team. He spoke perfect English, along with about four other languages, and was also very clever with electronics and explosives. He had been trained by one of the Middle East terrorist factions. Sahaed had yet again found the right price! Hank Marlin walked into the vast garage area. Without looking round he knew that someone was close behind him.

"Stay right where you are," said a voice with a tinge of an accent.

"Don't turn round. Put your hands on your head. You are on private property; you're not wearing an identity tag and have no authority to be here." Hank did as he was asked. He was quickly checked for firearms, and then told to turn around. He found himself looking into the dark bottomless eyes of a Middle Eastern man. Shorter in stature, physically fit, light on his feet, and extremely alert.

"What is your business here?" the man asked. Hank put his hand cautiously into his inside jacket pocket and brought out his police ID, showing it to the Arab.

"What can we do for the police inspector today?" said the man calmly.

"I want to talk to a Mr. Jones."

"There is nobody here of that name. In fact the only Jones I know is the singer Tom Jones," said the man with a sickly smirk on his face, curling his lips as he spoke exposing badly shaped yellow teeth, further emphasising the disrespect and sarcasm in his voice.

"I will give you just twenty seconds to come up with a better answer than that mister. If not I'll bang your backside into jail so fast you won't know what hit you. Maybe we'll take a look at your papers, and whilst we're at it we'll need the license for that gun in your pocket." He said pointing to the ominous lump showing through the Arab's trouser pocket. "Now answer my question you insolent piece of shit!" snapped a normally calm and otherwise pleasant Inspector Hank Marlin, of The Metropolitan Police Royal Protection Group.

"That won't be necessary, inspector," said a voice from an open office. A well-built man walked out of the door and came across to where Hank stood.

"Inspector Marlin, I presume," said the man in a broad Welsh accent. "I'm Gavin Jones."

"How very perceptive of you, Mr. Jones," said Hank. He didn't turn to look at Jones as the Arab and he still had their eyes locked in a mutual no-love-lost stare.....

"That will be all," Jones said to the Arab who reluctantly walked away.

"I'll see you again, Mr. Motor mouth," Hank snapped, as the Arab moved away

"I'm not being perceptive inspector. I have you on my computer profiles and also a mutual friend of ours speaks very highly of you." said Jones. "That was a very close shave you had in Brighton the other day inspector, a very close shave indeed. You had us all worried for a while there," the big Welshman said, holding out his hand to Hank.

"Come on into the office for a minute. I'll clear myself to leave, then maybe we'll go and have a pint and a sandwich."

"Sounds like a great idea to me," replied Hank.

Ten minutes later, after the Welshman issued instructions to various people, they were walking across the garage. Hank noticed that although the Arab was polishing lethargically on a Jaguar, he still kept one eye firmly on him. *I don't think I'd like to meet him on a dark night in the wrong mood*, Hank thought to himself.

They found a pub around the corner from the big store. Judging by the number of people in there it was a very popular haunt. After drinking a beer at the bar, a corner table was vacated quiet enough to talk without interruption, or more importantly being overheard.

Steel sat at the other end of the bar. He couldn't get near enough to hear, and he knew that neither of these two men would miss the ear attachment, if he were to connect up the device, so he had to sit and wait.

"I appreciate the chance to have a chat with you," Hank said. "I think you know where I stand as far as the princess is concerned. Any questions or comments I may have are purely in her interest. If you are aware of the unfortunate Brighton incident, then you are left in no doubt as to the seriousness of the situation. There are people who will, without any thought or question, kill one or both of your charges. I'll make no secret of the fact that I advised the princess to stop seeing the young man. I also advised her to cancel all of her public appearances. She refused on both counts and if you knew her as well as I do, you'd know she means no," said Hank.

"There have been one or two recent occurrences culminating in the Brighton affair. Incidentally, Mr Sahaed came to me first and said it was time to increase security. He was thinking numbers, I'm thinking quality," said Gavin Jones thoughtfully.

"We were with you all of the way in Brighton the other day. I almost missed you when you left the palace in the beemer though. Luckily we picked up your conversation in the car, and then I put a tracking device on it at the village store.

That was us behind you out at sea. I must admit we never saw the powerboat come out of the marina. In fact I know that it didn't, it must have left before any of us got there," he said, looking a little deflated at the thought of the boat attack.

"Those people meant to kill, but I don't think that they will attempt an actual assassination. I think they will want an apparent accident. What do you think, inspector?" asked the Welshman.

"I think maybe you're right, but remember desperate people will do almost anything to achieve their aims," answered Hank. "There's a lot at stake here."

"Inspector, who do you think we're up against?" asked Jones.

"Why don't you call me Hank; its Gavin isn't it?"

"Gavin, or Gav to my friends."

"The way I see it, beside ourselves, there can really only be two groups. I don't suppose they know of each other just yet, and each of them will naturally think the other is you anyway," Hank said smiling. "For sure the British government will want to see this relationship ended, so you're up against some of the finest of MI6. The others will be the Buck House mafia, another formidable group, selected from the M groups, and some ex-special forces, like yourself. I can't be seen to get involved, but I have more than a passing interest in Princess Anna's continued safety. Here is a number where I can be reached twenty-four hours a day. Any problems, don't hesitate," Hank said passing a card to the bodyguard.

Steel sat nursing his second beer in three quarters of an hour. He had picked up nothing of interest; both of these men knew their business. He left the half mug of beer, which was warm by now, got off the stool and walked out of the bar and crossed the street.

"There was an interesting man for you," said Hank.

"Who's that?"

"Oh, you couldn't see him, your back was turned, but if he'd had telescopic ears one of them would've been a foot longer than the other by now," said Hank smiling. "Don't worry son, he didn't hear a word," he added smiling.

"I feel quite a lot better having met you. What is your full background anyway Gavin?"

"Three years in the Para's, a couple of years in the 22, the SAS that is. Then I did a year as the personal bodyguard of the one and only Colonel Gadaffi in Libya. Then one year as bodyguard to one of the Dubai Sheiks. The last two years with the Sahaeds. Oh, and of course I did a spell in the Met Police when I first came out of the military," Jones smiled knowingly at his intended omission.

"Just checking to see if mine agrees with yours, didn't know about the spell with Gadaffi. Three years in the Met wasn't it?" Hank grinned nodding at the bodyguard. "Quite a formidable background, I'm impressed! Remember what I said Gavin, I have access to all kinds of information and people, but you'll have to let me be the judge as to what I am prepared to divulge. But don't ever hesitate to ask me first. I know that I don't have to teach my grandmother how to suck eggs. Don't trust anyone; don't talk to anyone; keep the couple off the phone; keep them inside as much as you can; keep them out of the air as much as you are able. You know the drill, be careful. Here endeth the first lesson," said Hank as he stood to leave. "Oh and by the way keep your eye on the Arab I met earlier, he looks a bit of a wild card, that one. I wouldn't trust him as far as I could throw the Queen Mary's anchor."

"Thanks for the chat. I'll try to bear in mind most of what you had to say and I'll certainly come for help if I need some."

They shook hands and left the pub together.

Hank spotted the blonde-haired man sitting in a Ford Escort at the opposite side of the street. He could see him fiddle with his right ear, and assumed that he was wearing a listening device.

Air France Flight Sarajevo-Cairo

Princess Anna sat in the first class section of the Air France Airbus. She had just completed a hectic self-inflicted duty. She'd had an exhausting four-day tour in Bosnia furthering her latest cause: the total world wide banning of land mines. She was just starting to bring the world attention that the cause needed. She had talked by phone to Michael Meadows who had missed this trip as he was still recovering from his *'sailing accident,'* as the press had so aptly put it.

Anna's mind went back to that day at sea, her recollections still vivid. After seeing some of the horrific scenes from war torn Bosnia, she realised how lucky she was.

"May I have your attention please? The captain has put on the seatbelt signs; we are commencing our descent into Cairo International Airport. Please stow your cabin tables and adjust your seats into the upright position."

"Let me take that glass Princess Anna," the cabin attendant said, as she cleared her table for landing. Anna looked around the cabin. She was without escort for the first time in an age. She looked across the aisle at the Arab man dressed in traditional garb, who nodded solemnly, his eyes covered by the small hexagonal tinted lenses of the glasses perched on his beak-like proboscis.

Anna felt the dull thud as the flight crew locked in the undercarriage, then the silence as her ears were affected by the change in cabin pressure.

She was first off the aircraft and escorted to an electric cart, then driven through the usual chaotic madness of a Middle Eastern international airport. She noticed that on the rear facing seat immediately behind, was the Arab who had sat opposite to her on the flight.

The driver took Anna directly to the VIP Lounge where she was shown into a private room reserved for visiting dignitaries.

"Have a good trip, Ma'am?" she heard the lilting Welsh accent of Gavin Jones, who walked across smiling and shook the princess firmly by the hand.

"Fine, no problems at all," she replied tiredly. "Are we leaving by helicopter?"

"No Ma'am we are travelling by car today."

They left by the rear of the building. Anna climbed into the back seat of a stretched Mercedes while Jones climbed into the front alongside the driver.

Anna had noticed the face of the Arab sitting in the front seat of the escort car behind. It was the Arab from the flight, now bereft of his robe and headdress, an automatic weapon strapped across his chest; she hadn't been alone after all. The convoy with motorcycle escort sped off for the Sahaed residence.

Since the day at Brighton Anna was starting to feel restricted and threatened. She sat alone in the rear seat of the limousine, the windows darkly tinted, *and no doubt bullet and rocket proof,* she thought to herself.

She wondered what it must be like to be able to stroll down a street in any town in any country, and not be noticed, or to ride on public transport.

Anna was brought back to reality with a jolt as the car swerved violently to avoid a young child crossing the road. They approached the high menacing walls that surrounded the estate. The car drew up to the massive solid gates that opened automatically. The limousine swept through and along the half-mile drive leading to the ornate residence.

Raffi stood beneath the towering pillars as the car drew up, by his side stood the short stocky figure of his father, Sahaed.

Later, in his room, Gavin Jones took off his shoes, loosened the belt of his slacks and crashed onto the bed emitting a long expulsion of air. It had been a long day. He had tied up a few loose ends earlier in London, and then flown across with Mr Sahaed in his jet. Jones had only arrived at Cairo International about an hour before the princess's flight. By the time Sahaed's plane had waited for a take off slot at Heathrow, and then later sat in holding patterns over busy Cairo, it had been five and a half hours since they'd left Knightsbridge. Add on the two-hour time difference, it begins to feel like an extra long day. At least everyone is staying in tonight, no late night protection exercises for me, he thought to himself as he heard a loud knocking on the door.

"Gav, the old man wants to see you in his quarters now," a voice through the closed door announced.

"Just my bloody luck," he cursed as his feet hit the floor one again. Within five minutes he was knocking on the boss's door.

"Come in," he heard the voice call out. He went through into the office.

"Sit down, Jones, I'd like you to meet my brother-in-law Mr. Agnin Armimi," said his boss. A stern faced Arab man came out from behind the masses of drapes in front of the open French window.

"Sit down," said the man to Jones without even looking at him.

"I want you to tell me exactly what took place last week out at sea off the coast of Brighton. Don't miss one detail," the brother-in-law of his boss said.

"Well, sir, I'm not sure that will be..."

"It's OK Jones, you can speak to Mr Armimi, he is close family," said Anwar Sahaed. So Jones related the happenings of that day. When he had finished the older man sighed and said, "You may leave now, thanks very much for your help in this matter."

Meanwhile, Anna had got out of her clothes and was sitting on the balcony overlooking the pool, wearing a white towel robe. There was a loud knocking at the door.

"Princess Anna, Ma'am, it's Gavin Jones here, could you open the door for a moment please."

Anna walked across and opened the door to see the cheerful smiling face of the bodyguard.

"What's up Gavin?" said the princess.

"Oh, I just got a call from the boys in the grounds. They spotted you sitting on the balcony Ma'am. That's not really a good idea at present, bearing in mind the recent problems we've been having. This being a foreign country and all, I think it's better to keep the windows closed and also the curtains Ma'am, if you don't mind."

"Whilst you're here, I'd like to talk to you for a moment, come in will you?" said Anna opening the door wide. Jones walked into the magnificent apartments. "Sit down, Gavin. There are a few things that I want to clear my mind on. After my recent sailing trip at Brighton, I arranged for you to have a meeting whilst I was in Bosnia."

Jones cut the princess short, at the same time putting his forefinger to his lips in a signal for the princess to stop talking.

"Ah, yes Ma'am and grateful I was that you did. I thought when you gave me the name of the osteopath when we were at the Dorchester, that those kinds of people were quacks, but how wrong could I be. I kept the appointment that you made for me, the man worked wonders. I have to call and arrange for another session when I get back from here, Ma'am," he smiled, pointing to his ear.

Anna had got the message, which only added to her feelings of being spied on from all angles, along with that hunted, lonely sensation. She knew only too well that there was always the chance that the odd fanatic or flake could endanger the life of any celebrity or member of royalty, but that was a chance to be taken, though not lightly. Now she felt certain that her life was in continual danger, and she did not enjoy that feeling one little bit.

"I am sure that you are by now apprised of the happening at sea. Do you have any idea who would wish to do such a thing?" Anna winked her right eye, and rolled her eyes around the room.

"Well no Ma'am, I don't," said Jones smiling, "but it emphasises the need to be doubly careful, wouldn't you say?"

"I'm afraid that I must agree, sad though it may be," added the princess. "Would you like a drink?" she asked. Gavin accepted, then excused himself and went to the bathroom.

After a pleasant rum and coke and some light conversation, he got up to leave, thanking the princess for the drink. As they walked towards the door of the apartment the bodyguard passed a note written on a tissue from the bathroom, which Anna slipped conspiratorially into the pocket of her robe. They bid each other goodnight as Jones left for the guest wing.

The phone began to ring as Anna walked across the room.

"Hello darling it's me," came the voice of Raffi, "shall I come across for a goodnight drink?"

"I think that I need to get some rest my love, I'm absolutely shattered. If it's alright with you, I'm going to take a shower and get an early night. We have a busy day ahead of us tomorrow. Besides, you need the sleep too darling," she added. "But I don't think that I'll be doing too much sleeping tonight myself, do you?"

"I don't suppose for one moment that you will, my poor dear," replied Raffi. They said their goodnights and arranged to meet for breakfast, Raffi mentioning that she was not allowed food prior to her visit to Cairo the next day.

The jets of water stung her and probed her head and the back of her neck, but the natural massaging, relaxing effect, was doing its job on Anna. As she stood there in the shower her mind moved from the coming events of tomorrow as she started to think of her two sons, she slowly began to relax for the first time that day. Changing the temperature to cold, the bracing exhilarating sensation shook the last vestiges of tension from her body.

Drying, then putting on a fresh robe, she walked out into the sitting room, where one of the servants had brought the hot chocolate she had ordered, putting it on the side table. Drinking the smooth beverage, she got up and poured herself a stiff brandy from the bar. *I'll make damn sure I sleep well tonight*, she thought to herself. She sat down again, and then suddenly sat bolt upright remembering the scribbled note that Jones had given to her earlier. Anna went into the dressing room to where she had put the robe that she'd been wearing before her shower she opened the laundry basket. The garment was gone; in fact the basket had been emptied completely.

Anna suddenly had a hollow feeling in the pit of her stomach. She knew that the note contained something that Jones would not wish any other person to see. At first she panicked and picked up the phone intending to call the bodyguard himself then thought better of it. *Calm down Anna, you know better than this you silly woman*, she thought to herself, swallowing the brandy in one slug.

She had stayed in this part of the house before, and remembered where the kitchens and domestic areas were as she and Raffi had made a midnight raid there on one occasion. She left her room, moving swiftly along the corridor, passing a servant who promptly stood to one side, putting his hands together and bowing respectively. Turning a corner, Anna walked slap bang into one of the household guards.

The man spoke no English, just as she spoke no Arabic, so the usual arm waving and slow deliberate speaking began. The other man kept pointing to a sign hanging on the corner that Anna had just turned. It could have read Piccadilly Circus for all she knew, but the guard would not stop, though he did not once lay a hand on the princess.

Anna could hear the sounds of crockery and machinery, she pointed in that direction. The guard continued to shake his head from side to side. In the midst of the scene, a stranger wearing traditional Arab robes came from the direction that Anna had left. As he appeared, the guard stood bolt upright. The other man spoke rapidly to the guard in his own tongue, his tone was by no means friendly. The guard left quickly.

"I do hope that you are alright," said the newcomer in impeccable English, "some of these servants can get a little bit too officious on occasions, Your Highness. Please forgive this humble household."

"I'm afraid that you have me at a disadvantage, sir," said Anna

"Forgive me. I am your humble servant, head of the household staff. May I be of some assistance?" he asked Anna, looking deliberately down at her attire.

"Maybe you can help," said Anna. "I am trying to find the laundry area. I put a valuable gold ring in the pocket of a bath robe. One of the servants rightly took it away to be laundered. I would like to retrieve it before the garment is put into the washing machine."

"Princess Anna, please leave this matter to me. You may go back to your room. I'll have the ring back to you in a trice," said the Arab.

For a moment Anna was lost for something to say when the welcome sight of Gavin Jones face came around the corner. He had obviously overheard the conversation.

"Princess Anna, is there a problem, Ma'am?" he asked as he walked towards them, not waiting for an answer. "It looks as though you have taken the wrong turn, Ma'am. Let me show you back to your room," the bodyguard said, lightly taking the princess by the arm and walking her away.

"Have no fear, I will look for the ring," the Arab said as he walked off towards the staff areas. Walking along the hallway, Jones said to the princess, "These corridors don't have any sound surveillance, but they do have cameras." He spoke quietly putting his head down as he said: "The rooms, however, don't have cameras, but do have sound detecting devices.

Oh, and by the way, Ma'am, when you get back into the room, you will find the ring you sought is right now in the left pocket of your robe that you're wearing." He tapped her left hip lightly and smiled, holding out his hand gesturing towards the Princess's room. "Have a good night Ma'am I'll see you in the morning."

"I'll try Gavin, and thanks for your help." Anna sat down to read the note, which had an addition in different coloured ink. The first part of the note warned her of room bugs and cameras in the hallways. The addition read said, "I already had the note, I checked the robe as soon as the servant brought it down to the laundry!"

Looking at the battery of TV monitors, the security guard had watched the meeting of the princess and the head servant. He had previously listened to the conversation between Jones and the princess. He was watching the princess and the bodyguard walk back along the hallway, when the door to the monitor room opened behind him. The chief of Sahaed's security walked into the room.

Colonel Boris Kiev was an example of physical perfection. He admitted to being thirty-nine years of age, a total disciplinarian both to himself and those below him. Kiev had formerly been a KGB officer. Before the collapse of the USSR, he had run the Western European desk, reporting only to the Chief, but with a line to the President of the Soviet Union.

Once again, Sahaed had found the right price. Kiev spoke some eight languages fluently, including Arabic in three dialects.

"What's the story here?" he said to the man at the desk.

"I'm not absolutely certain sir. The English princess seems to have lost something, Colonel." They both watched as Jones waved towards the door. The princess went inside then the bodyguard walked off shaking his head, with a condescending smile on his face.

"Seems perfectly alright to me," said Kiev.

"I think you ought to re-run the tapes sir," said the guard, "particularly the earlier conversation in the room. Something just didn't gel, I can't put my finger on it, maybe you should look into it, sir."

Anna awoke to the sound of a helicopter landing somewhere in the grounds outside. At the same moment a servant entered the room carrying a tray containing coffee and croissants. As the servant pulled back the drapes, the sun came streaming through the windows. Anna looked at her watch; it was 7:30am. She had an overpowering feeling of depression as she opened her pill container. The phone by the side of her bed rang and she picked it up to the sound of Raffi's voice.

"Raffi, come across and see me, I feel so down in the dumps. I'm not sure that I can go through with this today, and what's more important, I don't think that I want to!"

"I'll be over as soon as I am dressed and ready," replied Raffi.

After showering quickly, swallowing his coffee, wolfing down the croissants, Raffi went across the other side of the guest wing, and knocked on the door of Anna's suite. She opened the door looking tired and pale. Her eyes were red as though she had just been crying. She threw herself into his arms, bursting into a torrent of tears.

"What am I going to do Raffi darling; what am I going to do?" she said sobbing heavily. Raffi couldn't be sure whether her room was bugged or not, so he hugged her under his arm.

"Not one more word, let's go into the gardens for a walk and get some fresh air." She started to speak. "Now shush, not another word," he said, kissing her on the cheek.

They walked in silence through the main hallway and out into the extensive grounds, towards the private polo field. They sat down in the small grandstand. Anna saw Gavin Jones from the corner of her eye.

"Now what's all this?" asked Raffi.

"I'm so unhappy darling, I don't think I was ever this unhappy before. We are talking about taking a life you know," she said as she started to weep again sobbing heavily.

"I don't think it's exactly like that," he said. If you want to change your mind, I'll not stand in your way Anna.

The City of Cairo, Egypt

The helicopter flew over the busy city of Cairo. Anna looked down at the place teeming with people and traffic. It made London look like a walk in the park by comparison. She saw the windsock on top of the building as the chopper circled into the wind, then descended hovering over the big yellow circle before settling down as a butterfly selects his flower, onto the flat roof surface without so much as the slightest bump.

They had landed on the pad on top of the Ritz Palace, another hotel owned by Sahaed. They had booked in for lunch as a ploy to keep his father off the scent, in the hope that he would not discover their real reason for visiting the city. As soon as they had descended in the elevator, they ran through reception and out into the bustling street. Jones was right behind them.

Suddenly, without any warning, Raffi took off across the busy street, weaving in and out of the noisy traffic like a professional rugby player. At the same time Anna took off at a run in the opposite direction melting into the heavy pedestrian masses. For a second, the bodyguard was in a quandary, not knowing which one to follow. He screamed into the two-way radio as he ran after Anna, crossing to the other side of the road.

Jones could not see her. There were so many people that it was impossible to run. He just went with the flow, jumping and then standing on tiptoe. He had seen Anna throw a black head cover over her head as she ran. Unfortunately there were many other ladies wearing exactly the same!

As arranged, Anna only went a matter of two to three hundred yards, then she shot down an alley into the rear entrance of a small bar. After checking that he wasn't followed, Raffi also doubled back, going into the front entrance of the same bar.

The inside was dark and smoky as the two met up, slightly out of breath. He was wearing a khaki bush hat and hunters jacket.

"That's the first part of the plan. Let's put some distance between us and this place now," said Raffi to a slightly more cheerful Anna, who was starting to enjoy the chase; she smiled broadly between gasps for breath.

Across from the hotel, the figure of David Steel stood in the shadows of a shop doorway. He had watched what went on with intrigue. He had followed Raffi, and seen him enter the bar. Then he went back to observe the rest of the scene with interest. He was quite pleased to see the big Welshman in trouble at last and had no intention of changing that fact.

After a couple of minutes had passed, the entrance to the hotel was a mass of security staff. Men were being detailed in every direction. *All hell and no notion*, thought the agent, *running around like headless chickens*. He walked towards the front entrance of the bar, then paused outside for ten seconds, his eyes tightly closed to accustom them more quickly to the dark interior. Inside the smoke filled bar not only was it difficult to see, but it was equally as hard to move with any speed.

It became apparent that neither the princess nor the Arab were in there, so he exited quickly by the front entrance. Making his way around to the outside rear alley, he fully expected to see activity out there, but the alley was completely deserted, apart from a couple of mangy dogs scavenging the trash.

Meanwhile Raffi had gone into the men's room, changing into the full traditional dress of an Arab gentleman. Anna, in the ladies room, changed into the total black flowing garb and veil or burqa, of a Muslim's wife. They walked straight through the entrance of the bar behind a tall blonde-haired man who left just in front of them. They walked along the street; Anna a couple of paces behind Raffi, in the time honoured fashion.

Reaching a busy taxi rank, Raffi walked up to the second empty vehicle. He climbed into the front beside the driver, Anna into the rear in observation of Muslim custom. He instructed the driver, who shot off into the heavy traffic. In true Cairo style the traffic ground to a halt at the end of the first intersection, so the driver began to curse.

"The police are holding up the cars searching for an Englishwoman," Raffi repeated the driver's rapid guttural outburst, for Anna's benefit. Anna tapped Raffi on the shoulder; he leaned his head backward in the seat as she whispered into his left ear.

"I hope we don't have to get out of the car, take a look at your feet," he looked down at the black shiny shoes that he'd clean forgotten to change in the rush. The traffic was about five vehicles wide. The searchers couldn't hope to check every one before the traffic moved, or the whole of Cairo would soon come to a complete standstill.

Just then an armed man came past their taxi, looking into the vehicles on both sides as he hurried along, only pausing to rattle his firearm on those windows that were closed. He passed the couple without a second glance. Eventually the traffic began to move, slowly at first. Soon they were clear of the city centre and heading into a more rural area. The scenery began to change into manicured, green surroundings, which were obviously well irrigated. They left the cab outside a very exclusive country club.

Raffi held Anna back from entering the club until the taxi had disappeared into the distance. Then he began to lead her along the road away from the establishment. She was just about to question his action, when a very large white Rolls Royce slid up silently behind them and came to a halt.

Anna climbed into the rear seat, Raffi into the front next to an attractive mature European woman.

"I'd like you to meet one of my dearest and closest friends," Raffi said to Anna. "This is Margaret Weatherfield. Margaret, this is Princess Anna, formerly Her Royal Highness the Princess of Wales."

"Delighted to meet you, Margaret," said Anna.

"Me too," said Margaret, turning and giving Anna a broad smile. "You can both relax now, you are in good hands. Did you manage to get rid of the Gestapo?" Margaret asked Raffi.

"Yes we did, but it gets more difficult each time," he replied. The Englishwoman pulled up in front of a pair of gigantic solid gates that look as though they had come out of a biblical film epic, which opened as she pressed a button on the car's dashboard.

"Here we are, home sweet home," said the woman almost singing as she spoke. They drove some long way up a tree-lined drive, then pulled up in front of the most magnificent building that Anna had seen in many a year. As they got out of the car, servants opened every door. Anna could not help seeing how much security was in evidence. It seemed as though they had their own private army here.

They went through the palatial entrance, and as she looked around, although she had been in some rather sumptuous places in her time, she said:

"It looks as though everything is made of gold," in a semi jocular manner.

"Most of it is," replied Raffi, almost nonchalantly. "This is one of the many palaces owned by The Sultan of Dubai, by far the richest man on this planet. Margaret manages this and many other such residences. I went to school with her brother in England and Switzerland. Nobody will bother us here darling; we can talk and act with impunity."

"I have given you the diamond suite. I'll see you at the pool for lunch, dears," said Margaret.

"This way please, Master Raffi, sir, " said a kindly looking grey haired servant, as he led the couple to the elevator.

Boris Kiev sat in front of the security team. Though he spoke quietly he was livid. He had faced the ultimate disgrace of a severe dressing down from his boss, Sahaed; along with the other most unpleasant Arab man Armimi. No one had ever talked to him that way before and he wanted to impress upon the rest of the team that he would not tolerate such behaviour allowing it to recur. He was a trained leader, and like all responsible controllers of men, he knew where the buck stopped.

"I want that couple found, and I want them back here today. I have a list of the closer friends of Mr Raffi here in Cairo. As far as I can make out, the princess has no close friends in the city or indeed in the country. I have contacts at the British Embassy; no communication was made there.

I want every taxi driver that was on duty questioned. I want every hospital, emergency room, private clinic, hotel and bar covered. The rest of you get on with it and keep in constant touch with me. Gavin you stay here, I want words with you," said the Russian ominously.

"How the hell did they get away from you?" Kiev said to the Welshman. "This is not your style, how did you let them give you the slip?" he continued, looking Jones directly in the eyes.

"Why would I want to do that?"

"I'll ask the questions around here if you don't mind. You are British, you are a Welshman, and the princess was the Princess of Wales. If she decided to clear off why wouldn't you close a blind eye as a loyal Brit?"

"Because I work for this organisation, because my only responsibility is to take care of Mr Raffi."

"Well you didn't make such a good job of that either, did you man?" the colonel snapped, banging his massive hand heavily on the table. "Now get out there, and bring the couple back here before we're all out of a job."

"Yes sir," replied Jones, "I'm on my way."

"Coming back without them wouldn't be such a good idea!"

With the veiled threat hanging over his head, Gavin retraced his steps back into the busy city. He was crossing the road opposite the hotel where the couple had absconded earlier, when he saw two of Sahaed's men leading a man across the traffic. The man was apparently not enjoying the idea one little bit. He followed the three men into the foyer of the hotel and through to the room where his meeting with the colonel had just taken place. The Russian slammed the man down on a seat at the centre table. The conversation was brief and in Arabic.

"He took a couple out to the suburbs in his taxi at the time of the disappearance. They were dressed in Arab clothes. The woman never spoke, which is customary; the man did all the talking. He said that when they left the cab, the man was wearing shiny black laced European shoes and socks," said the colonel.

"Where did he drop them?" asked Jones.

"At an exclusive Country Club," replied Kiev.

"Did he hear anything that they may have said?" The colonel fired more questions at the cab driver, who gave an answer, shaking his head.

"He heard nothing. She whispered something in the man's ear. Could have been English. The windows in his cab won't close, he says, so listening to what people say is difficult above the noise of the traffic."

Jones took the address of the club, and was gone. In the meantime, Anwar Sahaed was beside himself with anger, as he spoke on the telephone to Dr Nasser, who said he had seen neither hide nor hair of the couple, nor had they made contact with his office.

"I want you to speak to every doctor in Cairo if you have to. On no account must any doctor touch that woman. Anyone who does won't even live to regret it! I put you where you are Dr Nasser, and don't you forget it. If this matter is not concluded to my satisfaction, today, you'll spend the rest of your miserable life as a missionary doctor in some remote African jungle village. Believe me!" the irate man screamed as he spoke, the veins in his neck bulging fit to burst. "That pregnancy must not be terminated under any circumstances!"

Meanwhile Gavin Jones pulled up outside the country club gates, which were firmly locked. He leaned out of the car window and pressed the button on the intercom, which was eventually answered in Arabic.

"I want to speak with the manager," said Gavin.

"I'm afraid that the manager is in a meeting. Call him on the telephone later today," said the woman's voice in perfect English.

"I must speak to him now. The matter is very urgent. I come with the authority of Mr Anwar Sahaed. I repeat the matter is very urgent. Maybe you will get your manager to phone Mr Al-Sahaed and explain why you won't be of assistance."

There was a loud buzzing sound as the locks on the gates clicked and the way opened up. Jones drove to the club's entrance. As he walked through the entrance, a tall Middle Eastern man wearing a morning suit met him. The man held out his hand.

"Good morning, sir. I am the director of the club. What can we do to be of assistance to you and to Mr Sahaed?" he said with an over emphasised look of concern on his face. Jones asked if Raffi were at the club. The man checked the visitor's book, spoke to the receptionist, and then came back to the bodyguard.

"No sir, we have not seen Mr Raffi for quite some time. He was last here some months ago at our annual polo tournament accompanied by a group of Argentinean friends," said the man, holding out the palms of his hands and shrugging his shoulders.

"We are reliably informed that they were dropped off here by a taxi cab not two hours ago. Perhaps you might want to reconsider your answers or maybe double check or something. Mr Sahaed does not take kindly to the wrong answers," said the big Welshman, leaning forward and putting a vice like grip on the man's upper arm. "Let's both take a look around," he said, leading the man into the club.

"You said that a cab driver dropped them here two hours ago," said the club director. "If that's the case, they must have been dropped outside the gate. There have been no cabs in here today, of that you can be assured."

"I need to use your phone please," said Jones.

"Certainly, it's over here." The man took the bodyguard to a kiosk. Jones immediately phoned Boris Kiev, who answered instantly.

"What have you got, Jones? Hang on, the boss is calling on another line, just a minute… Good morning, sir. I have Jones on the other line right now; please hold one moment, sir and then I can report what he's said," the Russian said to Sahaed.

"Looks like a blank here, Colonel. Will you find out from the cab driver if he dropped the couple inside the country club grounds at reception, or did he let them outside the gates on the main road? Call me back at this number. You got a pen?" He passed on the number to the security chief and sat in reception waiting for the return call, which came within a matter of minutes, confirming the club director's suspicions. He got in his car and drove down the driveway. He paused outside the country club gates while looking at the local terrain, trying to decide which direction to take and wondering why they would be dropped at such a remote location. There was no sign of life or buildings within a 180 degree sweep of his vision.

He did not take any notice of the old Ford van that drove slowly past in the opposite direction back toward the city. After some thought, he too drove in that direction. There were many large houses in the area; he went past one estate that had walls at least twelve feet high, which seemed to go on forever. He noticed the massive, solid gates and drew up into the entry. There was no name on the gates or a number.

As he sat considering what to do next, he noticed the old Ford van drive past again, but this time the vehicle was travelling away from the city. It had Arabic writing on the side along with the picture of a TV set, so he assumed it to be a television repair service. He drove further along the road heading for Cairo, but saw nothing that helped in his search for the couple.

Number 10 Downing Street, London

Prime Minister Tony Blain sat in his offices at Number 10, contemplating his forthcoming meeting with Sir Martin Fields. He had learned during his short term in office that the secret services were a law unto themselves and they didn't take too kindly to interference from politicians, and, in fact, regarded them as temporary nuisances. Blain knew the topic of the meeting, so he had prepared himself suitably. He had met with the Queen recently on the same matter. He had noted the Queen's concern, and had promised to see what could be done. At the time he'd made the position quite clear, that this was more a family matter than a matter of national importance.

The intercom buzzed. "Sir Martin is here Prime Minister."

"Show him in please and hold all calls," he said to his secretary.

The MI6 man entered the room. Tony Blain got up from his desk and walked across to a comfortable armchair. He shook hands with Sir Martin then gestured for him to take an armchair opposite.

"Would you care for a coffee, Sir Martin?" the PM asked.

"No thanks, I had one not a half hour ago."

"So, what can we do for MI6?" asked Tony Blain.

"Well, it's to do with Princess Anna. I don't know how well informed you are as to what's been going on over the past few months regarding the princess's private life, but a rather delicate situation has developed," said Fields.

"I was summoned to the Queen's presence last week. She apprised me of the situation regarding Princess Anna's association with the son of Anwar Sahaed. I assume that's what you are referring to, Sir Martin."

"Precisely, Prime Minister, but the situation is out of control. We have been keeping a close eye on the developments. The affair seems serious — we think serious enough for them to be thinking of marriage. That would create rather an untenable set of circumstances — the full ramifications of which do not bear thinking about, wouldn't you say, old chap?"

"I can see your concern, but what's to be done? We can hardly say to the princess, 'hey you've got to stop this, the Queen doesn't like it, and neither does the country, can we? They did throw her out in the first place, did they not, Sir Martin?

"Maybe a word from the Prime Minister may be of some help. She must realise what she's doing: that a marriage to the Arab would make any subsequent offspring from the union blood relatives to the future King of England, and in passing, would put Mr bloody Sahaed exactly where he would like to be. He would go from being refused a passport to being a damned in-law of the monarchy. It's unconscionable! What in the hell does the princess think she's playing at? Imagine if she decided to convert to being a Muslim as well? The mind boggles!" said the MI6 chief. "This whole affair makes the late Duke of Windsor's affair and abdication pale into insignificance by comparison."

"What suggestions do you have, Sir Martin?" asked the PM.

"Well, I'm afraid that there's more to come sir," said the other man.

"You mean it gets worse?"

"I'm afraid so; much worse!"

"It can't get much worse...Can it?" Tony Blain asked, showing his teeth in that grimace of his, somewhere between a grin and a snarl.

"We believe that the former Her Royal Highness, The Princess of Wales is pregnant." Tony Blain looked askance.

"Are you certain of this?" snapped the Premier.

"I'm afraid so," replied Sir Martin with a sigh. He opened his attaché case and took out a file from which he selected two pieces of paper, one in Arabic, the other in English.

"This is the medical report from a prominent Cairo doctor, after testing the young woman for pregnancy. You can see the results for yourself on the translated version here," he held out the English version.

"I suppose it is my duty to talk with the princess. She can just as easily tell me to mind my own damn business," said Tony Blain. "But I will talk to her."

"I think it would be in her best interest to pay attention to what you have to say, as well as in the interest of the monarchy, and most of all that of her children and her country. Let her think a little about her own country for once in a while. She seems to spend enough time concerning herself about others. Tell her that charity should begin at home."

Tony Blain did not like the MI6 man's tone of voice, or his inferences. There had seemed to be a veiled threat somewhere in what he had said.

"For your information, Prime Minister, she arrives back in England tomorrow, and for your further edification, she is flying in from Cairo." His latter addition held a tinge of the facetious. Sir Martin stood up. "I'll be on my way then, sir," he said to the Premier. "If anything of importance crops up, I'll be in touch." He shook hands with Blain, then walked briskly out of the office.

Blain was not sure how to react to what he had just heard, neither was he sure what had motivated the secret service man to talk with him. He had known that the matter was serious from the questions put to him by some Members of Parliament, and from the conversation with Her Majesty, but news of the pregnancy had shocked him considerably. He decided that he would meet with the princess as soon as possible.

"I want an appointment with Princess Anna, as soon as possible. Get onto her secretary, Michael Meadows. Tell him it's of paramount importance that I see the princess immediately on her return to the country, which I think is tomorrow. When you've done that get me the Deputy Prime Minister," Blain said to his secretary, sounding most unlike his normal ebullient self.

The Sultan of Dubai's Estate, Cairo

Anna and Raffi went down to the poolside as arranged. Margaret Weatherfield was sitting at a table by the pool. She had the table set for traditional English tea: bone china from Staffordshire, finger sandwiches of salmon and cucumber, a selection of pastries, and of course, scones with clotted Devonshire cream along with freshly made preserves.

"This could have come from a local Devon tea shop," said the princess.

"It did. We have the stuff flown in specially, every week, along with Whitstable oysters, and many other special British delicacies," their hostess Margaret said nonchalantly, a devilish twinkle in her eye.

Over tea they began to discuss the reason for their visit.

"I have talked to Margaret about our situation, darling," Raffi said to Anna. "I know that you said not to talk to anyone, but I just had to speak to someone, and Margaret here is my dearest and closest friend in the whole world. It's good to get out of my father's place. He has cameras and sound bugging devices all over the building. His security is possibly tighter than Buckingham Palace itself," said Raffi.

"What made you change your mind about agreeing with Anna to have the clinical termination Raffi?" asked their hostess Margaret.

"I'm not changing my mind at all. I just had to stop today's visit to Cairo. You see, my father is not the only one who can eavesdrop on people. He was having a meeting with uncle Agnin the other day. I overheard most of the conversation. He knows about Anna's pregnancy and was telling my uncle that he had instructed Dr Nasser to go through the motions of the operation today, but under no circumstances was he to terminate the pregnancy. His motives are, as usual, purely selfish," he said, his voice starting to shake, his lower lip to tremble as he spoke.

Anna reached across and took hold of his hand. "Don't upset yourself my dear, there has to be an answer to the situation."

"I think maybe that I can offer the ideal solution to the whole matter," said Margaret. Come with me," she said, getting up from the table.

The three of them walked across the expansive courtyard, just as the sound of a helicopter was heard heading in their direction. They had entered the building before the machine came overhead. Anna noticed that it hovered for a short while then sped off. *I am becoming paranoid*, she thought as she followed the others towards the elevator.

The doors opened into a room below ground. It looked like a hospital, except that it was deserted. There were no people down there at all. As they walked along the hallway, Anna and Raffi marvelled at what they saw. They were in a mini hospital, perfect in every detail. Margaret threw open two swing doors into a complete operating theatre. She went through into an intensive care unit. The place was absolutely incredible.

"Wow, I can hardly believe what I'm seeing!" said Anna.

"The Sultan has the same set up in every one of his residences," said Margaret.

"He always has his personal physician and a surgeon in attendance wherever he goes. If you would like, I can have a specialist here within the day. You can have your operation, and no one will know that it ever took place, including and especially *your father*." She emphasised the words as she turned and looked at Raffi.

They sat in the drawing the room before agreeing that this new suggestion could be the answer to their prayers.

"May I use the phone? I really ought to speak to my secretary and as he's not sure where I am I really should touch base with him," Anna said to Margaret.

"Sure you may, but I cannot vouch for the security of the conversation. You know how resourceful Raffi's father can be. He has most of the officials of this city in his pocket. Maybe you should wait until you have decided what your plan of action is going to be," said Margaret.

It didn't take long for the couple to decide that they wanted Margaret to organise a surgeon to carry out Anna's operation at the estate. They calculated that two days would see the matter solved. Margaret was to contact Michael and let him have Anna's revised schedule.

"How will you organise this without the conversation being overheard?" asked the princess.

"Simple. I will send a plane to bring the surgeon and team here." She looked at her watch. "I will have him here first thing tomorrow morning. Now why don't you two relax and take things easy, and let me get things moving." She got up to leave the room.

"Margaret," Raffi said, "you're a darling."

"I know I am!" she said with a big smile.

"Now just relax. Anna, if you will give me the name and telephone number of your secretary, and jot down a brief message, I will have it relayed safely and securely for you," she said as she swept out of the room.

"What a precious lady," Anna smiled as she spoke. "How lucky we are to have such a person at hand." She stretched across the couch putting her hand on his knee.

"Yes, she's a dear, isn't she?" Raffi took hold of Anna's hand. "I do hope things will be alright," she said with a sigh.

"I'm sure they will darling, try and relax. I love you," said Raffi.

The Sahaed Estate, Cairo

Boris Kiev sat in front of Sahaed and Armimi. "I want this city taken apart brick by brick!" Sahaed said, his voice hardly above a whisper. The phone rang.

"Yes doctor, and what did you find out?" He paused as Dr Nasser spoke to him. "That's not good enough, do you hear me, then speak to every doctor in Cairo!" He slammed the phone down.

"We know that they did not fly out of the city officially, either on a private plane or on a scheduled airline. I have had all roads out of the city checked by our choppers. The police have cooperated checking traffic, and there has been nobody answering their description booked into any hotel either in the city, or within a twenty mile radius," said the Russian. "Do you know of anyone they could be staying with, sir?" he said to his boss.

"Is the Sultan in residence here?" asked Agnin Armimi.

"I don't know," replied his brother-in-law. "Why do you ask?"

"Isn't Raffi close to his secretary?"

"Yes; he went to school with her brother. They are very close. Colonel, get me a detailed map of the whole area will you?"

"I have one right here sir," replied the Russian. He spread the map on the desk in front of the two Arabs. Sahaed pointed to the vast estate of the Sultan.

"Mr Armimi is right; they could be right here," he said pointing.

"Find out if the Sultan is here, or who else is here at the moment. But be careful, the Sultan has some of the best security and protection in the world. We don't need to make an enemy of His Serene Highness."

As the chopper criss-crossed the suburbs of Cairo, Colonel Kiev spotted the estate of the Sultan and signalled the pilot to go down closer. He noted the large number of security guards dotted about the grounds, and along the staunch walls around the estate.

He also saw what he thought to be sentry posts every few hundred feet. His trained eye recognised the camouflage covers over what were undoubtedly either anti-aircraft or anti-personnel rockets.

The place was a veritable fortress. His boss had been right about the security here. He told the pilot not to go any closer. Taking a look through his binoculars, he saw a military helicopter half under cover. He knew the machine, which was of Russian manufacture.

He'd seen enough. He signalled the pilot to leave the area and hoped that the couple wasn't in that place. As the chopper gained height he saw a white Rolls Royce limousine leaving through the main gates. He instructed the pilot to gain more altitude and follow the speeding vehicle.

The car eventually drove up to Cairo International Airport. It went through the cargo entrance at the rear of the perimeter fence, and then drove on through to the area where private jets were parked. The Russian saw the car drive straight up to a Cessna Citation with its navigation light flashing. The driver, a chauffeur, got out of the car, carrying only a small white envelope. He climbed the stairs into the plane and seconds later reappeared empty handed. He returned to the Rolls and drove out off the airport area. Boris Kiev put his binoculars down on the console, directing the pilot to return to base.

An Apartment in Down Town Cairo

"They seemed to disappear into thin air. I saw them come out of the hotel, she went down a side alley, he went off down the main street, and puff, they were gone," said Steel to Reilly, the CIA agent.

"Today I know that they were supposed to go into the clinic of the good Dr Nasser. Of course they didn't show. We've checked all exits from Cairo and come up with an absolute blank.

If we were dealing with a top Soviet agent here I could understand. But a princess and her boyfriend, I ask you? It's bloody hilarious! Where the hell can they be?" asked Steel.

"I fear that you are guilty of the worst crime a trained agent can commit, my good buddy," said Kevin Reilly.

"And what's that?" asked the Englishman.

"Underestimating your opponent," replied the American, with a shrug. "But look, this kind of talk won't get us anywhere. One of them must have a friend or friends in the city somewhere. Let's get onto some of our contacts and find out. Has there been any kind of communiqué from the princess to England?" asked the CIA man.

"No, none that we've picked up," replied Steel. "She would normally only contact her secretary, or her sons and so far, neither," he added.

"I seem to remember that Sahaed's son had a friend who is a close aid to the Sultan of Dubai. An English woman, as memory serves. The Sultan has a massive estate on the outskirts of the city. In fact it's more a god-damn fortress than a house, armed to the teeth and crawling with goons. Maybe you should start by taking a look out there then. I'll find out if the old man's in residence. I know that the woman's called Weatherton or Weatherby, spends quite a lot of time there. She's not a lady to be messed with. Met her at an embassy do last year, quite a looker too, as memory serves." the American said.

He went across to the cupboard next to his desk in his apartment. He took out a large map of the area and spread it across the centre table.

"Here's the estate," he said, pointing to a large area. Steel already knew where the place was, but hadn't had the chance to study a map.

"Getting into that place is not going to be an easy job," said the British agent.

"How right you are. You may find it easier to get into Fort Knox! I wouldn't advise night-time commando tactics here. You need to employ some kind of subterfuge, get through the front entrance under some guise or other. I have a local operative with passable English, if you need him."

David Steel picked up a glass and finished off the unpleasant contents of whisky and icy water. Thanking his erstwhile counterpart, he said goodnight and left for his hotel room.

Boris Kiev watched from the shadows as Steel left Reilly's apartment. He waited until the Englishman had got into his car and driven off. Then he quietly climbed the fire escape stairway to the apartment block. He stood in the shadows of the hallway and heard the phone ringing inside the room.

Moments later the American left, pulling on his jacket as he slammed the door, he went off towards the elevator. Kiev heard the elevator doors close with squeak as he went towards the door of the apartment. He had the lock open in seconds. He eased the handle open, cautiously pushing his head around the door. The room was in total darkness. Taking out his flashlight he walked over to a painting on the opposite wall. He raised his hand and was about to reach up behind it, when...

"Looking for this, Boris?" said the voice of Kevin Reilly as the lights came on in the room, temporarily blinding the big Russian, who then heard the distinct metallic click of a safety catch and a potentially fatal round entering a polished barrel.

"Get your hands where I can see them. Turn around very slowly. This is the second time tonight that I've had to chide someone for underestimating the opposition. You can turn round slowly, but keep your hands up there, if you want to see your pension," said Reilly as the Russian turned to face him.

"So, Colonel Boris Kiev KGB retired, we meet yet again. What the hell do you think you're playing at? You seem to be losing your touch. I hear that's not all that you've lost at the moment either! Fancy you trying to pull a stunt like that on an old warrior like me. I found your bug the day you put it there. I knew you'd be here tonight or pretty soon. Throw your weapon down on the table, handle first buddy, if you don't mind, please. There's a good man."

The Russian did as he was bid.

"Now sit down," said the American, pointing to a chair away from the table. Reilly picked up the automatic, putting it on a desk away from the table.

"You might as well give me the one in the ankle holster as well," he said to the Russian, who reluctantly passed the small pistol across. The American then put his handgun on the desk. Sitting on a chair opposite the colonel, Reilly picked up the whisky bottle and filled the two glasses that were already there on the table. He picked one up and slid the other towards the Russian.

"Nastarovia, Colonel," he said as he held his glass towards the other man.

"Nastarovia," replied the Russian as the glasses clinked. "Here's to old times, my Yankee friend."

"To old times colonel and here's to the Princess Charming who's giving you all the goddamn run around!" said the CIA man with a smile. He threw the micro tape recorder across the table to the Russian. Then he disarmed both weapons pocketing the rounds, then sent them sliding across to a deflated Kiev.

The small ford television repair van pulled up outside the massive gates of the Sultan's estate. The Arab walked towards the intercom on the wall and pressed the button. After a couple of minutes the speaker crackled into life. The Arab man noticed the cameras at both sides of the gate. One of them began to turn towards the vehicle. A voice in Arabic asked what he wanted.

He replied that he had come to do a routine check-up of the televisions in the building. The speaker went silent, then after three minutes or so, the voice came back.

"There have been no arrangements made to have the televisions checked. Make an appointment in the usual way, thank you." The speaker went dead. The Arab returned to the van, disappearing inside. After a short time the van drove off down the road.

Later that night, the same van again went past the gate of the Sultan's estate, disappearing into the darkness. Shortly after, two shadowy figures crept closely along the side of the wall, moving noiselessly toward the gates.

The taller of the two wore black tight pants, a black sweater, dark trainers, and a tight fitting knitted hood with two slits for the eyes. He had a long length of special light cord wrapped around his chest, an automatic firearm holstered to his belt and a vicious looking knife strapped to the outside of his right lower leg. Stopping short of the gates he looked up at the two cameras. He knew that they made a ninety-degree turn automatically. Further along the wall, and around the total perimeter, similar cameras performed the same function, each one set to turn a complete circle, looking into each other's lenses at the completion of each turning. The time-lapse in-between each full circle was just thirty five seconds, the height of the wall, all of twenty feet.

The second man had disappeared back into the darkness across the other side of the road. The other one began to adjust the tungsten fitting on the end of the cord, which he had removed from around his chest. He checked the retractable hooks, then crouched down against the wall and melted into the darkness, waiting.

Suddenly there was a burst of bright light. Two distress rockets soared into the night sky directly opposite the gates of the estate, their magnesium glow turning night into day. The man at the wall didn't move. He crouched perfectly still. Looking up at the cameras directly above him, he saw both devices lift skywards. They had been taken off automatic and were being controlled by the guards.

Quick as a flash the man below threw the tungsten device on the end of the cord. It sailed over the top of the wall. As he pulled down cautiously the hooks did their job and gripped the top edge of the masonry. The man scaled the wall, his legs at forty-five degrees to the surface, the soles of his special sneakers gripping to the joints in the stonework. Within seconds he was peering over the top. He could see no movement of the cameras from the corner of his eyes. He had a pair of goggles strapped to the top of his head, which he pulled down over his eyes with his left hand, the right gripping the top of the wall. The lenses were night sight lenses. Seeing no movement below, he rolled over the top and slid deftly down the cord, landing in the soft earth below inside the property. He could not see the main building from where he crouched.

There were security lights all around the grounds, and floodlights on the sides of the long drive. He adjusted his goggles and was able to pick up the masses of infrared lines that criss-crossing the grounds amongst the foliage. To walk through any one of those would bring the world crashing down on his head. He moved carefully along the wall towards the side of the drive, and then he froze on the spot. He heard the sound of dogs snarling and growling somewhere ahead.

Over to his left he could make out the main security building. With the help of the night sights he saw a compound filled with heavy, fit looking rotweillers jumping and crashing against the heavy chain link fence.

He made his way successfully through the first barrage of infrared sensors. He could see guards moving around the grounds. He knew that he would soon trade one danger for another, for if the guards were moving around there would be no passive sensors to avoid, just bullets, guard dogs and trained killers instead.

He looked at his watch as he moved on with caution. He was fifteen minutes into the operation. He had just twenty left before his borrowed accomplice would set off the diversion again. When he was within fifty yards of the main building, which seemed more like a palace than a house, Steel could see what Reilly had meant when he described the security. He had not exaggerated. The MI6 agent moved towards the building with much trepidation. He made his way around to the rear of the vast mansion, where he unzipped the front of his combat suit and pulled out a small pair of normal binoculars. He proceeded to look into each lighted window, of which there were many. He could see servants by the score, but he saw no one that he recognised.

Suddenly, to his left the whole area was bathed in brilliant light. He flung himself to the ground feeling sure that he had been seen. An area of some five hundred square feet was lit up like a football ground. Then he heard the distant and unmistakable sound of a high-powered helicopter as it came in at speed.

Steel had retreated carefully into the surrounding bushes. He watched the aircraft descend into the centre of the lit area, recognising the chopper as a Russian military machine, minus the armaments. The moment the helicopter had touched down the lights were extinguished, the subsequent temporary blindness, rendering him unable to identify the figures that moved quickly from the chopper into the rear of the building. Steel looked up at the windsock as it fluttered in the breeze. He was pleased to see that it was pointing in the direction of where he hid, for he saw a guard walk towards the chopper holding the leash of a large lean and muscular canine machine. Luckily his own scent was blowing in the opposite direction of the guard dog's sensitive nose. He had not been able to hear a word spoken above the noise of the jet engine and the heavy thumping of the rotor, but now both had just been cut, the rotor still spinning slowly to a halt.

Then came his first break. A woman came out of the rear of the building.

"Bring the doctor's cases and take them below will you?" she shouted towards the now silent machine. Steel was unable to move from his hiding place for some minutes until the chopper crew had put the machine to bed. Looking at his watch he had only ten minutes left to complete his task. He decided to call it a day and make his way cautiously back to the perimeter wall.

The Sahaed Residence, Cairo

"So please tell me, colonel, why do I pay all this money to have a princess and my son make fools out of what is supposedly one of the best security teams in the world? Don't bother to answer that question just yet, we will reserve the post mortem for later. Right now I want to know what you are going to do in order to find the couple. My own sources tell me that they may be in the palace of the Sultan, that some mysterious person was flown in earlier this evening from Dubai. It could be the Sultan himself, but I rather think not, as he doesn't like to travel at night. I will know for sure in about a half an hour's time. I may even know who the new arrival was. Now tell me, colonel, what are your plans?"

"I have had the Sultan's estate under close surveillance since the disappearance of Mr Raffi and the princess sir. With the exception of a Russian-built helicopter, nothing or no one has gone in or left the building during the day. Well err… that's not exactly true. An hour ago, a man who I know to be a British agent, set up a distraction outside the estate and scaled the walls, then came back out shortly after the helicopter arrived. We can hardly have him arrested, sir, and finding him would not be easy. He is one of MI6's best men. He certainly didn't cause any trouble whilst he was in there, or as the English say, the balloon would have gone up. In my opinion, without the use of open aggression, that place is impregnable. The only way in is by invitation," said the Russian looking defeated. "If you'll forgive me sir, there are other avenues to be followed. If you'll excuse me, I would like to carry on."

"You do that, colonel, but you remember, if one hair of my son's or the princess's head is harmed, I hold you totally responsible."

Back at the Sultan's Residence

"Miss Weatherfield, there is a call for you. It's Mr Anwar Sahaed. He says that the matter is urgent," said the girl from the main switchboard.

"Put him through," replied Margaret. "Mr Al-Sahaed, what a pleasant surprise. I am afraid the Sultan is not in residence."

"It was more you that I wished to talk with, Miss Weatherfield. There is a delicate domestic matter that I wish to discuss that involves my son. I know that the two of you were quite close, so I would like to seek your respected opinion," said the Arab trying to sound weak and in need of help, succeeding at neither.

"You flatter me, Mr Sahaed. When did you wish to meet? I could be across the city tomorrow afternoon," replied the woman.

"I do not wish to put you to any trouble, my dear. I can be across there in about ten minutes if I use the chopper," replied Sahaed." The matter is of a most urgent nature."

"I am planning to leave in about ten minutes. I will be here in the morning though. Why don't you come across then?"

"The matter will not wait that long. Please hang on for a few more minutes and I will be across immediately." The line went dead.

"Mr Sahaed, Mr Sahaed. Damn; damn it! Damn his hide," she added as she rang security.

"Yes, Miss Weatherfield, what can we do for you?"

"Mr Sahaed will be arriving by helicopter in a minute or so. Prepare the pad, but don't let him get out of the machine until I come there, have a couple of the dogs with you so he won't consider alighting. Under no circumstances is anyone to talk to him nor answer any questions that he may ask, any questions at all, is that quite clear?" she ordered.

A quarter of an hour later, Margaret sat opposite Sahaed.

"And what makes you think that he would come here? Granted we are friends, and yes I spoke to him a few days ago. He was full of himself and sounded so happy. He did tell me of his love for the princess, but then the affair is not exactly a big secret is it? Maybe they have eloped," she added smiling sardonically as she frowned inwardly. She noticed that the Arab did not return the smile. Quite the contrary, in fact. His face had set in a fierce, don't-mess-with-me grimace.

"Miss Weatherfield, I did not come here to be ridiculed. My son has disappeared without telling me, which is unheard of. I intend to find him if I have to search every building in Cairo," he snarled as he got up from his seat.

"Let me make one thing crystal clear to you; this is one building that you will most definitely not be searching, of that you may rest assured, sir," she said in her perfect English cut-glass accent. "You have my answer."

"Which answer is that, Miss Weatherfield?"

"I refuse to be spoken to in such a manner! As the senior representative of his Serene Highness I must ask you to leave immediately Mr Al-Sahaed." As she spoke, the two men standing inside the doorway came across the room.

Sahaed walked towards the door dwarfed between the two big men, then turned.

"You have not heard the end of this young woman. If I find that Raffi was here....."

"What will you do Mr Sahaed? Go on then, do tell me what you will do. This is one person who doesn't give a damn about you. You don't own me, and what's more you don't own your son either. Show Mr Sahaed to his helicopter," she said to the two burly guards. "I'll bid you good day sir," she said shouted tersely, as she walked out of the room.

After Sahaed had gone, Raffi came into the room. "Bravo, bravo!" he said clapping his hands. It's a long time since, if ever, my father got a dressing down like that."

"Your father can be a very determined man," she said trying to clear the frog from her throat. "Oh my, maybe I'm going to lose my voice. Perhaps I did go a little too far, but he has always rubbed me up the wrong way. His sheer arrogance really gets to me," she added. "How is the princess?"

"She's fast asleep. According to the doctor everything went just fine. She should be up and about by tomorrow then she can plan to go home the same day."

"Don't you think that's a little soon dear?" asked Margaret.

"The doctor says not. And we do need to get her back into circulation to silence my father," Raffi added.

"I suppose so," Margaret nodded reluctantly in agreement.

"I know that she has to get back to England tomorrow, she has a flight booked out of Cairo at noon," said Raffi. "I assume that Anna's message got through to her secretary OK?"

"Yes it went by plane yesterday," she replied.

The flight had been uneventful. Princess Anna was awakened by the distant ping as the captain put on the seatbelt lights and announced their descent into London's Heathrow airport. She was really feeling the effects of the operation physically; the thought of the act of abortion was weighing heavily on her mind. As she sat in the upright position she saw the lights of Middlesex flash past the windows.

"Please remain in your seats until the captain has brought the aircraft to a complete standstill," said the purser.

On the way back home in the heavy London evening traffic, Michael Meadows brought Princess Anna up to date on the past few days' happenings, in particular the urgent message from Number 10 Downing Street.

"What's that all about Michael?"

"I'm not supposed to know," replied her secretary, "but it's to do with your relationship with Raffi. They seem to be lighting fires everywhere. I hear that the Queen is furious, absolutely livid."

"So what's new," said Anna sinking back into the seat of the car, "What's bloody new?"

"If you only knew what I've been through in the past few hours, you'd realise I don't particularly care what the Queen thinks, or the bloody Prime Minister, Uncle Tom Cobbley and all. They can all sod off, as far as I'm concerned. I want to see my boys," she turned her face toward the window, as huge crocodile-size tears began to well up in those sad blue eyes and slowly ran down that famous face.

The Sahaed Residence, Cairo

Raffi had stayed in his room since Anna left earlier that day. His father had called on the phone a number of times, but he had feigned sleep. Since talking with Margaret, Raffi knew why his father was so anxious to talk with him. Margaret assumed his father already knew of the pregnancy. Raffi heard his attitude when he'd arrived at the Sultan's palace knowing it wasn't solely the posture of a worried parent. She had advised Raffi to tell him that they had been somewhere else.

"Lead him to believe that nothing has changed, then a little further along the way, maybe an unfortunate miscarriage can be concocted," Raffi did not like deceit, but he knew his father very well, and understood what his motives would be in the circumstances. He agreed with his friend's advice.

He was still feeling low as he sat by the swimming pool, reflecting on all that had really taken place and the unforgivable act committed by them and the doctor, with their full agreement. He stared into the sparkling blue waters, sipping a welcome wine spritzer. His father approached looking stern, but tentative.

"I did not wish to cause a scene when Princess Anna was here. Do you think that you might like to tell me where you have been for the last two days?" he asked.

"Anna was feeling very tired after her last trip, so we decided to get away for a short while. We had a private problem between us, on which we had previously agreed a course of action in the solitude of our own company. We decided to change our minds. Also, I didn't realise that I have to report to you on every action that I take, like some schoolchild. In case you hadn't noticed, I'm a big boy now, father. I'm a grown man for heaven's sake! I suppose the next thing you'll want to know is where we stayed." He stood up and marched into the house as he spoke, slamming the door behind him.

"Raffi my boy, Raffi, don't be upset," He followed him into the bar area where he poured a drink. "Raffi, I was only worried, as any father would be, particularly in the way that you ran off in the middle of Cairo like that. Half of my security people have been looking for you, and you know that I feel doubly responsible. What would I feel like if something were to happen to the princess? I would have a lot of explaining to do in England." He put his arm around Raffi's shoulder, giving him a hug. "You are sure that everything is alright?"

"Perfectly father," he replied, shrugging off the older mans arm.

"When are you seeing Anna next?" he asked, walking towards the door.

"We are meeting in Paris next week Father. I'm sorry if I sounded a little short earlier, but a lot of things seem to have happened within a short space of time."

"Don't you worry about a thing my son, everything will work out right in the end, you see if it doesn't." He held his son's shoulders with both of his arms outstretched, looking him straight in the eyes. "I'm very proud of you my only son, very proud indeed."

"Father, I may have some very exciting news for you in Paris!" Raffi said.

MI6 Headquarters London

David Steel walked out of the underground station, emerging into the daylight at Vauxhall Cross, the unusual modern edifice of the MI6 headquarters commanding the attention of all. He entered the building, cleared his ID with security, then took the elevator to the seventh floor, walking along toward the suite of offices used by all field agents visiting HQ. He had sat at an empty desk for no longer than ten minutes, when a secretary came up to him.

"Mr Steel, the chief wants to see you now," she said to the agent. He got up from the desk walked towards the elevator, inserted the electronic card into the slot, the bell pinged and the door opened. He pressed the button for the penthouse and was whisked up the one floor to the chief's suite, which also contained a complex communications centre connecting with the whole world. Steel emerged from the elevator and walked across to the outer office of the chief's secretary.

"Hello Mr Steel, Sir Martin is waiting for you. Go straight through please."

"Hello there, Moneypenny," he said, grinning, as he walked across to kiss her on the cheek, "how's my favourite secretary today?" she looked away feigning coyness, flicking her hair back from her eyes;
"Oh James you shouldn't do that, you know I'm crazy about you," she held her clasped hands close to her heart as she spoke. They both beamed with laughter at their mocking charade. He straightened his tie, then knocked on the door and walked directly into the chief's office with a smile still across his face.

"Sit down Steel, what's so damned amusing?" he asked the agent in a somber voice, not wanting a reply. "Close the door," said Sir Martin irritably, as he undid his tie.

The MI6 chief looked tired and drawn and unshaven. Steel took a seat in front of his desk. He knew what the subject matter would be, without prompting. Sir Martin looked directly at the agent for all of twenty seconds, sighing deeply.

"Well David, old lad, it had to happen sooner or later. I have set up a meeting of the four, to be held in Austria next week. You will meet in Vienna. Here are your air tickets and the details of your hotel. This job has to go without a hitch, and must remain undetected for time imme-morial. There is also the added complication of possible interference, or more to the point, the probability of running into other people with similar intentions, just different motives," said the chief.

"I understand clearly, sir," replied the agent.

"There have been one or two faces around recently that are unknown to me. I was not sure whether they were from other Governments or maybe the royals. I know everyone from the Sahaed side of the fence."

David Steel picked up the envelope from the desk and made his way to the door.

"Steel, if this goes wrong, you're on your own, you know that," said Sir Martin Fields both arms in the air, in a this-is-out-of-my-hands gesture as the agent's hand rested on the doorknob.

"I know, sir. As usual, if I mess up, it's my fault and I'm out in the cold. When I succeed, my rewards will be in heaven. So what's new? Please don't tell me, if I can't stand the heat I should get out of the kitchen, either. Trouble is, sometimes it gets lethally hot in that bloody kitchen! I was trying to remember only the other night how I got into the bloody kitchen in the first place. Seeing as we're into clichés, if I can't take a joke, I shouldn't have joined!" He walked out of the door without looking round, or closing the door behind him. With a carefree wave of his hand, he turned into the elevator.

Kensington Palace, London

Princess Anna sat in her apartments within Kensington Palace. She had been back from Cairo some two hours and already there were lists of calls to be made. She had noted the urgency in the request from the Prime Minister's office, and heard what Michael had to say regarding the Queen's attitude. She wondered why she felt concern; she had fully expected the reaction to be bad. She felt the royals had treated her so poorly; she really didn't give a damn.

"You have a free evening this evening. Did you have anything in mind, or will you just make a quiet night of it?" asked her secretary.

"I think that a quiet night seems to be the answer, Michael."

"Do you wish me to organise some food, Ma'am? I can have something sent up from the kitchens if you wish."

"No thanks, Michael, that airline food is all that a stomach can handle in one day. I'll give it a miss tonight. You run along and I'll see you in the morning. I need to look through the list you have there. Don't forget that I have to be in Paris on Friday. I shall be staying over the weekend at the Majestic Palace Hotel. I don't want that made public, in fact quite the contrary," emphasising her last words. "Get my maid to bring me a hot chocolate in about twenty minutes, will you?"

"Will do; see you in the morning then. Goodnight, Ma'am," he said, leaving the room.

Anna changed into casual slacks and a sweatshirt, went through to the sitting room and poured a stiff drink, picked up the papers that Meadows had left, and stretched out on the couch. She knew that the list of engagements would have to be reduced somewhat if she was to get to Paris by the weekend. She read the extensive pile of requests for her presence. As usual they all seemed important. Anna felt that she might have to cancel her coming weekend trip after all.

Vienna, Austria

Steel sat in the back of the cab as the driver took the vehicle at a walking pace through the centre of the famous historic city. It was a dreadful night, the rain had turned to drizzle and there was a bitter cold bite to the air. People were scurrying across the dimly lit streets, heading for home and a warm fireside, or maybe a cozy bar and mulled spiced wine. The cab pulled up outside the Hotel Kieserhoff. He paid the cab driver and strode quickly into the warmth of the foyer, closely followed by a porter carrying his one piece of baggage. He booked in under the name of Jim Arkwright, a cutlery rep from Sheffield, England. His passport along with other ID bore the same name. A letter from a Sheffield firm too had confirmed his hotel booking. He went directly to his room and saw that the light on the telephone was flashing, indicating that there was a message awaiting him.

Walking across the room he plugged in the electric kettle and tore open the packet of instant coffee, tipping its contents into a cup. He sat on the bed picked up the phone, dialling the usual zero. While he waited for the operator to reply, he thought how all hotel rooms looked the same in any city in the world, the only difference was the alternate language of the instructions on the coffee packs.

Steel spoke a number of languages fluently, German being one, but he chose to speak to the operator in English. She told him, in impeccable English, that there had been two calls, and gave him the information. He took his coffee through to the bathroom, and then climbed into the shower. After a few minutes he dressed.

The agent put on his coat. Before leaving the room he took an habitual, mental picture. He walked the full length of the hallway in the opposite direction of the elevators. He opened the door to the fire exit, and then descended the stairs passing the sign to the hotel foyer, eventually exiting by the door to the car park. He walked around the parked cars until he came to an Opal Cadet, parked with the interior courtesy lights aglow. He walked to a nearby concrete pillar. Lighting a cigarette he looked around carefully then walked back to the car. Putting his hand under the right rear fender he pulled out a key, opened the door and drove out of the car park.

After driving for some miles and leaving the outskirts of the city, David Steel drove into the parking lot of a bar. Inside, the bar was busy and extremely noisy. The agent walked to the far corner of the room where he found an empty kiosk. A waitress took his order. He sat nursing a foaming stein of Austria's best beer. A dark haired woman came across and sat at his table. She had somewhat of a masculine appearance about her, which was emphasised by the jagged scar on her left cheek. Another waitress came across and the woman ordered a mulled wine. Her German was faultless.

"Well David, how are things with you lately?" she said holding up her glass. "Prost," said the woman as she chinked her glass against his. "It's nice to see you again. I trust you are keeping well?" She said in equally impeccable English. "Le'xayeem!"

"Same here. How have you been lately?" Steel said raising his beer stein to the Israeli woman, one of Mossad's finest.

The Majestic Palace Hotel, Paris

Gavin Jones sat in the offices of the underground garage going through the latest reports of the drivers, and more especially the reports of the mechanics that carried out the routine checks and maintenance on the many vehicles that made up the transport section of the big hotel. He was mainly concerned with those cars that stayed on the locked side of the barred gates, those that were used exclusively by the Al-Sahaed family and visiting dignitaries or relations.

This coming weekend, Raffi and Princess Anna were to spend the weekend at the hotel. In view of the last major catastrophe in Cairo, security was to be doubled in both numbers and quality. Gavin's boss, Boris Kiev, was to be there on Friday. Already the paparazzi were beginning to stir. It intrigued Gavin as to how they always seemed to know that something was afoot long before the event took place. They were like the buzzards of the desert.

Reading through the reports, all private vehicles had checked out and none of them had been moved for the past seven days. Jones alone had the keys to the compound, which was very securely locked and protected, both electronically and physically. He re-checked the drawings. There was only the one entrance, the other three walls were solid concrete blocks and underground.

The bodyguard went into the private compound and walked around the two main vehicles. The first was a new Bentley Turbo, a gleaming black specimen built especially for the Al-Sahaeds. The car was bullet proof; without the extra weight normally expected, it still weighed two and a half tons and was capable of reaching sixty in under seven seconds, and was able to top one hundred and forty. The other car was a Mercedes five hundred. It too, was very fast when needed and just as secure. Built like a tank, in fact.

Gavin Jones' job was to protect Anna and to keep the cars untouched: two very tall orders, bearing in mind that most of the time both charges were quite a way apart from each other. The only time he could physically see the car and people was when they rode together.

Like Boris Kiev himself, Jones had to trust the abilities of others, or at least one another. He locked the massive barred gates, turned out the lights, and then set the infrared and laser security systems. Looking at his watch, he walked quickly to the elevator and his meeting with the chauffeurs.

Walking across the lobby of the magnificent hotel, he saw the face of one of the local paparazzi sitting next to a well-known English member of the same low-life fraternity.

"Somebody died then, or somebody must be about to?" said Jones to the two of them.

"What seamy low life activities are you scum up to?" his dislike and aversion was blatantly apparent to the two long-haired specimens, who gave no answer.

He beckoned to a large ominous looking man standing by the elevators, at the same time putting his foot firmly on the long telescopic lens of a camera lying on the carpet. The men got up to leave, the French hippie-like man, tried to pick up his camera, but failed. As he pulled harder there was a resounding snap as the lens connection to the camera broke, leaving the expensive tubular part remaining firmly under Jones' foot.

"These two pieces of shit are just about to leave. If they do it too slowly, assist them," Jones ordered, in no more than a whisper.

"The next time I see any of this type of scum anywhere in this hotel, it'll be your head that rolls," he said to the security man.

"I want my lens," whined the photographer.

"If I did give you this," he said bending down and putting the broken part in his jacket pocket, "you won't be able to sit down for the rest of your miserable scavenging life. Now get him out of here before I do something that we might all regret," Jones said to the big man.

"And you," he said pointing to the other English man, "if I see you within ten miles of this place again, you'll end up swimming the channel back to England, got that!" He poked the man fiercely on the chest, turned and walked to the reception, then beckoned one of the assistant managers across.

"If I see one more member of these damn paparazzi in here again, you will be explaining yourself to Monsieur Al-Sahaed in person, is that clear?" he roared at the dark-suited man, banging his fist on the counter as he spoke.

"Bloody inefficient ass holes," he muttered as he went to his office, which overlooked the whole lobby area from behind a two-way mirror. As he entered, the four full-time drivers were waiting. He sat down at the table and threw the telephoto lens into the trash bin with a loud clatter.

"Do you all speak English?" he asked the assembled group. One of the men shook his head. "I won't be requiring your services then," he said, as one of the other men translated. "Tell him, no hard feelings, but I need fluent English for this weekend. Tell him there'll be plenty of other work around the place," he said, as the man got up to leave, a disgruntled look on his face.

"I'll need a replacement for him," he said picking up the phone and asking for personnel.

Aboard the Sahaed Jet

Raffi sat in the rear of the Sahaed's jet. He was deep in thought; he really was in love with Anna. He hoped that they had done the right thing in ending the pregnancy. He was pleased that they'd been able to keep the matter from his father, which in itself was a gargantuan achievement.

He had brought up the subject of marriage whilst she had still been pregnant as any gentleman would in the circumstances. He realised that his feelings had not changed, quite the contrary. *If I really love her nothing else should matter*, he thought to himself as he sipped his orange soda. *Only time will tell*, he sighed at the thought.

"Everything alright?" said Raffi's father from the other side of the cabin. "You seemed deep in thought. Soon be there." He picked up a phone and spoke in Arabic to the flight deck. Raffi went forward to the toilet and as he returned stuck his head into the tiny galley. His favourite stewardess sat there.

"Seeing the princess this weekend Raffi?" He was surprised at the warm feeling he experienced when he answered in the affirmative. Just then the plane hit a spot of turbulence. Raffi lost his footing and slipped to the floor. Sahaed came scurrying from the back, just as the captain spoke on the PA system asking them all to be seated, and to fasten their belts until further notice.

Raffi took his seat and adhered to the captain's request. Shortly after, the stewardess came back to check on his welfare and to see if he required anything before they landed. Minutes later, he saw the lights of Surrey as the plane entered the holding pattern, awaiting its turn to descend to the tarmac.

At the same time the princess was being driven to London's Gatwick airport, although she had a booking on British Airways to New York's Kennedy airport the following morning from London's Heathrow. That booking had been set up as a smoke screen, and carefully leaked to the gutter press. It seemed to have worked judging by the lack of followers from the capital.

Anna's car entered the rear gates of the airport, just about the same time as the private jet had landed and taxied to a remote corner of the airfield. Anna was checked by security police, who until her arrival, knew that a celebrity was arriving, but weren't sure of the identity. There were no press or onlookers as the car drove through towards the waiting Lear Jet. As the car approached the plane, Raffi stood by the steps and welcome his princess. He hugged her warmly, and then they both hurried up the stairway into the aircraft.   The engines roared into life. They must have been given royal preference, as the jet taxied around the perimeter and soared instantly into a take off for its short hop across the channel to France's Orly airport and the city of Paris.

Chelsea, London

Just between Chelsea High Street and the Fulham Road there's a nice little enclave with a quiet pleasant pub called the Red Anchor, frequented mainly by a wide selection of locals, ranging from stage and screen celebrities to those whose means of income would be purely a matter for conjecture.

Michael Meadows sat at the end of the bar passing the time of day with the landlord, Ken. He always enjoyed a stop here, though not directly en-route to home, it helped him to unwind after a hectic day. Most of the customers knew what his job was, but didn't ask too many questions and tended to protect him from prying strangers, certainly against the press. This particular evening he was to meet up with his old friend, Inspector Hank Marlin, former police bodyguard to the Princess of Wales.

Hank had called Michael earlier in the day and asked for a meeting. He had asked after the princess. Michael had been unable to say anything on the phone about her Paris trip, as secrecy was the order of the day. As he ordered another half of beer, Hank walked in looking more harassed than Michael had seen him for some time.

"How's it going, my old friend?" said Michael.

"Oh, alright I suppose," replied Hank.

"Ken, I'd like you to meet Hank Marlin, an old friend of mine. Hank meet Ken, the boss here."

"Pleased to meet you," said the policeman.

"Same here," said Ken.

"Aren't you the policeman who was Princess Anna's bodyguard?"

"The very same. If you'll excuse us Ken there are a few things that I need to talk to Michael about."

Behind the Majestic Palace Hotel, Paris

The Paris Water Company had been working outside the hotel for a day and a half. The everlasting sounds of the pump and ancillary air tools were proving to be an irritant to most of the hotel's guests. Then, after management complaints, it had been stopped abruptly, much to the relief of the director, as the owner of the hotel was arriving the very next day.

That night, as the security guard sat in his small office by the side of the massive barred gates that lead to the private motor section of the hotel, a strong fluid that broke down cement was being carefully used on the other side of the back wall facing the big gates. Slowly the cement bonding the concrete blocks was being eroded away and silently raked from between their joints. If the guard had looked closely behind the parked vehicles, he would have seen the damp sandy mortar as it fell silently to the floor of the underground garage, much as though a mole were hard at work there.

Eventually the block began to move as the tool being used went clear around the concrete cube. This was then lowered to the floor; shortly followed by a second one, then a third and a fourth, after which a head followed by shoulders attached to a lithe body wearing skin-tight clothing slid quietly through the small opening.

The guard was unable to witness any of this as the Bentley stood in front of the whole proceedings. The intruder slid under both cars in turn, working diligently for at least twenty minutes on each vehicle. At one point there had been the clink of a wrench on a nut. The alert guard came out of his office, shone his flashlight around, then he returned to guard the only entrance to the garage, assuming that a cat had gone through the bars of the gate.

Afterwards, the intruder cleaned the residue from the concrete. A few feet away a flat metal sheet had been left leaning against the wall. Before crawling back inside the small hole, the heavy sheet of steel was pulled in front of the orifice, then the blocks repositioned from the outside.

The whole operation had taken no more than an hour. Outside, the lithe shadowy figure surfaced at the water company workings and disappeared into the darkness that surrounded the night-time city of romance.

Meanwhile, the guard sat fully alert at the only entrance to the motor pool. He was still looking in the wrong direction, completely unaware of what had taken place behind his back.

Later that night the blonde hair of David Steel shone under the over-head lights in the bar behind the Majestic Palace Hotel. He sat with the severe-looking woman, a nasty scar on her left cheek. They awaited the arrival of another. Within a few minutes the same man who Steel had met earlier, entered the bar still wearing the hotel uniform.

"Fancy seeing you here again," he said, first in French then in English.

"It's been quite a while. How about another game of your English darts?"

"No thanks, I don't have the time right now." They moved over to the corner where the dartboard hung. The hotel employee picked up the darts and began throwing them at the board as he talked.

"Did you get the names?" asked Steel.

"I got what you need, yes," said the darts man, as he came across and sat with the other two. Steel introduced the woman with the lithe figure as Esther Ben-Sheed, a friend from Israel. They sat in a huddle for ten minutes, not noticing the big man sitting in the shadow of a pillar, a hat pulled down over his eyes. After a while the British agent wearing the Majestic Palace Hotel uniform left the bar. The other two finished their drinks and left shortly after.

The Majestic Palace Hotel

Earlier that evening, after a meeting with Jones, Boris Kiev had meticulously gone through the records of the hotel staff, looking for any recent changes in the full-time members. He knew from years of experience that the floating population of temporary staff in catering made it almost impossible to keep an absolute check on everyone.

Colonel Kiev scanned the monitor looking at the usual array of faces, some pleasant, some looking as though they belonged in a criminal records department. *Some maybe are* he thought, as the computer record files slid by. He occasionally stopped and rolled the files back, checking the accompanying details of a face.

Kiev paused at another face, went back to the man's records, and then returned to the face. Henry Duval. The man seemed vaguely familiar to the Russian. Duval had been at the hotel for only three months. His records were scant: he had worked as a porter in three different hotels before, two in London, one in the south of France; bi-lingual, English and French; born in England of a French mother and English father; hobbies: martial arts and golf.

The security chief picked up the phone and pressed the buttons for the personnel office.

"Kiev, security, here. Can you tell me if a Henry Duval is working today? He works as a hall porter." There was a pause, then:

"Oui Monsieur Kiev, he goes off duty in one hour. Is there anything else we can do for you?"

"No thanks, you have been most helpful." Kiev then ran a print of the man's complete record, including the photograph, put on his jacket and walked out of the office.

A few minutes later Kiev looked across the bar, his face hidden under the brim of a trilby hat. He watched with interest as a member of the Majestic staff left, followed by his old MI6 adversary David Steel. He did not recognise the woman who accompanied Steel, but his trained eye told him he was looking at a professional. He noted the way the woman had walked. Her feet seemed to glide catlike, and her Middle Eastern eyes did not miss a thing as she had continuously scanned the room. He had no doubt at all that he was looking at one of Mossad's finest and, *if so, what the hell is she doing here with Steel, and talking with the man Duval?*, the Russian thought to himself.

He too finished his drink, walked out of the bar, and then drove off in the direction of the hall porter's address on the outskirts of the city. The man Duval was an MI6 agent, placed in the hotel reporting back to Steel. Kiev had talked with old friends in Moscow calling in the odd debt, who had confirmed Duval's connections with the agency.

The Majestic Palace Hotel Paris - earlier that evening

Gavin Jones sat at the computer terminal looking through the personnel files. He had run into a bit of a problem regarding the driver's duty list for the visit of the princess and Raffi. One of the only two cleared drivers had gone sick with the flu and would not be able to drive that evening. This put Jones in a bit of a spot, so he went through the possible alternatives. He drew a blank at every attempt. The only possibility seemed to be that of using a chauffeur agency. He could bring a driver over from London, but he did prefer to have one who knew Paris well, and was born a driver on the left hand side of the road.

After another fruitless foray through the files, he had decided that the computer records were well out of date. The phone rang. It was Kiev, who wanted to see him right away. Gavin decided to sort out the driver situation tomorrow. After all, he had a couple of days in which to handle what was a relatively simple problem. He signed off the computer and made his way to the office being used by Colonel Boris Kiev.

The Red Anchor Pub, Chelsea, London

Michael Meadows carried two more pints of beer across the bar to the corner table where Hank Marlin sat. He thought that Hank was beginning to look a little older, but decided to keep his opinions to himself.

"So what's up Hank? You sounded a little worried on the phone. Has something gone wrong?"

"Well, yes it has. I'm beginning to hear things that worry me to death regarding Anna. There's a lot of talk about her relationship with the Sahaed man," said Hank, deliberately keeping his voice down, looking around the small bar as he spoke.

"I'm assuming that this one is serious, and not just another one of the princess's flings."

"This one does seem a little more serious than any of the others I must agree," answered Michael. Hank leaned forward with a very severe expression on his face. He beckoned Michael closer.

"I'm worried Michael. I am frightened for Princess Anna's life," he said in a whisper. "I overheard a conversation a couple of nights ago. I won't tell you where or who." He paused looking around the bar again. "I think the powers that be are very concerned, and are capable of doing anything to end this relationship. As a result of what I heard I've been keeping my ears open in various quarters. My suspicions were proven correct, or let's say they were not disproved." He took a long drink of his beer, looked around the bar yet again, and then added: "There seems to be two separate camps as usual, obviously the palace mafia, and of course the Government's agencies. Which one, I don't know, but it will have to be MI6, as they handle most everything outside of the country. Also, if the Israelis get a whiff of this, they'll be delighted to help MI6 in their endeavours. That's a scary outfit, the Mossad. They take life very seriously and they take it quite often too. They always play for keeps." He spread his hands in a gesture of despair.

"What's to be done, Hank?" asked Michael, looking quizzically at Hank.

"Not sure," replied the policeman, "but something has to be done, and done quickly."

There was a long pause, the silence broken by a voice from across the room.

"You two ready for another pint?" shouted Ken the landlord from behind the bar.

"Sure," answered Hank. "I'll get these," he said to Michael, as he stood up, taking the now empty glasses back to the bar. Michael's mind raced as Hank stood at the bar. He too, had thought that the relationship was bound to raise the odd eyebrow or two, but he had never considered such a potentially dire outcome.

Hank put the drinks on the table and returned to his seat.

"Imagine what would happen if they married," said Hank. "The thought would be totally unconscionable to the palace, and for that matter to the nation. Now imagine if they married and had a child. That child would be half brother or sister to the future King of England, born of a Muslim father, being half Arabic. The only person who could be delighted would be the one and only Anwar Sahaed. He would escalate from not being able to get British citizenship, to being a relative to the King of England!" said Hank, looking around as he had raised his voice in the excitement of making his point clear.

"Can you see now, Michael, what's at stake? They won't let it happen, and you can rest assured that the two main parties who have the most to lose won't work together on the matter. They can't, which means that there could be attempts on the lives of either or both Anna and Raffi Sahaed from at least two different directions. On the other hand, there are the massive resources of the Al-Sahaed family and relatives who will pay any price and go to any length to see the marriage take place." Hank took a long drink from his pint. He lit a cigarette, looking around for an ashtray.

"I'm sorry Michael, mind if I smoke?" Hank asked his hands spread in apology, as he flicked the ash from the end of the cigarette.

"You carry on Hank. It's your funeral, not mine."

"This time Anna doesn't have the might of British security to protect her."

"Quite the contrary, Michael. In fact, she hasn't anyone, apart from the Sahaed security, which may well be good, but it's no match for specially trained secret service people who kill as a profession. Also, who is to know whether they will co-opt other Government agents? USA and Brit secret services are joined at the hip! Hank paused and finished the remains of his pint.

"I understand clearly what you say, but what the hell can we do against such overwhelming odds, Hank? What can be done to protect the princess," he added, furrows appearing across his brow.

"Where is she right now?" Hank asked. "We have to get to her and place her out of harm's way before it's too late, or at least until we can get her some real protection."

Michael pulled up the cuff of his jacket and looked at his watch.

"At this precise moment, she's in Sahaed's aircraft flying towards Paris where she is to spend three nights at the Majestic Palace Hotel. They made a circuitous trip and stopped at Gatwick to collect the princess on their way over from Cairo. I gave the press false information. They think she's flying out of Heathrow to the States tomorrow."

"It's not the press that we're worried about!" said Hank, somewhat sarcastically. Who else knows that she's flying today? How many people know that she is to stay at the Majestic Palace Hotel for the next few days? A very delicate question I know, but did she carry out her plan as far as the doctor was concerned?" The policeman asked with a note of concern in his voice.

"She intimated that she'd gone through a lot on her trip to Egypt. She didn't actually say that the procedure had been carried out. Not the kind of question one could ask really. Now you have me worried to death," said Michael. "Do you really think that matters are as serious as you say?" He put the palm of his hand to his forehead, a look of total disbelief across his face. He finished his drink and looked at his watch again. "What do you suggest I do Hank? You've painted a very glum picture indeed. I don't know what to do next."

"I have a lot of leave due to me, left over from my time with the princess," said Hank. "I was told that I could take it whenever I wished," he said, taking out his pocket diary. "I think that right about now would be a good time. I have about five weeks to come in total. It seems that to spend it on Princess Anna would be poetic, though I must not let the powers that be get to know what I'm doing or that would be the end of my career and my pension," said the policeman, one of the most experienced protectors available.

"That would be fantastic," said Michael. "When can we get started?"

"I'm free right away," he replied. "If the matter is as serious as you say, we ought to get onto it quickly. You have the contacts Michael; can you get me some tickets to Paris as quickly as possible? I am prepared to go in the morning. The Royal Family is in Scotland, so I'm a bit redundant until they return in a few weeks."

"I can do better than that. I will fly you there myself. My airplane is at Redhill airfield in Surrey. Meet me there first thing tomorrow morning. I can't fly tonight after drinking. Do you know where the airfield is?" he asked the policeman.

"Sure, it's off the A25 at the village of Nuffield, in Surrey. Some of the police helicopters are serviced there and I've been there a few times so know it well." They finalised arrangements in a very short space of time, had a last half of beer and went their separate ways.

Michael drove along the Fulham Road, his mind on the conversation with Hank. The points raised by the policeman seemed very valid. Why was the princess being so blind to such serious circumstances? Hank was right: *those in opposition would not allow this relationship to go any further*, he thought to himself. He, above all, knew what 'they' were capable of doing. A cold shiver passed through his body at the thought. He had not noticed the car that had followed him from the princess's offices, and subsequently from the pub, or the driver talking into his cell phone.

Michael pulled into the small mews where his house was located. He parked his car and went into the house. Picking up the phone he called his mechanic at Redhill airfield and gave instructions for his plane to be prepared and ready for an early flight to Paris the following morning. He then asked to be transferred to operations, where he logged a flight plan, with a 6:30am take off. He then called Hank, informing him of the schedule for tomorrow, made himself a hot Horlicks drink, and then went to bed. At the same moment a car drove out of the mews, its lights extinguished until turning out onto the main road. Michael lay in bed going over the conversation with Hank Marlin.

Meanwhile, Hank had already reported to his office that he would be away visiting a sick relative in Europe. He had contacted his boss and cleared the taking of three of the many weeks vacation time owed to him. He had agreed to report in on a weekly basis. He packed a suitcase then retired to bed, his mind too, going over some of the things that he had been privy to hearing during the past few weeks. He began to formulate a plan of action for the days to come.

The Majestic Palace Hotel that same evening

Jones was having quite a time trying to fill the driver's roster for the following few days during the visit of the princess.

He had to find a driver for the car that would be taking the couple to their favourite Paris club following dinner. The couple were to dine at the hotel first. He had organised a decoy car, which would be parked in front of the Majestic Palace Hotel, but he would have the real car parked behind the hotel, in readiness to slip quietly away, avoiding the ever-increasing crowd of press photographers outside the main entrance. Jones made his last call before deciding that he himself may have to drive the car, which he did not relish. Night-time Paris driving, on the right-hand side of the road was not exactly his idea of a walk in the park. Besides, Colonel Kiev had instructed him to bodyguard the couple. Kiev had emphasised the need for absolute top security and not a single mistake was to be made. He had referred to the fiasco in Cairo with some sarcasm.

Gavin dialled a Paris number. A woman speaking French answered the phone.

"May I speak to Paul Gastard please?" he asked the woman in English. After a pause she spoke in highly accented English.

"Who is that speaking?" she asked.

"It's Jones, security at the Hotel. Is he there please?"

After another elongated pause, she said something in French. He felt the bang as the receiver was thrown down heavily. He then heard her foot-steps on a wooden floor as she stomped away. After what seemed an age he heard the receiver being picked up, then the voice of a man, sounding sleepy and slow.

"Hello, who is that calling?" Jones heard the man say.

"It's Gavin Jones here, Mr Sahaed's personal security. Is that Paul Gastard? he asked.

"Yes, Gastard speaking. What can I do for you? I am off duty for the next two days," said the Frenchman wearily.

"We have a small problem; we need someone to drive Princess Anna and Mr Raffi tomorrow night. There is a number of staff away due to illness. I am told that you stand in sometimes for the drivers, Monsieur Gastard. Though you are off duty, are you able to come in tomorrow and drive the couple around Paris? It will be worth your while, I can assure you. Mr Al-Sahaed will hear of your loyalty," said the bodyguard, hoping that the man would agree.

"What time do you need me to be there?" asked Gastard. "My daughter has an engagement party tomorrow afternoon. I must attend that, on pain of death."

"We need you to be standing by from eight o'clock onwards. The couple wants to leave after dinner. Let's see, seven o'clock will be fine," said Jones crossing his fingers. "Will you be able to make it then? It will be greatly appreciated." There was a pause, during which he heard the Frenchman speaking heatedly to a woman who Gavin assumed to be the man's wife.

"Ok I'll be there. What do you want me to wear?" asked the Frenchman.

"Just a normal suit," replied a relieved bodyguard. "There's no need for a uniform. See you later Paul, and thanks again."

"Yes!" Jones exclaimed, thrusting his clenched fist to the ceiling like a victorious boxer, relieved by Gastard's agreement. *You've saved my life.* He said as he put the phone down. Sighing and smiling, he left for the garages with a spring in his step.

The scene at the hotel was hectic to say the least. Outside at the front entrance there were large numbers of the press. They were like a hoard of scavenging vultures, haggling arguing, pushing and jockeying for position, colloquially known as 'The Paparazzi.'

Inside the hotel, security was at a peak. Jones waited in the plush main foyer, his earphone in his right ear, watching every move made around him. There were large numbers of his men stationed at every vantage point throughout the building, some sitting, some reading newspapers, others talking to colleagues, some even out on the roof of the hotel.

Colonel Boris Kiev stood up on the main balcony overlooking the whole of the busy hotel foyer. He too had his eyes peeled, not missing one move. Gavin's earphone crackled, followed by the voice of Kiev.

"Is the male who just came through the swing doors a reporter? He looks it to me," Kiev said into the wrist microphone.

"I've got him sir." He moved to intercept the man who had an ominous bulge beneath his overcoat. He found himself very quickly in a room off the reception area trying to explain his presence in the hotel, as his pockets were turned out onto the desk of the security office. The man complained bitterly. At the same time behind his back, his camera was being dismantled and rendered useless. He was seriously warned and then bundled unceremoniously out of a side staff door of the hotel.

Sahayed's Aircraft over Paris

Princess Anna had been aboard the plane for what seemed only minutes. As the pilot put on the seatbelt lights, she held Raffi's hand as she reached across the armrest, whispering into his ear, making sure that the older man could not overhear her words.

"Has your father had anymore to say since he spoke with you after my departure from Cairo?"

"No. He seems totally convinced that the situation is as it was, and that you are still pregnant, though we have never discussed the matter at all. He's too quiet to think otherwise. As a matter of fact I don't think that I've ever known him keep so silent for so long before, or seen him play his cards so close to his chest. I know my father like the back of my hand," said Raffi squeezing Anna's hand as he spoke."

"Do you think he has any idea of our plans?"

"What do you think darling?" His question and smile said 'don't be ridiculous.' He turned to look across at his father, the remnants of a smile on his face. As their eyes met the look came back, seemed to be that of a proud father.

The tone of the engines increased as the jet began to lose altitude on its approach into Charles De Gaulle airport, Paris. Tyres screeched as the plane touched down and the engines roared as the pilot applied reverse thrust. The jet reduced speed and turned off the main runway, then wheeled across towards the executive area, where it drew to a halt.

Gavin Jones stood on the edge of the apron next to the Mercedes as the aircraft engines whined down to a stop. The upper door was slowly raised, then the lower part housing the stairs came down to the ground. The flight attendant came out of the plane first, followed by the rest of the crew. As Jones stood waiting, he saw Anwar Sahaed come down the stairs followed closely by Raffi and Princess Anna. The three walked directly towards the waiting car. They climbed in and the car swept off with Jones seated in front with the driver. There was a motorcycle escort in front of their vehicle and behind them another car followed closely. The cavalcade sped off towards Paris, whilst the luggage was loaded into a waiting van.

Meanwhile, back at the Majestic Palace Hotel, the Bentley, which had been driven slowly around the block, pulled up to the front entrance of the hotel, carrying five passengers. The press, disappointed to see that the occupants were of no significance to them, left the area. At the same time, the Mercedes swept through the rear gates of the underground car park, the massive gates closing down behind. The *passengers,* along with Gavin Jones and one other security man, walked to the elevator smiling at the thought of having managed to get into the hotel un-noticed. They stepped from the elevator heading to their various suites. Jones positioned a security man outside the elevator as he followed the couple along the corridor.

Once inside her suite, the princess sat down with a sigh. She knew that she was playing with fire and was fully aware of the attitude of the Royal Family, and indeed that of the British establishment. If only they all knew what she had planned.

Her last brief conversation with her friend, Inspector Hank Marlin, had left her in no doubt as to the attitude of the Royal Family. Hank had made it clear that they would stop at nothing to bring this relationship to an end. She was also well aware of the Prime Minister's concern, having successfully managed to avoid the meeting recently requested by him. Anna's life had been such a misery over the past few years and now things were starting to become enjoyable. She really liked the idea that she was at last upsetting the royals, perhaps even more so, soon. *What could the Prime Minister wish to do anyway? She asked herself. He has enough on his plate having just taken over the Premiership without pushing his nose into my personal life, Anna thought.*

Sitting there, her mind began to go back over some of the more recent happenings, back to the near accident at sea; who was behind that? Who had been bugging their hotel rooms in London? That time during their cruise in the Mediterranean, was the helicopter that flew over the Sahaed's yacht really carrying members of the press or was it someone more sinister?

Anna looked around the luxurious suite. For the first time in many months she felt totally alone and a little worried, perhaps even slightly afraid. Her thoughts were halted by the warbling tone of the telephone. She reached out and picked up the handset.

"Hello darling, it's me." The voice of Raffi jolted Anna back to the present. "Shall I come across, or will you come over to my suite?" he asked. The very sound of his voice had that warm feeling coursing through her body; she was really becoming fond of him.

"I was just about to take a shower, I'll be over in about twenty minutes," replied Anna.

She replaced the receiver then went across towards the bathroom, taking off her jacket as she went. Meanwhile, the phone rang in Raffi's suite as he was just putting on his shirt in the dressing room.

"Mr Raffi, there's a man on the phone who wishes to speak with you, from a Paris jewellers. Will you take the call?

"No, that won't be necessary. Tell him I'll call him back in a few minutes, but you'd better take his number, please." Raffi began to fasten his tie, a knowing grin across his face.

The A23, South of London

The journey south to Redhill in Surrey was rather quicker than Michael had expected. Though it was five o'clock in the morning, the roads were virtually deserted. Forty minutes after leaving his house he drove into the airfield and over to the side of the hangar that housed the Piper Navajo. The aircraft was already standing outside, its fuselage glistening with the reflections of the arc lights of the airfield, its navigation lights flashing ominously. As he climbed out of his car, he saw Hank walking across the grass.

"What kept you?" he said to Michael.

"Have you been here all night?" Michael replied to the policeman.

"I thought I would give myself plenty of time, but the roads were so deserted I got here in next to no time. The young man here kindly got me a cup of coffee," said Hank gesturing towards the man walking towards them.

"Morning, Mr Meadows," said a fresh faced young man.

"She's gassed up, checked out and ready to go. The forecast looks good; the usual fog over the channel."

"Thanks Charlie, and thanks for taking care of the inspector here."

"It's always a pleasure to be of service Mr Meadows, you know that," he said, smiling as some folded crisp bank notes slid surreptitiously into his hand. He looked down grinning.

"Always a pleasure," he repeated, as he went towards the hangar. The two men walked across and climbed aboard the plane.

Michael's father, a retired naval pilot, taught Michael to fly at an early age; he had made him a present of the Piper when he had been appointed private secretary to the princess.

The Navajo was set up to seat six, and could carry up to eight passengers including the pilot. As they strapped themselves into their seats Michael brought both powerful engines to life, and then began to wheel the aircraft forward. An indication of dawn could be seen across the night sky as Michael waved to the mechanic. He completed his pre-flight checks then rolled the aircraft out onto the active runway. He applied the brakes, finally opening the throttles partway and checking engine gauges as the plane pulled and shook quite violently against the restriction.

"Redhill tower, this is Golf Echo Delta two zero, requesting clearance for take-off on pre-ordained flight plan."

"Roger Golf Echo Delta, two zero, you are cleared for immediate take off, runway 2".

Michael acknowledged the call.

"Golf Echo Delta two zero, rolling."

The engines roared once more as he released the brakes. The plane leapt forward gathering speed; Michael rotated the nose wheel off the runway as they lifted into the air in textbook fashion. He cleaned up the plane, retracting the gear and flaps.

"Golf Echo Delta two zero, left climb out,"

"Roger, left turn Golf Echo Delta, have a good flight. Redhill out and standing by."

The bright lights of London's Gatwick airport glistened and twinkled in the distance to their right. Hank could see the flashing of the plane's strobe light reflecting from the underside of the wing. As they climbed to their cruising height Michael indicated to Hank to put on the headset, which hung on the right hand side of the co-pilot's seat.

"Everything alright there, Hank?" asked Michael once the headphones were connected.

"Fine thanks, Michael." He replied adjusting the volume.

"If you'd like to go into the rear, you'll find a couple of thermos flasks of coffee or tea, with some milk and sugar. Pour yourself whichever you prefer, I'll have a nice cup of tea myself, if you don't mind, two sugars please," Michael said with a smile, not taking his eyes off the instrument panel as he spoke.

He'd got the aircraft to cruising height then engaged the autopilot, the plane then locked onto the pre set heading or way point of the GPS.

Hank passed him his cup of tea, put on the headset, then settled into a seat behind Michael which had far more leg room than the co-pilot's seat, which was quite restricted by the rudder pedals and yoke.

The Navajo could carry a maximum of nine people. This plane was configured for P1 and P2 up front, then four passengers in the rear, with two seats facing two seats, providing lots of leg room, plus plenty of baggage space to the rear.

"Not long before we get to Paris?" asked Hank, rhetorically as he enjoyed the luxury of stretching his legs.

The Previous Evening, Paris

Princess Anna nodded to the security man outside her door as she walked along the corridor towards Raffi's suite. She had changed into casual gear, feeling quite relaxed. They had planned to stay in the Hotel this evening, perhaps have a light snack in the suite, and then just relax for the rest of the night. There was much planning to be discussed, and some special shopping to be done the following day. Anna could hardly wait to see the faces of the royals when they heard the news.

Gavin Jones sat in the main security office watching the surveillance cameras as they switched from one location to another. He could see the increasing crowds of press outside the main entrance and also at the rear, and some were even outside the gates to the entrance of the underground parking lot. He sensed the unrest of what could quickly become a nasty mob out there.

His phone rang. "Gavin, I don't like the look of those press people out there, far too many of them for my liking," said the voice of Colonel Boris Kiev. "I think that we should disperse them, don't you?"

"It won't be easy sir," replied Jones. Technically they're not breaking the law or at least I don't think they are. I'm not too clued up on French law."

"Since when did we care about the law?" asked his boss. "I don't like the looks of the situation so just go out there and get them out of here. That's an order!" said the Russian quietly but firmly as he put the receiver down with a bang. Outside the hotel, the manager was talking to the mob of press photographers as they haggled and jockeyed for position. They began to close in on the man, some shouting obscenities. Someone threw a plastic soda bottle as Jones and a number of burley security men got in between.

"We know that Princess Anna's inside," shouted one of the paparazzi.

"Raffi's in there too. Do you think we're stupid or something!" yelled another woman in a cockney accent.

"When are they coming out?" an English voice snapped.

"Alright, that's enough!" shouted Gavin as he went forward toward the leading man, who was now shouting about the freedom of the press. "It's time to go home. There's nothing here for you tonight," he shouted. There was a scuffle amongst the crowd toward the rear. It seemed that two of the reporters were arguing. Then one of them hit the other, a powerful blow to the jaw and further back another skirmish began. Within seconds it seemed that a full-scale riot would break out; cameras flew through the air and bodies fell to the ground and women cried out. Then police sirens began to scream and the sounds of whistles pierced the air. As police batons began to fly, men were being hand cuffed and crammed into the rear of black vans. Soon peace and calm reigned once more. There seemed to be half the stock of a camera store littered across the ground. In the darkness of the side street opposite, a group of some fifteen men and women climbed quietly into a small bus unseen by the television camera crews that had arrived on the scene.

Boris Kiev looked out from his third floor window with a smirk on his battle-scarred face. He knew that there were forces at work other than a few disgruntled reporters.

Across the other side of street, two men sat in the back of an undercover van watching the scene. Its antennae turned back and forth on top of the vehicle, which bore the name of a well known French television channel.

"What's all the commotion outside, Raffi?" Anna walked towards the window of the suite. She was about to pull back the drapes, when she remembered the words of Hank Marlin and Gavin Jones. Instead she peered through the semi-transparent material, looking at the scene below. "Looks like some sort of a riot or demonstration, love; nothing that we should worry about," she said, as she walked back to the couch.

The tall blonde man sat in the hotel reception, surveying the scene through his dark tinted glasses. He smiled knowingly as he watched the mayhem unfold outside. David Steel continued to read the newspaper in his hand. A false beard irritated his face. The beret he wore was pulled down to one side. His clothes were those of a bohemian artistic type. The cigarette he held between his teeth in the plastic holder was unlit. Steel finished his coffee, slowly folded his newspaper and got up from his seat, and with the help of a walking stick limped slowly towards the revolving doors of the main entrance. As he left the hotel, he was not aware of the small Arabic figure that followed him into the darkness of the Paris night, nor did he see the smile on the face of Boris Kiev as he watched the British agent, followed by his man.

It was now 10:30pm. Gavin Jones walked around the rear of the hotel and seeing nothing out of the ordinary he nodded to his security man and then walked around to the underground garage. The gates were locked and the security office was manned. He saw the floodlit cars parked securely behind the gates as he made his way back into the hotel. He checked the main entrance to the lobby. Seeing all of his men in place, he entered the elevator, getting off at the private floor. He spoke to the man outside the elevator, checked his men outside both Princess Anna's and Raffi's suites.

"They're both in here, Gav," said the security man nodding towards the door of Raffi's suite. Jones nodded in return, smiled and bid the man goodnight. He went back to the princess's door and knocked twice. Receiving no reply he took out a master key, entered and checked the rooms, then came out. From the security office he rang Raffi's suite, spoke to Raffi and the princess, wished them both goodnight then sat watching the bank of surveillance monitors.

Aboard Golf Echo Delta two zero

Daylight had broken shortly after the plane had entered Dover airspace. The sky was clear as the sunlight came up on their left. As forecast, there was low lying fog blocking out any vision of land below. They were given a new heading by Dover air traffic control, taken up another three thousand feet and were on course for Paris's Orly Airport.

"Should be there in about thirty minutes," said Michael as he turned on the cabin radio speakers in time to hear the morning news.

"There were riots outside of the Majestic Palace Hotel in Paris last night. Photographers who'd gathered, expecting to see Princess Anna, and her latest friend Mr Raffi Sahaed, seemingly started to argue amongst themselves. Fights broke out and a number of arrests were made. There were no serious injuries, though a number of the press received treatment for minor wounds, our Paris correspondent reports.

"The affair between Princess Anna and the son of the flamboyant Egyptian entrepreneur Anwar Sahaed has recently been the subject of much speculation around the world. The couple is rumoured to be in Paris; some reports say they are to become engaged, others have even hinted at a possible pregnancy. A spokesman from the Al-Sahaed's headquarters here in England at his famous Knightsbridge store, Harrobys, said that the couple were just good friends. A Buckingham Palace spokesman refused to comment. The Prime Minister, Tony Blain, questioned on the subject during a recent by-election, said that he would not comment on the private life of Princess Anna, particularly on such wild rumours." Michael looked across at Hank after the newscast.

"Sounds odd to me that the press would attack each other, especially this new breed, the paparazzi or whatever they're called." said Hank.

"Sounds more like someone stirring up trouble to me," he added.

They sat in silence for a while, which was eventually broken by Orly air traffic control.

"Golf Echo Delta two zero, this is Orly air traffic control."

"Go ahead Orly,"

"Reduce your altitude to two thousand, you are on the flight path and clear to land. Weather on the ground is clear, scattered cloud at two thousand feet".

Michael brought the Navajo down through cloud to five thousand feet. The cloud began to clear, leaving partial vision of the countryside below.

As the plane reduced altitude and came down through four, three and two thousand feet, Hank could see the airport runway ahead in the distance. Michael put down the landing gear then executed a perfect landing, skimming along the runway, eventually losing ground speed then turning off to the light aircraft area as instructed by the controller. Michael parked in the space indicated by the traffic marshall, turned off the engines, completed his log, and then prepared to leave the plane.

"Welcome to Paris," he said to Hank. "Let's go and get a rental car, find some breakfast, then work out a game plan," he said as they walked towards the customs and immigration building. As they entered the building, a man shouted, "Hey Hank, this way." Michael followed Hank towards the man.

Hank said. "I would like you to meet a very good friend of mine. Michael, this is Chief Inspector Pierre Lacoste of Interpol. Pierre, meet Michael Meadows"

The Suburbs of the City of Paris

Henry Duval made one last stop on the way home to his apartment after meeting with Steel and the Israeli woman. The MI6 agent always called at his favourite bar one block from home. He usually met up with a few people whom he had befriended during his many visits to the great city. Though born in England, his French mother had made sure that he had been brought up as a Frenchman. He considered himself French, and often said that he wanted to be buried on French soil. When he entered the bar, the bartender nodded in greeting. As Duval looked around, it seemed that most of his friends had already gone home. He had spent too much time with Steel. He ordered a glass of his favourite wine, then sat at the bar passing the time of day with the bartender. Two or three people came into the bar, to which he paid little attention.

Boris Kiev had followed the hall porter into the bar. He watched him order a glass of red wine, then sit on a stool at the bar. Kiev ordered a beer. After a while Duval finished his drink, said goodnight to the bartender then left the bar. He did not take notice as Kiev followed seconds later; however, he did hear the footsteps as they came closer behind. He turned into the back street of his apartment block. The footsteps followed, a voice in English said:

"Excuse me."

Duval took two quick steps to the right then turned, fully expecting and ready to be attacked.

"Don't you work at the Majestic Palace Hotel?" said the big man smiling.

"I saw you in the bar on the corner there." As the big man turned to point in the direction of the bar, he spun back with speed and force driving his right elbow into the temple of Henry Duval.

The agent fell to the ground, his body giving a couple of involuntary twitches.

"Trust nobody," the Russian said to the corpse lying at his feet. "You should know better!" he said aloud as put his hand to the side of Duval's neck. Feeling no pulse, he looked around carefully then walked away casually, returning eventually to his office in the hotel. *That's the inside source of MI6 stopped. That'll slow them down*, he thought, but he knew it wouldn't stop them.

As for the agent, perhaps he'd be buried on French soil after all.

Gavin Jones heard the door open behind him in the monitor room. He did not look round as he had already seen Colonel Kiev on a monitor.

"Take a break," said the Russian, "go and get some sleep. I'll call you when I want relieving. Good job with the crowd earlier."

"Thanks. I'll just take one last look around before I hit the sack," said the Welshman as he got up from his seat to leave the room.

"There's coffee in the pot if you need some," he added as he closed the door behind him.

Orly Airport, Paris

Inspector Lacoste whisked Hank and Michael through customs and immigration. Basically, it was just a matter of following him through the building. With their passports duly stamped, they were driven to a small hotel on the outskirts of the city, which had been booked in advance. The inspector gave Hank the keys to a small Renault car, the property of Interpol, on the basis of international police cooperation. The three arranged to meet for dinner later that evening.

Their rooms were small and clean — adequate would be the best description. The hotel had a small bar, which lead to a side street and turned out to be a favourite and therefore busy local hostelry.

Michael and Hank sat in the bar eating fresh croissants and butter, accompanied by a large pot of coffee, as they worked on their plans. It was decided not to telephone the princess right away, but to take a look around the Majestic Palace Hotel first. Hank said that he would like to speak with Gavin Jones before seeing Princess Anna.

With breakfast over, they changed into city clothes, then went down to their transport. Only after receiving directions from the concierge did they drive off in the direction of the Hotel Majestic Palace. It was now rush hour; the Paris traffic was the usual fast moving, noisy free-for-all. As they made mistake after mistake, finally sitting in a cul-de-sac, despairing of ever finding their way, they put coins into the meter by the side of the Renault, and decided to walk the remainder of the way. As they rounded the second corner they were confronted with the elaborate canopied frontage of The Majestic Palace Hotel.

The princess and Raffi sat in his suite eating breakfast. It was a magnificent morning. The windows were open and a gentle breeze pulled the drapes out onto the balcony. The noise of the Paris traffic could be heard far below them; the room presented a magnificent view across the famed city. Anna lifted a napkin to her lips.

"What a beautiful day it is," she said, "isn't it just great to be alive?" She looked out across a beautiful Paris morning as she spoke.

"Sitting here, opposite the most beautiful woman in the world, what more could a fellow ask for?" said Raffi

"I do love you Raffi." She got up from her chair, walked to his side of the table and threw her arms around his neck. "I've never been so happy, I keep waiting for something to burst my bubble, or to wake up and find that it was only a dream," Anna said, as she kissed him on the cheek.

She later stood on the balcony looking out across the city. *Can this really continue? Were my friends and advisors right? Will someone try to put a stop to my happiness? Am I being selfish?* she thought to herself.

A quarter of a mile away, the morning sun sparkled on the glass of a very high-powered lens attached to the barrel of an equally high velocity rifle, the cross hairs of the sight aimed perfectly at Princess Anna's heart. The princess turned and walked into the room.

At the same time, Esther Ben-Sheed lowered the rifle, slid the window down, and closed the curtains. She turned.

"Her security is non existent, or she just doesn't care. I could have put two bullets into her heart right there," she said to David Steel. "For some reason she seems to have no concept of the problems she is about to cause, or the ramifications of her actions. You're right, apart from the Sahaed's team, she is unprotected.

"Don't forget that our old friend Colonel Boris Kiev is in Paris. He heads their security, so don't you get too cocky and don't relax too much. That man is a perfectionist and he's as wily as a fox. He's got more notches on his gun than all the Wild West gunfighters put together, and he's still around to tell the tale!" added the MI6 agent, a genuine look of warning on his face.

She made no comment as she carefully, dismantled her weapon, placing it almost lovingly into the velvet grooves of the case. She walked across the small room and began putting the remainder of her belongings into a small shoulder bag.

"Tonight looks like being one of action my British friend; everything is in place, including our backup plan," she said, patting the rifle case as though it were a precious pet.

"I have things to take care of," said the agent as he got up to leave the room. "From what my surveillance boys tell me, there don't seem to be any changes of plan by the couple. I need to get some final details from Duval. I'll be in touch before the day is out."

He walked out of the room closing the door behind him and looked both ways before moving along the corridor. Through the crack of the slightly opened door opposite to the room Steel had just left, the small Arab from Kiev's team watched the British agent turn down the staircase. He closed the door and took a small case from the bed, then removed a pack of plastic explosive along with detonators. Placing them on the table in front of him he began to assemble a small explosive device. The detonator was the electronic version, the type activated by a radio transmitter. He placed the device in a rolled up newspaper, sticking it to the inside of the roll with strong duct tape. Placing the newspaper in a clear plastic bag he put it into a canvass bag along with twenty or so identical packages. He took an automatic silenced handgun, checking the action. He placed it in the canvass bag along with a small transmitter then threw the leather case under the bed, put the strap of the canvass bag over his shoulder and left the room, closing the door quietly behind him.

Walking to the opposite end of the corridor where Steel had just exited, he began to drop a newspaper on the ground at the foot of each closed door. When he reached the door of the Israeli woman he knocked and continued to knock on each door, dropping papers as he made his way towards the staircase.

Esther Ben-Sheed cautiously opened the door of her room at the sound of the knock. She had heard the voice of a man announcing the delivery of newspapers as he walked along the hallway. She looked after the man who continued without looking round.

The *phut phut* of a silenced handgun was the only sound to be heard as the Arab literally stopped dead in his tracks, then fell face down on the carpet, his hand still inside the canvass bag. The Mossad agent crouched, legs apart, both hands on her gun, waiting for any movement. Both shots had entered the man's skull: he was very dead.

She took the bag from his shoulder then dragged the body into her room. Carefully she emptied the contents of the bag onto the table. Placing the gun to one side, she gently picked up the transmitter.

There were no lights flashing, she cautiously took the newspaper from the plastic bag. Looking down the inside of the rolled up paper, she saw the device, at the same time smelled the un-mistakable odour of Semtex.

Placing the firearm and the transmitter into her bag, she put the bomb into the washbasin then threw the bag over her shoulder, picked up the case containing her rifle, stepped over the corpse then quickly left the room.

She noticed the large bloodstain on the hall carpet as she exited by the fire door at the rear of the small hotel and was very soon a couple of miles away. She stopped at a public telephone booth, made a call, then slowly went on her way.

Princess Anna and Raffi were just about to leave the hotel. There was a knock at the door of the princess's suite.

"Come in," shouted Anna. The door opened as Gavin Jones entered the room.

"Are we ready to go Ma'am?" he said to the princess, just as an enorm-ous explosion shook the whole building. Princess Anna automatically fell to the floor. Jones dragged a surprised Raffi to the thick Persian carpeted floor. The force of the explosion had rattled the windows and blown the heavy drapes into the air of the open balcony doors as though a gale had blown through the room.

After a few seconds Gavin Jones crawled towards the balcony and cautiously began to raise his head to look over the ornate balustrade. As he did so he saw a large pall of smoke rising into the air some three or four blocks away, no more than five or six hundred yards off. His radio crackled.

"Is everyone alright up there?" Boris Kiev asked.

"Yes sir, as far as I can make out it was an explosion a few blocks to the east of the hotel. No damage here."

By now the princess had joined the bodyguard on the balcony.

"Excuse me Ma'am, please go inside," he said to the princess leading her by the arm. At the same time he closed the doors and drew the drapes closed. "I must ask you to cancel your trip out for the time being, and please stay in the room. I will be back as soon as I can, Ma'am". He left the room. "Go inside and don't let either of them out of the room until you hear from me and keep them away from the window!" Jones shouted at one of the bodyguards, as he rushed towards the elevator.

Michael and Hank were just about to enter the hotel when the explosion went off. It blew Michael against the front of the building; cars screeched to a halt at the shock, a woman screamed as pieces of debris fell to the street.

"What the hell was that, Hank?"

"It was a bloody enormous explosion!" Hank replied.

"Jesus, look at the windows in the building opposite, they're all cracked up," said Michael as people began to pour out of the Majestic Palace Hotel, as though a bomb had actually gone off in there. Hank spotted Gavin Jones who stood in the middle of the sidewalk, looking from left to right.

"Hey Gavin, what the hell's going on here?" said Hank to a surprised bodyguard who came running across towards them.

"Hello inspector, hello Michael. I might ask you what the hell you're doing here," he said with a grin.

"Looks like some lunatic let a bomb off. Quite a big one judging by the sound of things."

"I've got a bit of a panic on at the moment, why don't you come inside?" He led the way through the revolving doors into the foyer.

"Go and get yourselves something in the coffee shop there, and I'll be back down in a minute or two," he said as he strode off.

"Gavin!" Hank called after the bodyguard, who turned and came back to them. "I would rather that you didn't say a word to anyone, about our presence here until we've had a chat, I mean anyone."

"OK, got the message," said Jones as he rushed off talking into his radio as he went away. As the two sat in the coffee bar enjoying a strong coffee, a television newscaster was reporting on the explosion. Michael, who spoke excellent French, said that an Arab terrorist organisation had phoned a ten-minute warning of the bomb going off. The building was totally destroyed with no report of fatalities. A shot from the camera showed the building was reduced to a pile of rubble.

The hotel's proprietor said that to the best of his knowledge, all of the residents had evacuated the building. He said there were no answers to any of the room telephones. The fire alarms had been set off, as a further warning to evacuate.

"Excuse me Monsieur," a waiter spoke to Hank, "Is your name Marlin?"

"Yes," replied Hank.

"There is a message from Monsieur Jones, will you follow me please?" The two of them walked after the man who led them to the bank of elevators.

"Please go to the tenth floor. Monsieur Jones is waiting for you there." He bowed and walked away.

David Steel, like most other residents within three miles of the explosion had felt the shock. He sat looking at the television news.

In another area of the city Kevin Reilly watched his TV set.

At the security office of The Majestic Palace Hotel, Boris Kiev watched the same program.

In the privacy of his suite, Anwar Sahaed was also glued to the screen. Esther Ben-Sheed sat in her new hotel room, listening to the announcer.

Following the television coverage on the bombing, the announcer reported that the body of a man wearing the uniform of a Paris hotel bellhop had been found in mysterious circumstances in another area of the city. The body had been discovered lying in a side street. Foul play was suspected and the police were carrying out a full-scale enquiry.

Princess Anna looked up from the television screen.

"There will be something else soon, you'll see. Bad things always seem to happen in threes," she said to Raffi who, against the instructions of Gavin Jones, were peeping through a gap in the window drapes. The phone rang, and was answered by the security man.

"Yes sir. Excuse me Mr Raffi, it's your father, and he wishes to speak to you." The bodyguard passed him the phone. Princess Anna continued to watch the scene of the bombing on TV as Raffi transferred the call to the bedroom.

Steel switched off his TV set, picked up his jacket left his room a worried man. Had the Mossad agent been killed in the blast, and whose was the body of the hotel employee? He had the distinct feeling of a change of role, from the hunter to the hunted. *Another thirty minutes in that hotel and I would now be a statistic*, he thought to himself as his mind worked overtime.

He had a left the building by the rear exit, and now stood in a doorway opposite, looking across at his parked rental car. The cell phone in his pocket began to vibrate he pressed the send button.

"Yes," he said curtly."

"Meet me as usual in ten minutes."

An open look of relief crossed the usually impassive face of the MI6 agent, as he heard the voice of Esther Ben-Sheed.

He decided to leave the car where it was parked. In fact, as far as he was concerned it would stay there forever. He would also move to another safe house.

He walked a few blocks, crossing the street a number of times, checking reflections in shop windows and doubling back on himself until he was certain that he was not being followed. Pausing in the doorway of a derelict cafe he took off his jacket, turned it inside out, the reversible side being a Scottish plaid. He pulling on a beret and sauntered across the street, mingling with the busy pedestrian traffic.

He took out the cell phone, dialling the Majestic Palace Hotel. His face puckered into a scowl as he was told that Monsieur Duval had not reported for work. He walked on towards the centre of the city.

Michael and Hank stood in the elevator as the attendant announced their arrival at the tenth floor. Gavin was waiting as the doors slid silently open.

"I'm sorry about the delay, come this way," he said as he moved across the thick lush carpet. The two men followed him into an area of offices where the open part in the centre had a number of desks. Three or four obvious bodyguard types sat there: thick necks, massive forearms, short hair with modified facial features, pens dwarfed by hands the size of shovels. They passed an open door where a complete wall of television monitors flickered. A woman sat at a radio control centre relaying messages in verbal shorthand, amidst crackle and squelch.

They followed Gavin Jones into a small office with a desk, computer monitor and two guest chairs. He gestured for them to sit down.

"So what brings you two to gay Paris, if you'll pardon the colloquialism," he said with a smile. "Like some coffee?"

"Not for us, thanks," said Hank.

"If we have one more cup, the stuff will be coming out of our ears," added Michael.

"So what's going on?" Jones asked again.

"Frankly Gavin, we're worried about Princess Anna," said Michael.

"Hank's been hearing stuff that leads us both to believe that Anna's life could be in danger."

"Things like what?" asked the bodyguard.

"I'm afraid I can't go into detail," said Hank

"Then how can I help?" asked Jones, a genuine look of confusion on his face.

"You can begin by telling me what level of security is being given to the princess," said Hank.

"I have to be careful exactly what I discuss. Whatever you may think, security is tight here. My boss will have my guts for garters if I discuss anything to do with the couple. It may not have escaped your notice that we are in France, which doesn't come under your jurisdiction," said the bodyguard to the inspector.

"I am asking you as a friend, but let me remind you that things have changed immensely in the last couple of years. We are now all part of the European Union. I could pick up the phone right now and have you transported to the local nick for questioning," said Hank with a sincere and threatening look on his face, "So don't even think that you won't answer my questions, and don't forget that you will be back in England next week, or next month. If I so desired I could lock you up and throw away the key. There are at least three question marks on your file to my knowledge, for using undue force in executing your duties as a minder; I believe one using a ping ball hammer was suggested at the time, but all verging on grievous or actual bodily harm. Do you want me to continue?" asked Hank.

"Hold on a minute, Hank," said Jones, his big hands spread in a gesture of hurt.

"No, you hold on, and it's inspector to non-friends. I'm concerned about the life of a British princess, not some two-penny halfpenny bouncer." Hank shouted, banging his fist down on the desk. As Hank spoke, the door to the office opened. Michael and Hank turned to see the frame of a large man enter the room.

"What's all the shouting about in here?" the big man asked. Jones got up from his chair quickly.

"These are friends of mine: Michael Meadows and Hank Marlin," he said to the big man. "Gentlemen, this is my boss, Colonel Boris Kiev." They both got up from their chairs and shook hands with the big Russian.

"A strange way for friends to talk to each other. Mind you, some English habits seem very strange to we Russians, wouldn't you say, inspector?" He had emphasised the word inspector as he walked out of the small office. He stopped and spun on his feet.

"Don't come in here with empty threats, inspector. You're not going to be arresting anyone; you're out of your jurisdiction and you don't work for the princess anymore. Here's a word of advice for you. Keep your nose out of this business and go home, or the next time we meet it may be under less pleasant circumstances. You're not wanted here. My office, when you're free, Jones." he said in an authoritative and somewhat threatening tone. He slammed the door as he left.

After their meeting, where Gavin had been as helpful as he could be, Hank left Michael sitting in the hotel foyer and went around the interior of the hotel. He was gone for a full hour, after which he went outside and spent a further half hour looking around. His trained eyes didn't miss the television van parked across the street. He took care not to offer a full-face view of himself in its direction.

When he returned Michael was nowhere to be seen, so he took a seat and waited. Within twenty minutes Michael returned, holding an armful of newspapers, both French and English.

"Been waiting long?" he asked Hank.

"No, not too long," replied the inspector.

They decided to go and get some lunch. Michael said that he knew of a place on the river. Outside the hotel they hailed a cab then went off heading for the banks of the Seine.

Colonel Kiev watched them depart the hotel then picked up the phone.

"Gavin, get in here when you have a minute will you," he growled. Gavin knew that meant right now. He knocked on the door of Kiev's office. Receiving no reply, he walked in. Kiev was on the phone. He held his finger to his lips as Gavin entered and indicated for him to take a seat.

"Yes sir, I agree. I have tightened up in every area. Yes, I will. Yes, I do understand what the consequences would be, Mr Sahaed. Please try to remember that I am a professional. Hello, hello?"

Kiev threw the receiver into its cradle. He glared at the Welshman with such ferocity he looked as though he had murder in his eyes. The bodyguard had never seen him like this before.

"Mr Sahaed wants the answers to some questions and also assurances that it is impossible for either of the couple to come to any harm. His secretary saw your friend Inspector Marlin in the hotel foyer. Gavin, I want to know exactly why the inspector is here, and also what is Princess Anna's secretary doing here? To the best of my knowledge Princess Anna has never mentioned that Meadows would be in Paris."

For a moment Gavin seemed lost for words. He stood up and walked across to the window. He turned, looking the Russian directly in the eyes.

"They are both extremely concerned for the safety of the princess, sir. They believe that her life is in great danger; that there could be an attempt to kill her. Their interests are the same as ours sir," he added, as he sat down with a sigh. "I don't think that the inspector intends to leave in a hurry either. It can't hurt our cause to cooperate with him."

"I don't agree," said the Russian. "Too many cooks spoil the broth, isn't that one of your British sayings?" he asked with a smirk. "Besides, Mr Sahaed views them as a danger, and for that matter, so do I. If they do not return to England, and they continue to interfere, they are to be taken care of. You'd better be very sure which side you're on Mr Jones." He banged the palm of his hand on the desk, as he stood, indicating that the meeting was over.

Jones left his boss's office equally concerned about Kiev's open threat to Hank and Michael as he was about Hank Marlin's fears for Princess Anna's safety. He had a great respect for the Inspector, and knew that if he was concerned, then there was good reason for him, too, to worry. He intended to meet with Hank and cooperate with him fully, despite the words of Colonel Boris Kiev, and, yes he did know which side he was on!

Charles De-Gaulle Airport, Paris

The British Airways Jet taxied towards the main airport building as the driving rain bounced off its fuselage. The waiting ground staff sheltered under the building as the screaming engines blew water in every direction. The plane had left Cairo earlier en-route for London's Heathrow airport, but with a scheduled stop in Paris first. The unexpected rainstorm had slowed everything in the busy airport to half speed.

As those passengers for Paris began to leave the aircraft, the baggage handlers below removed their belongings from the belly of the plane.

In the customs and immigration hall, an Arabic couple dressed in European garb had collected their baggage. They were pushing a trolley through the green area for those with nothing to declare.

"Excuse me Monsieur, Madame," a customs official said beckoning the couple towards his station. After he had thoroughly gone through their cases, finding nothing of concern, the couple went out into the main concourse. They left the building and went across to the taxi rank, joining the long line, and then eventually heading towards downtown Paris.

At the same time, David Steel, having met with his Israeli counterpart earlier, was in another apartment preparing to get a report off to MI6 headquarters.

Meanwhile, inside the surveillance vehicle with the television station insignia, its occupants watched a taxi pull up to the hotel. A porter carried the baggage of a young Arabic couple. The Arabic man paid the taxi driver, and then followed his partner into the hotel foyer. Inside he filled out the registration form, and then he and his attractive partner followed the porter towards the bank of elevators.

Boris Kiev, who had watched from the balcony above, went back to the security offices. He was concerned, as he had not heard from his Arab agent who he had sent to eliminate the Israeli woman earlier. Kiev knew she was good. *Maybe I should have gone myself,* he thought. He knew deep down that the man had died in the bomb blast earlier. *Such is life,* he smirked as the thought crossed his mind.

Inside the van, cameras had clicked and timed reports had been made.

David Steel had watched the police activity in the alley behind Duval's apartment, his worst fears confirmed. *This had to be the work of the Russian,* he thought. *This man Sahaed really plays for keeps.* He lit a cigarette and walked away from the crowd that had gathered, his mind working overtime on the coming events of the evening, and more heavily on the most recent happenings. Duval had been assassinated, and a serious attempt had been made to kill the Israeli woman. He slid into a doorway checking behind him. One mistake could prove fatal. He moved quickly heading towards his rendezvous and final meeting with the Mossad agent. At the same moment, Gavin Jones was checking that the arrangements were still in place for vehicles, bodyguards and drivers to cover the coming evening. He was in the middle of a phone call to the transport department when the door swung open and Mr Sahaed himself walked through the door. Gavin jumped up with a start.

"Sit down Jones," snapped the Arab.

"I just want to be absolutely sure that everything has been done to protect the couple. After that bomb blast today, I am seriously considering getting them out of this city right away." He leaned across the desk looking as though inspecting every particle of Gavin's face.

"I don't think that will be necessary sir," he replied. "We have doubled up on our security; I have gone over the plans a dozen times. Apart from a commando attack by the SAS we have it all secure, I think that you can rest assured, sir." The bodyguard sat down relieved as his boss walked towards the door of the office, he opened the door, and then swung around quickly.

"I asked the colonel what the British police inspector was doing here, which is certainly no coincidence and neither is the arrival of Princess Anna's private secretary," he said with a sickly smirk on his face.

"The only interest that either of them has is the safety of the princess," replied Jones to the unasked question.

"The Inspector is on leave, and of course Michael Meadows is still Princess Anna's private secretary, though admittedly the princess doesn't know that either of them are here. I suspect they'll make contact with her soon."

"There are many forces working against the relationship between the couple, now that the friendship seems to be getting stronger. We can't be too careful. Remember the inspector is not just a British policeman; he is a part of the royal protection group. I want them both out of here, and I don't much care how it's done." He turned to walk through the open door, then again spun quickly on his heels and came back towards Gavin Jones, his arms spread, both palms of his hands flat on the surface of the desk, his face inches from Jones' face. He squinted, looking deep into the other man's eyes as though looking directly into his soul.

"If one hair of their heads is damaged there is no place that you can hide from me, do I make myself clear?" said the Arab in a harsh whisper, still locked in a stare as he spoke.

"Yes sir, very clear sir," he replied, standing as he answered.

Sahaed walked away, nearing the door, his back still towards the bodyguard, he spoke again.

"Don't forget what I said. Remember my words." Without turning around he walked out of the room, leaving the door wide open.

Jones shuddered as he sat down looking at the open door. *Shit, that was no idle threat, that man was not joking*, he thought to himself. As he looked down he noticed for the first time in many a year, that his hands were shaking slightly. He stared down at the desk blotter, deep in thought and did not notice Boris Kiev enter the room.

"A penny for your thoughts, as you Brits say." Jones jumped up with a start.

"Hey, take it easy man, what's got you so nervous?" asked the colonel.

"Can I talk to you for a minute?" said Jones.

"Sure what's bugging you?" asked Kiev as he pulled a chair up to the desk.

Before the Welshman could begin, the phone on his desk rang. He picked up the handset and listened in silence.

"I'll be right down Michael; I'll see you in reception." He replaced the receiver, and then looked across at the Russian.

"That was Meadows. He has spoken with the princess who told him to have me take him and the inspector to the princess's suite. Now what?"

"You can delay for a while, but if that's an instruction from the princess, you'll have to comply," said the colonel. "Now what did you want to talk to me about?"

"Oh it's not important, it will keep," said Jones as he got up to leave the office.

As the Welshman left the room, Kiev picked up the phone and hit three keys.

"Yes, Kiev here, do you have the information I asked for on the Arab couple in room 854?" He waited in silence for several seconds.

"Good! Photographs were taken by the reception cameras I assume, fine. I want those pictures faxed immediately to the usual number. Do it now," he barked throwing the handset into its cradle, and striding out of the office.

Gavin Jones walked across the vast reception area towards the two waiting men, smiling as he approached.

"Come on then, let's get you up there," he said and beckoned them to follow.

The CIA agent, Kevin Reilly, saw them from his seat at the cocktail bar, his head, to all intents and purposes, buried in a newspaper. He finished his drink, left a generous tip, folded the paper and left the hotel by the rear exit. He walked along the street a couple of blocks, checked behind him and went into a bar. He ordered a beer and strolled over to a kiosk table in the far corner. Already sitting in the dimmed space was the MI6 agent.

"You look a tad harassed," he said to the Englishman.

"Yes, you could say life has been a little hectic during the last few hours," replied Steel.

"I take it that the body in the alley is one of yours?' said Reilly, a look of concern on his face. "What about the bomb?"

"That was a close shave," said David Steel.

"Very close! How did you get on at the hotel?"

"You were right, the security guy Jones took two people up in the elevator just a few minutes ago. I recognised one as the princess's secretary, the other I didn't know." Steel showed Reilly a picture of Hank Marlin.

"Yep, that's the secretary. Who's this other guy then?"

"A British police inspector." replied David Steel.

"God damn it! This situation gets more complex by the minute," said Kevin Reilly.

"Who are the Arabic couple you were interested in?" asked the American agent.

"Don't know yet, central records are checking out their mug shots right now."

"Do you want me to do a double check at our end?" asked the CIA man.

"It can't do any harm," Steel replied reaching into his inside pocket, passing an envelope containing the Arab's picture to the American.

"Also, as you requested, I went to Paul Gastard's daughter's engagement party. Here is the film you wanted. I should think he'll be well inebriated by now. He seems to like his drop of Pernod; quite a drinker for a chauffeur," said Reilly, smiling as Steel picked up the small yellow film container.

Back in the Hotel

In room 854 the woman lay on top of the bed watching the television, which played at almost full volume. The young man opened a sealed box that had been left in the closet under some extra pillows and blankets. He placed a black leather jacket, matching pants and a pair of black boots on the bed. He passed an ominous-looking case to his partner. She threw her legs to the ground and opened the case, then started to assemble the marksman's rifle silently and expertly. Neither spoke one word as they carried out their chores. The woman examined every piece of ammunition then equally quickly and silently dissembled the firearm. She took one of the two automatic handguns that her partner had put there, smiled, and then walked across the room.

She put on a figure-hugging black leather suit and calf high boots. Taking two Samsonite cases, each bearing a BMW insignia on the side, she began to pack the firearms and other items. The man put on the pants and leather jacket. She left the room empty handed, walked toward the elevators, a leather purse swinging heavily from her shoulder. Reaching the foyer she made her way across to the cocktail lounge. Taking a seat at the bar opposite the entrance, she sat there sipping a cocktail.

Ten minutes later her partner left the room carrying the two lightweight cases. He turned in the opposite direction, and left by the fire exit stairs.

In the underground parking lot he walked across to a gleaming black BMW bike. He clipped the cases to the sides, then took one of the two helmets hanging from the rear, pulled it over his head, flipped up the tinted visor, took the ignition key from his pocket and rode out into the early evening traffic.

The telephone rang in the sitting room of Princess Anna's suite.

"Yes, hold the line please," said the security man.

"It's a Michael Meadows for you Ma'am," he said, as Anna put down the newspaper. "Do you wish to speak to him Ma'am?"

"Good God man, of course I want to speak to him," she said as she walked across the room.

"The princess will be right with you sir, hang on a sec," the man said as he handed the phone to Anna.

"Michael, what a pleasant surprise. To what do I owe this unexpected pleasure?" asked Anna. "You're where? Here in Paris, why? What's wrong Michael? You have Hank with you too! Is there some kind of a problem? You're down stairs in the hotel? You'd better come up here right away. You'll need to go to security first, ask for Gavin Jones. He'll bring you up here, I'll see you then," said Anna as she replaced the receiver. *What the hell's that all about? Michael's here and with Inspector Marlin and can't talk on the phone. What now?* she thought to herself as she pulled out her silver pillbox.

Anna went across to the bar, poured a soda and swallowed a cocktail of pills then walked across to the window and looked out as the early evening sky began to lose its brightness. She leaned forward to open the French windows.

"Excuse me ma'am, I'm instructed to ask you not to open the windows," said a concerned security man, walking across the large room as he spoke

"Damn it, one begins to feel like some sort of a prisoner. You should have me locked in the Tower of London. I'm expecting two visitors, so perhaps you'd like to contact your man Jones and see where they are. Give him a call now; there's a good man."

Just then there was a knock at the door. Gavin Jones entered the room.

"I have your visitors here Princess Anna: Michael Meadows and Inspector Marlin."

"Show them in Jones, please," said the princess.

"Hank, it's so nice to see you. What a pleasant surprise. I was just thinking about you recently. You must be clairvoyant." She then turned to her secretary. "Michael, you too! Is there some kind of problem? Why the deputation?"

"Well Ma'am, there are a couple of things we would like to discuss, er... particularly in private," he said looking round at Jones and the other security man.

"Would you mind," said the princess, turning to the Welshman.

"Well Ma'am, I am under strict instructions not..." The princess cut across his conversation abruptly.

"Damn it man, get out of the room! Don't argue, and take this oaf with you!" the princess shouted

"Yes Ma'am," replied Jones, jumping to attention, and then leaving the room, closely followed by his colleague.

When the room was clear, Hank walked over to the window. At the same time he put his forefinger to his lips, indicating silence to the others." What a fantastic view of the city from here," he said as he wrote on a sheet of hotel notepaper. He passed the note to the princess which read. *Don't discuss anything of importance. Talk small talk. Is there somewhere that we cannot be heard? Answer by note.*

"So what's happening back home, Michael." said the princess as she began to scribble on the notepad.

"Nothing in particular ma'am. Hank here had some leave he had to take. As you were away, I thought that I would take a few days off and join him," said Michael Meadows.

"Sounds like a splendid idea to me, take all the time you want, as long as it's not more than two or three days," said Anna smiling, as she continued to write. She passed the note to Hank then the three walked across to the bedroom.

"There are some papers that I would like you to take with you on the Bosnia visit, Michael. Come through here, and I'll give them to you now." The princess winked as she beckoned them into the bedroom, closing the door behind them. Once inside the room, the princess continued: "There are no sound detectors in here Hank."

"If it's alright with you I'll just make sure ma'am," Hank replied. He swept the room carefully with a small electronic device, finally checking the telephone instrument. He pronounced the room clean. The three sat down and talked, the princess listened intently to what Hank had to say, after which he asked a number of questions. It was agreed that on her return to London, the princess would select and employ some full time protection, under the expert guidance of Hank and would employ such protection 24 hours a day. Whilst here in Paris, she would not expose herself unduly to danger, apart from this evening's trip out, already planned, and would head back to London tomorrow and begin the security programme.

"Well that's fine, Ma'am," said Hank.

"I must say that I feel much happier."

"Me too," said Michael Meadows.

"One more thing, Ma'am," said Hank. "I'd like to see the arrangements for this evening. Try and get Jones, or even the Russian colonel, to take me through their security plans. We'll tag along whether they like it or not, and please Ma'am, try to remember some of the points we just covered. Keep your eyes peeled for the unusual." Hank opened the door into the sitting room. As they walked through Colonel Kiev walked into the room from the hallway.

"Ah gentlemen, I am just checking that everything is in order for this evening's outing."

"I can't think of anything untoward colonel," said the princess. Then the door to the suite swung open as Raffi Sahaed entered.

"Excuse me, colonel," he said as he brushed passed the Russian.

"Raffi, my dear, I would like you to meet two very dear friends of mine: Inspector Hank Marlin and Michael Meadows." Raffi shook hands with Hank.

"It's my pleasure. We met once before at the Savoy Hotel," said Raffi, as he shook hands with Michael Meadows.

"That's right sir, and it's still my pleasure to meet you again," he said smiling.

"Colonel, Inspector Marlin here is expressing concern for my personal safety, which he successfully took care of for a long time. I would like you to go over your plans for this evening with the inspector."

"I will have to get clearance from Mr Sahaed before I can do such a thing Ma'am," replied Kiev.

"I will accept nothing less colonel, so please go and make the arrangements now."

"Come this way, gentlemen," said Kiev to Hank and Michael, as he led the way out of the suite.

"If I don't see you before, I'll look forward to seeing you in London next week inspector." said Anna with a great big smile, as she followed them to the door.

Number 10 Downing Street, London

Tony Blain sat at the desk in his study at Number 10. He had gone through a tiring day in the House. Prime Minister's Question Time always presented him with a challenge. He loved the theatrics involved and the banter kept him on his toes as the adrenaline flowed when he had to answer questions, sometimes off the cuff. This was far more reward-ing, challenging, and scintillating than his earlier chosen career as a barrister. This was not just question time in the House, to him it was national television performance time, or indeed international, and he was a natural born performer. Today some of the questions could not be answered with his usual panache and flippancy; particularly those refer-ring to the princess and her relationship with the Arab man, Raffi Sahaed.

He looked down at both issues of the London evening newspapers on his desk. **'Princess Anna and Raffi in Paris'** was the headline in one, whilst the other read: **'The Princess of Peace Flies on a Different Mission'**. It showed an earlier picture of the princess climbing aboard the Sahaed yacht. *What is this woman playing at?* the **PM** thought to himself as he read the body of the articles.

The phone rang; it was the Home Secretary commenting about the same articles and informing the PM that the French and German newspaper issues were worse and a lot more suggestive. The Spanish and Italian papers had also headlined the couple.

"Princess Anna must be the most popular woman in the world today," Tony Blain said aloud, replacing the receiver. His irritation was apparent, as he scowled down at the newsprint. His thoughts went back to a recent meeting with the head of MI6. He remembered the innuendo and the veiled comments made. Blain could also see the ramifications of such a relationship, were it to become permanent. He thought of the Arab father of the man in the limelight, and knew that sooner or later he would try to collect the fruits of his recent investments made in the political arena. How he wished that the princess would stop this frivolity and tire of this particular relationship, as she had done so on many other occasions.

The door to his study opened and in walked his wife, Cheryl, carrying two glasses of gin and tonic. She put one glass on his desk, and held the other in the air.

"Cheers, Prime Minister," she said with a smile. "They tell me you were great at question time today." She walked across and turned on the television set.

"There's a hell of a lot going on in Paris tonight. Princess Anna is staying at the Majestic. That new boyfriend of hers is there too. Look at the crowds of reporters!" she said, pointing to the TV set. "Anna must get fed up with all those people chasing her everywhere; she must really tire of it all. Do you think this relationship will last?" she asked.

"I bloody-well hope not," said the PM. He walked across and turned the set off, swallowing the gin and tonic in one swig.

"That's one thing I don't need, and have no control over whatsoever," he said as he walked out of the room, leaving his wife sitting there.

"Pardon me for speaking Mr. Prime Minster," she said to nobody in particular. "What's bugging you?"

The Majestic Palace Hotel, Paris

After his reluctant meeting with Hank Marlin and Michael Meadows, Colonel Boris Kiev looked out of the window and down onto the forecourt of the hotel. He wondered why the crowds were increasing. *Where the hell do these parasitical reporters get their information from?* During the last twenty-four hours there had hardly been a sign of even one reporter, *now those irritating bastards are everywhere*, he thought.

The phone on his desk rang.

"Everything's in place sir, all the drivers and bodyguards are here. As arranged, I will go in the car with the couple and handle them personally; the Bentley will be the decoy. By the way, there's bloody hundreds of those damn paparazzi outside, they seem to come out of the woodwork like sodding termites," said Jones. "Will you come downstairs, sir? I think there are one or two other members of the press in the bars and restaurant. The couple are scheduled to come down for dinner shortly. I think they'll find privacy a little difficult; their presence here is all over the TV and the international newspapers. Just our bloody luck, on the last evening," said the Welshman sounding very irritated.

"Just try and relax and I'll be right down. Where are you now?" Kiev replaced the receiver and pulled out a Glock, checked the magazine and the action then returned the handgun to the rear of his waist belt under his jacket.

Anna and Raffi were in her suite at the hotel. She sat on the couch sipping a fruit punch; he stood over near the window. He had just asked the security man to leave the room.

"There's something I want to say to you, my darling," he said, walking across the room. As he crossed he took a small leather box from his jacket pocket. Sitting by her side he took hold of her hand, placing the box in her hand. "I'd like you to have this, my dear." She opened the box. There sitting on the velvet lining was the most gorgeous diamond solitaire ring.

Anna looked into his eyes.

"I haven't been this happy for such a long time," she sighed.

"I think that soon we should consider a more permanent relationship," he said with a slight wobble in his voice.

"Are you proposing to me?" asked the princess.

"Yes, I suppose I am," replied Raffi.

"There's a lot to consider before such a big step. We have to be absolutely sure that it's the right thing to do, my love," she said squeezing Raffi's hand.

"Let's get our other plans into action first. But I would love to marry you." They kissed and held each other for minutes.

"Let's go downstairs and celebrate. I'm dying to get out of these rooms. This will be our secret until we have worked out the details," she said to him, steering him towards the door, her arm around his shoulder.

A Small Bar in the Suburbs of Paris

The engagement party was in full swing. Paul Gastard, one of the Majestic Palace Hotel chauffeurs looked down at his watch. It was 4:00pm. Across the smoky room people were dancing and singing and his wife, for once, was laughing as she danced with the owner of the bar. His daughter danced cheek to cheek with her fiancé. He looked on with pride and happiness, emptying his glass. A hand slapped him on the back.

"Come on buddy, have another one," said the voice of an obvious American tourist. "It's not every day that your daughter gets betrothed."

The flash temporarily blinded Gastard as the American took pictures with the camera hanging from around his neck. The bartender passed him another Pernod; he took a swig then went into the men's washroom.

Looking at his reflection in the mirror of the dimly lit room, he flicked his thinning hair with his fingers, straightened the knot in his tie, then fluted the handkerchief in his top pocket and felt the slight stubble on his chin. As he did so, he staggered backwards slightly. *Whoops, you're drunk captain; drunk on duty,* he thought to himself.

Paul Gastard was a retired French Air Force fighter pilot. He would never have flown a plane after a drink; he would never have been allowed to, though he had drunk much more on other occasions and still driven his car. He considered himself a good drinker; he'd really taken it easy tonight. *Let's see, how many did I have anyway, one, two, three...*he began to count to himself just as the door to the men's room opened.

"Hey Paul, great party, she's a lovely girl, that daughter of yours," said the man, slapping Paul on the back. "You should be proud," he added, banging the toilet door behind him.

Paul went back into the crowded bar, took one more look at the happy scene then left quickly by the rear door. To try and say that he was leaving would have taken too long; he was late already. The cool evening air hit him with a jolt. As he inhaled deeply, his head began to spin slightly. He got into his Citroen and opened all the windows in an attempt to clear his head. His vision seemed fine. *A couple of black coffees and I'll be fine,* he thought as he drove off towards the Majestic Palace Hotel.

A car behind hooted and flashed its headlamps. Paul looked down at the unlit dashboard and quickly turned on the cars lights, waving his hand in thanks.

Back at the Hotel

Hank sat back in his seat as Boris Kiev concluded his run down on the security plan for the evening.

"I can't see any obvious glitches in the plan," said Hank. "The only unknown element is the usual one, the human element: either error, bad judgment or a surprise from an outside force. But, something just doesn't feel right, and it all seems so unnecessary. It would be much easier to cancel the whole thing. After all it's not an event of national importance, is it?"

The colonel shrugged his shoulders.

"I'm doing as I'm told. It's just another job to me. But you're right, by the look of the crowds there will be a lot of people trying to get in on the act, I suspect." Kiev walked across looking out of the window as he spoke. The VHF radio on the desk crackled into life.

"One, come in Control."

The Russian picked up the handset.

"Go ahead one."

"I have subjects in the restaurant. There are people approaching from all angles, not just press, but members of the public and other diners, offering best wishes and asking for autographs. I need permission to leave the restaurant, and return upstairs over."

"Yes, take the couple back to their suites. Attention all stations. Apart from door surveillance, all other stations to the restaurant. Keep your eyes peeled for any unusual movements. Report now," said Kiev

"Two moving now, sir."

"Three moving."

"Four in place."

"Five in position, sir."

"One, moving subjects now sir, out."

"I have to leave now inspector, if you'll excuse me," said Kiev as he strode out of the room. Hank and Michael followed the Russian through the offices and out onto the balcony. They saw the scene, as Jones led the princess and Raffi through the foyer towards the elevators. They were completely surrounded by people, a camera flashed and an angry guard snatched it.

Kiev and his staff quickly dispersed the scene. Those that were diners returned to their tables, the press was ejected from the hotel by both front and rear doors, the hotel returned to its usual calm and quiet efficiency.

Meanwhile the princess and Raffi, more determined than ever to have a night of enjoyment, ordered the restaurant to serve the full meal in their suite. Jones had stationed a guard on the door and was on his way down in the elevator. He met with Kiev in the main foyer.

"That was a pain in the backside, sir," said Jones. As he spoke, Hank Marlin joined them.

"Maybe that was a blessing in disguise," he said to the two men.

"Perhaps they'll just stay in and give you all a quiet night."

"No such luck, inspector, they seem more determined than ever to have a night on the town," Boris Kiev said.

"Are all the transport arrangements still in place, Gavin?" he asked.

"I'm just on my way to the car pool now, sir," answered Jones.
As they spoke, the Arab woman in the leather suit walked past. The aroma of expensive perfume wafted in their direction.

"Cor, I'd sooner be guarding that body tonight," said Gavin as the woman went through the exit to the car parking lot. He followed the leather-clad apparition.

"If you'll excuse me, gentlemen," said Kiev with a nod of his head.

"I must get on." He too went in the direction of the underground car park.

"Let's go and have ourselves a quick drink," said Michael to Hank.

"Better still, let's go and have a couple of slow ones," said Hank with a smile. They went off towards the cocktail bar.

In the corner of the stillroom, off the Majestic's main kitchens, Paul Gastard stood drinking his third cup of black coffee. He went across to a water fountain and poured a large glass of cold water, knowing that the hangover feelings that generally followed excess drinking was the result of dehydration, rather forgetting that Pernod, along with it's Greek and Italian counterparts, is a drink that gets re-livened when water is added to the contents of the stomach. He swallowed the water, looked at his watch and then made his way around the rear corridors heading towards the car pool, at the other side of the underground car park.

Gavin Jones watched the fluid movement of the woman in the skin tight leather suit, as he followed her across the dimly lit indoor car park. He admired the sway of her tight buttocks, the purse swinging from her shoulder tapping her rump as she glided across the concrete floor. *I'd like to be that purse,* Gavin thought, as he watched her turn the corner. *Ah well, they can't lock you up for thinking boyo. Best get to work.* He sighed and walked towards the iron gates of the car pool. Around the corner the woman walked up to the little white Fiat car, she stooped to put the key into the lock.

"Excuse me, Miss," said a voice from behind. Her hand went instantly for the purse. It was pulled away, and the butt of a pistol was slammed hard into her kidneys. "Not so fast, my dear, I have a few questions for you." Boris Kiev pushed the woman unceremoniously against the Fiat, kicking her legs into an undignified widespread position. He grabbed her purse and stepped back pulling an automatic handgun from the purse.

"Well, look at this little beauty — not exactly the sort of thing a lady would carry," he said with a grin. He did not need to frisk the woman for further firearms, as her clothing seemed incapable of hiding anything."

"You'd better come along with me," said the Russian.

"Stand up slowly, and walk backwards towards my voice," he instructed.

As she obeyed his instruction, a voice echoed across the parking area,

"Is everything alright there colonel?"

In the split second that Kiev was distracted by Gavin's interruption, the woman spun round, following the sound of his voice, as instructed, delivering an accurate blow to his throat. Kiev fell to the ground. She leapt into the Fiat, with tyres screaming as the vehicle shot out of its parking space, narrowly missing Jones as he dived for cover between rows of parked cars.

"You alright, sir?" he asked, as his boss got to his knees pulling himself up by the door handle of a parked car.

"I was fine until you stuck your stupid Welsh nose in." replied Kiev in a rather husky voice, rubbing his throat.

"What was that all about?" asked the Welshman.

"That was the attractive ass you were admiring a short while ago. She is the trained partner of a very highly skilled and equally highly paid international hit man. If I'm right someone's paid a high price to get that pair into town. Let's hope they're on vacation and we're not their targets. He doesn't miss too often. Thanks to you, we have little or no chance of nailing that desirable ass, before she nails somebody else's; maybe even yours, eh?" Kiev continued to massage the side of his neck. Here, take this," he said kicking the woman's firearm across the concrete floor.

"Well, don't stand there looking stupid, we have work to do. Come on, move it!" shouted the Russian.

Paul Gastard walked through the open gates into the car pool. The Black Bentley Turbo came towards him.

"Hey Paul, I see they got you out tonight. I thought today was the big party!" said the driver as the Bentley pulled up beside him.

"They were a bit shorthanded, so they called me in," he replied. "As far as I know the party's still going. I could really do without being here tonight."

"All I'm doing is decoy out front tonight," said the other man. "They should have put you on that and let me drive the couple. It's a bit late to change now, I suppose," he said as he pulled away in the car.

Gavin was waiting for Paul as he walked up.

"You're cutting it a bit fine aren't you? Come on let's get this Merc out there," he said climbing into the passenger seat. Gastard climbed in and drove the car around back.

Meanwhile upstairs, the couple had finished dinner, having eaten in Anna's suite. The bodyguard knocked first then opened the door to the suite.

"We're ready when you are, Ma'am," he called through the opening.

The couple emerged. She wore a headscarf and tinted glasses, and he wore an American baseball cap and wrap-around sunshades with his collar up around his face.

All went according to plan. The Black Mercedes 500 stood in the shadows at the rear of the hotel, awaiting its celebrity passengers. It was parked in the shadows; its lights extinguished.

At the front of the hotel the black Bentley Turbo stood gleaming in the bright lights. The car was almost totally surrounded by members of the unpopular tabloid press, hoards of vulture-like photographers, haggling, arguing and fighting for position: the paparazzi were here in force.

A chauffeur sat in front with an expressionless look on his face, knowing full well that these parasites were about to be disappointed. They continued to shout and argue amongst themselves, pushing and jockeying for position like a bunch of seagulls after one piece of bread. They almost totally engulfed the decoy car.

A couple came out of the hotel entrance, surrounded by body guards, the woman wore a shawl over her head and the man held a newspaper over his head and face. They hurried towards the waiting Bentley as the crowd descended on them.

At exactly the same moment the revolving doors at the rear of the hotel began to spin noiselessly. Paul Gastard was first into the night air.Close behind, only seconds later, came the passengers holding hands. Gavin, who stood slightly away with his back to the vehicle, heard them giggle as they dived quickly into the rear seat of the Mercedes. His eyes never left the darkness as he scanned both directions. Hearing the thud of the rear door, he turned, and then jumped into the front passenger sea next to Gastard.

Two or three photographers came running out of the darkness as the big car took off with a squeal of tyres; two motorcycles were in hot pursuit.

As soon as the big car took off from behind the hotel, the airwaves began to buzz with activity

"Desert flower, your mother is on her way, do you copy?" said a male voice with a strong Arabic accent.

"Perfectly, I'll await her arrival. Everything is prepared," replied the voice of a woman.

"Damn!" said Hank Marlin as he heard the message on the special scanner he had borrowed from his French police host. Then another transmission hit the airwaves.

"The doctor will be there soon, do you read, darling?" said a perfect male English voice.

"I can wait. I read you loud and clear," came the reply of a woman's voice with a slight Middle Eastern intonation.

Hank heard most of the transmission.

"Control, this is Unit One. Everything seems A-OK, though I have two motorcycles behind me. Come back."

"Keep to the original plan. I will be at first destination. I'm right above you in the bird."

"Roger, Control, I have you in view. One out."

Hank sat in the back of their car. They were now about five or six vehicles behind the Mercedes.

"Try to keep up with the Mercedes, Michael," he said as he listened to Gavin speaking with the Russian colonel. Hank looked up to see the black helicopter. He knew that it was the latest Russian military version, by standards silent, armed to the teeth and equipped with every conceivable detection device. They were still about five vehicles behind as they headed for the tunnel nearly two miles ahead.

The helicopter gained height then took off in the direction of the underpass. Boris Kiev instructed the pilot to hover around the tunnel's exit. He began to scan around the area carefully through his night sight glasses. He covered every building, top to bottom.

The Royal Retreat, Scotland, earlier that evening

The motorcycle wound along the dark country lanes of the Scottish countryside, eventually turning in to the road that led up to the ancient Balmoral Castle, the Scottish residence of the Royal Family. In the distance, the rider could see the Royal standard way above the floodlight turrets fluttering in the night breeze, announcing to all that Her Majesty the Queen was in residence. The bike pulled up to the closed gates; there was a slight whirring sound as a camera zoomed in on the new arrival like the evil eye of a cyclops.

A small side door in the solid gate opened as a uniformed man came out and spoke to the rider of the bike who took off his helmet and shook his head emphatically.

"No sir, I have to deliver this one personally to the Queen's secretary," he said in his broad Scottish brogue. The guard disappeared through the doorway. After a couple of minutes one of the big gates swung open. He was beckoned towards the guardroom. He and the motorbike were thoroughly searched. He was then given directions and sent up to the main building.

The Queen sat in her study reading a selection of evening newspapers from around the world. She was also watching televised coverage from Paris. She heard the knock on her door.

"Come in."

The door opened and her personal secretary, Sir Geoffrey Bowles, entered the room. "I have a special delivery for you, Ma'am," said the equerry, passing a large brown string and wax sealed envelope to the Queen. She took a paper knife and hesitantly, then fiercely, opened the envelope. She looked at the contents for some time then put the document down on her desk, taking off her reading glasses. She pinched the bridge of her nose with her thumb and forefinger, both eyes closed and then stared down at the document again as though hoping that it had somehow disappeared. She leaned back into her chair and threw her spectacles down on the surface of the desk in a gesture of despair and defeat.

"Will there be a reply Ma'am?"

"No reply, Sir Geoffrey."

"Shall I take the document, Ma'am?"

"No thank you, that won't be necessary," she answered, placing the palm of her right hand firmly and protectively onto it.

"I'll keep it here. That will be all, thank you, Sir Geoffrey." She looked pale and worried, perhaps even a little frightened.

The door closed silently, as her private secretary left the room.

The Queen re-read the letter a few times before walking across and throwing it angrily, as though it were contaminated, into the centre of the glowing embers that burned in the fireplace. The glare from the flames immediately illuminated her lined face as she watched the paper change from white to bright red, then to black, as it disintegrated into small sparks that floated aloft into the dark cavernous chimney. *Ashes to ashes, dust to dust,* the involuntary thought came to her mind.

She looked above the fireplace at the portrait of her grandfather, King George V, who seemed to have a look of sympathy on his face, aptly befitting the current situation.

"I wonder what you would have done, Your Majesty?" she said aloud. "The family future was never jeopardized in your day," she added as she turned and walked back towards her desk. *I did warn the silly young fool, she couldn't say that she wasn't forewarned. God help us all.*

Her thoughts troubled her as she heard the faint chatter of her grandsons playing in the hallway outside her study. A large lump formed in her throat as she went to the door to speak with the future heir to her throne.

Back in Paris, France

Colonel Boris Kiev sat in the chopper, meticulously scanning every window that offered a view to the exit of the tunnel. He spotted a slight movement in a fourth floor window of what looked like a partially constructed office building, nearing completion. He saw the unmistakable flicker of a red laser sight as it paused on the windowsill.

"Fourth storey five windows along, hit it now!" he said into the microphone hanging from his headphone.

"Yes sir," replied the pilot as he brought the machine round. He adjusted the sight on the screen in front of them, then lowered the chopper in line with the window and pressed a button. As the sight locked on, a rocket grenade shot from the underside of the chopper, its destructive power obliterating three windows of the fourth and fifth floors of the building.

The Arabic woman looked up as the helicopter ascended to her level. Too late to react, she never felt a thing. The chopper had instantly climbed, disappearing silently over the buildings, seen only by a woman no longer of this world, and the eyes of Esther Ben-Sheed, as she watched from behind the curtains of a nearby hotel window.

The Mossad agent held her rifle and returned her attention to the now still exit of the tunnel. She smiled at the lack of traffic. *Plan number one seems to have succeeded*, she thought, as the VHF by her side crackled into life.

"The doctor won't be there, he's tied up elsewhere," said the English voice.

"I can wait," replied the agent. "I'm in no hurry now the main source of my pain seems to have gone. Out." She began to dismantle the firearm, wiping clean each piece before putting it into its case.

Paul Gastard was becoming increasingly irritated by the small white Fiat in front. *It's obviously some silly old fool, who shouldn't be on the road,* he thought. He could see that in front of it the road was totally clear.

"Paul, get round this twit in front and lose that bike behind," said the bodyguard sitting next to him. Gastard reacted as asked. He slammed the accelerator down hard. The big car leapt forward and drew level with the Fiat. The road ahead was absolutely clear with about three-quarters of a mile to the tunnel's entrance. The Mercedes gained speed instantly. Gavin saw the speedometer reading of 129 kmh, which he knew was close on 80 mph. The motorbike was caught napping and still held up behind the slower car. The small Fiat, travelling at around the same speed, began to pull away from them as they approached the entrance to the underpass. Both cars shot into the brightly lit interior of the tunnel. The Fiat driver, who was by now some two hundred yards ahead, suddenly swerved into the right hand lane. Smoke poured from its tyres.

Taking his foot off the gas pedal, Gastard slammed his foot hard on the Mercedes brakes. He screamed at the top of his voice as the big car continued to accelerate.

"My God, I can't stop it. It's accelerating on its own!" he screamed in French, as he threw the wheel to the left to avoid the Fiat ahead, which accelerated rapidly forwards.

There was an ear-splitting screeching of tyres and steel as the big car's wheels gouged deeply into the curb of the central reservation. Concrete dust filled the air as the uncontrollable vehicle mounted the emergency footpath. All four passengers stared in total horror, frozen to their seats, waiting that split second for the inevitable. The man in the rear was yelling at the top of his voice as the Mercedes continued to accelerate. He stopped as he was flung forward by the massive jolt, as the left front of the car bounced off one of the enormous centre concrete supports of the tunnel, its engine now screaming as it neared full throttle. The vehicle was thrown violently to the right, climbing straight up the wall on the right hand side of the tunnel, glass shards and sparks flying in all directions as the two ton projectile hit the top of the tunnel, flipping over completely and crashing to the ground on its roof, with a massive impact.

Gavin could hear nothing but the tearing of metal on concrete as his world spun round, rolling over four or five times before smashing into another central support. He felt warm liquid over his face then blackness, then nothing.

The mangled unrecognisable twisted mass finally came to rest further along the tunnel, the roof flattened down below the level of the door handles. Inside the car was mayhem. Both rear passengers had not been wearing seatbelts and were thrown up against the front seats. The man was killed instantly. Gastard was smashed to a pulp; the whole of the steering column had been driven through his body. Gavin Jones was slumped in the front seat, his safety belt secured, an air bag pushing his smashed head and face back against the headrest. He thought he could hear a female voice, and then he slipped back into total oblivion.

When the big car had collided with the first central support, the small Fiat in front had accelerated away and was nowhere to be seen. Of the motorbikes, one, a BMW, had paused then driven on, the other rider had parked and was performing the ghoulish task of photographing the horrific scene as traffic began to jam up behind the accident.

"Unit one, this is Control. Come in. One, do you have a copy on Control. I repeat, Unit One this is Control come back......... All units this is Control. I can't raise Unit One. Anyone: report please. What the hell's going on down there?"

Kiev showed no sign of panic; his voice was cool and controlled as he continued attempting to make contact as he looked down from where he sat in the helicopter. The traffic coming out of the tunnel had thinned to a trickle. One last small white car came out followed by a motorbike, then the traffic flow had stopped.

"Control, this is Unit Two, traffic has come to a standstill and we are at the entry side of the tunnel. We are a couple of cars behind the British cop's car. The Mercedes has gone into the tunnel. Traffic is still flowing out the other direction, but we're jammed solid here. The cop and his buddy have just got out of their car and are running towards the tunnel. I'm going to follow them. Unit Two, out."

"Control to Unit Two, report back ASAP."

"Roger Control, will do."

"Something's wrong Michael," said Hank throwing the radio scanner down on the rear seat. "Come on!" he yelled as he threw the car door open. "Let's go Michael!" he shouted as he took off between the two rows of parked cars, some already loudly hooting horns in typical French fashion.

The two of them ran the quarter mile or so, then rushed into the mouth of the tunnel. Within another few hundred yards or so, the sight that met their eyes was one of total mayhem; glass everywhere, pieces of shattered metal, fuel, water, lumps of rubber tires, half a rear seat, a complete wheel. A woman's purse lay in the middle of the tunnel. Blood had splattered on the tiled walls of the underpass. Further along, they saw a mangled mass of metal that once could have been a car.

"My God, look there," said Michael, pointing at a man bending down with a camera in his hand, flashes coming from the instrument. They both ran towards the stricken vehicle shouting. The man ran forward, jumped on a motorcycle then drove off into the tunnel. They reached the twisted mass of metal, just as another man came running up. He was holding a VHF radio in his hand. Hank recognised him as one of Raffi's bodyguards.

"What a bloody mess!" he said.

"Someone get an ambulance!" the man screamed to nobody in particular as other people began to come towards the scene.

"Control, this is Unit Two, do you read, Control? Do you have a copy on Two.... come back!" he yelled into the radio.

Hank grabbed his wrist.

"It's going to be impossible to get a signal out of here. Do you have a mobile phone?" he asked.

The man threw the radio on the ground and pulled a tiny Motorola out of his inside pocket. The bodyguard was yelling into the phone.

"I think they're all dead sir, oh God, what a bloody mess!" he shouted, as many others clambered around the scene, some taking pictures others just staring.

Inside, the vehicle was an indescribable mass of blood, metal and body parts. Michael came across; Hank tried to prevent him from looking into the mangled car, but was not quick enough.

The royal aide ran across to the wall and threw up violently. A doctor came across towards the remains of the car carrying his bag and offered his services. The bodyguard and Hank managed to rip open one of the rear doors. The doctor clambered through the small space, a stethoscope clutched in his hand. After some time he came out asking for the ambulance, saying that the driver and the rear male passenger were dead; the latter's head was squashed to a pulp. He held out little hope for the front passenger. The female in the rear was still alive, but badly smashed up; her features irreparably unrecognisable. He returned to the rear seat to give what help he could to the woman. It seemed an age before Hank heard the welcome sounds of police and ambulance sirens, and saw the flicker of blue strobe lights coming towards the sorry scene.

"There's nothing more we can do here, Michael." As he spoke he looked around the scene one more time, and then looked across at the faces in the crowd, which was already being rapidly dispersed by the police and fire service. He had a quick glimpse of a face that he recognised and could not quite remember from where, but it certainly rang bells.

The two of them walked back to where they had left their car standing alone in the centre left of the road. A very large gendarme officer stood beside the Renault writing down notes as they approached.

"You'll need to handle this one Michael as your French is better than mine," said Hank as they walked tentatively towards the car.

"Try and get out of this one without his making enquiries. Remember, it's an Interpol vehicle," Hank said.

An irritated officer glared at Michael, awaiting his excuses, hands on hips.

After some long explanations the gendarme took one more look at Michael's driving license then went off towards the accident. Another gendarme made him turn around and drive some distance along the wrong side of the road, where they were eventually filtered into the right hand lane.

The first ambulance came up fast behind them, sirens blasting, lights flashing. Michael moved the car over quickly as the vehicle flew past. Close behind came an equally noisy police car.

"Follow them," said Hank,

"The doctor said that one male and the female passenger were still alive," said Michael.

"Let's pray to God that he was right," said Hank as they went after the fast moving vehicles. "If anyone ever needed your prayers, the princess needs them now."

After a fast ride into the centre of Paris, they pulled into the hospital grounds, just in time to see a stretcher case whisked into the emergency department.

They parked the car and walked up to the main hospital reception as more and more officials poured into the building. Two more ambulances arrived, heavily escorted by police. Two more bodies arrived, this time in body bags. A third casualty was brought in, attendants holding drips in the air, as the injured person was rushed into emergency.

Michael had hurried over as the stretcher came through the door. He sat down next to Hank.

"I heard one of them say English bodyguard," he said to Hank." Maybe Gavin Jones is still alive."

A white Jaguar pulled up to the door of the hospital. Three people came hurriedly into the foyer. Hank recognised the face of Colonel Boris Kiev and close behind was the figure of Anwar Sahaed himself.

The Arab looked distraught and for the first time, Hank thought he looked frightened and helpless. The arrogant strutting gait was missing. He sat quietly in the waiting area whilst Kiev spoke with the staff on reception. The Russian walked across to his boss, he bent down and spoke quietly in the Arab's ear. Hank looked towards the door where numbers of the gendarme were already stopping members of the paparazzi from entering. He thought that they had an impossible task as hospital buildings always had so many different entrances. And of course even paparazzi had hospital appointments. In a short while two white-coated

officials came across to Sahaed. He followed them through a door marked
"Private."

Number 10 Downing Street, London

"We interrupt your programme this evening to bring you an important announcement. News has just reached us of a serious motor accident involving Princess Anna. The accident is said to have taken place earlier this evening in a Paris vehicular tunnel. The princess was rushed to hospital after suffering life-threatening injuries. It was reported that of the four people in the car, two were killed, and the other is critically injured. One of the dead is reported to be Raffi Al-Sahaed, son of the well-known Arab multi-millionaire owner of Harrobys. The other was the driver of the car."

The newscaster went on to say:

"We will interrupt your programme with further information as news comes in. This is Janet Snow, BBC Television News, reporting at 8:30pm."

Cheryl Blain, the wife of the British Prime Minister, jumped up from her seat as the news broke. She almost ran out of the sitting room towards the open door of her husband's private study. Tony Blain was speaking on the phone, his expression a mixture of shock and sadness. He put his forefinger to his lips, and then indicated that his wife should take a seat.

"Thank you, Monsieur Le President, I do appreciate your calling me." He nodded his head a number of times. "I will, and again thank you for your call. The same to you. Goodbye, Monsieur Le President," he said, replacing the phone. "My God, what a shock! I assume by the look on your face you've heard the news," said the PM to his wife.

"Yes. The BBC just this minute interrupted normal service to make the announcement. I wonder if she's going to live."

"The President said that the injuries are of a most serious nature," he said as the phone rang again.

A hotel in the Suburbs of Paris, the same evening

Michael and Hank had eventually left the hospital, saddened and shocked, Michael who had been closer to Anna was totally distraught as they returned to their hotel in the suburbs. They had showered and changed and were sitting in the busy bar, its occupants a mixture of hotel guests and locals. From where Hank was sitting everyone seemed to be French.

They had learned, before leaving the hospital, that Anna was undergoing a long surgical procedure, which would continue through the night. They could see from the television sets over the bar that the accident was the only subject on French TV at that time.

"Now what?" asked Michael, as he toyed with the beer glass in his hand?

"I want a meeting with our friend the Russian Colonel as soon as possible," said the British police inspector. "Do you have the number of the Majestic Palace?" he asked Michael. Hank lit a cigarette as he spoke.

"What about the matchbook in your hand?" asked Michael, smiling. Hank shrugged his shoulders.

"You got any coins?" asked Hank.

He stood up, taking a number of coins from his colleague, and then walked over to the phone on the wall. Hank looked round the room. The bar was old, but very French, with a most convivial atmosphere. On any other occasion, a very pleasant place to while away an evening, he thought. Hank returned to the bar.

"He'll be here in a few minutes or so. I thought that he may feel like talking after today's events," he added confidently. "How about another beer, perhaps you'd like something a little stronger?"

"Beer's fine," replied Michael. The TV set flickered above as the camera showed scenes from outside the tunnel entrance. As yet no footage had been shown inside.

"You lads English?" asked a man sitting next to Michael. He wore a leather jacket and had his hair tied back in a ponytail. He looked as though he needed a shave, and to Michael, he smelled as though a shower wouldn't go amiss either.

"All of this is a bit sad isn't it," said the stranger, pointing to the TV set above.

"Don't I know your face?" he said to Hank.

"I don't think so," replied the inspector.

"What are you doing over here, on business or holiday?" asked the man.

"You sound like a policeman with all these questions," said Hank sarcastically. "Now let me ask you a few. Get some good shots of the bodies in the tunnel today, did you? Follow us here from the hospital, did you then?"

Hank pulled out his ID, shoving it under the nose of the man. "Now let me see some identification from you."

"France is not in your jurisdiction, I don't have to do anything that you say here."

"In a way you're right, but how would you like me to call some of my French colleagues and have you arrested for leaving the scene of an accident, and before you try to leg it, I have the registration number of your motorbike, and we both saw you at the scene earlier."

The man jumped off his bar stool, and set off to leave the room. He walked slap-bang into the broad frame of Boris Kiev.

"Hey, slow down little man," roared the Russian, placing a vice like grip on his arm, leading him back towards Hank.

"This little hippie giving you trouble, inspector?" asked the Russian.

"Give me your driving licence lad and stop being an idiot," said Hank.

When the man pulled papers from his pocket, Hank saw the edge of his passport.

"We'll take a look at that too," he said pulling out the hard-backed document. "Make a note of these, Michael, please." He passed both across. Kiev then released his grip on the reporter.

"There's a nasty odour in here. Smells like paparazzi to me," said the Russian screwing up his nose.

"Hey, these two have different addresses!" exclaimed Michael .

"No matter, write them both down," said Hank. He then thrust them back to the man. "If I see your scavenging ugly face again I swear that you will go inside and I'll throw the key away. That applies here or home. Am I making myself quite clear, you disgusting piece of garbage? Now get out of my sight before I change my mind!" The three of them watched him scurry from the bar.

"Well colonel, let's find a table and talk. Like me, I'm sure that you and your boss want to get to the bottom of this nasty mess. As we say in England, two heads are better than one, and we both have the same interests at heart, do we not?" The Russian held up his hand. "There is nothing to discuss at the moment. I came here to tell you personally to come to the hotel tomorrow and we will help as much as we can, but there's nothing to tell you that you don't know already. Kiev turned and left the bar.

Hank and Michael had slept fitfully. They were awakened by the sound of a street sweeping truck, the engine humming, the circular motion of its brushes swishing and hissing as it passed under their window. Michael leaned across to the centre bedside cabinet and picked up his watch.

"What time is it?" asked a gruff voice from the adjoining bed.

"Morning Hank, it's 6:15," he replied, climbing out of bed and walking across to switch on the room kettle. He emptied the contents of two instant coffee sachets into the two available mugs, and leaned across to switch on the TV set.

Across the channel in England, daylight had dawned on what would prove to be one of the saddest days in the long history of the country. Hank and Michael listened to the French newscaster. At the same time a very large percentage of the British population were glued to their TV sets; most had been awake throughout the night, awaiting news.

"Good morning this is the BBC news. It was announced from Paris early this morning that Princess Anna died during surgery. She passed away in the early hours of this morning as a result of the massive injuries sustained in last night's accident. Over to our Paris correspondent for more details on this devastating situation."

The picture changed to a woman standing in front of the entry to the fated tunnel. There was still much activity going on behind her: the tunnel had been closed off to traffic and in the background a crane was lifting a mass of metal that looked for all the world like a compressed car from a wrecker's yard.

"This is the scene of last evening's tragic accident. As yet there are no suggestions as to where the fault lies. We know that a Mercedes left the Majestic Palace Hotel with a driver and three other passengers inside. It was said by a spokesman for the Sahaed family, that one was a bodyguard and the other two were Princess Anna and Raffi Sahaed. The only re-maining survivor, who could shed any light on the disaster, the Welsh bodyguard, is in a hospital bed fighting for his life.

"An eyewitness reported that the car was travelling at a speed in excess of eighty miles per hour. The atmosphere here in Paris is sombre as an air of sadness seems to have descended upon the city at such a sad loss. This city normally associated with lovers and romance, is now the scene of tragedy and loss.

Since her break away from the Royal Family, Princess Anna has become one of the most popular and loved people in the world today, known as the People's Princess. Her death has already struck a note of sorrow into many hearts internationally. This is Mary Holmes reporting from Paris, handing you back to the studios of the BBC in London."

The camera switched to a scene outside the gates of Buckingham Palace. Large crowds were beginning to gather as hundreds of people were placing bouquets and bunches of flowers at the gates and around the walls.

"This scene here in London is being repeated in many cities throughout the whole of our country. The princess's death seems to have pierced the very heart of the nation," said the newscaster.

"The Royal Family is staying on at Balmoral Castle in Scotland. So far there has been no comment from Her Majesty The Queen, Prince John, or for that matter, any spokesman of the Royal Household."

Paris the same morning

Hank walked up to the reception desk at the Majestic Palace Hotel.

"I have an appointment to see Colonel Kiev," he said to the man standing there. After a couple of minutes the man returned.

"The colonel will be down shortly, please have a seat," he said pointing towards the seating area.

"You have carte blanche. You may go anywhere you wish; our security staff will not hinder you in any way," said the Russian to Hank as they sat talking in Kiev's office. "All I ask is that you keep me updated on anything that you find pertaining to the deaths."

"I don't think that will present a problem," replied the policeman, who got up and shook hands with the other man. As he went to leave the room, Boris Kiev said,

"You understand that I shall be carrying out my own line of investigation, and shall handle the outcome in my own way?" The innuendo in his voice left Hank with the thought that somewhere was a veiled threat to keep out of the Russian's way.

Hank started his look around in the garage section. When he and Michael walked through the entrance they were stopped by a security man, who questioned their authority, then made a phone call.

"You may carry on sir," he said gesturing them into the large area, where a number of very expensive cars were neatly lined up, some being polished, others with their hoods open receiving attention. The tall man with the chauffeur's uniform came over towards them.

"You must be Mr Marlin, how can I help?" he asked.

"Where was the Mercedes usually parked?" asked Hank

"In bay 5, sir, right here, next to the Bentley," said the man walking across and standing in the empty space next to the gleaming limousine.

After a thorough search on the ground, Hank walked across to a metal sheet leaning against the wall.

"Give me a hand with this," Hank called to a nearby mechanic pointing to the steel sheet, but as he pulled the metal it moved more easily than he had thought. "It's alright, I can manage," he said as the sheet slid along the wall revealing the unevenly placed blocks, and the loose pieces of concrete that littered the floor.

Hank squatted down on his haunches, picked up the dust and crumbling it between his thumb and fingers.

"What've you found?" asked Michael looking over the policeman's shoulder as Hank ran his fingers along the jagged open joints of the concrete blocks.

"Don't know yet, but it looks as though this part of the wall has been disturbed very recently." They dragged the steel plate further along the wall, revealing an area of some four or five square feet where the structure had been disturbed.

Hank walked across the garage and picked up a tyre lever, which he forced between the joints of the blocks.

As he did so one of them fell out with ease, followed by fresh loose earth and clay.

Looking closer at the floor where the Mercedes had stood, he saw traces of the same earth along the ground.

"Will you come over here for a minute?" Hank called to the chauffeur, who walked briskly towards the two of them. "I'd like you to move the Bentley carefully please. Don't start the engine, just release the brake, put it into neutral and let the three of us push it over there," he added. When the car was moved he found the same traces of earth along the floor where it had stood.

"I'd like you to cordon off these two bays where both cars stood. Take great care not to stand on the area, don't let anyone else walk here or touch anything."

"As you wish sir," replied the chauffeur.

"What's all that about?" asked Michael, receiving no answer, as Hank walked towards the office at the entrance to the garage area.

"Whatever you do, don't touch, move, or start the engine on that Bentley," he said to the chauffeur who stood by the door to the office looking concerned.

"Is there a problem?" asked the man.

"Just do as I ask," Hank said irritably, picking up the telephone and pressing three numbers.

"Marlin here, colonel, I need to see you right away, I'll be in your office in five minutes," said Hank. He replaced the receiver. "Come on, let's get a move on," he said to Michael, and strode out of the car pool office.

The chauffeur watched them disappear around the corner, shrugged his shoulders and turned back into the garage. As he did so he let out a yell.

"Hey, get out of that car now! For Christ's sake don't you start that engine!" He ran across the floor waving his arms. A confused garage hand got out of the black car looking a little bewildered.

"That car must not be moved. Here, give me the keys," he said with a sigh of relief and holding out the palm of his hand to the confused man.

Boris Kiev's Office, later that day

"I checked the area directly above. There has been excavation very recently. According to the staff here, the Paris Water Company were working there for a couple of days, but the company has no record of any work being done here," said Hank to the Russian. "And, I found this in the bushes." He threw a small black leather glove that had been soaked then had dried into a wizened ball, onto the desk. Read the label. It was made in the State of Israel."

The Russian passed the glove back to Hank, and walked over to the window.

"I have had the Bentley checked by my expert, who has spent more time placing devices on vehicles than having to find them. You were right. The car had been fixed. Come, let me show you," said Kiev walking out of the office.

Down in the garage, the Bentley sat in the centre of the area, black coachwork gleaming under the lights. Standing next to it was the Arab who Hank had met at the garages under Harrobys in London. His beady eyes glistened, as he smirked.

"Hello inspector. So we meet again," said the man in a strongly accented voice. "Allow me," he said as he climbed into the driving seat of the big car.

Hank turned to Boris Kiev, a look of concern on his face.

"Don't worry, inspector, it's not an explosive device, or at least we don't think so," Kiev added with a grin — the first time Hank had seen anything resembling humour from the Russian. Michael moved uneasily as the Arab started the engine, which immediately purred into life. He then pressed down on the accelerator, bringing the revs up to a high level. The Arab jumped out of the car as the engine began to scream, the revs went up automatically to maximum.

The sound was unbearable. Hank saw the Russian look across to the Arab drawing his forefinger across his throat in a gesture telling him to cut the engine. The man grinned at Hank, jumped into the car, pulled the keys from the ignition, but still the engine continued to roar. He then flipped the hood, putting his hand inside and the engine stopped. The relief on every face was apparent.

"What are you trying to do? Melt my car? What the hell's going on here Kiev?" They all turned around to see the figure of Anwar Al-Sahayed standing there, hands on hips, glowering.

"My office, now!" he yelled as he marched out of the garage.

"What the hell happened?" Hank asked the Russian.

"Someone fitted a device to the throttle linkage, so that once the engine passed a certain level of revs, three things happened simultaneously: firstly the throttle was opened to the max, secondly the ignition was bypassed and could not be turned off, and thirdly, the inhibitor switch on the gear selector was immobilised, locking it in the drive position. It would be impossible to do anything but increase speed. My people tell me that it would take about fifteen minutes to install; it's a very clever and fatal device. Ali here reckons that it would kick in at around sixty miles per hour. The Bentley was used as a decoy last night therefore it only went around the block, stopped out front of the hotel, and then was brought back here. Thanks to you, nobody got the chance to take it out again, though Mr Sahaed called for it a half hour ago. And again, thanks to you, he's still safe. And on that note I'll have to go, you heard him yourself. When he hears what happened he may change his attitude," said the Russian walking away. He turned. "On the other hand he may not!" This time there was no sign of humour.

Hank and Michael sat in the coffee shop of the Majestic Palace Hotel.

"So, what do we have?" Hank asked.

"We have an obvious forced entry into the garage — a very complicated and professional entry, which was carried out meticulously. Then a very sophisticated device fixed to one car that we are certain of, and we can assume that a similar one was put on the Mercedes."

"Damn, they killed Anna!" said Michael, slamming his fist down on the table with a loud bang. It seemed to be the first time that he had thought of murder. A number of other people looked across at the disturbance. Kevin Reilly sat at the next table reading his newspaper; he too had been surprised by the bang. The CIA man lowered his head back into the newsprint.

"Hey, take it easy!" said Hank. "This looks like a very messy business," he added, as he squeezed Michael's shoulder. "Now where was I? Ah, yes, and we think that the person who made the entry could be of Israeli origin, and of course, could be the same person who placed the device or devices." He paused, looking around the café.

"Until yesterday we had the company of a tall blonde guy who has followed us consistently both here and back in London. He was also with us that day in Brighton. He's conspicuous by his absence and I think I know who he works for," said the policeman. "I suppose his job is done and now he thinks he can disappear. If he does, he reckons without me." As he spoke he noted the reaction of the man sitting at the next table. He had continued to read the same front page of the newspaper in his hands; his head had jolted when Hank had last spoken.

"Who is the man? Who does he work for?" Michael asked.

"I'd rather keep that info to myself at the moment. At least until I've covered a few more angles, then I'll tell you."

"So, you really think the princess was murdered too?"

"It's beginning to look very much that way," answered Hank.

As they spoke the man at the next table threw a bunch of francs on the table, folded his newspaper and left the coffee shop.

"Don't look up and don't follow me, but I'm going after that man who just left. Wait for me back at our hotel. Take a cab; I'll need the car." With that he got up from the table moving quickly towards the exit. Entering the main foyer of the hotel, he spotted the man walking towards the bank of pay phones at the other side of the elevators, leading to the banqueting rooms. He stayed where he was, sheltered from sight by large palms and plants. Eventually the other man went out of the main front entrance. Hank followed at a safe distance. The big man took off at a good pace among the busy morning pedestrian traffic. Hank was lucky, for the man was over six feet tall and relatively easy to keep in view. One thing he had learned over the years was never to underestimate your quarry and had recognised the man as a professional. He had gone to the other side of the busy street and rightly so. The man had checked behind him at least three times and then stopped in the entry to a busy newsagent's store, his head back in his own newspaper, at the same time inspecting the passing pedestrians.

After a couple of minutes he seemed satisfied. He again folded the newspaper under his arm and took off at a leisurely pace. Hank followed him for at least ten blocks where the man then turned right. A few hundred yards along he entered the foyer of an apartment block. The policeman walked another fifty yards along the street and then watched the entrance for another half hour. The man did not come back out.

Across the other side of the street, David Steel in his artist's disguise stood watching the British policeman. The MI6 man had got the call from Kevin Reilly. He had followed the policeman and watched him tail the CIA man. Reilly had given the cop the slip. Steel smiled to himself as Marlin wrote down the address of the building, then took off down the street and hailed a cab.

As the vehicle pulled away, Steel grinned. *Not to worry, my copper friend, we will meet soon enough. If you had any sense at all, you'd be on the next plane home, or even better, take your secretary friend and fly away whilst you're still able*, he thought to himself.

He walked back into the mainstream of pedestrians, just another Parisian limping along with his walking stick.

Michael was sitting at the bar of their hotel as Hank walked in.

"A bit early for this isn't it?" asked Hank sarcastically.

"I'm only drinking coffee. In fact if I drink one more cup of coffee today, I swear I'll never sleep again. How did your investigations go?"

"Fine," replied Hank. "I think I know where he lives now."

"Who's he?" asked Michael.

"Not sure, but I have a jolly good idea. He wears American clothes and American footwear and I don't think he's an amateur, not by any stretch of the imagination. He's a pro, more than likely CIA."

"Now what?" asked Michael.

"I want to talk with our Russian friend. There are quite a few things that just don't make sense to me. I'm sure he knows more than he's telling. But will he tell? Don't forget the warning he gave us when we first met him with poor old Gavin. He will know who these mystery men are. After all, it's not that long ago since he was a very senior KGB officer himself. Why don't you leave the coffee and let's go see our friend Boris," said Hank.

Charles De Gaulle Airport, Paris

An aircraft of The Queen's Flight, bearing the roundel insignia of the Royal Air Force, landed at the French airport. Hundreds of cameras from across the world filmed its arrival.

British television had shown nothing else all day. They had followed the activities of Prince John who had flown down from Scotland directly to Paris where he was to collect the body of his ex-wife and accompany her back to London.

There had been much unrest in the country. The royals still had made no official comment. Most of the nation felt that too much time had elapsed since the tragedy and a comment was well overdue. The scenes across Britain were unbelievable. Thousands of people stood outside Buckingham Palace; such crowds had not been seen since the wedding of Prince John and Anna years before. The crowds were heard to be shouting for the palace to fly the royal standard at half mast, and in some areas ugly scenes were controlled by police who were becoming more concerned as similar reports were coming in from many other pars of the country. In general, an air of sadness and loss had settled on the whole population.

A cavalcade of vehicles left the airport heading for the Paris hospital where the body of Princess Anna lay at rest. Outside the hospital, crowds of photographers waited, along with hundreds of onlookers. Eventually, a procession of French police bearers emerged through the doors carrying the coffin, which was draped in the Royal Standard of the House of Windsor, a point noted with some pleasure by those staff commentating for British television.

The French Premier stood silently as the cavalcade left on its slow journey to the airport.

The Security Offices — Majestic Palace Hotel, Paris

"Surely you must know the people I refer to, colonel. To say otherwise would insult my intelligence and make you look like an inefficient fool." At this comment, the Russian literally levitated from his seated position, shot into the air pushing his chair back with such force that it fell over with a thud. The anger on his face defied description.

"Listen here, you stupid London copper! Nobody talks to Boris Kiev like that! I have put people into Lubianka prison for life who said less than you just did." Instantly he seemed to realise that he had overstepped the mark. Turning and picking up the chair, he sat down and slowly interlocked his fingers. He stared at his hands for a moment, seemingly unruffled with no sign of a shake.

"Forgive my outburst, inspector. We have all been under much stress." He looked Hank directly in the eyes.

"That's all right, I'm sure that recent events would test the patience of a saint," Hank replied, knowing full well that this was not a man to be trifled with.

"Yes, there have been a number of different groups operating in Paris during the past few days. Your blonde man is an MI6 agent by the name of Steel, David Steel. He used to be one of their top operatives, or should I say your operatives," he smiled, correcting himself.

"He was, and I'm sure still is, a clever and worthy opponent. Your other man is, as you suspect, a CIA agent. In fact, not just an agent, though quite some distance from his bailiwick, which I believe is your description, as he runs the Cairo desk for the agency. His name is Reilly, Kevin Reilly, another crafty clever old warhorse. Those Yanks and you Brits always stick together like glue, if you'll pardon the description," he said with a smirk. "As for the Israeli connection, I can only assume that they sent help to both groups. Sometimes those Jews are as thick as thieves with the Yanks and you Brits as long as it suits their own interests!" he added sarcastically. "I can tell you no more, other than three people are dead, and that nobody can change. Now, if you'll excuse me, there are many things to be done, and much explaining to do. Again I'm sorry to appear so touchy."

The three of them shook hands and Hank and Michael got up to leave the room. As they reached the door Hank turned to the Russian, still inwardly smarting from Kiev's description of him. I do appreciate your somewhat clumsy way of trying to use English colloquialisms; however, for your further edification the word bailiwick refers mainly to an area of specific knowledge, or chosen academic field of expertise, that's unless you happen to be a bailiff! A term used by the less sophisticated would be 'Manor'. More fitting in the circumstances, wouldn't you agree, colonel?

Walking down the staircase Michael turned to Hank.

"You certainly got him going, didn't you? I should think he's eating the table after your last dig, I'll bet you wish your Russian was as good as his English." Michael looked around him on the stairs as though half expecting to be followed by the former KGB super boss.

"Yes, we touched a raw nerve-end there," Hank replied with a grin. "But something's not right though. I can't put my finger on it, but somehow he doesn't seem upset or worried enough, unless he really is Mr Cool, and that certainly didn't show when I got the end of a raw nerve. That outburst was just professional pride. As he said, nobody talks to him like that. What he meant was that he's not used to being in that sort of position, or he doesn't normally make those kinds of mistakes. I don't know, but something just doesn't gel. I'll work it out, just give me time."

As they passed the coffee shop they glanced inside at the television and saw a group of police carrying a coffin. The two men almost ran across the room in time to see Prince John standing alongside the French Premier. A squad of French police was carrying a coffin draped in the Standard of the Royal Household.

They both stood there, Hank with a lump in his throat, unable to speak, Michael with tears streaming down his face. May God rest your soul, my princess, he thought to himself. He covered his face with his hands, turning away and biting his lips as uncontrollable sobbing overtook him.

Sympathetically, Hank put his arm around Michael's shoulder and led him from the room. There were not too many dry eyes in that small room. For that matter, there were thousands of tears being shed around the world. A few minutes later they climbed into the small Renault. Michael turned on the radio advising Hank that there was little else on the French channels but the constant reports of the tragedy and the departure status of Princess Anna's body. They pulled into a parking lot; the sign over the building read "Interpol."

A Roadside Cafe on the Outskirts of Paris

The Englishman and the American sat across the table from each other. The café was noisy and occupied mainly by truck drivers and tourists. The conversations were multi-national mixed with sounds from the jukebox and the clatter of cutlery. It made the place seem reminiscent of a street in a Cairo kasbah.

"It looks as though the man could become a bit of a nuisance. He's asking questions all over town and he also seems to have the ear of our friend Colonel Kiev. I also have a 24-hour watch on the Russian, as you suggested," the American agent said, nonchalantly.

"Kiev is bound to be after us soon; he's no fool. He must be seething at the deaths. He is not used to such failure. Come to think of it, most of his past notable failures were down to us, Kev," said David Steel grinning. "This time there's money involved and not just nationalistic pride. He'll be around, you can be sure of that," he added.

"In the meantime what are we going to do about the interfering cop?" asked Reilly.

"He needs a severe warning, let me take care of that," said Steel.

"What do you have in mind?" asked the American.

"This, you don't need to know about, but you can take your men off him for the time being," said the Englishman. I think that the Palace Mafia will leave Paris in the next day or so. Maybe it's time they were blamed for something. Besides, the cop knows most of them — remember he works on the special Metropolitan Police Royalty Protection Group. We could give him a sharp warning and put him right off the scent in one fell swoop. Fancy another coffee?"

"Not for me," said Reilly. "I must be off. I'm getting a lot of flack from my boss. Evidently, the reaction in England and the world is unprecedented. He wants absolute assurance that the USA cannot be connected with the tragedy."

Interpol Headquarters, Paris

Inspector Pierre Lacoste led the way to his office amid the usual organised chaos of a busy police department.

"Take a seat gentlemen." he said to the two men.

"You have my deepest sympathy. It's tragic,"

"Half of our staff has been moved onto the disaster. As the Americans say, the shit has really hit the fan."

"I suppose you'll be making your way back home now?" he added.

"No we won't, not right away." Hank replied. "I want to make a few discrete inquiries. I was hoping that I could get a little help from you, Pierre.

"I'll do all that I can, you know that Hank, but right now the pressure is on. The last thing we need here is more mud stirring up, until it's a bit more settled. Have you seen the reaction throughout the world, Hank? Every eye across the globe is focused on Paris right now. Princess Anna must be the most popular woman in the world, or so it seems," he said, slumping into his chair. "I'll have to take the car back now as we need all the transport we can get." He shrugged his shoulders, a resigned look on his face.

The phone rang.

"Yes sir, right away." Sorry guys, that's my boss I have to go. Contact me before you leave. Oh, and remember Hank, no mud stirring. We have enough on at the moment without another international incident. I know what you can be like if you get your teeth into something!" he said as he rushed out of the room. Leave the car keys on my desk will you?

The two men stood on the sidewalk.

"Well that wasn't very fruitful," said Hank.

"Not only didn't we learn anything, but we lost our transport to boot."

"There's a Hertz office across the road. Let's go and rent something decent; that Renault was a bit of a squeeze for two big lads like us," said Michael.

"Why not, blow the expense!" said Hank as they crossed the road.

The Majestic Palace Hotel, Paris

After getting clearance from Kiev, Hank had the keys to both suites used by the couple prior to the fatal night. Unfortunately, the rooms had since been cleaned, but were kept unoccupied. They first went to the suite that the princess had used.

When they entered the luxurious surroundings, everything seemed immaculate and in its place at first glance. Michael sat down on one of the sumptuous couches; he could almost hear the voice of Princess Anna as she sat there.

"Michael, bring me one of those small plastic bags will you please?" Hank called from the bathroom. As he walked into the bathroom Michael saw Hank scraping something off the side of the washbasin.

"What's that, Hank?" he asked.

"Looks like makeup, but it could be from a previous occupant. It's just that old habits die hard. It seems quite fresh, so we'll see if it matches up with anything in the other suite," he said, putting the scraping into the bag, then squeezing the seal across.

He collected another two or three different samples from around the rooms: hair, minute pieces of tissue, and then he opened the French windows and walked out onto the balcony.

"There's the site of the explosion," he said to Michael, pointing over to the obvious pile of debris with crime scene tape all around, clearly visible from the room.

"I wonder where the princess's belongings are?" asked Michael.

"That's a very good question, let's ask."

Michael opened the drawer of a writing desk.

"What the hell?!" he exclaimed, as he held up Princess Anna's silver pill case.

"That's odd, Anna wouldn't go too far without this."

"Interesting," replied Hank.

Then he suddenly remembered. Putting his forefinger to his lips, he pointed to his ear, then put the palm of his hand across his mouth indicating silence to Michael.

"That's not Princess Anna's. It's too big and besides, it smells of snuff. Look it's not even solid silver; it's obviously a snuffbox that belongs to someone else. Go back into the bedroom and put it where you found it Michael," said Hank holding open the plastic bag.

They looked into the closet, which had been cleaned out completely, then left the suite and walked across to the other rooms that had been used by Raffi. Looking to the right, Hank saw movement in the surveillance room, which had been empty when they'd arrived. On entering the second suite, Hank walked over to the writing desk and took some of the hotel notepaper.

"Don't talk about anything specific to this room or the inquiry," he wrote on the note, which he passed to Michael.

Hank went to the bathroom and again began to scrape the same light brown coloured substance from the surface of the marble. He collected hairs from a space down the side of the hand basin and found a soiled tissue behind the waste bin. Underneath the bar he found a used glass, which also found its way into a plastic bag.

"It will soon be time for me to return home," Michael said aloud.

"I suppose I'm out of a job now," he said following Hank into the bedroom of the suite.

"I hadn't thought of that," replied Hank.

After another ten minutes or so they left the room and headed for the elevators. Hank noticed that the door to the other suite was not closed properly, which he knew he had done when they'd left earlier. The elevator doors opened into the hotel foyer. Standing there was Boris Kiev.

"Find anything interesting gentlemen?" he asked.

"Just a dirty glass," Hank said to Kiev passing a crystal glass across. Walking towards the door, Michael asked:

"Why did you give him the glass?"

"I soiled another one and gave that to him," Hank replied, tapping his jacket pocket, a grin across his face.

The replacement car was quite an improvement on the Renault. It was a late model Citroen with a large engine and big comfortable seats. They drove through the city towards the headquarters of Interpol. It was late afternoon and the traffic was beginning to build up to the usual evening crescendo.

"This is a much better car than the other," Michael said settling into the seat.

"No it's not," said Hank. "The other was free, and besides this one still has the wheel on the wrong side," he laughed as they pulled into the police headquarters. They were lucky and were able to catch Pierre. He also agreed to have the fingerprint experts at the lab check those on the glass with those on the pill box, and have answers on the other items as soon as the next day. Hank had also asked if Pierre could ascertain the blood group of the dead Raffi Sahaed.

As they drove back through the increasingly heavy traffic Hank said;

"How about we give it a rest for today, and have an evening out on the town? What do you say Michael? Remember what Princess Anna used to say?"

"Come on chaps, a girl has to let her hair down occasionally; can't stay locked in a box for ever."

"I remember. You're right Hank, we've earned a night out. You're on. I know one or two good spots. You got plenty of money?"

"I've got plenty of plastic," replied the policeman.

"Let's get changed, get something to eat, and hit the town."

Hank parked the car behind a small Renault, and then they both went into the hotel. Pausing, Hank turned.

"Let's go into the bar first, I could use a quick one," he grinned at his colleague.

"After all, we are on holiday."

"Lead the way, inspector, mine's a large gin tonic."

The noise was terrifying! The explosion that followed shook the whole bar; windows shattered while debris flew everywhere. Shocked, Michael looked down as Hank lay on the floor, blood pouring from his head wound. It was like one of those slow motion dreams where one seems neither to have control of their movements nor to have any effect on their surroundings. It is simply the state of being there, but not actually taking part.

Everywhere people were either lying on the floor or standing petrified or wandering stunned by the shock. Amazingly, every single window in the bar was gone. The mirrors behind the bar were shattered while light fittings hung hideously from wires along the walls. One bulb had some-how remained lit. In the distance, women were screaming. An old man lay slumped across a table with a cigarette still burning between his fingers. Slowly, Michael bent down to Hank who lay twisted and still amongst the broken shards of glass and debris. He felt for a pulse and detected only a faint response.

"Call an ambulance, get a doctor!" Michael yelled in French. Suddenly the place was teaming with police and ambulance staff, a young man with a stethoscope around his neck pronounced the old man dead. A woman was carried past on a gurney, her right arm ripped open to the bone. Two medics carried Hank away as Michael followed to the waiting ambulance. He noticed their rental car was badly damaged, but the car that had been in front of them was nothing but small pieces of black metal. It had been blown over the other side of the street.

Sitting in the ambulance next to Hank, Michael asked the young doctor if his friend would be all right.

"I can't say, his pulse is weak, but as you can see he is breathing," he said pointing to the oxygen mask as it inflated and deflated sporadically.

"Your leg needs some attention too." He added, pointing to the blood seeping through Michael's trouser leg. Until then he hadn't noticed his own injuries.

Hours later, as Michael sat outside the emergency room; he saw Inspector Pierre Lacoste come rushing along the corridor towards him.

"My God, what next?" asked the inspector.

"I got a message from the lab. When I called your hotel I heard about the explosion, I came as quickly as I could. How is Hank, is he hurt badly? Are you alright?" Just then a doctor came out of the emergency room a serious look on his face.

"Mr Meadows?" he asked, as Michael stood up.

"Yes doctor."

"I'm afraid your colleague is going to have to stay here for at least another day. He has a pretty nasty head wound, which required a number of stitches and we want to be sure that he was not badly concussed."

"Can I see him now?"

"I'm afraid that won't be possible, we've sedated him and he's well separated from his senses right now; he will be out of it until the morning. I suggest that you go home and get some rest; you look pretty badly shaken up yourself. Let me give you something that will help you sleep. Nurse come over here for a moment will you?" he beckoning to a passing nurse.

Pierre drove Michael back to the hotel. There was still much activity in the bar area. Salvage workers were still sifting through the debris.

"I think that you ought to come home with me," said the French inspector

"Let's go, we can come back tomorrow and collect your belongings."

Michael was quite happy to have some company that night so he gladly took up Pierre's offer. After a light meal with the inspector and his wife, he was soon fast asleep, thanks to the pills from the doctor.

The city of Paris seemed to be undergoing a run of terror and misfortune. Three explosions in as many days, one of them claimed to be the work of a terrorist faction. The most unusual bombing of an empty building, and some reports of the presence of a helicopter at the time of the explosion, now a car bomb, outside a popular local suburban bar. And above all was the unfortunate death of Princess Anna.

Paris was now the centre of international attention. There had also been more than the average number of killings in the city; a recent shooting of a hotel employee had helped to boost those statistics. The French Premier sat with Government leaders:

"We cannot allow these happenings to pass by without comment. I want more details on each of these situations. I want chapter and verse. There are also accusations from the British TV and press that it took an ambulance half an hour to reach the scene of Princess Anna's accident. If this is so, then I want to know why. I want a crack down on these damn paparazzi. A round up of all those present at the scene of last night's disaster would be a good start. Remember, we are all members of the European Union, and we will be required to supply answers to all of these points sooner or later. Make sure that France is not caught with her trousers down!" he roared, waving a clenched fist.

"Get to it gentlemen. I want you all here the same time tomorrow morning and this time without the vacant looks and with lots of answers. I bid you good night," He stood and walked across the silent room. He turned as he reached the door.

"Mark my words the death of this princess will have a knock-on effect throughout the world. Take a look at the reaction of the British public. Answers gentlemen, we need answers. France will not be found wanting!" He left, closing the door with a bang.

Hank opened his eyes to the feel of hands wrapping the arm piece of a sphygmomanometer around his upper arm, then felt the increasing pressure as air was pumped, tightening the strap around his arm muscle. He could not understand what the woman said to the man standing next to her.

"How long have I been here?" he asked

"Good morning. I am Dr Mayer. You were brought in here last night, unconscious from injuries sustained in a bomb blast. You received quite a nasty injury to your head. We are keeping you here to be sure that you were not concussed." The doctor leaned forward, lifting Hank's eyelids and shining a light into his pupils.

"Your vital signs seem fine this morning. How do you feel?"

"Apart from a bit of a headache, I've felt worse," he replied.

"What happened to my colleague, Michael Meadows. Was he hurt badly doctor?"

"He's waiting outside right now. He had some injuries to his leg and a couple of minor cuts to his face; he'll be alright. Nurse, you can bring Mr Meadows in now if you will, please."

Michael walked into the room, looking tentatively at Hank,

"Hey, my mother always said that drinking was bad for me." Hank smiled as he sat up in the bed. He threw his legs gingerly over the side of the bed, and looked around the room. His eyes focused fine.

"That was a hell of a mess last night, the bar was totally destroyed, I don't think that Hertz will be too pleased with their car." said Michael. "I stayed with Inspector Lacoste last night. He took me home as I was a bit shaken. He phoned the hotel and said he had results back from the lab for you. When he heard about the bomb he came straight here. He and his wife were very kind and to be honest I didn't much fancy staying in that hotel last night."

"I don't blame you," replied Hank.

After a couple of hours, more tests, and a mound of the usual form filling made easier by Michael's command of the language, the two of them left the hospital by taxi, calling first at the Hertz office, who had already been notified by the French police. They would deliver a replacement car within the hour.

The ends of the street behind the hotel were sealed off to traffic, both vehicular and pedestrian. Michael spoke to a gendarme who allowed them to go under the tapes. The officer spoke into his radio as they walked towards the busy scene.

A tall man in civilian clothes, who introduced himself as Pierre Lacoste, Chief of Police for Paris, met them.

"How are you feeling, Hank?" inquired Pierre Lacoste.

"Hello Pierre. I've felt worse. What are you doing here?".

"There's a lot of pressure from the top on this one. They've asked me to work with the locals, and specifically, to liaise with you."

"Why me? What did I do wrong?"

"Come on, Hank, you are a British police officer, you are in Paris. Not only are you both of the above, you are an active member of the Royalty Protection Squad. Princess Anna is killed in an accident then the following evening somebody blows up a car outside your hotel bar. Could be coincidence, but I don't think so, Hank."

The Frenchman walked into the building, climbing over debris. Hank followed inside. He turned and pulled a brown manila envelope from his inside pocket and passed the lab results to Hank.

"This is for old times' sake. I tried to contact you last night. I hope you're able to understand them as they don't mean a thing to me. And I hope you appreciate my comments of a moment ago. Hank, I'm sure that bomb was meant for you. That was no coincidence. Let's go up to your room."

After they had talked for some time, Hank looked down from the bedroom window. For the second time, he saw the mangled remains of a vehicle being craned onto the back of a truck. He could not help shuddering slightly, as though someone had just walked over his grave. He had levelled with Pierre and told him most of what he knew and suspected. The Renault that had been bombed was the same model, year and the colour as the Interpol car they had borrowed. It had most definitely been meant for them.

Michael and Hank booked out of the hotel. As they went to leave, Pierre had to caution them formally, telling them not to leave Paris without first seeing him, and to let him know where they were staying while they were in France.

The man on the front desk told them that Hertz had delivered another car to the front of the hotel, but first they had to sign more paperwork before he could give them the keys. They then threw their bags into the rear seat and drove off.

David Steel watched from his car as the two came out of the hotel. He saw them climb into the Renault and drive off.

"You got away with it this time copper, but no more," he said aloud. "I think you know too much old lad!"

Though he didn't hear the agent's comments, Hank knew that his life was in danger, and for that matter so was Michael's as it would be assumed that he knew as much as Hank. After he'd read the contents of the envelope from Pierre Lacoste, Hank knew that he had to go to ground immediately. He had to get Michael away to safety too.

Even Lacoste did not understand the significance of the contents of the envelope, nor would their lab. Since reading them, Hank knew that he would be hunted by at least two of the groups involved; each with differing motives and all operating separately — but all of them with the same intention: to kill Hank Marlin as quickly as possible. His life had become worthless.

Hank drove around the rear of the Majestic Hotel. Instead of driving, as normal, into the underground parking lot, he accelerated and turned quickly into a side street on the right. He waited a few seconds then sped along the street. Turning left, he joined the main flow of traffic, looking continually into the rear view and wing mirrors.

"What in the hell was all that about, Hank?"

"We had a tail on us then; it was the man from MI6. He went into the hotel car park."

"Why should we have a tail? Who wants to follow us?"

"Him for one, a few others too if I'm not mistaken, Michael."

"Is there something I should know?"

"There sure is, but first we need to get rid of this car then put some distance between us and this part of Paris." He turned into a side street and parked the car.

"Come on Michael we have to go. Get your bag and follow me and I'll tell you some of what's going on. Not all, as it's in the interest of your safety that you don't know everything!"

Michael ran after Hank as he sprinted off and disappeared down the stairs of a convenient entrance into the busy overcrowded Paris Metro. After they'd boarded a train, Hank followed the station indicator printed above, they decided to get off at La Chapelle. As they surfaced they saw that they'd made a good choice, as the area turned out to be a well populated working class suburb in the northeastern part of the city. They came out of the metro station, found a café, and were soon enjoying coffee and hot croissants.

"I think it's about time you told me what is actually going on here."

"I think you're right," replied Hank. They sat outside at a curbside table and Hank began to explain. After some ten minutes, in which time Michael had sat perfectly silent listening to every word, Hank said:

"There is more, but in your own interests I won't tell you. I have to decide now whether I drop the whole thing and take the risk that I will get through this alive and kicking, or if I should continue until I get to the bottom of the matter. Either way I'm a marked man.

"You should go home right away Michael, and try to carry on as though you know nothing. There is a good chance that you will be left alone, if you follow some of the guidelines that I'll give you, such as making a few statements to the press, that obviate the fact that you know absolutely nothing.

"If I were you I wouldn't fly in your plane until it has been checked thoroughly, and as callous as it may sound, you may want to let somebody else try it first. You saw what they're capable of with those devices on the cars!"

"What are you going to do Hank?"

"I really have no choice but to continue, and try to confirm my suspicions; maybe expose the whole situation. It's a classic case of heads I lose, tails they win, and quite frankly, Michael, I'm not a very good loser."

Michael jumped up from his seat.

"Goddamn them all! I'm staying too then. Garçon, deux biers si'l vous plait!" He shouted to a nearby waiter, who returned with two foaming glasses of beer.

"I trust you appreciate what you're letting yourself in for, Michael. This will be no Sunday school outing. The chances of beating some of the best that three leading countries have to offer is quite a task."

"Here's to stupidity," replied Michael, holding his glass in the air.

"I'll drink to that." Two glasses chinked together. "Let's go and find somewhere to stay, then we can work on our plans," Hank said, throwing down some money and picking up his bag. "We've got a hell of a job on our hands, and a dangerous one at that!" They walked up to a small hotel with Michael leading the way through the door.

A Street Corner Café Close to the Eiffel Tower

The area was, as usual, packed with tourists. Kevin Reilly never ceased to be amazed at the number of people wanting to reach the top of the tower. He held the same thoughts when watching the Empire State Building, or the constant clamour to climb the Statue of Liberty. *Think of the money they bring. Helps to pay my wages*, he thought to himself.

He sat sipping his coffee and enjoying the morning air, the words of the CIA chief still ringing in his ears, the unveiled threat of a desk in Arlington Virginia still hung freshly in his mind. The typical sounds of French accordion music and the laughter of children mixed with the noise of traffic made the prospect of leaving Paris seem unpalatable to him. The eventual return to Cairo was even losing its attraction in comparison to Gay Paris. The sudden appearance of the Brit agent brought him back to harsh reality.

"Morning," said David Steel, joining him at the table. "What a gorgeous day."

"Maybe for you, but I got my ears chewed off earlier," Reilly growled. My boss is flipping his lid. The president has made it very clear that the States must be seen to have no involvement in this whole affair."

"That's OK then, you're clean as a whistle. The only man who could have possibly identified you is the French driver, and he certainly won't be too talkative, unless its to his Maker, or maybe Lucifer, so relax."

"Nevertheless, this is the last time I shall meet with you, until things quiet down. What's the problem anyway?" asked the American.

"I've lost that bloody English cop and his friend. They disappeared last night. I think the cop spotted me so they ditched their rental car and vanished.

"So, what's the big problem? What harm can they do now?"

"That cop's no fool. He's been asking a lot of questions. He went to Interpol Headquarters twice in the last day. I found out that he was given permission by Kiev to go over the rooms used by the couple. He was also nosing around the back of the hotel. I think he worked out where we entered and maybe he even found the other device. Somebody must have or it would have gone off by now, who knows? All I do know is that he is a bloody danger to the whole of this Goddamn operation, and will have to go."

Kevin Reilly stood, pushing back his chair to leave the table.

"I'm having no part in this!" Steel looked him straight in the eyes.

"Kevin, my old sport, you're already involved. It's too late to back out; the job has to be finished, with no loose ends. Remember what you were told. Give the Brits whatever help they need on this one."

"I just told you that their position has changed now," Kevin Reilly said.

"Well, ours hasn't my dear chap. Don't forget the English cop followed you the other day, so he can ID you."

"Yes, but he doesn't know who I am," Reilly added!

"How do you know he doesn't? Maybe your old friend Boris told him. It's no skin off his nose, and you tell me you pissed him off the other night! You'd better hang around and give me a hand to find him just in case, eh? I'll be in touch then."

The English agent put two fingers to his brow in a mock salute as he disappeared into the crowd just as quickly as he'd arrived.

Boris Kiev watched with interest from his position on the first balcony of the tower. He put another coin into the tourist telescope. He grinned, watching Steel walk away, then returned to the disturbed face of the American. The allies begin to argue amongst themselves. I wonder what brought that on, he thought to himself, watching Kevin Reilly throw down money and hurriedly leave the café. Kiev smiled, turning the telescope to where Steel had walked, but he was gone, nowhere to be seen.

The Suburb of La-Chapelle

Michael and Hank had found a small pension in a busy part of the suburb. It was a guesthouse used by working people visiting the area. The small parking lot was filled with vans and trucks bearing the names of carpenters, electricians and plumbers. Across the street was a market area, which had come to life at about 5:30am. The two of them sat in a small bar-cum-café, drinking coffee amid the hustle and bustle of the busy arcade. Michael had just returned to the table with the inevitable four fresh croissants and butter.

"We need to get to the airport somehow," said Hank. "I want to take a look at the area where light aircraft are kept; where your plane is now, Michael."

"That shouldn't present a problem, should it?" asked Michael.

"I'm afraid it does. They may well be watching your plane and the whole area. Like all such places, you'll have to give some sort of ID to get back in there, of that you can be sure. First, we need transport. Car rental is out of the question because we would need to use a credit card as no rental company takes cash these days. I'm quite sure that our friends have the facility to find out if we use a card anywhere. So it looks like public transport is going to be the answer. In any case it's less conspicuous as we can get lost in the masses.

"Why don't you go and find out which is the best form of transport to Orly Airport. I'll take a walk around the market and meet you back here in ten minutes." Half an hour later they were back in the Metro underground railway, packed like sardines heading for the airport, with two more changes of train to make.

They got off the train one stop before the airport and grabbed a cab, getting the driver to drop them off at the rear of the airport perimeter near the cargo area. They walked along the fenced off perimeter for what seemed to be miles, eventually coming up to a part that was obviously devoted to helicopters. The entrance didn't have a checkpoint and the gates were open, so they walked right through.

"What are we looking for?" asked Michael.

"Sahaed's chopper. That sleek black Russian job that flew over the tunnel the night of the trouble." Hank put his bag on the ground and took out two lightweight black bomber jackets and two black baseball caps. "Here, put these on. At least they offer some form of disguise or anonymity. I picked them up in the market earlier." Hank winced as the rim of his hat smartly reminded him of the recent stitching to his head.

They had walked the complete area ,but saw no sign of the black machine, having looked into every hangar. There were only two buildings that were locked, and in both cases grass was growing around the base of the doors.

"Well, I thought for sure that the damn thing would be here. I know they don't keep it on the roof of the hotel, and there is no other place that they could keep it and have the required servicing done."

Just then they both heard the whistling whirring sounds of a chopper. They saw the machine coming in low from the roadside, its shadow crossing their path as it went overhead. It hovered for a few seconds, and then disappeared behind the buildings on the far side of the area. They strode off in its direction. As they approached, a technician already had a ladder up to the rear jet engine on the right side of the chopper. Another man, obviously the pilot, stood hands on hips shouting up to the other man; he spoke perfect English with an American accent. When the two approached, he looked around seeing the two matching hats bearing the badge of the LA Lakers.

"Hey! How's it going guys?" he said with a grin

"Great," said Hank smiling back at the pilot. "Hell of a machine you got there. Looks more like a military chopper than a civilian one. Bet that thing can move along a bit."

"Sure can, I just came back from the south of France in just over two hours. We came from right down there on the Med, near to a place called Toulon, if you know the area."

Just then the side door of a hangar opened thirty yards away, and the figure of Colonel Boris Kiev emerged from the building. Both Englishmen saw him at the same time. Hank pulled his cap down over his eyes. Michael turned away slinging his bag over his shoulder as he walked off.

"Have a good day, buddy," Hank nodded to the pilot as he too turned and strolled off behind his partner, walking with an exaggerated sailor's gait, his bag over his shoulder.

Kiev was talking to a stranger as he walked. He headed in the direction of Hank and Michael; he had been half turned to the stranger as he walked towards the aircraft.

"Who were those two?" he asked the pilot as he came up to the chopper.

"Don't know, sir, just a couple of fellow Yanks." he replied, smiling.

Kiev leaned towards the stranger speaking quietly then the man walked off behind the two Englishmen.

"Don't look round now, Michael, but the guy who was with the Russian is following us. Just keep walking." Hank leaned across putting his arm around Michael's neck.

"I never knew you cared."

"You should be so lucky," replied the policeman. "Follow me." He turned to the right walking across a grass-covered area, towards the offices of what looked like a large helicopter company. They both went into the building as though they knew their way around.

Once inside they went along a corridor. Hank spotted the international sign for the men's room and went straight in followed by Michael. The washroom had a second exit at the other end. Hank opened the door, which led out into a large hangar and repair area. There were a number of aircraft in different states of repair.

They walked out and across the workshop. Michael spoke to a couple of mechanics as they passed, and smiled at the old man who was sweeping the floor. Once outside again, Michael followed Hank who crossed to the next line of buildings, then he turned right to the end of the block. Crossing back over, he went around the end building and carefully peered around the corner from behind some shrubs. The stranger was still standing opposite, leaning against a telegraph pole.

"Come on let's get the hell out of here. He thinks that we're still in there. Let's move it before he goes inside asking questions. I've got most of what we need to know for the time being," Said Hank.

Taking off at a brisk pace they had to make a complete circle in order to reach where they had entered the perimeter fence. Nearing the gate, Hank heard the noise of the helicopter taking off again.

"Quickly, follow me over here." They ran towards a bus parked at the gates, both jumping aboard just as the doors closed with a hiss and a thump behind them.

Hank watched through the window at the black aircraft as it hovered over the rows of hangars. The bus driver spoke to Michael, who answered, then offered him money, which was refused.

"What's all that about?"

"He said this bus only goes to the airport terminal, which is just around the corner, but he wouldn't take any money," replied Michael. As he spoke, they both leaned inwards as the chopper came low casting an ominous shadow over the top of the bus.

"Phew! That was close. We need to get out of Paris as soon as we can. We really could use your plane Michael, but I can't figure out a way to get it out without our being seen."

"You're right Hank. I'd have to file a flight plan, and then ask control for clearance to take off. At that point anyone with a radio will hear."

"There has to be a way," said a worried Hank. "We just have to get that plane into the air."

"Remember what you said earlier about possible sabotage."

"I remember," replied Hank.

"That too is another problem we have to overcome."

The bus pulled into the terminus. They waited until most of the other passengers had alighted. Hank asked Michael to stay where he sat, and watch carefully for any overly interested onlookers. Just as he was about to give the go ahead, he froze.

"What's the matter Hank?"

"Get your head down," snapped the policeman,

"It's that bloody MI6 man. How in the hell did he get on our tail? Keep down. We can't get out here."

Outside Buckingham Palace, London

The scenes outside the royal residence were unprecedented. Never had such crowds gathered outside the palace. Not even in those euphoric days at the end of the Second World War had so many people shown the strength of their feelings. The Queen had returned from Scotland along with Prince John and his two sons. The reaction of the British public was beyond all belief, forcing Her Majesty The Queen to speak to the country the previous day.

"Quite a turn round, because a few months earlier she had commanded that the name of Princess Anna should not be spoken within the walls of the palace," said a member of a panel of celebrities watching the scenes from the television studios.

Thousands upon thousands of wreaths and bunches of flowers had been placed outside the palace and along the Mall leading to the gates. Similar scenes were taking place throughout the country. The Queen had announced that a full state funeral would take place.

An enormous roar had come from the hundreds of thousands of people, who now crowded the route, as the Standard above the palace was lowered to half-mast. Though the funeral was not scheduled until the next day, the published route was already packed with the dead princess's loyal supporters.

The previous day, the funeral of Raffi Sahaed had taken place at a North London Mosque, a much less publicised family affair. His body had been flown back from Paris earlier.

British newspapers announced in large headlines, that the Royal Family was at their lowest point of popularity; some even questioned their chances of survival.

"Nobody in his or her wildest dreams could have forecast such a public reaction to the death of the woman who had become the most popular royal in history," said a BBC television commentator.

"Businesses throughout the country are being brought to a halt as people continue to pour into the capital from every city and village in Great Britain. Trains are packed to capacity and roads are blocked with traffic as a nation mourns the loss of its fairy tale princess," she continued.

"It has been announced that the multi millionaire singing star and friend of the late princess, Alton James, has had the lyrics of a song re-written and dedicated to the princess, which he will sing at the funeral in Westminster Abbey." The screen switched to the tunnel in Paris.

"Meanwhile in Paris, police are still searching for clues as to the cause of this terrible tragedy. Even there, people are placing floral tributes at the entrance to the fated tunnel. Some are even risking serious injury by walking the narrow central reservation to place flowers at the exact point of impact, as traffic continues to flow. This is Mary Holmes, in the studio handing you over to Sir Geoffrey, who is with the crowds outside Buckingham Palace. Over to you Sir Geoffrey."

Orly Airport Paris

"Got them!" shouted David Steel as he punched the steering wheel of the rental car. "Goddamn it, I have them!" he said, again out loud. Paying little attention to a helicopter as it hovered low overhead, he kept a safe distance behind the bus as it pulled away from the gates of the heliport.

The MI6 agent drove along the perimeter of the airport and followed the vehicle as it turned into the main terminal. He held his breath as he watched the passengers leave the bus. He was sure he had seen the two Englishmen rush onto the bus, but now it seemed to have disgorged its entire cargo. Outside, the driver leaned on the front, lighting a cigarette.

Steel turned as a loud rap on the driver side window had his nerves jangling.

"You can't wait here," said a French policeman.

Steel wound down the window.

"I don't speak French," said the agent, spreading his hands.

"That's alright sir, I speak English, and if this car is not moved instantly, I will have it and you taken away. The signs are in both French and English. I assume you read, sir?" the cop said, with the usual unfriendliness afforded the Brits by the French.

Inside the bus, Hank peered over the window ledge, seeing the French policeman gesticulating and blocking the agent's view of the bus as he pointed towards a no parking sign. Hank jumped up from the seat.

"Come on let's go. Quickly, let's get out of here!" he shouted as he ran to the front of the vehicle with Michael hot on his heels.

Steel glimpsed the rear of the second man as he fled the bus. He took off with a screech of tyres, leaving the policeman glowering at the noise and other passers by standing staring.

The two men shot through the main doors into the terminal, and were soon rushing headlong into a seething mass of travellers. Michael kept as close as he could to Hank, his legs bashing painfully into suitcases and baggage trolleys.

Above, on the second floor balcony, a large man spoke into a radio mike clipped to his wristwatch, a hearing aid-sized receiver in his ear. Steel had left the car where it was and had rushed into the building with the policeman shouting and blowing his whistle as traffic built up behind the offending unoccupied car in the centre of the road.

Hank ran through the baggage hall, as carousels filled with suitcases and boxes were surrounded by hundreds of milling people all trying to grab their belongings at the same time. He jumped between two women, climbed onto the moving beltway, and then ran along, leaping over cases and packages, eventually forcing his way under the heavy flapping rubber skirt leading to the baggage handling area. A couple of men looked aghast as Hank catapulted through the small opening, closely followed by Michael, still clutching his bag. One of the handlers shouted after them as they disappeared out of the building towards the area where large jets stood next to the hydraulic ramps towering way above. They ran underneath the massive nose wheel of an airliner. Hank paused for breath. They both leaned against the cab of the unoccupied tractor that was connected to the aircraft. Before either of them could speak, they heard the unmistakable thud and zing as a bullet ricocheted off the side of the tractor; a second bullet completely shattered its windshield. They ran off, at first under the fuselage of the big jet, and then Michael followed as Hank climbed the metal staircase leading up to the passenger ramp.

Out of the corner of his eye, Hank saw flashing strobes as two police cars arrived at the side of the tractor. He dived into the extended passageway of the ramp, joining the mad rush of passengers as they came off the parked aircraft to his right; Michael was some twenty feet behind. They wound along the tunnels, eventually climbing onto the moving walkway and were lost to view among the hundreds of other passengers heading towards the main terminal. Hank followed the sign to the washrooms. He turned to the left, walking twenty yards or so. He looked round to see Michael trotting along behind. They went into the men's room heading to a door with a French sign. The door opened as they turned the handle and entered the small room.

Hank pressed the door lock behind them. Michael sat on a pile of towels and Hank leaned on a trolley. The room was in semi-darkness. They became aware of each other's heavy breathing as they realised the magnitude of what had just taken place. Hank felt around and found the light switch. The room flooded with light; it was the cleaner's supply room.

It didn't take the two of them very long to put their jackets and caps into their bags and don a cleaner's uniform each. There were three trolleys in the room; they took one each, loading them with all of the usual supplies. They emerged separately from the room; Hank a couple of minutes after Michael. They headed down the long concourses towards the main airport building, as well hidden as couple of fir trees in a pine forest. Hank paused to empty a trash can. As he did so he saw the figure of Colonel Boris Kiev sail by on the moving walkway, looking everywhere, but at him. An involuntary shudder went across his stomach as the Russian passed by.

Hank had agreed with Michael that they would go through the main building, then on to the executive and light aircraft section of the airport. He was wearing a black beret with his coveralls, and Hank wore an airport uniform cap.

They had separated, skirting around the main check in desks and shops, and were well on towards their goal when Hank spotted an armed airport security man in full uniform who seemed to be giving his colleague a bit of a hard time. The man took out his radio and was speaking rapidly to someone on the other end, whilst Michael looked on uneasily. Hank went around a corner behind a large self-service café. He hurriedly took off the coveralls, put them into his bag and put on the black bomber jacket and cap.

He walked across to the security man.

"Excuse me, do you speak English, officer?"

"A little," replied the security man.

"There is a man robbing a woman at gunpoint behind the café. Come quickly!" Hank had shaped the two fingers of his right hand into a gun as he spoke. The security man snapped something in French at Michael; then he ran off in the direction of the café.

"Grab your bag, let's go Michael!"

Minutes later they were both walking towards the light aircraft section of the building. Michael pointed to a gift shop. Where they bought two Paris tee shirts and sunglasses and then changed in a men's room..

"I have a plan to get the aircraft out of here," Michael said as they walked along the concourse. "It's a bit complicated, but I think we can pull it off with a bit of luck. Let's find a phone where I can talk and you can keep a look out. Then we need to find somewhere to hide until it gets dark, preferably out near the light aircraft park. The security won't be quite so intense there. Oh, and I'll need some black electrician's tape. And Hank, you have blood running down the side of your head under the cap."

Steel had covered the whole of the airport site and drawn a blank. He had spotted men from the Sahaed team; at one stage he'd seen Kiev himself. He had phoned Reilly to get some back up. There had been no reply to either the apartment phone or the cell. Steel's section was moving another agent over from Spain who was scheduled to arrive within the hour. He passed the desks where the small charter companies ran their flights to places that he'd never heard of, and then followed the signs to the private plane park. He could see lines of small aircraft through the window and next to them were a number of private jets. He walked over to take a closer look and recognised the sleek plane belonging to Anwar Sahaed, its fuselage glistening as the strobe lights flashed, engines screaming as it turned and headed for the main runway. Maybe we've seen the last of that lot. I should be so lucky, the agent thought to himself. He walked across and sat on a seat near a cluster of pay phones. Picking up a newspaper that had been discarded and putting it in front of his face, he waited.

The two Englishmen passed the small charter company desks. The remainder of the concourse was almost deserted and away in the distance the could see the end of the building. Hank took out a pair of pocket binoculars and scanned the empty area. He focused on a man sitting near a battery of phones, holding up a newspaper. Fine-tuning the glasses, he turned to Michael.

"Here let me look at your newspaper." He took the paper looking at the front page then putting the glasses back to his eyes again. "I thought so, that man there is reading an old newspaper."
Michael took the glasses and adjusted the focus.

"I don't see anybody."

"Over on the right near the pay phones."

"Got him." Michael moved quickly into an adjacent doorway, pulling Hank along as he did so.

"Hey what's up?"

"It's him, I think it's the MI6 man," he stuttered. Hank peered around the corner.

"Give me the glasses, will you Michael." He looked back to where the man sat and as the paper was lowered, he saw that it was indeed the MI6 agent. Turning towards the direction they had just come from, Hank saw two faces that he recognised instantly. Way in the distance he could see the large frame of Boris Kiev, but much closer he saw the thin pointed features and beady eyes of the Arab from the garage at Harrobys.

"Damn it," he exclaimed as he pulled back quickly out of view.

"What's up?" asked Michael.

"We need to get out of here, and right now," he answered abruptly, walking across to the door at the end of the short corridor. The door was firmly locked and bolted; without tools and a lot of noise it would have to remain that way. They were boxed in with no visible means of escape; the shifty-eyed Arab would certainly not miss them as he passed. Looking upwards Michael spotted a manhole entry in the ceiling above.

"Quick, Hank, give me a leg up here will you," he said pointing to the small door. "See if I can get into the crawlspace." Hank formed his hands into a stirrup, hoisting Michael into the air.

"Damn the bloody thing," he cursed as the metal trap door refused to budge. After another hefty slam with the heels of both hands, the door flew up inside the roof space, dust and muck covering his face. Michael made a mighty heave as he pulled himself up into the space, and then appeared back in the opening his hands held down towards Hank. The distance was too great for them to reach each other and there was nothing for Hank to stand on. He peered around the corner. The Arab was within view without the aid of binoculars. Six feet around the corner Hank spotted a flip top waste bin. He hurriedly leapt out and grabbed the receptacle, rushed back into the corridor, put it under the hatch, clambered up and grabbed Michael's waiting hands, and was dragged upwards, legs flailing in mid air, as he disappeared into the roof space.

The Arab's attention was drawn towards a man's figure. He saw the man grab a trash can, then disappear round the corner. The Arab lengthened his stride.

Hank looked down at the trash can. Luckily the top was still securely fixed. Apart from dust on the floor around the bin, there were no visible signs of their presence or hurried departure. Hank let go the steel door, as it clanged into place. The roof space was completely pitch black and smelled musty. He very quickly learned that the height was about three feet, as his eyes watered from the pain when his injured head hit the concrete roof joist.

"Here, stand on this trap door with me." Hank whispered.

"Why?"

"Don't ask questions, just stand here," he snapped, groping for Michael's arm, and guiding him to the space.

The Arab reached the corner standing perfectly still; he peered cautiously into the empty corridor, and then walked briskly towards the exit door. After finding a staunch metal door securely locked, he looked around with an angry grimace on his dark features. Spotting the trap door above, he leapt lithely onto the top of the waste bin and began pushing upwards on the metal cover, which remained solid. His radio crackled into life.

"What's going on Ali?" growled his boss Kiev. "Ali come back, you hear me?"

"Yes, I am hearing you good my colonel. I am theenking I see someone turning in here, but the door she eez locked."

"Where are you?" snapped Kiev. The Arab stepped out into the main walkway, just as Kiev came up to where he stood.

Hank and Michael felt the knocking and thudding under their feet, as they stood on the door. After a short while it went silent. They heard the crackle of static from a VHF signal, but could not hear any conversation. The area was flooded with light as Hank struck a match. Near them was a pile of concrete blocks, four of which they hurriedly and quietly stacked onto the trap door.

Further down the concourse, Steel spotted the Russian. He had turned off to the left, along with what appeared to be an accomplice. He realised that he was sitting in an open and relatively quiet area, so he took the opportunity of moving off towards the very end of the building, eventually exiting out into an area packed with light aircraft.

Kiev had looked around the short corridor carefully.

"You were right Ali, someone has been in here recently, and either left by the door which they locked behind them, or they went up into the roof space." He moved the trash can as he spoke, noting that there was dust underneath the receptacle.

"You say that the trap door is solid?" he asked the Arab, who nodded in reply.

"And the exit door is locked?" The Arab spread his hands in a gesture of resignation.

"Then where the hell did they go? Do you suppose they disappeared into thin air?" he yelled at the little man. "Maybe you imagined that you saw someone come here in the first place".

The Arab looked his boss directly in the eyes and shook his head slowly. Kiev knew that the man was too well trained to make such a mistake. He too was sure the English men had either gone out the door and locked it behind them, or had gone up into the roof space, somehow locking that behind them. Kiev issued instructions to the other man and snarled more orders into the radio as he strode off in the direction of the private aircraft area. *Now I'm sure that they know too much. They have to go at all costs.* Kiev muttered to himself.

In the dusty roof space, Hank had managed to work out some of the geography. The shallow area was there to carry air conditioning ducts, along with many electric and electronic cables. The main pipes that fed the sprinkler system were up there and there was no apparent way out above. They began the long trek bent double, heading in the direction of the main walkway below them. Hank, the smoker of the two, took out the book of matches from his pocket, and counted the last remaining three. The floor under their feet had concrete ribs every three or four feet. Luckily there seemed to be no upright supports between them and the roof above. They continued to make slow progress, both of them puffing and grunting under the strain.

"How much longer do you think we'll have to put up with this?" asked Michael.

"Shssh," Hank hissed. Above the continuous rumble of aircraft they both heard a metallic click. "What was that?" whispered Michael. At the same moment Hank, who was leading the way, had been following the air duct with his left hand, felt the metal casing terminate as it bent away at a right angle to his left, he turned to the left, followed by his colleague. Ahead he saw a pinpoint of light and began to move towards it just as a blinding flash shot along the main roof space behind them. They both turned, temporarily blinded by the beam of a powerful searchlight as it flooded the area with light.

"Jesus, that was close!"

"Sure was," replied Hank. They both heard voices, and metallic echoes.

Hank lit a match; they saw a metal hatch in front of them held by a number of wing nuts.

"Damn it!" hissed Hank as the match flame reached the end, burning his finger and thumb.

The beams from the powerful searchlight continued to flash along the roof space out in the main tunnel. They still heard metallic sounds and occasional voices. Michael crouched, expecting to see someone to appear round the corner and discover them at any moment. He could hear the scratching squeaky sounds as Hank worked at undoing the wing nuts he had seen on the metal plate.

"Damn, I wish I had a pair of pliers. Some of these screws were put here to stay!" cursed Hank. Out in the main crawl space things seemed to be quieting down. The lights were still shining, but Michael couldn't hear voices getting any closer, or indeed any sounds of movement. He moved slowly towards the corner and cautiously peered out.

He could see a bright stationary light coming from the direction of the private aircraft end, but there was nothing in the direction they had just come from.

"Got it!" whispered Hank as another equally bright flash of light poured in from behind Michael, which was quickly extinguished as Hank replaced the plate.

"I think we have a major breakthrough here. Apart from a grill behind this plate there is nothing to stop us getting out to the light aircraft area. I just saw clear out there, but we'll have to stay put until it gets dark," he said with a sigh of resignation. "Make yourself comfortable."

"Everything seems to have gone quiet out here. I think they put out the lights and closed the trap doors," replied Michael, a note of some relief in his voice.They settled down in much discomfort, awaiting the coming night.

"Well come on, let's have it then!"

"Have what?" asked Michael. Sounding confused

"Your plan of escape, we've got plenty of time to refine it now," his colleague replied as he fidgeted on his uncomfortable seat.

"I have one thing to say now. Mr Boris Kiev has now confirmed my suspicions. He and his cohorts have plenty to hide so he must be just as big a danger to us as the others, if not more. I was just thinking back to our meeting with Gavin at the Majestic. I believe that poor bugger was ready to talk to us, you know. I had a feeling he had something to say. Pity he never got the chance."

Princess Anna's Funeral Ceremony, London

The country had never seen such crowds in its long history. Every single inch of the planned route to be taken by the funeral procession was packed. Lines of people stood patiently waiting to sign the book of condolence. Already some ten thousand had signed and the lines were growing by the hour as the number of completed books grew beyond all expectation.

Wreaths and bunches of flowers covered the entire route. Outside Buckingham Palace the whole of the frontage was a mass of colour, the floral tributes there were up to twenty feet deep.

"One begins to wonder if there are any flowers left growing anywhere in the country," said a television announcer. Television cameras panned along the never-ending miles of devoted people paying their respects. Commentators spoke in reverent tones.

"It is staggering how popular this princess of ours had become," said one of them. A camera zoomed in and moved along one side of the road.

"It's almost impossible to find a dry eye here today."

At the palace the Royal Standard fluttered gently in the breeze at half-mast. The gates were opened and the royal procession made its way slowly down the Mall towards Westminster Abbey. In the rear of the leading car sat Her Majesty The Queen along with the Duke. In the cars behind could be seen the Queen Mother, followed by the brothers of Prince John accompanied by their children. The body of Princess Anna had left St James Palace for the shorter journey to the Abbey. Prince John walked slowly behind the flower-decked hearse accompanied by his two sons, George and Edward. A Military Guard of Honour walked solemnly alongside the vehicle. Thousands of people stood silently and tearfully as the sad procession passed by.

After the coffin had been carried into the ancient Westminster Abbey, sombre music was relayed to the crowds outside and along the route. Then followed the service read by the Archbishop of Canterbury. Then as the voice of the well-known pop singer, Alton James sang his song, My English Rose, hundreds of thousands of people stood silently. In fact the whole of Great Britain and most of the world followed suit. The funeral had the largest worldwide media coverage of any one event in history.

Later, the cortege undertook the slow journey across London to the M1, then north to the final resting place in the grounds of Princess Anna's family estate; where a special grave had been prepared on an island in the centre of the estate's lake; a very special place to the princess when she was a child.

Orly Airport, Paris

Hank took off the last two wing nuts that held the hatch temporarily in place. Pulling it away from its position he peered through the opening. It was dusk, and the ground was wet from the constant drizzle. Large puddles reflected crazy images from the airport lights. A stiff breeze drove rain into their hiding place covering Hank's face with water and disturbing the dust in the roof space. Michael crawled across to the light, squinting as his eyes became accustomed to the sudden glare.

"Looks as though we're right in the middle of the light aircraft park," he muttered, peering over Hank's shoulder. "Can't see our plane, can you?"

"No, but I can see about twenty others." Hank replied enthusiastically. There was a building between them and the planes, which blocked some aircraft from their view, but it would also shelter them from being seen by others. Hank had, by now, taken the plate completely away from the opening. The vent outside was more delicate than he had first imagined; he was able to pull it inwards with ease.

"Thank God for sloppy workmanship," he said pointing to four empty holes that should have contained screws, as he passed the lightweight frame to Michael. Looking out of the hole he saw a very convenient down pipe only about a foot to the left, which he pulled hard. He hoped that the same sloppy workman hadn't installed that. It felt firm.

"OK, let's go then. You first and I'll pull this vent back into place behind me," Michael said.

Hank threw both bags down to the ground, pulled himself through the hole then slid down the water pipe, his colleague close behind.

It took all of five minutes to get their joints back into working order after being in the cramped space for so long. They both put on the coveralls and the headgear of airport cleaners that they had kept in their bags, and began walking towards the building opposite. The area was quieter than they had anticipated. A single engine plane taxied past them, blowing the heavy drizzle into their faces. Rounding the corner of the building they saw that it was a long open fronted hangar, in which a number of planes were sheltered. Looking from that angle they recognised the area into which they had taxied on their arrival. Michael saw that the Navajo was just where he had left it.

"There she is Hank, right where we parked her."

Apart from an airport catering truck passing by, the area was like a tomb. The rain became much heavier.

"Now what?" asked Michael?

"In for a penny, in for a pound," said Hank. He entered the hangar from the rear, took out the binoculars and scanned the whole of the surrounding area wishing that he had a night scope as rain covered the lenses. Unless there was someone who may be hidden behind a window, he could see nothing out of the ordinary. He walked along the rear wall and came to a workbench. On it was the usual assortment of old and broken tools: a screwdriver that had been used as a paint stirrer, bits of wire, a flashlight with a broken lens and a half roll of black electrician's tape, which he instantly put into his pocket along with a full box of matches. His foot caught something on the floor that went spinning under a nearby aircraft. It was a box knife, which he also pocketed. He picked up one of the larger coils of wire and went back to Michael who stood inside the hangar sheltering from the driving rain, which had now become torrential.

"Got the keys ready?" he asked. Michael held them up by the tag, jingling them.

"Well, what are we waiting for? I'll go first, you wait until I signal the all clear. There's no sense in both of us getting shot — besides I can't fly," he added with a grin, grabbing the keys and disappearing into the dismal rainy night.

Michael suddenly felt scared. An involuntary shiver ran through his whole body as he remembered the whine of bullets earlier. He had stood in the hanger for a full five minutes having seen the shadow of Hank's feet from the other side of the Navajo. He looked at his watch as the seconds ticked by, waiting for a signal, but what kind of signal? There's a flashlight in the plane, but he won't know where it is, he thought. He looked at his watch. Seven minutes had elapsed. Come on, Hank! What the hell's keeping you? He picked up both bags and began to walk towards the plane anyway, rain driving into his face making it almost impossible to see ahead.

"Psst, Psst, over here Michael," he heard the whispered words from his cohort. He followed the sounds with his eyes and saw the door of a nearby plane open. He ran across, and climbed up sitting next to Hank in the twin engine Cessna. Hank had slid the window open and was watching the Navajo from the pilot's seat.

"What's the big idea?" asked Michael.

"Are we going to steal this one?"

"Well not exactly, more like we'll borrow its identity. Your idea of changing the numbers with tape was good, but how about we use the actual identification number, and call sign. Look, they're both blue. To the average person, they look alike from a distance. Yours has square windows, this one has oval," said Hank. Looking at the instrument panel Michael said:

"We only have to change two letters and one number. Let's get started. We need tape and a knife first, though," he added.

Hank passed the items across with a smug grin. They hopped out and started work immediately on each side of the Navajo's tail, the heavy rain not making things any easier. The new number AVR50 meant changing DG and 2 of the Navajo's ADG 20. They took one side each, working feverishly, replacing both sets of figures with electrician's black tape, and looking around for the slightest sign of any trouble.

By the time they had finished, they were both soaked through to the skin. They climbed back into the Cessna using the rear door. Looking around the large cabin space, Michael spotted a pile of clothes and a number of towels stacked neatly at the back of the fuselage. Stripping down to their underwear, they dried themselves on the towels and put on a pair of slacks each, and were able to find a couple of sweaters.

"I wouldn't like to argue with the guy who owns this one," muttered Hank. His sweater reached to his knees and the sleeves were a good six inches past his hands. After a spot of light humour, both faces became serious when they looked across at the Navajo, rain pouring from her fuselage. Her new decals looked less than professional, but would not be noticed from a distance. The big unspoken question they both shared.... Has the plane been tampered with?

"OK, what next?" asked Michael.

"I think that we have to make a few checks first before we risk our lives unduly," Hank replied. "I know what the device looked like that was put on the car and we can easily check all the control cables. As for small explosive devices and contaminated fuel, well, that's anyone's guess.

"The fuel's not a problem. Father always insisted on having total security on the fuel input. Like him, no person other than me supervises loading avgas. It's always been that way. Besides, I know precisely how much was on board when we left. As it happens, we could do with more."

"Not if we leave here and make a stop elsewhere," said Hank.

"What exactly do you have in mind?"

"A spot of subterfuge maybe? Let's say we leave here and make a long detour. That way we'll draw any attention away from us if we don't go directly for England. Here, pass me those charts across will you?" While he looked at the charts, Michael had his nose into an atlas locating French airfields.

A couple of hours earlier, David Steel had crossed the light aircraft area, searching for Michael's plane. He had gone into an open hangar and spoken with a mechanic who was working on the wheels of a small Piper. The man could not or would not help him locate the aircraft. Eventually he had found the location of the tower and gone in there to ask for assistance. He had been amazed at the security: he'd been asked for ID and eventually escorted off the premises then taken back into the main airport building.

Meanwhile Boris Kiev moved around the inside of the hangar at the helicopter section of Orly Airport. He began to pull up the zipper of the body bag containing the remains of the American chopper pilot. Just before closing it completely, he pulled down the eyelids of the corpse with the first and second finger of his right hand.

"Sorry comrade, you know too much, you've seen too much, you were too much of a danger to us. As you Americans say, that's how the cookie crumbles." he smiled at his own humour, then frowned as he remembered the salutary and sarcastic comments he'd received from the English cop. He pulled the zipper closed. Opening the door of the aircraft the Russian bundled the body into the rear section, stretching it across the floor, then closing the door. He slid back the door of the hanger, just as the VHF crackled into life.

"Control, this is Three. I still have no sighting. Do you want me to continue surveillance, come back?"

"Have you located the plane yet, Three?"

"Negative to that Control, though I did see the blonde guy go into the control tower. Security put him back into the main building, over."

"Good work, Three, continue surveillance. Report every five minutes, out."

"Roger Control. Three standing by, out."

"Two report."

"Nothing at gas centre, nobody's been here to refuel. Two standing by, sir."

"Control, this is Four, you copy?"

"Go ahead Four."

"Roger on blonde in main building. He just met male passenger off flight from Madrid, over."

"Tail and report Four."

"Roger, Four out."

Kiev called for help and had the helicopter pulled out of the hangar, slid the big doors across and then climbed into the machine. As the engines started he received clearance to fly over to the refueling area.

Michael was first to venture across to the Navajo. He approached the plane cautiously, checking the doors and hatches for any sign of forced entry. He put the key into the lock of the main entry hatch, which hinged upwards from the bottom, lifting it sufficiently to jump up without dropping the steps. He hoisted his backside onto the floor of the aircraft, swinging his legs up into the cabin.

Sitting in one of the passenger seats, he began to take stock. To the best of his memory nothing seemed to have been moved. The thermos flasks were still on the seat opposite where Hank had left them. His clipboard was where he had left it on the co-pilot seat, his log on the top of it.

There was a tap on the side of the fuselage.

"Psst, it's me," said the voice of Hank. His head came up under the partially open door. He climbed into the cabin and fastened the door shut.

"So far, so good. Does everything seem to be in order? I don't see anything out of place, and I do like everything tidy and in its place."

Michael switched on the plane's radio and also a hand held VHF, while he checked the rudder and flaps. Hank flipped through all the channels on the hand held VHF.

"Good work Three. Continue surveillance. Report every five minutes. Control out."

Michael's head, as he turned, nearly came off his shoulders. Hank sat bolt upright.

"Christ, its Kiev!" said Michael.

"Nothing to report at the gas centre; nobody's been here to refuel. Two standing by, sir." They listened to the remainder of the conversations.

"Where the hell are they then?" asked Michael, peering through the rain outside.

"That rain's a blessing in disguise. If we can't spot them easily, they must be having the same problems Michael."

The main radio in the aircraft then relayed Kiev's request to airport control, for permission to move over to the fuel storage area.

The interior of the plane began to steam up. Hank wiped the windows with the over length sleeves of his borrowed sweater. The rain outside and the presence of their wet clothes and their own body heat added to the condensation.

"I suppose we ought to make a move and get on with our plan," said Michael, his statement somewhat lacking enthusiasm and motivation. He climbed out of the plane and moved around the edges of the buildings until he was almost outside of the main terminal building. Then he spotted exactly what he was looking for. It was a small canteen used by the baggage loaders. He went inside, ordered a cup of coffee, and then went over to the payphone on the wall.

Finding the number for flight control, he proceeded to log a flight plan. His point of reference was the town of Bourges, some 155 miles due south of Paris. He had given all of the details and had written down the waypoints. He was about to thank the controller when two men walked into the canteen. He recognised the larger of the two as one of Sahaed's security men; he did not think he knew the other one.

Michael turned his back as the men went to the counter. By now he had finished his conversation and stood pretending to talk, cupping his hand over the phone's cradle, he waited until the other two looked as though they were well occupied.

He put the phone down, walked to the door and straight into a man coming through it. His coffee went flying. The Frenchman yelled from the heat of the liquid as it hit his face and the cup crashed to the floor. The two men looked round at the disturbance. They saw the back of Michael's head, as he leapt through the door. Both men took off after him as he disappeared into the dark rain-swept night.

He had a good start on Sahaed's men. At first he had run off blindly then realised that without thinking he was heading directly back towards the plane. He veered off to the left, and found himself running towards a large building. He could hear the shouts of the men behind him as he began to tire. A tractor pulling baggage cars swept across his path covering him in water. He jumped between two of the containers, landing on the connection device. He crouched there, rain pouring down the back of his neck. He saw the smaller of the two men holding a radio to his face as the baggage train swept on. Michael looked round and could see his pursuers, both carrying flashlights, now heading back towards the building he had left.

Jumping from the train, he stood in the shadows. It took him seconds to re-establish his bearings, and then he headed of towards the Navajo. Moving cautiously from building to building he stood for a full minute in the open hangar watching his plane for any signs of movement. Either Hank was not there, or he was being overly careful. He crept up to the plane and, as arranged, tapped five times on its fuselage. He did not receive the agreed reply. He resisted his instant reaction to open the door, but followed the advice of the voice in his head: *make yourself scarce*. He moved swiftly from plane to plane, until he reached the comforting shelter of the hanger. He had stood in the shadows for at least a minute. Then his heart nearly came into his mouth.

Without any warning, from behind, an arm was wrapped around his neck. Before he could utter a sound, a hand was clamped tightly across his mouth and nose. He froze, not knowing what to expect next.

"Don't move, keep quiet, it's me," Hank whispered into his left ear as he released Michael.

"Not a sound."

Michael turned and bent forward, supporting himself on the wing of an aircraft, his knees weak from the shock.

"What are you trying to do, give me a damned heart attack?" He whispered hoarsely.

"When I heard the commotion on the radio, I waited a while then came out of the plane looking for you. It's a bloody good job that I did. As soon as I left two men walked the length of the aircraft parks, checking aircraft then went off to the other batch of planes over there. I'm pretty sure that one of them was the MI6 geezer."

Hank held the VHF to his ear. He listened in silence for a while.

"It seems they didn't recognise you and have given up the search," he said to the royal aide, who still looked pale and shaken.

"Are you alright? Are you OK to fly that plane out of here?"

Michael nodded. "I think it's time we made ourselves scarce. Ideally I'd like to wait until at least one other plane moves out."

"That's not very likely on a night like this," said Hank, looking out at the continuing rain as it bounced off the water-covered tarmac. Hank stared into the lake around his feet.

"You know what? We need a diversion. Yep that's exactly what we need." He stood in silent thought for a few seconds, then disappeared into the back of the hangar. He returned carrying a gas can with 'paraffin' written on the side.

"Now, this is what we're going to do. Here's the Navajo, here's the way out to the apron, and this is the fuel area." He drew a diagram in the dust on the wing of the plane next to them in the hanger. "And here's where the short runway starts…….."

Buckingham Palace, London

It had been a long day. London had witnessed scenes beyond comprehension and now, most of the crowds had gone home. Many people had visited pubs and hotels, the majority of which had been packed beyond capacity. The mammoth cleaning up job had already begun in the streets of the capital.

The Queen sat in her study staring down at her desk. A cloud had fallen over the palace — indeed over the whole family. *Damn the woman. Damn her hide. She's even more powerful when she's dead*, she thought to herself. For the first time in her memory she had heard subjects shouting derogatory comments as she and the Duke had passed by following the harmful eulogy given by Princess Anna's brother.

His words had been very damaging to the Royal Family. In answer to a suggestion that the title 'Her Royal Highness' should be given back to the princess in death, he had said from the podium in the Abbey, that taking the title away had made no difference. In fact, quite the contrary, and that in the eyes of the world, Princess Anna was, and still is, royal. The Queen sat in stony silence; she could feel her world crumbling around her. She looked at her hands and imagined she saw the blood of the princess there. One thing she did know for certain: the future of the monarchy was in jeopardy and more so now than ever in its long history. Now she was at a loss at what to do next. She had also heard from her informants that Meadows, the princess's secretary, was asking questions around Paris. *We must cover every angle; we can't be too careful*, the Queen thought to herself.

"We're fighting for survival!" she said aloud.

Orly Airport, Paris

There was a small flicker of light around the wheels of the twin-engine aircraft. At first it was almost invisible. Nobody saw the figure of a man run quickly from the plane as the rains poured down. Then the right side tyre burst alight, flames licking up the strut of the undercarriage igniting the fluid from the hydraulics. Within seconds flames began to burn fiercely inside the cabin. The first explosion went off within minutes, the sound shattering the relative silence of whole area. Soon fire trucks were on the scene, and all hell was let loose.

Other planes were being dragged away from the blazing frame of the ill-fated aircraft as debris flew in all directions. The falling rains helped to reduce the danger from flying sparks. Two or three planes were started up and taxied away hurriedly from the dangerous area. More fire appliances ambulances and police vehicles arrived at the sorry scene further adding to the confusion and chaos

"Orly control, Orly control. This is Cessna Golden Eagle, Alpha Victor Romeo Five Zero, requesting permission to takeoff on scheduled flight to Bourges. I am one hour earlier than logged, due to improving conditions at my destination." Michael spoke in strongly French accented English.

"Stand by Alpha Victor Romeo Five Zero, we have an emergency and have many aircraft holding above. There is a fire on the ground, stand by. Do you need the long runway?"

"That's a negative, tower."

"Take up position for a short take off Golden Eagle."

"Roger tower, standing by."

Michael moved onto the runway as two other aircraft requested permission to take off, and got in line behind the Navajo. He looked through the windshield as the rain poured incessantly down the glass, then through his distorted vision he saw the figure of a man running through the deluge towards the plane.

"Alpha Victor Romeo Five Zero, you are cleared for take off. Climb to one thousand feet, heading one two zero, and maintain until further instructions."

"Roger, Orly control. Alpha Victor Romeo Five Zero commencing take- off to one thousand feet, heading one two zero."

Michael heard the sounds of Hank lifting the partially open door, followed by heavy breathing and groans as he collapsed onto the floor of the plane. There was a thud and the snap of door locks falling into place. The red door warning light went out on the panel indicating that the door was secure. Michael applied the brakes and opened the throttles, completing his final checks before take off. There was a silent prayer on the lips of both men as the Navajo sprang forward fighting against the drag of inches of water under her wheels. He used every bit of the short runway and was still below the normal take off speed, as he lifted the nose and then climbed laboriously. He eased back slightly on the throttles, as the RPMs increased. The plane slowly reached one thousand feet, where he awaited further instructions from the tower to get on course for Bourges.

When Michael looked round Hank was stretched out on the floor between the seats.

"Are you OK back there?" Michael asked

"I'm as right as can be expected in the circumstances. A bit damp though" Hank replied sarcastically.

"That was a hairy few minutes down there you know." Looking back Michael could see no trace of the fire on the ground.

"Now we have to see if our ruse has worked," said Hank as he climbed into the seat behind, sitting sideways as the seat was back to back with Michael's. Looking around him, the sky was pitch black; there was no light to be seen anywhere apart from the distant glow of Paris below.

"Alpha Victor Romeo Five Zero. This is Orly Control. Go to your scheduled flight plan and climb to three thousand feet, heading two one zero. "Roger Orly, three thousand feet, heading two one zero."

"No coffee on this flight," said Hank sarcastically,

"It seems like a year since I ate or drank. What I wouldn't give for a nice cuppa," he said as he settled back into his seat.

"Try and get some shuteye, we'll be in Bourges in just over an hour," said Michael.

"Jesus, shit! Get back on the floor Hank, on the floor right now!" he yelled at the top of his voice. Michael pulled the collar of his sweater up under his ears, at the same time pulling his beret down to his eyebrows. Hank had obeyed and had thrown himself onto the floor between the two rows of facing seats. Michael looked again to his left and saw the shape of the mat black helicopter in the dark. Its navigation lights and strobe flashing seemed dangerously close to his left wing tip. He had also put on the interior cabin lights, making the occupants of the chopper aware that there was only one person aboard the plane. He could not see past the dark tinted windows of the other craft, only the reflection of his own lights. He hoped that whoever was inside the chopper, didn't know the difference between a Cessna Golden Eagle and a Piper Navajo, though that too would be more difficult at night.

He sat uncomfortably for sometime then he relaxed visibly as the helicopter suddenly veered off to the left, disappearing from sight.

"Goddamn it! That was bloody uncomfortable, Hank."

"What the hell was going on man?" A muffled voice asked from the depths.

"That was Sahaed's chopper. He came far too close for comfort. I don't know if they spotted the switch or not

"It looks like Plan B then. Is it all right for me to get up now? This floor's a bit hard on the bones!" Hank said.

"Wait there just a little bit longer; it's better to err on the safe side." As he spoke he pushed the menu buttons on the Northstar GPS as he searched for the alternate waypoint on the satellite navigation system. They had made a contingency plan for such an event. The new heading would take them over the small town of Auxetre, which on the charts had shown a light aircraft field, close to the local church.

The plan was fraught with danger, as they would not be able to communicate with the small airfield without giving their plan to all and sundry on the airwaves. Also to deviate unauthorised from their original flight plan would not only put them into air space that could well be occupied by other traffic, but Orly tower was bound to be onto them very quickly.

"Here goes, Hank," he said as he switched off the autopilot and pressed enter on the Northstar, turning to the new heading. Luckily it was only a few degrees deviation from the original one. The plane began a slight move left heading eastwards. Michael had decided to keep to his existing altitude until they were over the airfield so as not to draw the attention of air traffic control. Then, if the lights were on, he would attempt a landing, if not, well!

"You can get up now Hank. Keep your eyes peeled for any sign of lights and yell if you see anything at all."

"Don't worry, I will," came the prompt reply. The rain clouds beneath them formed a blanket. It was impossible to see any sign of land below. *"Thank God for electronics,"* Hank thought to himself as the plane droned onwards in the darkness.

Orly Heliport, Paris

"Control, we have a negative here, none of the three aircraft matched descriptions or decal numbers we checked, two of them were on course for Bourges, the other went eastwards. Standing by for further instructions."

"Have you sufficient fuel to reach Bourges?" asked Boris Kiev.

"Roger Base, but that would be about the safe limit sir."

"Go there, report to me on a land line when you arrive, Control out."

Meanwhile, David Steel phoned Kevin Reilly's apartment. There was neither reply nor voice mail. He had also been onto a French secret service contact recalling an outstanding debt. He had obtained the destinations of the first three light aircraft to leave Orly after the fire.

"I can't raise him at all. Either he doesn't want to be contacted, or there's some kind of problem here," he said to the other MI6 man standing at the small charter company desk, who'd already requested a flight to Bourges, which seemed the more likely of the three flight plans.

"Yes sir, we can get you to Bourges first thing in the morning, leaving here at 7:30am. We have two seats on a six-seat plane," said the young man behind the desk.

"That's no use, we have to go tonight."

"I'm afraid that's out of the question, sir."

"How far is it to Bourges?" asked the agent.

"Around three hundred, three fifty miles," replied the young man.

"We'll pay whatever you want!" said Steel.

"We'd love to take your money sir, but the only plane available is being serviced right now for the morning flight." Steel and his colleague walked away from the desk.

"Hang on one moment, sir. I may know someone who will get you there," said the young man, lifting the phone to his ear.

The Arab, who had earlier booked into The Majestic Palace Hotel in Paris with his female accomplice, sat nearby wearing leather motorcycle gear, his eyes and ears alert to everything that went on around him. As Steel and his colleague went back towards the desk clerk, he stood and walked across to stand in line behind them. He listened to the charter company assistant as he gave Steel his alternative.

The Navajo over France

A loud buzzing noise jolted Hank from his half sleep.

"Well, we're over the town of Auxetre. Now comes the hairy part," Michael said, as he turned off the autopilot. "Here we go then," The small hand on the altimeter began to spin quickly in an anti-clockwise direction as he took the plane down.

While Hank had dozed off, Orly Control had attempted to make contact, but Michael had foxed them by switching his radio on and off, after every two words, as he'd replied to them. Praying that they would assume he was having trouble, hoping they would watch his heading regarding any other traffic hazards. He did not hear anymore transmission from them.

Clouds began engulfing them. It was a bad feeling knowing that another plane could come out of the cloud at any time. After what seemed an age, along with some serious fingernail biting, the cloud cover thinned out. Hank saw the welcome glow of lights from the town below them. He began his descent in a wide spiral until they were at one thousand feet. They both saw the runway lights, way ahead, at the same time and were so elated that they both spoke at the same time.

Michael brought the plane around then lined it up on the approach. Still at a thousand feet, he needed to lose some height quickly, as he switched off the left engine feathering the propeller.

"Aircraft approaching Auxetre airfield, please identify yourself.......... Unidentified aircraft on approach to Auxetre airfield please identify your... Unidentified aircraft if you are experiencing radio trouble and you copy, you are on course for correct landing. We have sufficient runway for most light aircraft. We will have our limited emergency equipment quickly available." The same message was then repeated in French.

"Hold on tight, it's a long time since I did a single engine landing," said Michael, he had full flaps and gear down as the runway came rushing up at the plane a little too quickly for his liking, he flared the plane by lifting the nose as the main wheels touched down very firmly. Hank was strapped into one of the rear seats. After one slight and embarrassing bounce, Michael had the nose wheel down as they were shooting along the sparsely lit runway. He brought the plane to taxi speed then turned round towards three oncoming vehicles, drawing the aircraft to a halt.

Hank already had the door catches undone. He lifted up the door and put down the short steps. Michael stooped as he climbed out into the glare of headlamps.

They were met by a pleasant faced man in his late forties. They spoke to each other in French as a truck came over and towed the plane slowly towards the airfield buildings.

Hank followed the two men across to some offices where they were given coffee. The Frenchman greeted Hank in perfect English, and then continued his conversation with Michael in French. After a short while they were driven to a nearby village where they were shown to a couple of comfortable rooms at a local pension, which also had a small bistro.

The pleasant faced man bade them good night. They sat at the bar amongst locals.

"Let me get you a drink," said Michael.

"Best news I've heard all day. I need a large scotch."

"Me too," said a smiling pilot. Michael beckoned to the patron.

"I'll see if we can get some food as well."

"Bloody good idea, my stomach thinks my throat's been cut. Then maybe you'll tell me exactly what's going on," said Hank.

The Patron found a bottle of Johnny Walker Black Label Scotch. They both drank a very large and very neat one. Then they ate paté and toast followed by boeuf bourguignonne, with a fine bottle of Burgundy. Relaxed, they sat in a quiet corner, sipping the remainder of the bottle, accompanied by some French brie and crackers.

"So tell me," said Hank, "I'm all ears."

"While you were dozing I took a transducer out of the radio. I broke one of the connectors, and put the broken part back. Then I simply turned the engine off. While you opened the door, I turned off the emergency fuel valve to the left engine."

"Won't they know that those things were done intentionally?"

"Why would any pilot in his right mind switch off an engine then disable his only means of communication simultaneously? I don't think so, do you?"

Michael grinned as he looked across at his partner in crime.

"I suppose you're right, but won't they look at the plane?"

"No, I told them not to touch a thing until daylight. And just in case we have any other snoopers, I asked them to put the plane inside for the night. They're all fliers, they understand."

"What happens if they notice the decal changes?"

"Now that's the million dollar question! Let's turn in. We've had a hectic day, and both need the rest," said Michael.

Hank relaxed in his bed, cognizant of the recent repairs to his head, his mind going over the day's events. He knew though they had gained some respite, he was also aware that it was temporary. Right now powers much greater than they, were searching for them as they lay there. His mind went back over the detail of the Interpol lab reports. Though he was still somewhat confused, the pieces were slowly beginning to fall into place. He drifted off into a sound sleep.

Bourges Airfield, Champagne, France

There had been some slight rain earlier in the evening, but now the weather was clear. The helicopter had landed near the buildings belonging to the local flying club.

Across in the main part of the airfield, a rather busy little place, a good number of older charter cargo planes carried on business. Two ancient DC3s and an old Fokker Friendship stood near hangars. The flying club was a busy social centre. That night the bar was very hectic. Some twenty to thirty old by-planes were visiting from Holland — the Dutch Tiger Moth club was staying in town for two days.

Normally, the appearance of a stranger would not go unnoticed. But tonight the whole area was filled with foreigners speaking in many tongues. The two-man crew of the helicopter sat at a corner table next to a dance floor. David Steel was sitting at the bar with a fellow agent. They had just returned from a fruitless search for Michael Meadow's plane.

The helicopter crew had earlier completed the same exercise and reported their findings to Kiev. They had been instructed to await further orders from the colonel.

Meanwhile the Arab motorcyclist sat in Orly airport awaiting the departure of the early morning six-seat charter plane to Bourges.

Hank had awakened Michael at 4:30am. They had left money for the room, borrowed a couple of cycles and made the airfield by five o'clock. Unfortunately, the hangar door had been locked, but thanks to the more devious part of Hank's training, it had not proved to be too much of a problem.

"England here we come!" shouted Michael above the sound as both engines roared into life. Hank, who sat in the seat behind the pilot's position, tapped Michael on the shoulder pointing to the headset he wore.

"What's up?" asked Michael, after switching on his phones.

"I'm afraid that you're not quite correct in your assumption, Mon Capitan. Please set course for the southern coast of France. Marseille would be an ideal spot," said the policeman, passing a chart across, already circled in pencil. Michael turned with a grin on his face; his expression did not contain too much surprise.

"I had a feeling there was something else afoot. You're telling me that we have to reach Marseille without air traffic control permission and with hardly any fuel in the tanks?"

"Is that possible?"

"Not on your life! The fuel is imperative and also the southern part of France is extremely busy air space. Lots of private light aircraft, at least three busy small- to mid-size airports and, in addition, there's a French Air force base there. Afraid not old chap — not possible this time."

"I suppose we still have the changed registration numbers and they should be of some help."
Hank added tentatively, sounding somewhat despondent.

"Don't you think you ought to tell me exactly what it is that you have in mind? I'm just as keen on finding Princess Anna's killers as you are."

"Yes, I suppose you're right," Hank said with a shrug, but quickly changed the subject to the matter of fuel. Michael turned off the engines and they both left the aircraft. Hank worked yet again on the more devious part of his skills. He took the lock off the fuel supply pipe, which, by a stroke of good fortune, was hand pumped direct from a large tank above ground, he also disconnected the actual gauge so that their self service would go unrecorded.

Meanwhile the Sahaed jet purred along on its flight to Nice in Southern France. The only occupants aboard were Sahaed himself and his chief of security, Colonel Boris Kiev. Sahaed had just collected Kiev at Paris's Charles De Gaulle Airport on his way back from his son's funeral service. They were heading for the Arab's villa in Monaco.

"I want a complete debrief on every aspect of the last few days, ending with the funerals. I have a lot of questions for which, I trust, you can supply the answers." The Russian looked across as Sahaed spoke, knowing full well that there were many answers that he did not as yet possess. Kiev had never given over half let alone all the information he possessed, to anyone, ever.

"Where are the two troublesome Englishmen?" Sahaed asked. "They seem to have temporarily vanished."

"We had them at the airport in Paris where they logged a flight plan for Bourges. I believe they set up a distraction by way of a fire at the fuel centre, then slipped out during the panic."

"Do you mean that they took off in their plane?"

"Well... er, yes, I believe they did," said an embarrassed Kiev.

"And where do you suppose they are right now?"

"I am assuming that they are either on their way to England, or somewhere in France preparing to leave for England, sir."

"And suppose that your assumptions are wrong, then what, colonel, then what?! It's not the first time that this London bobby has made a fool out of you all. I don't know how you managed to handle some of the world's top agents if you can't find one damned English policeman.

The Arab turned away opening his attaché case, signalling that the conversation was ended.

Kiev looking black as thunder, the muscles on the side of his jaw flexing in silent rage as the attendant light overhead began to flash. He stood up and walked forward, his broad shoulders stooping in the cramped cabin space. Pushing his head into the compact flight deck he spoke to the pilot, then put on a set of headphones that were handed to him.

"Roger Marignane, Alpha Victor Romeo five zero, out and standing by on frequency for Marseilles beacon." He heard Michael's voice, as a grin broke out across his face.

"They are somewhere below us right now, heading for Marignane airport outside of Marseilles, said the pilot to a smirking Kiev.

Interpol Offices Paris, two days earlier

Kevin Reilly sat with the Chief of Interpol. At first the police commissioner was not very forthcoming.

"I'm here at the direct request of the CIA chief. The President of the United States himself, in turn, instructed him. We are working closely with the Brits on this one. Any information, no matter how small, could be of enormous assistance, commissioner."

"We, too, have massive pressure from the President of France himself. He wants this whole affair brought to a head, leaving France blameless. One of my inspectors, Pierre Lacoste, worked with an inspector from the Royalty Protection Squad. They came up with some findings, but I'm not sure what they amounted to as they were contained in a report from our laboratory — a bunch of chemical results. I'll arrange for you to meet with him right away."

The Frenchman picked up his phone and issued his orders to Lacoste.

Later that day, Reilly met with the inspector, then afterwards spent a fruitless couple of hours trying to make contact with David Steel. He had no idea what the results of the report in his possession meant. As the French inspector had said, they are only meaningful to the person who called for the tests and report and only he would know what to compare them to.. He assumed that it was of importance and therefore communicated through official channels for the British agent to make contact urgently.

French Airspace

The Navajo droned onwards towards its new destination with a record-ed flight plan.

"Michael, do you think we could pull a similar stroke to the one we pulled en-route for Bourges?"

"You mean a little deviation from course Hank? I don't see why not. Half the world must have heard us by now. After what you've told me, assuming you're right in your assumptions, I'm convinced that these people will stop at nothing," Michael said, resignedly.

Having already anticipated Hank's request, he had found a tiny airfield in a village called Brignoles some thirty miles east of their destination and only ten miles or so north of the town of Toulon and the coast. They were blissfully unaware that some three thousand feet above them was Kiev's crew in the helicopter. Not only up there, but knowing of their presence and destination.

At that same moment Kevin Reilly was speeding, by agency chopper, towards the airfield at Bourges, as indeed was the Arab motorcyclist in the small charter plane. He was cramped into the rear of six seats, elbows tucked in, holding a mat black BMW pannier case on his lap containing his explicit instructions to tidy up all loose ends.

Some of those very loose ends had been airborne for over half an hour and still on their original course.

"That's Avignon down there. I think it's about time to change course." Michael said as he fiddled with the buttons on the GPS, and then hit the new waypoint for Brignoles. Switching off the autopilot he turned steadily to the left following the new heading.

AnwarAl-Sahaed sat in his ultra modern villa overlooking Monaco. Though the extent of the grounds by comparison to his other homes was small, the villa was magnificent; the views stunning. He looked down across the packed marina area, lined with its array of mega yachts with the famous casino in the background — the absolute epitome of a play-ground for the super rich.

Boris Kiev sat in a small room in the staff quarters at the rear of the building. He stared intently at the wall, deep in thought. His concentration was broken by the low warble of the phone.

"Kiev. Yes, sir, I'll be there right away." A short while later he knocked on the door of Sahaed's sitting room and was told to enter.

"Sit down, colonel," Sahaed pointed to a chair. We really have to do something about this interfering policeman and Princess Anna's secretary. We don't need them poking into our affairs." Bearing in mind the circumstances, the Arab did look somewhat relaxed. He still maintained the cocky attitude; still had the arrogant tilt to his head.

"Colonel, you told me that the Steel fellow had gone to Bourges. why would the MI6 man be interested in going there? I would have thought that as far as he is concerned, now Princess Anna is dead, what more does he need?"

"I think, sir, that he has it in mind that maybe the inspector knows more than he ought to. If he thinks the inspector can prove they're involved in the deaths of the couple, then he will have to silence both Marlin and the secretary, Meadows." Kiev paused. "I also have to inform you, sir, that the CIA man, Reilly, has been snooping around the Interpol people in Paris. You'll remember that one of their inspectors by the name of Lacoste, is quite a friend of the English cop." He waited for a retort from the Arab, but none was forthcoming. "I have a sneaking feeling that Marlin lifted a few things from the apartments used by the couple, then had Interpol's laboratory test whatever he found. I knew it was risky letting him go over the rooms, but it would have been difficult to do otherwise. I did supervise the initial cleaning up operation personally." Sahaed leaned forward conspiratorially.

"What about the Palace Mafia in all this? Where are they? Do you have information on their whereabouts?" asked Sahaed smugly.

"They employed the two Arab specialists, a real top class team. The woman was handling their attempts at the tunnel. She was placed to shoot the couple if the car had come out of the tunnel, but we terminated her. As for the remaining male team member, I think we shall see him arrive at Bourges sometime today. You see sir; he too cannot allow the British cop and his partner to live, just in case they're able to point a finger at the Palace. He was spotted earlier at The Majestic, and yesterday was seen at the airport in Paris hanging around the small air charter companies at the same time as Steel, the MI6 agent."

"So really, Colonel, what you're saying is that one or other of the two groups involved will terminate the two of them anyway?" He said, smirking.

"Yes sir, with extreme prejudice," Kiev continued:"In keeping with your instruction to ascertain exactly what they do know, we must get to them first, and squeeze every last drop of information from them, but at the same time we need to know what the CIA man got from Interpol. I do possess some very impressive powers of persuasion, sir, believe me!" The Arab looked down admiringly at the colonels massive hands, nodding in agreement.

The Russian continued: "We can be sure if Reilly did get anything of interest, he'll show up looking for his MI6 cohort. Those two agencies are as thick as thieves; always were." The big Russian looked up with the expression of an afterthought on his face. "It seems we do have one other bonus: it looks as though the Israeli contribution may have gone back to the Promised Land." He seemed relieved by his own words.

"It's imperative that we find them first. I know Mr Reilly, the CIA agent, like the back of my own hand. I have a team standing by at Bourges airfield, and I am in full possession of the movements and destination of the two Brits." Sahaed stood and walked along the window surveying the colourful panoramic vista, hands on his hips. Turning to the colonel he smoothed his thinning hair with his hand, his brow furrowed.

"So! It seems that everyone wants to catch up with our friend the inspector and his sidekick. What do you think prompted the two of them to come down this way rather than return to England? You don't think that they're susp......" The colonel cut off his boss in mid word.

"There are a number of questions that I intend to get answered, sir, before I can answer yours." Kiev paced back and forth irritably like a caged animal, and then stood perfectly still, staring into space. The Arab broke his concentration slapping his hand noisily on the side of his knee.

"Colonel, I wish to make a visit to Toulon in the next day or so. Be sure that the helicopter is available." Sahaed waved his hand in dismissal of the Russian. Kiev nodded and walked out of the room.

Brignoles Airfield, Southern France

Michael brought the Navajo down onto the tarmac runway in a textbook landing. He taxied across towards the only two buildings in sight. There were no noticeable signs of life as both men climbed out of the aircraft.

Walking towards a van parked near the larger building, Hank noticed an English registration plate on its rear. On the side it bore the name 'Hertz Van Rentals'.

Michael walked across and tried the door to the building, which was locked. He walked round to the side trying unsuccessfully to peer through the darkened windows. The smaller building, no larger than a single domestic garage, was also securely locked.

Hank opened his jacket pocket and lit a cigarette. He leaned against the fender of the van.

"Now what?" asked Michael.

"We seem to be a long way from civilization and it could be quite a long walk to the nearest village," said Hank.

It was still early morning — a little too early for the general public to be up and about yet. They couldn't leave the plane unattended. If someone were to come along and see it there, it could cause a stir and maybe get onto the airwaves giving away their position. They decided to sit it out and wait.

"We aren't in any desperate hurry; we have some time to spare," said Hank, "and anyway, the wait will give us the chance to go back over our plans thoroughly; make sure that we agree and understand exactly what has to be done." Michael sat down on an upturned oilcan, Hank on the steps of the Navajo.

"You did say that you were going to bring me up to date on what you are up to, and all that you know." Hank walked over to the small building as Michael spoke.

Bourges Airfield, the same morning

The three-man helicopter crew, as instructed, spent the night in the chopper, taking turns to keep watch as the others tried to sleep in the confined space available. One plane had arrived early that morning and disgorged its seven passengers before departing with cargo and one other passenger aboard.

David Steel had gone downtown earlier and had returned with a small Renault van in which he and his accomplice had kept vigil through the night. They were currently checking every building by daylight, paying little attention to the helicopter that landed and parked behind the make-do airport terminal, nor did they take note of the Arab who had landed earlier and now followed their every move.

Kevin Reilly climbed down from the noisy machine carrying a brief case with one hand and holding down what was left of his fast thinning hair with the other as the rotor blades continued to turn. He made his way over to the main building. His arrival was instantly relayed by telephone to Boris Kiev in Monaco.

Reilly looked around the almost empty terminal, and then walked back to the door where he stood looking out into the dull misty morning. Two men entered the building and sat down close to where Reilly stood looking through the window.

"Where the hell is that Limey asshole," The American thought to himself. He turned and walked towards the men's room.

David Steel looked at his watch.

"Those bastards seem to have disappeared into thin air. Jesus, look at the time. Kevin Reilly should be here soon. Let's get over to the main building," he said to the other man. A helicopter took off as they walked across the tarmac. They entered the deserted terminal building. A second helicopter took off as Steel looked impatiently out of the window. He recognised it and the registration number, as the one owned by Anwar Sahaed.

"There's someone coming."

"What?" said Michael as his head came out of the plane's doorway.
The sound of a car's engine in the distance pierced the silence of the early
morning countryside and seemed to silence the singing of the birds. As it
came nearer, it had the unmistakable sound of a car with muffler problems. The bright yellow Volkswagen Beetle came into view, trundled
straight across the runway and headed for the larger of the two buildings.
The passenger door opened letting out a pretty, curly-haired young
woman, followed by a fresh faced man in his early thirties, struggling
gamely to climb past the lowered front seat. He pulled out three packages,
went around to the driver's door, gave the man money, then the Beetle
chugged off.

The couple walked towards the hangar.

"Morning. Lovely day. Nice plane you have there," said the young man
cheerily to Hank, as he passed. He took out keys and opened the hangar
doors revealing a single engine light aircraft. He walked across to the
rental van carrying a fan belt. Lifting the hood, he began to install the
belt.

"Having a spot of bother?" asked Michael as he walked across.

"You could say so," said the young man, standing up from the van.

"My name's Phil and that's Jane," he said pointing, to the young
woman.

"Hi," she shouted from inside the hangar.

"I'm Michael, and this is my colleague, Hank. You live in these parts?"

"No, we're from England. We've just had an absolute run of bad luck,"
said Phil. "One thing on top of another. We come down here every year
with the parents, bringing the plane and the boat. We had a crew bring the
boat to Toulon and we came down in the plane. Jane and I hit fuel problems and had to drop in here. My father eventually came down with parts
in the rental van, then that damn thing broke down too. Dad went to the
village. We should be out of here today — with a bit of luck that is."

"We had a similar problem early this morning," said Michael.

"We're en-route for Marseilles. One engine was missing badly, so I
dropped in here. I seem to have cleared the problem now though"

"Don't I know your face?" the man said to Hank.

"I don't think I've had the pleasure."

"Where are you from, anyway?" asked Michael, quickly changing the
subject.

"We live in Hamble, near Southampton."

"Who owns the hangar, Phil?" Hank asked.

"It belongs to an old couple who also own the local bar-cum-cafe in the village."

"I'd like to talk to them and rent the building for a few days, until I can get my man out here to check the engines properly."

"I'm sure they would help. Why don't you go into the village with Jane? She's going to collect Dad and drive down to the coast while I fly the plane. If you wait, I'll get the plane out then we can push yours into the hangar. Here, take the key to the padlock."

Within minutes they were in the van shaking and rattling down the narrow country lane. The young Englishman, Phil, had taken off in his plane a couple of moments before.

After a pleasant meeting with the owner of the airstrip, Michael paid a week's rental for the hangar.

"Where are you driving to Jane?" Hank asked as they walked from the café.

"Dad and I are meeting Phil at Toulon where the boat is moored, then we'll sail round to Nice. Why, do you need a lift somewhere?"

"If you'd kindly drop us off in Toulon, we could kill a few days while they come over and fix the plane."

"Hop in, let's go then," Jane said cheerily.

"Dad, this is Hank and Michael, the chaps I was telling you about." Jane said to Phil's father.

Bourges Airfield

Steel sat around for another half hour before he began to realise that all was not right. He had seen two helicopters take off, one after the other. He walked across to the control room where the man inside at the desk was talking continually to various aircraft. Steel stood and waited for a break in the conversations, which came after some ten minutes.

"What can I do for you?" asked the air traffic controller.

"I was waiting for a friend to arrive by helicopter. He was coming in from Paris, supposedly about an hour ago. The machine is owned by the United States Government."

"Yes, that flight did come in about an hour ago." The operator's fingers clattered on the keyboard of the computer.

"Actually it was fifty minutes ago, to be precise."

"Who would know if anyone got off the aircraft?" asked Steel.

"Go over to the main terminal, ask for Michele, he will know. He takes care of arrivals. 'Go ahead Bravo Charlie Six, this is Bourges, repeat this is Bourges'...." David Steel left the control room.

Michele informed him that the chopper had arrived and that a man answering Kevin Reilly's description got off and went into the terminal building carrying only an attaché case. He and his agency colleague then searched the whole area without finding any trace of the American.

Earlier, Reilly had walked into the men's room, put his case on the floor and was just about to relieve himself when he felt the sudden jab of a hard metal object, thrust without finesse into his kidneys. "Don't try anytheeng seely Meester Cee I yay," snapped the small Arab.

Reilly spun to his right, the handgun struck him over the ear and he fell to the floor, unconscious. The two men dragged him out of a rear door, which led into an alley way filled with garbage cans, where he was handcuffed. In seconds he regained his senses and was dragged to his feet by a very large man.

"Do yerself a favour mi old mate, and don't give Ali here an excuse to blow yer away, cos he won't 'esitate." The big man spoke with a London Cockney accent, as he unlocked one of Reilly's hands and fastened the bracelet to his own wrist.

"Now cam on Guv, unless you want somefing worse than a mild 'edache I suggest yer wawk across to the 'elicopter normal like."

Reilly's case was put into his cuffed hand as he half staggered towards the waiting chopper. He was pushed through the rear door; the Arab's small beady eyes never left him until he sat between the two of them in a rear seat. He heard the pilot checking for clearance to leave and saw the agency chopper take off above them for the return trip to Paris. The engines began to whine and the rotors began to turn. He could feel the hot sticky blood that dampened his shirt collar.

The helicopter lifted from the ground. As it turned and took off, he saw the figure of David Steel and another man walking towards the terminal building. He seemed to look directly at the aircraft, but the windows were too darkly tinted for anyone to see inside.

The City of Toulon

The ride from Brignoles to Toulon, though short, was quite a painful experience. They had both sat in the rear of the rental van, Michael atop a cardboard box; Hank perched on the wheel arch. He had picked up from the floor an old copy of the London Daily Telegraph. Seventy five percent of the publication covered the funeral of Princess Anna. He put the paper into his bag, closing the zipper. Jane dropped them off on the oceanfront, alongside the great expanse of harbour.

"I hope you get the plane fixed soon," said Jane.

"Thanks very much for all your help. Tell Phil I said thanks." Michael and Hank waved as she drove away.

"That's the police inspector who used to protect Princess Anna. I met him on a number of occasions at polo club matches," said Jane's father-in-law. "I wonder what they are really doing down here."

"I've met the father-in-law before," said Hank as they walked along the quay.

"He's a polo supporter. I think he recognised me too, but I don't think it's of any import though."

"Not really, Hank. Let's find somewhere to stay for a couple of nights. How much money do we have left?"

"Can we afford the luxury?" asked Hank with a smile.

"I always carry a supply of different currencies in the plane. I brought all of the francs, some marks, and a few pesetas. I also have pounds and quite a few dollars, so we should be fine."

"You know something? You'd make someone a very good secretary Michael!" said Hank. They walked off laughing, heading towards the centre of the city, wearing their baseball caps and jackets.

Toulon is a very busy port, as well as being one of the largest naval bases in France. It also serves as the base for a large fishing fleet and has massive shipbuilding and repair yards. The harbour has five principal basins: the eastern part is used by merchant shipping and the western portion by the French Navy. The centre sports a private yacht area.

The city has an old section with narrow crooked cobbled streets, and a new quarter with handsome avenues and large public buildings. Michael and Hank found accommodation at an old inn in the old section, which seemed to be used only by merchant seamen. It was tucked away down an ancient narrow street. They walked back towards the centre of the city, wondering if they would ever find their way through the maze of streets.

"Well that's the first part of the plan completed. We're here unan-nounced and as far as I can see, not seen and not followed; here in secret, so let's try and keep it that way." They sat in a bar on the quay opposite the private yacht basin.

"Now the fun starts. Where do we go next? What are we looking for? How do we prove those secretly kept suspicions, whatever they are?" Michael said with a facetious tone in his voice

"Whoa, slow down, one step at a time," said Hank cutting across Michael as he spoke. "First, we need some form of transport. I saw a place selling used motorbikes further along the waterfront. Why don't we start there?" Their late lunch finished, they walked along the busy quay.

After some extended haggling, thanks again to Michael's excellent French and the strength of the American dollar in Europe, they left astride a powerful Kawasaki 750, this time with Hank at the controls.

"Part of my training old chap," he'd said nonchalantly as he'd thrown his leg over the machine and gone for a test run earlier.

They rode west along the coast road towards Marseille. The Northern part of Toulon was surrounded by hills, which were the sites of many ancient fortifications and private estates, some equally as daunting as the seventeenth century ramparts of Toulon. Reaching the outskirts they followed the signs for Marseille airport, which was ten miles further west at Marignane.

They pulled into the main airport entry. They had cajoled the salesman into including two full face helmets with drop visors, more for camouf-lage than for safety. They drove towards the private plane area. After a complete search they could find no trace of either the Sahaed jet or the helicopter. They retraced their steps to Toulon. Driving east along the coast road they followed the sign to Hyeres Airport, a smaller airport serving the Toulon area, and the French navy, situated on the Isles of Hyeres. Here, after a full search, they found no traces of Sahaed's air-craft. A search of the private marinas proved equally fruitless.

Driving back towards Toulon, Michael was starting to get the hang of being a pillion passenger, as Hank banked the bike from side to side through the long curves of the coast road. They came out of one particu-larly sharp bend and something shone on the perspex of Michael's visor. He looked up into the sun and saw the shadow of a low flying aircraft, as it blocked the light for a split second. He turned and saw the rear of a black helicopter heading out towards Hyeres Airport in the direction they had just left. He tapped Hank on the shoulder, flipped up his visor, and yelled for him to stop the bike. Hank pulled over.

"What's up? I was just beginning to enjoy the ride."

"I think I saw Sahaed's chopper go out to the airport."

"Let's go! What are we waiting for?" Hank spun the bike around. The Japanese engine screamed down the road.

Hyeres Airport, Toulon

The white convertible Mercedes was parked on the apron off the runway. The sound of an approaching helicopter became louder as the sleek black bird came into view. It was flying quickly then slowed to a hover above the car. The sports car was driven off to the left, pulling up next to other cars. The aircraft followed then landed some thirty feet away, rotors still spinning. A figure got out of the car, and stooping ran across to the helicopter then jumped quickly into the front passenger seat of the aircraft, slamming the door. The chopper took off, gaining height rapidly, then sped off to the north.

Kevin Reilly sat in the rear between the Arab and the big Englishman. He instantly recognised the rear view of his old enemy Colonel Boris Kiev. He could not ignore the cold shudder that coursed through his body at that moment. There had been no time to get rid of the information in his attaché case: a series of DNA lab reports. Another expert could soon decipher them.

Reilly knew he was in deep trouble. Kiev turned and stared him in the eyes, a cold deathly look with no traces of sympathy. His thoughts raced ahead of him. *Where in the hell is that goddamned Englishman when I need him? And if ever I needed anybody I reckon it's round about now.* He turned and looked straight into the dark bottomless eyes of the Arab. *Well Kevin, you've got out of a few tight spots in your life, but I don't fancy your chances this time,* he thought to himself. He looked out the window as the aircraft raced towards the hills.

Bourges Airport

After a thorough search of the whole area, Steel and his colleague could find no trace of Reilly or any evidence that he had been there, other than further confirmation from the Frenchman, Michele. The agent stood staring at the floor, his mind dissecting every angle, when he became aware of whistling.

A sweeping brush caught his foot as an old man swept the floor beneath him, whistling as he went by. After a brief conversation the cleaner remembered seeing a man answering Reilly's description enter the men's room, and also seeing two men follow him. He did not see them leave; out of interest Steel went into the toilets. They were unoccupied, and the rear door was open. The cleaner thought no more of the issue. Steel gave the surprised man a fifty-franc note. He and the other agent went out into the rear alley. It was impossible to tell whether a struggle had taken place as the area was a total mess and had obviously not been cleared for a long time.

There were now two men back in the control room. The man Steel had talked to earlier was preparing to leave, his replacement was already at the desk.

"I wonder if I could have a couple of minutes of your time?" he said to the controller.

"I'm in a bit of a hurry, can't he help you?" he said nodding towards his replacement.

"It's you I need to speak with," said Steel irritably. The controller sensed the change of tone.

"What can I do to help?" he asked.

"I would like to know the destinations of both helicopters that left earlier today. I have been unable to locate my friend who missed me and obviously left. I'm not sure which aircraft he was in," Steel put five hundred francs on the table.

"That's no problem, sir." He walked across to the computer and his fingers rattled the keyboard.

"The first aircraft returned to Orly Airport, Paris, the second went to Hyeres Airport, Toulon." The controller looked up from the screen towards Steel, but apart from his replacement the room was empty, the door wide open. The five hundred franc note had fluttered to the ground. He shrugged his shoulders, picked up the bank note and kissed it before shoving it into his pocket, threw his bag over his shoulder and walked out of the room.

David Steel ran across the tarmac towards the flying club. Around the back were rows of aircraft, including the vintage Tiger Moths. He went up to a mechanic who was working on a twin-engine plane.

"Excuse me, do you know where I can charter a plane? I need to get to Toulon right away. There are two of us."

"This plane is about to have a post service check flight. The owner is in the clubhouse; let me go and talk to him."

The mechanic returned with a short jolly-looking man. After a chat in the clubhouse, and the traditional exchange of money, he agreed to fly the two men to Toulon.

During their conversation, none of the three men noticed the leather clad Arab talking to the mechanic who packed his tools and fastened down both engine housings. The mechanic wiped off a number of greasy finger marks as he spoke to the stranger, then picked up his tool kit and walked away.

For the second time, in a few short minutes, Hank and Michael drove back into the airport at Hyeres. They were just in time to see the Sahaed helicopter rise above the buildings and take off at high speed towards the coast road. It disappeared out of sight behind the airport buildings.

"Damn it, what in the hell's going on here?" Hank said wincing as he pulled the restrictive helmet over his head.

"Are you sure it was the same chopper you saw coming in a moment ago Michael? If so, they hardly had the time to touch down."

"I'm pretty sure it was them, but let's have a look around and see which others are here."

After a good search, the only other chopper apparent was a twin seater Robinson. "Now we have to find out where they went, or maybe wait until they return," said Michael.

"I don't think that's such a good idea," said Hank, pulling on the helmet and starting up the bike. He drove the machine around to the fishing port, where there was an old disused lighthouse that was more of a tourist attraction. They got off the bike; Michael followed Hank to the top of the lighthouse tower.

"Got any coins?" asked Hank, pointing to the telescope. Hank spent the next five minutes scanning the whole of the area, including out to sea.

"Damn it, there's no sign of them anywhere." he growled as the coin mechanism expired with a click. They were just about to descend from the lighthouse, when Michael let out a yell

"There, over there, what's that? See it way above the trees up in the hills there. Isn't that a helicopter?" Michael thrust another coin into the telescope, as Hank swung it round in the direction of Michael's finger.

"I can't see a thing. Is it still there?"

"I've lost it now Hank, but I'm sure it was Sahaed's helicopter."

"Try and get a bearing on where it was. Look for a different colour in the trees, a telegraph pole, a pylon or something. I can't help, I never saw it," said Hank.

The helicopter flew low and fast over the tree tops for three miles or so then came in to land. A clearing appeared in the forest. Kevin Reilly saw a magnificent estate nestled in the wooded terrain, completely surrounded by high walls. Close by he could see what looked like the ruins of some old fortress. The chopper came to land in an extensive courtyard area. There was no sign of life, though he could see a number of vehicles in the surrounding garages. The rotors began to slow.

"Wait there, keep him here until I tell you." snapped Kiev. He jumped down and went across the courtyard into a side door. He returned within a couple of minutes, waving for the others to follow. The big man got out first, pulling at the agent's handcuffs. "I want yer ta walk across normally," he said unlocking the cuffs. "Follow me, and remember what I said, Guv. Ali here will be behind yer wiv a shooter in 'is hand."

Reilly followed as instructed. They went down a long flight of stairs, into a cavernous complex underground area. They walked through two enormous storage warehouses, filled with packing cases. There were many large objects covered with canvas and he could see wheels beneath them. They eventually went through a door into an office area.

"You can leave now," snapped Kiev to the other two. "Leave him with me." He pointed for Reilly to sit. "What was the phrase again, underestimating the opponent, trying to fool an old warhorse? Like you, wasn't it Kevin? So let's see what you have to tell me, old warhorse? It's time to talk! We both know that, and we both know what happens to people who don't cooperate with the colonel, now don't we?" He pointed to the attaché case, and beckoned with the fingers of his right hand for Reilly to pass it across.

The Sahaed Residence Monaco

Sahaed sat talking on the telephone. He had just received a call from his brother-in-law.

"Yes he has the American at your estate in Toulon.......... it's hard to tell yet,.......... it appears that the CIA man has some Interpol laboratory reports on materials taken from the hotel suites in Paris. The British police inspector took them. The MI6 agent is still sniffing around. Kiev says that the Englishmen are somewhere in the vicinity and there is also the Arab, who is working for the palace. With a bit of luck they will terminate each other then perhaps we can all relax." He pulled the phone away from his ear.

"That was meant in jest....... Yes, I do appreciate the delicacy of the situation. I am going up there in about an hour. I will get the answers to your questions and call you back, my brother."

Sahaed threw the instrument into its cradle with a crack, and then began to pace up and down the room. He picked up the phone and tapped out a number.

"Get me Boris Kiev," he commanded as the phone was answered.

"Have you got any information out of the man yet Colonel?"

"Not yet, but I am about to get some answers on what's in the DNA lab reports. I faxed them to a contact of mine, sir."

"I want you to have me collected right away. There are answers to a few questions that I insist on having and I want those answers now. Is the helicopter available or do I drive?"

"I'll send the helicopter right away, sir."

Hank threw the bike around the tight bends. Michael hung onto the handles behind his seat. They wound up the hills climbing higher into the heavily wooded terrain. Most of the trees touched overhead, making it feel as though they were driving through a grotto. Every now and then the road would burst into light as the sun shone intermittently between the branches.

They came out into a clear area where the blue sky and sunshine blinded them for a second or two, then, whooomf, the helicopter shot from their left, nearly touching the tree tops. It was only visible for a moment, and then it was gone. Hank stopped the bike. They dismounted, took off their headgear, and sat on a grassy bank by the roadside.

"This is getting ridiculous, Michael. That bloody helicopter is like a ghost — now you see it now you don't. It came from over there; it went off towards the ocean. It was very low, maybe it just took off. Let's get over that way." He pointed to the left.

They cruised around narrow roads for the next twenty minutes and saw no signs of property or even civilization. They pulled over and sat on a roadside tree stump. They could see the distant ocean through the trees opposite. The water sparkled like silver in the late afternoon sun. Hank got off the seat and stretched out prostrate on the grass, hands behind his head.

"On any other occasion this would be called paradise, lying here in the sun-drenched Riviera."

"Listen Hank, listen." Michael cut across his conversation. Way in the distance the sound of an aircraft could be heard. As it got nearer, the whistle of the jet engines and the whine of the rotors became discernible, then it was on top of them, right overhead. It began to slow, it began to hover, and then they heard it make a landing not far away.

"Hope nobody saw us; they were very close."

"We got 'em; we've found 'em!" Hank said rolling over on to his stomach punching the ground with his fists. "Come on, Michael, let's go. I think at last our luck is beginning to change." Putting on their helmets, they climbed onto the bike and went off down the road; taking a turn down a lane that led in the direction they had heard the machine land.

At around the same time the twin-engine aircraft carrying David Steel and his partner landed at Hyeres Airport. Shortly after, Steel stood looking out of the window at the blue Mediterranean, wondering where Kevin Reilly could possibly be, knowing that his task was a difficult one. He went towards a payphone. After speaking for some minutes they walked across to the airport manager's office. As they did so Steel saw the man who followed their every move. He took little notice of the Arab standing at the car rental desk, or the man who watched the Arab's every move closely from behind tinted glasses, as he was shown outside to a Volkswagen Golf convertible.

After a short conversation with the airport manager, Steel had learned that the small airport of Hyeres had one of the best helicopter service centres in the south of France. At one time or another most machines came here from as far away as Monaco on the Italian border, some hundred miles away.

After describing the Sahaed helicopter, the manager had said there was one such machine that was owned by billionaire Armimi, who had a chalet in the hills above Toulon, but there were similar machines that came from other areas of the Riviera. Moments later the two men took a rental car and drove off in the direction of Toulon.

"This idiot behind is a total novice," said Steel as he looked through the rear view mirror at the car that followed them. The man he had spotted so easily back at the airport drove it.

"I would have thought that Boris Kiev could do better than that," he remarked, smirking, as the car behind stayed close on his tail. "Damn it, why didn't I think of that before?" he said aloud.

"Think of what?" said his colleague.

"Let's lose this idiot behind, then when he gives up; we can follow him to where he came from. If he is from the Sahaed camp, he'll lead us right to them, and hopefully to Kevin Reilly," he said, slapping the car steering wheel with the palm of his hand.

The City of Toulon

Meanwhile the Arab climbed into the convertible, throwing his case into the rear seat. He too drove off in the direction of Toulon. He was followed, but a little more professionally. The Jeep Renegade tailed him some four or five cars behind as traffic flew along the coast road. Driving into the centre of downtown Toulon, the Volkswagen pulled up outside a small hotel. Its passenger grabbed his bag and went inside. The Jeep pulled up a couple of blocks behind, the driver peering through his dark tinted glasses. Shortly afterwards the Arab came out and drove the car to the rear of the hotel, re-entering the building by the rear door.

Minutes later the jeep parked next to the Volkswagen. The piercing eyes of Ali, Boris Kiev's number one exterminator, scanned the area. He climbed from the seat and slid effortlessly to the ground, pulling himself underneath the rental car. Within a couple of minutes he reappeared from beneath the car, climbed into the Jeep, replacing his tinted spectacles he drove off towards the hills, but not before completing one circuit around the town's one way system, checking his rear view mirror as he went.

Within minutes of his parking the Volkswagen, the driver again left the small hotel by the front entrance, carrying the black case. He had watched Kiev's man go under the Volkswagen. He smiled as he strolled off towards the outskirts of town.

The conversation between Kevin Reilly and Colonel Boris Kiev was not progressing as well as the Russian would have liked. He was under the added pressure of the imminent arrival of his boss, which would only serve to slow the process. Though he had a sneaking respect for the American who, over the years, had kept him on his toes from Berlin to Afghanistan, Kiev was reminded that he was not pursuing the interests of mother Russia now, but more the contents of his personal bank account, along with his professional pride.

He had little time for sentiment, which became apparent to the American as Kiev paced the room then walked behind his chair.

"I have a feeling that you know too much for your own good," he snapped, as he paced irritably around the small room. "I don't see why you have to be involved in this affair. It's purely a matter for the damn Brits, and their Royal Family. My boss will be here any moment. Now for the last time, tell me what you know about these lab reports, and the whereabouts of Steel, the British agent," He thrust the papers under Kevin Reilly's nose as he spoke, receiving no reply.

The door to the room opened.

"You got a minute sir?" asked one of his team.

"Don't go away. I'll be right back, my old warhorse," he said facetiously to the American. Kiev walked through into the adjoining warehouse, and was handed a phone.

"Kiev............. Good! That's exactly as I expected, keep your eye on the two agents for the time being, and whatever you do don't lose them. You can forget about the Arab, Ali is already close by and he'll take care of him. Just keep me posted on the British cop and his colleague. Stick close to them, lose them and you're a dead man!"

Activity at the Chalet was beginning to heat up considerably.

The helicopter carrying Anwar Sahaed arrived within minutes of Colonel Kiev replacing the telephone receiver.

"This could be the place, Michael," said Hank as they watched from their vantage point on the other side of the road. They were hidden from view by the dense undergrowth around the base of the trees.

"I hope they haven't seen us here already," he whispered looking at the solid gates.

"If they had, someone would have been out by now," said Michael. Minutes earlier they had driven past the gates twice then left the motorbike further down the road.

"Looks like this is the place though," he added, a note of satisfaction in his voice.

"Shhhh, listen, there's a car coming."

A large white stretched Mercedes limousine pulled up to the gates, which were opened almost instantly. The windows were so darkly tinted it was impossible to see inside as the vehicle swept off into the grounds. Seconds later another car pulled up to the gates; its hooter blasted.

"That's one of Sahaed's goons. I recognize him from the hotel in Paris," said Hank, as the car went through the gateway.

A moment later another car went past, slowing as it came level with the gates. They saw the blond hair of the driver through the open window.

"Shit, it's the MI6 man," said Hank. Michael jumped up in surprise. Hank pulled Michael's shoulder down behind the foliage as he spoke "Don't be a fool, get down!"

As they crouched there uncomfortably, another vehicle sped past their hiding place; Hank caught a glimpse of the rear of a yellow Jeep renegade as it shot past.

The Arab man carrying the BMW pannier case made his way towards a taxi rank in the centre of town. He stooped down and spoke into the window of a taxi for a few moments, and then climbed into the rear of the car. The vehicle took off towards the hills as it began to climb out of Toulon.

The Arab spoke good French. He talked to the driver as the taxi made its way towards the distant tree-covered mountains.

The driver continued to make conversation. After about twenty minutes he began to slow down as they approached a clearing in the trees.

"This is the chalet that you seek, Monsieur."

"Keep on driving," replied the passenger in the rear seat. The driver then felt the chilling cold touch of the point of a knife blade on the main artery of his neck.

"Keep on driving, don't stop," snarled the Arab, the man's hot breath now touching his ear as he hissed his instructions through clenched teeth.

The driver was absolutely petrified as he adhered to the man's instructions, pulling into a layby a couple of miles further up the steep hillside. There was no other vehicle parked in the layby; the area was overgrown and deserted. The knife had been taken away from his throat, along with a warning not to try anything stupid. He heard the click of an automatic weapon as the magazine slammed into place, and then there was silence. He could see the face of the man reflected in the rear view mirror.

"Move the mirror," snapped the voice from behind. At the same time the Arab reached between the front bucket seats, pushing the handgun fiercely into the driver's rib cage.

Without warning the rear passenger door of the taxi was wrenched open. The driver was petrified as he heard the sound of three rapid silenced shots, phut...... phut phut. He waited for the pain, but felt nothing; he froze to the seat mortified, as he smelled cordite and the odour of his own excreta.

After what seemed an age, he plucked up the courage to turn around. What he saw made his whole being shake with horror and fear. His passenger lay across the bench seat. Half the top of his head had been blown away; blood was everywhere, dripping from the roof and down the windows. He jumped out of the car yelling for help, throwing up over the inside of the open door, down the front of his pants and over his shoes. He rushed off blindly shouting and screaming for help, fully expecting to feel the pain of a bullet. The whole area was deserted, the silence shattered as he tore off up the hill, the sounds of his screams muffled by the overhanging trees and surrounding vegetation.

Some moments later the bushes behind the taxi parted, the figure of Kiev's man Ali, emerged. He climbed into the taxi and drove it away in the direction of the Chalet.

Michael and Hank were just about to leave their hiding place when the sounds of yet another vehicle could be heard approaching in the distance.

"This seems like quite a busy road," said Hank. They got out of sight as the sounds of the engine came closer and began to slow down. They spotted the car coming down the hill, and saw that it was a taxi. As it pulled up to the gates, Hank instantly recognized the driver. He saw the beady eyes of the Arab from Sahaed's garage in London, his fingers drumming the steering wheel as he waited impatiently for the gates to be opened in answer to the taxi's hooter. As the way opened up and the taxi moved along, Hank thought that he saw something that looked remarkably like blood splashed across the rear and side windows of the vehicle. He dismissed the thought as his imagination.

"Jesus, did you see what I just saw?" said a startled Michael. "There was blood all over the windows of that cab." he began standing up as he spoke.

"Get down, don't be a bloody fool! Those cameras never sleep," Hank hissed, as he dragged his companion to the ground.

"Yes, you're right, that was blood in the vehicle, and quite a lot of it too. We need to find some way of getting into this place, and I suspect that's not going to be easy. We certainly can't use the main entrance, that's for sure. It's going to get dark soon. Now that we know we're in the right place, why don't we go back down into Toulon, get a good night's sleep and then work on a plan of action. We need to use night-time hours to get in there, but we need some further daytime reconnoitering in order to find some other way of getting in. We know that the dodgy Arab is here; we know that Kiev is here; we have also seen the MI6 agent. What we need to know now is who was in the helicopter, and the limousine? Whose blood was all over the inside of that taxi, and how the hell are we going to get in there?" Hank let out a heavy sigh.

They crept along with great difficulty in the rough undergrowth, for quite some distance, before reaching the motorcycle. They pushed it cautiously out onto the road after checking carefully that they were unseen. After they had climbed aboard, Hank free-wheeled the machine some way down the steep road before bump starting the bike into life.

They pulled into the old section of Toulon, drove down the ancient cobble streets, and parked the bike outside the centuries old inn, where they soon retired to clean comfortable beds.

Though their minds were troubled and somewhat confused, they were soon fast asleep, unaware of the goings on back at the chalet, or indeed the consternation of the staff at the local taxi rank just a few streets away. As yet there was no panic. Maybe the errant driver had taken a fare down to the Italian border; maybe he had broken down; maybe his radio was not working or perhaps he was with his mistress.

"Let's wait and see what tomorrow brings," was the general consensus of opinion.

Buckingham Palace, London

The Queen and her husband sat in their drawing room in the palace. They had just watched a recording of an American television news show where the whole hour had been devoted to the death of the princess. Some British press had been involved; the end result was a damning report on the Royal Family and further glorification of the dead princess. Daily newspapers lay on the couches and coffee tables. Every copy from England and around the whole world served to worsen their image.

"There are reports that Meadows and that interfering policeman are still poking their noses into the affair," said the Queen,

"I have made arrangements to have them stopped, and permanently if necessary," she added, throwing a copy of a particularly damaging German newspaper across the room as she spoke.

"Was that a wise thing to do, dear?"

"Wise? Wise?! What has wise got to do with it? The whole affair is a disastrous mess. We are about to lose the monarchy and all you can say is, 'was that wise dear?'" She walked across the room then stood hands on hips looking out of the window down the Mall.

"John's image is at an all time low, the nation seems to want to bypass him and put George on the throne. That damn woman has, without doubt, become the most popular member of this whole family."

"Hold on my dear, she's not a member anymore. Remember?

"Damn, damn!" The Queen roared as she stormed out of the room, banging the big doors behind her.

Number 10 Downing Street, London

Prime Minister Blain sat at his desk, having just watched a transatlantic television interview with a popular member of the House of Lords, a former Member of Parliament. He had been a close friend of the dead princess. Though the Peer had handled himself well, he had struggled notably in order to seem impartial in some of his answers to the American panel of journalists and the TV host.

Blain picked up his private phone, tapping out a number.

"Sir Martin, it's Blain here."

"Yes Prime Minister. Good day to you. What can I do for you sir?" asked the MI6 chief

"I had the Queen on the phone a few minutes ago. She is rather perturbed about a report she has received, that a British policeman is carrying out enquiries in France. She says that the man concerned is not only a current member of the Palace Protection Squad, but is the man who was previously Princess Anna's personal bodyguard. Don't ask me how she knows, but she wants the man brought back immediately and says that no purpose can be served now. What do you know about this?"

"We know that Inspector Hank Marlin has taken paid leave that was due to him, and that yes, he is somewhere in France. It may interest you to know that Michael Meadows, the princess's private secretary is also holidaying in France. I wasn't aware that was a crime, Prime Minister!"

"The Queen was adamant that the policeman is carrying out enquiries. I want you to find out, and when you come across the man, please tell him of our concern, and indeed my own feelings, which are to let sleeping dogs lie."

"I will do what I can Prime Minister. Will that be all, sir?"

"Yes Sir Martin, for the moment, that is all."

The Armimi Chalet, Toulon

Boris Kiev climbed into the elevator in the basement of the chalet and ascended to the main foyer of the residence. He walked across to the study, where he had been summoned to meet with Sahaed. Knocking on the door, he heard the command.

"Enter." He walked into the room.

"Sit down, colonel. We have a lot to talk about and a lot of ground to cover. I want you to apprise me of all happenings right up to the current moment."

Kiev was never a man to tell all, so he brought the situation round to questions and answers, giving only information relative to specific questions rather than a complete run down of all events leading up to the present time.

"What was the outcome of the results on the DNA tests done by Interpol?"

"They told us nothing that we don't already know, sir."

"Do you think that the English policeman knows what the results show?"

"I suspect that he must do, sir."

"Where is the American?"

"He's down below, sir."

"Does he know what the results contain?"

"I'm quite sure that he does. Why else would he be here if not, sir?"

"Is the English policeman here in the south of France too?"

"So far we don't think so. We lost track of him after he flew out of Orly Airport. There is no trace that he landed in England, but he could have landed in some remote country airfield, or even gone to Ireland."

"Is there anything else that I should know about, colonel?"

"There is one thing, yes sir. We had to get rid of the other half of the Arab team that was working for the palace. He got a little too close. He actually made it here. We'll drop his body out at sea later tonight on the outgoing tide."

Sahaed looked a little concerned for a brief moment then asked,

"What about the CIA man. What do you intend to do with him, colonel?"

"He's going to have a genuine accident, a fatal one, sir. But first there are a few things that we need to get from him.

"What of the MI6 man? Where is he?"

"He's here in Toulon. He arrived today with a colleague. Unfortunately he gave one of my men the slip. One of my former men that is, sir!"

Sahaed noted the innuendo contained in the Russian's comment.

"What's next colonel?"

"Well sir, mostly things have gone according to plan. The MI6 agent is not going to come into the chalet neither is the English cop, or anyone else for that matter. We just need to sit here and let life go on as planned. When the blood tests are completed on Paul Gastard, the driver, there will be no doubt what caused the accident. The funerals are over and done with. Soon things will be back to normal then the rest of it is up to you sir."

The colonel stood up and walked towards the door.

"If it's alright with you sir, I'll be getting on with my chat with the American."

"Carry on, colonel, and well done."

"Thank you, sir." Kiev walked out of the study, just as a man in a wheelchair was pushed along the corridor.

"Good evening sir, I trust that everything is OK." The man in the chair did not turn around but raised his hand in recognition of Kiev's words.

The Inn, Downtown Toulon

As the Inn was almost totally occupied by fishermen and some members of the French Navy, all were early risers — sleeping late within the establishment was not an option. Michael and Hank sat at a table eating breakfast and enjoying the fresh coffee. It was 5:30am.

"Have you come up with a plan yet?" asked Michael.

"Not as yet. I still think that we have to find some rear entry."

"I don't know why we don't just drop the matter and go on home," said Michael. "Princess Anna is buried and there's nothing we can do to change that. Is it really necessary that we know who did it? There were reports in the paper that the driver had three times the alcohol level in his blood. Won't that be sufficient to convince the general public?"

"I told you before, if you want to quit, go anytime, but I'm going to see this through. I still have some doubts and I want to clear them before I give up. I owe that much to Princess Anna, and to myself. I told you that there were some anomalies contained in the DNA results. Interpol didn't spot them. It's still a very new field; I just completed an advanced course some weeks before and I'm curious. I have great faith in the use of DNA. If you want to go I won't stop you, but I could use your help, Michael."

"OK you win, but would you like to tell me a little more."

They sat and talked for a good hour and a half, during which time they formulated the outline of a plan. After another coffee, they climbed onto the bike and left for the hills.

During their discussions earlier that morning they had both come to the conclusion that it would consume too much time to try and skirt the whole of the estate looking for a means of entry, assuming that much of the rear was rough terrain and unapproachable on foot. They also had to take into account that the MI6 man and maybe others could be contemplating the same ideas.

They had decided to take one final look around the whole area. They skirted what could be the rear of the estate, but had no way of knowing how far the grounds spread out, nor could they assess the distance between the road that they were on, from the one that ran past the front entrance, as the road wound around circuitously.

Driving along past the main entrance to the chalet, they continued on for a couple of miles and were suddenly confronted by a number of police cars with blue lights flashing. A policeman stepped out into the road and waved the couple to a halt. Michael got off the bike, removed his helmet and began to speak to the man. Hank moved the bike off the road and sat watching as police dogs moved across the layby and entered the thick undergrowth behind. There was a very pale, thin-faced man gesticulating to a man who appeared to be in charge. Michael walked across to Hank.

"There was an incident here last evening involving the thin guy over there, who is evidently a taxi driver. He reckons he brought a fare up here and says that the passenger was killed in the cab. He's burbling on that someone stole his taxi. The police don't seem to be able to make head or tail of what's going on."

"You didn't tell them that we saw a cab here last night did you, Michael?"

"No, I told them we are English tourists, here for the first time."

Later Hank pulled up at a public phone kiosk where Michael went and called a number, then waited for a reply. After some time speaking in French, he beckoned Hank across, passing him the handset.

"Pierre, how are you? How are your enquiries going? I'm down in the south of France at the moment. I've come across something that maybe you ought to take a look at, my friend." Hank stood silent for a few seconds.

"Pierre, you have known me for a long time. But just check with the Toulon police about a suspected murder down here. It is alleged to have taken place right outside the chalet of none other than Agnin Armimi. I also believe that Sahaed is in the same building at this moment." There was a long pause.

"Good I'll meet you down here at Hyeres Airport this afternoon. By the way can you get your hands on a helicopter down here Pierre? Good, I'll see you later then, bye."

Hank put the phone down, knowing that the Interpol inspector would waste no time getting there.

"Was it a wise thing to involve him?" asked Michael.

"I can't think of another alternative. There's no other way we can get in there, at least not without the SAS backed up by a Royal Marine Commando team. Besides, the French are desperate for answers, and at least they don't want to kill us! But if my suspicions are founded, everyone else sure does! Now Michael, tell me exactly what the police said at the crime scene earlier. I have the strangest feeling that there is one person less for us to concern ourselves about."

Anwar Sahaed sat in the magnificent drawing room of the chalet feeling quite pleased with himself. He had just put the phone down after speaking with his brother-in-law, who, for a change, seemed quite pleased with the way things were going, though he had made his annoyance very clear at losing this once-in-a-lifetime opportunity resulting from the unfortunate deaths. At first he had questioned the solution regarding the CIA agent, but later agreed that there was no other safe alternative. He picked up the phone, and pressed three numbers.

"Yes colonel, we shall be flying back to Cairo in the next couple of days. I would like to hear what the American has to say for himself before he, er, before he leaves. I don't much care whether you think that it's a good idea or not, colonel; it wasn't a request, it was an order!" He replaced the receiver, and walked out of the room.

Down below, Kevin Reilly sat uncomfortably in a small bunkroom, his hands cuffed together around the upright timber of the lower bunk. He had noticed that the pressure had left the Russian's tone of voice when he had last spoken to him some hours ago. He assumed that they had either got, or located David Steel, and quite possibly had the DNA information deciphered. Reilly knew full well, if he were right, he would not be long for this world. He had to get out of the place as quickly as possible. Though right now that seemed a physical impossibility. Maybe he could reason with Kiev — after all they did go back a long way. This was not a cold war issue anymore; maybe he could deal with the man. Maybe not!

A Toulon Ocean Front Hotel

David Steel came off the phone after a conversation with the head of MI6. He walked back to his room at the beachside hotel. His new partner stretched out on the second bed in the room.

"I don't see why we should get involved here anymore. Getting into that place is going to be one hell of a feat, and all to find out if the American is in there. We're not even certain he's there, and we both know that Kiev plays for keeps."

"That's not the issue anymore. Evidently the British cop and maybe his royal secretary pal are around, still poking their noses into things. They have to be eliminated, or persuaded to go home, and that's right from the top. Whilst we're here we may as well see what we can do about Kevin Reilly. After all he was helping us, wasn't he?"

"I suppose that if the rest of Kiev's men are anything like the tail we had, perhaps getting in won't be that difficult."

"Maybe you're forgetting who owns the damn chalet, and the security that he'll have in there," Steel replied. "Our people are sending us a load of equipment and another agent today. He should be here in a couple of hours."

"Good let's spend the time in the sun looking at some of those gorgeous ladies out there," said the other man.

"I think not. There's a lot of planning to be done. Don't forget who we are up against."

"All work and no play make Jack a dull boy!"

"I'd rather be a dull boy than a dead one. Come on let's go," said Steel. He pulled one his colleague's legs off the edge of the bed, and walked towards the door.

Hank stood in the arrival hall of the airport at Hyeres. He heard the announcement on the arrival of the flight from Paris; saw the usual rush of passengers heading towards the baggage area. As the crowds thinned out, he spotted the figure of Pierre Lacoste. He was alone and looked tired and drawn as though he lacked sleep. They shook hands and greeted each other; Lacoste was carrying only a small canvas carrier bag.

"I'm using a motor cycle at the moment. I trust you don't mind riding pillion."

"No, not at all, it's been a long time since I did though. The fresh air will do me good."

They left the airport and were soon coasting along the oceanfront towards the centre of town. Michael had booked another room at the same inn; the three of them were soon in the bar. Hank proceeded to re-tell the inspector of the incident with the taxi. The local police had already briefed him.

"What is it you want from me Hank, and why are you so interested in the goings on inside the chalet?"

"I just want to satisfy myself that the death of the princess was indeed an accident and there are a few loose ends that I want tied up then I'll be on my way."

"Oh! Hank, there is something that I think you ought to know." Lacoste looked serious as he spoke.

"We have been told that you are not here officially. We are instructed not to assist you, or cooperate with you in any matters connected with the accident. We are to report your position directly to England, Hank." The comment stopped Hank dead in his tracks.

"Told by whom — you mean your bosses?"

"No, the instruction came from England. I happen to know that it came from the chief of your MI6." Michael's eyes were wide open as he listened to the Frenchman. Hank sat in stunned silence.

"They know that we're here then, do they?"

"No, I don't think they do. They know that you didn't return to England. They are looking for you both at this moment. They have been careful not to issue an international APB, just an unofficial request for assistance. That's one of the main reasons for my coming down here, to warn you. Hank you are both in very grave danger! The last thing that you should do is to enter the chalet. If there is anything that you shouldn't see there, then your life would be in double danger — worthless, I'd say" said Lacoste. He beckoned the barman to replenish the drinks as he spoke.

"You aren't telling me anything new, Pierre."

"I'm afraid I don't accept what you say. Your face displayed shock when I mentioned the involvement of MI6. Come on Hank, it's time to be on your way home."

"And don't you think that I'm in just as much danger going home as I am staying here?" Hank snapped irritably.

"I suppose that's a valid point. Somehow though, I don't think you're telling me all there is to know. They must think that you are in possession of important information. Your pictures are on fax at Interpol right now. I know you Hank Marlin; you're up to something. Either you level with me now, or I keep my nose clean and we put this on an official basis right now!" There was silence between the three of them, broken by the bartender's interruption as he noisily placed fresh glasses in front of them.

"I don't see that we have much of a choice," said Hank to Michael.

"You can say that again," said the Frenchman. "I know that there's something somewhere in the DNA report that I gave you a copy of, though for the life of me I can't see what it is. I didn't log that test as official nor as part of any specific case, though my boss did ask what it applied to. I told him it was a favour to you. To the best of my knowledge yours and mine are the only copies in existence. So come on, spill the beans, as the Americans say."

They retired to Lacoste's room, where once again, in the space of twenty-four hours Hank explained most of his theories, without actually telling the French police inspector or Michael, what it was that really concerned him. He had however, said sufficient to get the continued support of the Frenchman.

They discussed plans over dinner that evening, deciding that if the two were to try getting into the building how best it could be achieved. Lacoste was still against any involvement from the two, but after some convincing pressure, he gave in. After a long brain storming session, they came up with a plan on which they were all in agreement. It was also agreed that before any approaches were made, they should first fly over the chalet in the helicopter that would be supplied by Interpol.

It was in fact to be a charter and not a police aircraft, which made it easier for Hank and Michael to accompany the inspector on the flight. First thing in the morning Inspector Lacoste had to meet with local police and get an update on the latest progress in the missing taxi case, and the alleged murder without a corpse.

On that note they retired to bed. The small restaurant and bar was beginning to get rowdy as it filled with international sailors and members of the French Navy.

The helicopter ride provided a totally different concept of the surrounding countryside. The pilot had taken the aircraft straight up to a height of some two thousand feet and then given a running commentary as they flew along. The difference between the congestion of the town centre compared with the tree covered hills was quite stunning. To Michael, as a fixed wing pilot, everything seemed as though it were in slow motion. It was late morning and the sun was almost directly above them as it shone on the ocean; its reflection like a million watt bulb.

They had flown at first along the coast road with its manicured tree-lined median in the centre. The beach was multi coloured from the bright sunshades and clothing worn by some, for as Hank saw through the binoculars, most sun worshipers of the female variety were topless.

This fact had not been omitted by their commentator, thought the fact had gone completely over Hank's head when the three French-speaking men had laughed at the pilot's wry comments, before Michael had translated.

They began to fly towards the hills. As they did so the tree density of the area became apparent. At some points the road could be seen winding and twisting then disappearing. Occasionally a rare open area came into view. The pilot who had listened to Michael's earlier jocular translation now spoke in English, pointing out two ancient fortresses, one a complete ruin the other the result of some preservation and renovation.

They were still at a height that would draw no attention to them. The magnificent chalet was pin-pointed and the binoculars were quickly passed around the three men. Pierre turned around from his seat beside the pilot.

"We're going down now, the pilot will make two low passes," he said as the chopper swooped sideways, then began to descend in a large circle. The first pass was quite slow. At about five hundred feet it felt as though they would touch the tips of some of the tall fir trees that reached up towards them. The tower on top of the chalet protruded over the trees as the pilot turned and flew directly over the estate.

The area it covered was vast; the surrounding terrain provided a stark contrast to the manicured grounds within. Ornamental fountains sparkled in the sunlight and there was a large area of water in the centre of the drive where vehicles turned around. Hank counted five or six cars, including the jeep, but did not see the taxi. The front of the limousine protruded from an open garage.

One car was parked at the steps of the entrance, at the other side of the building the menacing black helicopter stood motionless on the lawn, its rotor blades drooping like the wings of a tired bird.

Hank counted five men. He had spotted the figure of Boris Kiev who was with another man, coming down the main steps of the entrance to the chalet. He lost sight of the two as they flew over, but not before he glimpsed the shiny metal of handcuffs on the wrists of the other man, who held his hands forward as he descended the stairs walking with some difficulty. Hank recognised the man as the one he had followed from the coffee bar at the Majestic Palace Hotel in Paris, and who he had eventually lost.

At the instruction of Lacoste, the pilot swung round in a circle. Below them was the layby where the police had been searching earlier. A black van was parked there bearing the insignia of the French police with a white number painted on its roof.

On their second pass over the chalet, Hank saw no signs of the Russian or the handcuffed man. He noticed the car that had been parked at the foot of the steps was also gone.

He had been correct in his assumption that an uninvited visit to the chalet would have been difficult, to say the least. As they completed their pass he could see the formidable walls that encompassed the whole estate topped with barbed wire, *no doubt live with electronics and cameras*, he though to himself.

Completing the circle again they passed over the layby once more, this time the area was deserted. The pilot gained height, and then flew off in the direction of his base back at Hyeres Airport.

Meanwhile, as instructed by Kiev, one of his men spoke to a helicopter charter company in Toulon.

"Yes sir we do have two machines of that type, would you like to charter one of them?"

"Yes we need to charter a machine right away," replied the man.

"I'm afraid that won't be possible for at least three hours sir. You see one is being serviced and the other is out on charter already. Let me just make sure. No I'm wrong, Interpol should be ending their charter any minute," said the woman.

"Would you like me to make arrangements for you now, sir? ...."

Hello..., hello..., hello. Can you hear me sir?" The line was dead. The woman replaced the receiver, and then went on to answer the next call.

Steel squatted in the undergrowth opposite the entrance to the chalet. In the light of day he could see the surveillance camera as it made its ninety-degree turns with monotonous regularity. Further along the road in the layby, his two colleagues sat in the van filled with sophisticated listening devices. The latest arrival was one of the agency's top eavesdroppers who'd complained bitterly that he had been dragged back from a vacation with his family, said he had seven months owing to him as a result of continuous call outs of so-called top priorities.

"Got anything yet?" Steel whispered into the radio.

"No, nothing decipherable. These damned trees and that bloody great wall don't make life any easier," replied the expert.

"I think we need to get further back or higher up."

Suddenly he ripped the earphones from his head as a helicopter screamed overhead almost blowing his eardrums.

"Shit, where did that come from?" he said into the radio.

"Are they onto us?"

"I don't think so. That's not their chopper. Could be the police, could be anyone, but it's not theirs," said the agent.

"Hang on, someone's coming out, the gates are opening. Oh Christ he's here, it's Reilly, they've got him in a car. Get ready to leave. I'm coming across right now."

He hurried through the undergrowth as he spoke, ferns and branches whipping his face as he ran. He tripped continuously over cumbersome roots in his haste to reach the vehicle.

Once inside, the van accelerated off in the same direction the car had taken.

"Other than the driver, there was only one other man with Reilly," Steel said, looking ahead with keen anticipation, as they rounded each tight bend in the road.

"Drive straight to the marina," said Kiev to the driver. He was in the rear seat next to Kevin Reilly. Both men sat in silence as the car descended the tree-covered winding road.

"We have a police van behind us sir," the driver said to Kiev.

"So don't do anything stupid. What kind of vehicle is it?" he growled without turning around.

"It's a larger van, like the kind of thing they carry prisoners in, sir."

"Maybe it's nothing, or maybe it's a surveillance vehicle, don't talk anymore just in case. Turn on the radio," whispered the Russian, as they came out onto the ocean road.

"There's nobody behind us now sir. They disappeared coming down the hill."

"Good, get a move on to the marina and let's get this over with," said Kiev. He studied a sea chart as they drove along, then scrutinised his watch.

"Yes, we have an outgoing tide, that's good," the colonel said. He then closed the chart and they travelled the rest of the way in silence until the traffic began to slow down, eventually coming to a complete standstill. Kiev began to curse the French road system as they sat looking at the rear of a stationary taxicab. The road was clear from the opposite direction. An ambulance came up on their left along the emergency lane with its siren blasting, followed by a police car and a police van.

"It looks as though there's been an accident up front, sir."

"There's going to be another one soon if you don't get this damn car out of here," said Kiev.

"Do you want me to go along the emergency lane sir?"

"Don't be an idiot." replied the colonel.

Reilly sat silently, and then suddenly made a grab for the door handle as Kiev talked to the driver.

"Don't be a fool," snarled the Russian as the door handle refused to budge. "That door is locked on the childproof system. You should know better." Just then the traffic began to move. Steel and his colleagues had followed the car down the hill. Suspecting that they had been spotted they had dropped behind at the risk of losing the car. When they had emerged from the trees they saw that southbound traffic had come to a halt. They could not at first see the car amongst all the other vehicles.

They pulled over, then Steel climbed onto the top of the van. Through his binoculars he looked along the road northwards, which was clear. He then scanned the lines of blocked traffic, spotting the Citroen. As he jumped down from the roof of the van an ambulance rushed along the nearside emergency lane followed by a police car, both vehicles' sirens howling.

"Quick, get in behind them," he yelled as he dived into the van.

"Where's the siren on this bloody thing? " he shouted as the van lurched onto the curb almost turning over, tyres screeching as it flew past the traffic jam.

"There they are. Reilly is in the back with our friend Kiev. They must be headed for the port or further on towards Monaco. They're past the turn for the airport. Let's try and get across the traffic and go into the port entrance."

They drove along the emergency lane for a mile or so. Steel pulled on a policeman's jacket from the back of the van. They stopped and he parted the traffic, then they drove down the sidewalk and entered the port, pulling over just past a taxi rank. Steel and the other agent left the new arrival with the van, got into a taxi, and sat waiting at the side of the road that led to all three parts of the massive port complex. Steel's fast thinking was rewarded; Kiev's car drove past and turned towards the private marina area of the port. The taxi took off and followed unnoticed at a safe distance behind.

Inspector Lacoste's Peugeot station wagon pulled up to the gates of the Chalet, its horn blasting as the gates were opened. As it entered the grounds the car was stopped by two armed guards who began to question the driver. He quickly shoved the badge and ID of an Interpol Inspector under the nose of the nearest man.

"Wait here, inspector," said the man as he went into the gate office.

"Drive up to the main house." The other guard tried, without success, to look into the rear of the vehicle as it sped off up the driveway.

Inside the chalet one of the security men was speaking on a mobile phone.

"I don't know colonel, he just arrived at the gate, and his name is Inspector Lacoste. He is from Paris and has the ID of an Interpol Inspector. What do you want me to do? OK, will do. No I won't. I'll make sure he stays outside, sir."

Pierre Lacoste drove around the circle with its lily pond and fountains, to be greeted by a large and unfriendly looking man.

"Inspector Lacoste, I assume?"

"That's me," he replied.

"What can we do for Interpol?" asked the big man.

"I would like to speak with the owner, or whoever is in charge," replied Lacoste, holding out his ID.

"I'm afraid that won't be possible. Neither the owner nor the chief of security are here at the moment."

"I can wait."

"That won't be possible either, Inspector."

"Look, there's been an incident involving a French citizen who has reported an alleged murder just outside the grounds of this house. Now either you find someone in authority for me to talk with, or I shall leave and come back with a search warrant, and when I leave I will arrest you for obstructing me in the execution of my duty."

"That won't be necessary, inspector, if you'd like to come this way perhaps we can help you." Anwar Sahaed stood smiling at the top of the steps.

Lacoste went up the steps and was shown through to a magnificent drawing room.

"Now what can I do to be of assistance? My name is Sahaed, Anwar Sahaed. This is the home of my brother-in-law Mr Agnin Armimi; we have just had a terrible tragedy in the family, as no doubt you are aware. We are here to mourn the loss of loved ones."

"Please accept my deepest sympathy, sir. I am very much aware of your loss, and was actually working on the Paris tragedy before I was called here. I have no wish to add to your pain, but there have been some serious allegations made by a local taxi driver, who witnessed a killing outside your grounds before his taxi was stolen. We wondered if any of your gate security saw or heard anything two nights ago."

"My security chief is not here at the moment. His name is Kiev. If you would give me a number where you can be contacted, I will have him meet with you and he will give you all the information he can. I'm sorry I can't be of more assistance. Will that be all for now Inspector?" The Arab rose to his feet as he spoke.

Outside in the grounds Hank cautiously lifted the blanket that covered both him and Michael in the rear of the station wagon. He lifted his head and peered over the window frame. He could not see anyone on that side. After a complete look around through the tinted windows, he decided the coast was clear.

"OK, you can get up now," he said to his partner.

"I'm going to go first. Remember I shall head for the garage with the limo. After a couple of minutes, if the way is clear, you follow."

Hank opened the side door, and was gone. Michael locked the door, and then heard voices approaching the car. He got back under the blanket quickly, as he heard someone lift the door handle of the Peugeot. The voices got louder. He froze as he heard a key being pushed into the door lock. He felt movement of air as a door was opened and he held his breath, waiting for the blanket to be lifted.

"Thank you again, sir, I will contact your Mr Kiev, as you say, and I'll ask the men on the gate if they heard anything on the night in question." Michael heard the voice of Pierre Lacoste as he climbed into the driver's seat. Closing the door behind him, he started the engine and the car moved off.

"Are you there by any chance?" asked the Frenchman.

"I am," replied Michael. "Hank got out, but you came back a bit too quick for me to follow. Let me get out before you reach the gates."

"I'm not so sure that's a good idea," replied Lacoste.

"Why not?" he asked

"I'm just looking at a man walking across the grounds leading a damn great rottweiler."

"I can't just go and leave Hank on his own in there."

"I don't think there is any other choice." The inspector pulled up at the gatehouse and got out of the car. He spoke with the two guards, and then drove through the gates and along the road back towards Toulon.

"Well what's our next move to be?" the Frenchman asked. "You got any good ideas, Michael?" There was no reply. Lacoste looked round to see a crumpled blanket in the rear of the station wagon. Michael was gone. *Crazy fool, what does he think he can do in there?* he thought.

Back at the chalet a few moments earlier, Hank had moved quickly across the drive and was soon inside the garage. He ran to the rear, crouching down behind the stretched Mercedes limousine. *So far so good.* He heard voices coming from the direction of the chalet, but could not see who was speaking, so he moved carefully towards the entrance, keeping close to the limo.

Peering round the corner of the garage he saw Sahaed walking towards the Peugeot. Pierre was already standing by the car door. He could not hear what they were saying. Pierre climbed into the vehicle and drove off down the drive, he assumed with Michael still inside.

He went back into the rear of the garage and sat down on the corner of a workbench. *Will Michael get out of the car and come back, or will Pierre make him stay in the car?* He decided to wait for a while. As his eyes became accustomed to the lack of light in the garage, he could vaguely see the shapes of four other vehicles besides the limousine, one a Mercedes sports, another a beach buggy, a Rolls Royce, and one other that was under a plastic cover.

He moved cautiously over to the far corner where the covered vehicle stood, he felt the warmth of a recently used engine under the cover as he moved to the rear and began lifting the plastic sheet, pulling it over the trunk. As he did so he saw the French government plate of a taxicab riveted to the bumper bar. He continued to pull the cover over the top of the car, until the rear door was clear.

As Hank opened the door, the stench of vomit and excreta, mixed with the smell of blood and death was totally overpowering. He stepped back covering his mouth and nose with his hand. From the glow of the interior lights he saw the bloody mess. There were still pieces of drying flesh and bone fragments clinging to the material of the seat and on the window surfaces. Bile rose in his throat as he gulped for air.

He was just about to close the door when his attention was drawn to a dark shape on the floor of the taxi. Holding a handkerchief to his mouth he bent and looked closer. Reaching down to the dimly lit floor, he found the handle of an attaché case. He stooped and felt further under the front seat, his fingers touched the butt of a gun, and he lifted the firearm into the light. It was a Glock semi automatic. Groping under the other front seat, he pulled out a very nasty looking knife with a switchblade.

He placed the items on the floor of the garage and closed the car door. As darkness fell again he re-covered the car. He went across to the workbench, struck a match, and examined the gun. He had seen a few of them before on firearms courses; he had actually fired an identical weapon. It was made of a lightweight polymer material stronger than steel and light as plastic. He pulled out the magazine which was fully loaded, then he closed the seriously serrated blade of the knife, tried the release a couple of times, then put it into his pants pocket. He put the loaded Glock into his jacket pocket, taking care to engage the safety catch before closing the zipper. He then flipped the two catches of the case, which released with a very loud snap. He turned to make sure that he had not been overheard. Inside were a number of items: a pair of gloves, a flashlight, a box of ammo, a mobile phone, a pair of infra red night sights with clip-on headgear and a note book with Arabic handwriting. He gratefully turned on the flashlight.

Clipped into the lid were a long length of special spider wire, a pack of Semtex explosive and a small box of electronic detonators with an electronic sender. He put the flashlight in his other jacket pocket. He was just about to clip the case shut when he heard a commotion coming from the outside. There were men shouting, and the spine chilling snarls of a large excited dog. Then he froze as heard a single shot ring through the air, followed by an eerie silence.

He put the case under the bench and crept cautiously towards the entrance, crouching down and peering around the side of the limo. He was not ready for the sight that met his eyes.

Two men were dragging Michael Meadows along the drive, blood running down the left side of his face and from his left hand, which he grasped with his right. His face seemed distorted in pain. Hank watched helplessly for a while, then hearing a second dog whining to his left, he scurried quickly back alongside the limo, opened the passenger rear door and dived gratefully into its dark cavernous interior.

The Marina, Toulon

Steel and his partner sat in the rear of the taxi. They followed the Citroen as it went off into the port. There were so many cabs moving around the port that they were virtually invisible in theirs. Eventually, the car in front went into the private sector of the port, driving up to one of the main jetties. The iron gates were closed. A guard came out of the small kiosk, looked at a card passed by the driver then he nodded to his colleague who opened gates to let the Citroen drive through.

"Damn," Steel said. "I didn't anticipate that we'd need ID to get in here." They got out of the cab and paid off the driver, giving him a generous tip for such a short ride.

"Drive to the very end pontoon," Kiev said to his driver. "Right next to the Sunseeker, on the end pontoon there," The car drew to a halt next to the sleek craft.

"Come on, Mr Reilly, are you going to sit there all day?" he asked the CIA agent, who reluctantly climbed out of the rear door next to the boat. The big man was waiting. He took the American's arm and led him across the gantry onto the boat and then below into the salon. Kiev paused, looking back along the jetty, as though waiting for someone.

At the same moment the two British agents walked towards the guard post. They both spun to the right as they saw the Russian looking directly at the gates. They strode off behind a parked truck, peering over its hood, seeing Kiev turn and walk over the gantry onto the boat.

"Whew, that was close. I thought for a moment there he'd spotted us," said Steel.

There was a small coffee and ice cream bar just beyond the parked truck. Its canopies offered shelter from view, and afforded them a partial view of the boat.

"It looks as though the only way over there unseen is a swim!" said the other agent.

"I don't think so," said Steel with a smile, pointing across to a twin seat pedalow. A bright yellow craft blundered past; its big inflated wheels being turned energetically by two young lads. They pedalled for all they were worth, in order to escape the oncoming bow of a pleasure craft.

"There's our answer. Let's go and hire one. I can see them on the floating dock over there. They may even have motor boats for hire," said Steel as he walked off followed by a none-too-enthusiastic colleague.

As the two British agents went to the other end of the marina, a truck arrived at the gate to Kiev's jetty. After passing inspection it drove down to where the Sunseeker was moored. The Citroen was moved as the truck pulled alongside the boat. The driver activated the built-in crane and began to unload three large packing cases, labelled 'Suzuki personal watercraft'. Two of the cases were laid on the concrete jetty; the other was lowered into the rear cockpit of the boat. The driver of the truck then opened the two crates on the jetty with his crane, lifted the two jet skis onto the rear swim platform behind the boat where they were then strapped into place by Kiev's man.

"What's going on there?" Steel asked. They came around the corner of the jetty aboard a small powerboat, wearing sunglasses and baseball caps pulled down over their eyes. Steel also had a life jacket around his neck to complete the disguise.

"Search me, looks like some sort of delivery by truck."
They were just in time to see the second jet ski lowered onto the rear platform, and the empty cases put back onto the truck. Finding a good vantage point under the jetty opposite, they watched as Kiev and the big man manhandled a packing case from the cockpit of the Sunseeker, over and into a Cigarette powerboat, moored on the port side of the Sunseeker.

Once the transfer was complete, the other man went back aboard the big boat, whilst Kiev raised the rear engine cover of the Cigarette. He spent some time with his head inside, and then he too went back aboard the Sunseeker.

After ten minutes Steel took the small rental boat over towards the rear of the Cigarette. As he neared the boat he could see the packing case inside the hull. The front seats had been removed; the case somehow didn't seem large enough to house a jet ski. Before he could look more closely he had to leave quickly. Kiev's man came out of the big boat's salon, and jumped aboard the fast boat. He started the noisy engines, and then undid the ropes that rafted her to the side of the Sunseeker.

Kiev stood on the deck of the big boat watching as the other man reversed the noisy Cigarette out of the slip and head towards the exit of the marina.

People sitting on motor yachts and sailboats turned as the noisy, irritating, spluttering ear-rending engines passed on their way out to sea. As the Cigarette cleared the entrance to the harbour the sound of its engines being opened up was heard by most of Toulon. Its bow shot into the air, a mass of creamy white wake rooster tailed behind her, as she leaped up onto plane, quickly reaching fifty knots or more.

Kiev went back into the salon of the big boat.

"Well my friend, that's one problem out of the way, or to be more correct, it's two really," he said smirking as he slumped into a comfortable leather armchair.

"Now all that's left is you, my American combatant."

Steel had followed in the wake of the fast Cigarette boat. Though the boat he had hired was supposed to be a speedboat and would easily pull a pair of skis, it was no match for the power of the other vessel. Steel's top speed was possibly thirty-five or forty knots. He was soon some distance behind, but did not lose sight of the faster craft. He had left his compadre ashore to keep track on Kiev.

He still had the Cigarette in sight when the boat began to slow down considerably. He judged it to be about six miles off shore, and maybe a mile from him. He slowed to a crawl, and then looked through his glasses. The boat was rocking from side to side, and seemed to be listing to starboard more than it had been in port. He could see the big man struggling, and then he saw something go over the side. He lowered the binoculars to the water level and saw the wooden case on the surface for some seconds before it sank beneath the waves. The man then looked around as though making sure he had not been seen. Then the boat sprang back into life.

Steel opened the throttles of the hired boat, heading south.

"Christ I hope that wasn't Kevin Reilly. They couldn't have had the time to get him in there, provided that was him in the car." He brought the boat round in an arc to the east, meaning to come into the harbour at about the same time as the Cigarette.

Meanwhile, Kiev looked across the salon at Kevin Reilly. He stared for quite some time, and then said very quietly;

"Do you understand what those DNA reports were about? Do you know what they really mean?" He leaned across and looked Reilly straight in the eyes.

"No I don't. I know they are very important to you and to the English, but their true translation has not been given to me. When I spoke to the French inspector, he too knew they were of importance, but did not quite know the reason either," Reilly added.

"I see, I see. Does the MI6 man know what they mean?"

"He doesn't even know of their existence yet; that's why I'm here. I came here to give them to him, and then get out of this stupid jamboree for good. This is their problem, not ours."

"I'd like to believe you, but I can't afford to take the risk, my old antagonist. Though it does seem a shame to end all these years over somebody else's problems, but then that's what we always did, wasn't it?

Always other people's damn problems! Come on, Mr Reilly. We all have to face the music one day," said the big Russian as he rose from the chair and walked to the door of the salon.

Reilly followed, still wearing the handcuffs. He had a raincoat over his wrists as he walked across the gantry toward the car with Kiev now behind him. Kiev closed the car door behind Reilly and then sat in the driver's seat of the Citroen. The phone in Kiev's pocket began to ring.

"Yes," he spoke into the small plastic device.

"Good, can you slow the boat down a little; I can hardly hear what you are saying. That's better. Where are you now, exactly? Good." He took another equally small plastic device from his pocket and pressed a button. A red light came on, and then a very loud explosion was heard.

"Yes, that's very good," he said smiling, as he put the device back in his pocket. "That's very good indeed." He drove the car to security, then out of the port.

Moments earlier, Steel had looked across at the sleek boat as it skimmed across the water. It was about a half mile away on his left. The Cigarette began to slow, and then it turned in his direction. He thought for a moment he'd been spotted. The vessel's bow dipped as she came almost to a halt. She stood wallowing in her own wake for just a few seconds. Then Steel saw the white flash. The explosion was tremendous; the black crimson-edged cloud that seemed to billow in slow motion followed it. The movement of air and the sound of the explosion blew him off his feet, as pieces of the doomed craft began to land all around. Soon there was no more to be seen, but small bits of the craft, like flotsam on the edge of a tide.

Steel sped into the marina to see that the Citroen was gone and his partner nowhere to be seen. He pulled his small craft up to the jetty, tied it to a cleat, and then gingerly climbed a ladder next to the Sunseeker.

Cautiously he clambered aboard, kicked open the salon door, both hands on his firearm, sweeping left then right. The boat was deserted. He returned the hired speedboat, then, as agreed, took a cab back to the hotel, and waited for contact from the other agent, which came immediately as he'd entered the room. He picked up the room phone.

"Where are you? What's happening?" A pause. "I'll be right over in the rental car."

Kiev had driven the Citroen out of the port, then north towards the centre of Toulon. Shortly after that he turned into the airport.

"Where are we headed now?" asked the American.

"You ask too many questions, but then you always did!" Kiev parked the car, and then leaned across, pulling Reilly's wrists roughly to the centre armrest. Pushing the key into the lock of the handcuffs, he released first one hand then the other. The agent rubbed his wrists, flexing them, round and round.

"Come with me," growled Kiev, who climbed out of the car waiting for Reilly to follow suit. They walked towards the main building of the airport with neither of them speaking a word.

"I want you on the next flight to Paris, and then the very next flight to America. Don't ask me why I'm doing this, just get on with it and be grateful that you are still alive. The next flight to Paris leaves in fifteen minutes. I want to see you on that plane. I'm having you met at the other end, and you will be escorted onto the plane to the US.   If you are sensible, you will do as you are instructed. You will also show respect for this gesture by not discussing this affair with anyone. If I see you back here, or sniffing around any of the Sahaed properties anywhere in the world, I will personally kill you on sight."

Kiev pointed towards the Air France desk. "Go and buy a ticket, you are running out of time in more ways than one, old war horse."

He watched as Reilly took out a credit card, signed the counterfoil, then picked up his ticket and walked through the departure door. He never looked round.

Boris Kiev watched through the window as his old enemy climbed aboard the aircraft. He waited until the doors were closed and watched as the plane taxied out and took off for Paris.

Steel's colleague looked on with interest as the Russian walked back to the Citroen. The car drove away just as Steel walked up beside him.

"What's going on? Why did you let him go? What the hell's happening here, talk to me?"

"If you'd like to pause for breath, and let me get a word in edgeways, I'll explain." After Steel had heard what had taken place, he rushed across to the Air France desk, obtained the Paris phone number then walked quickly towards a carousel of pay phones.

"Just a minute, what are you going to do?" his partner asked.

"I'm going to get a call put out on the PA system in Paris for him to contact me here."

"Don't you think that they will have someone meeting him at the other end? And wouldn't such an announcement attract them? Couldn't they pretend to be him and get find out your whereabouts and maybe have the call traced?"

"I suppose you're right there. Let's sit down and work this one out," said Steel.

Kevin Reilly sat aboard the Paris bound plane with mixed feelings. He couldn't really believe what had just happened. Deep down he knew there was an ulterior motive. He decided that even though his own situation was a hundred percent improved, the British agent was still in jeopardy. Apart from getting the captain to turn the plane around, he couldn't seem to come up with a quick solution.

Out of duty and loyalty, he knew he must get a message to Steel. He knew he really ought to go back to Toulon. The words of Kiev still rang clear in his head. *"It's not your problem, let the Brits and the royals sort out their own problems."* He also remembered the last words he had heard from the lips of David Steel as he had walked away from the Eiffel Tower that day. *Kevin, my old sport, you are already involved. It's too late to back out now; the job has to be finished."* He sat feeling unusually indecisive and equally uncomfortable as the plane headed for Paris.

The Chalet Above Toulon

The sounds of the dogs had stopped. Hank sat in the rear of the limousine. Dusk had begun and he could see the long shadows of evening falling across the grounds as he moved to the front of the vehicle. He was about to open the door when he saw the sidelights of a vehicle coming up the drive towards the chalet. The car pulled up directly in front of the limousine. As he looked through the tinted glass divider, he saw the lights go out then the interior lit up. He froze as he saw Boris Kiev climb out, slam the door shut and stride off towards the chalet.

Hank waited for a few minutes keeping his head well down. Eventually he looked over the glass divider and opened the rear door of the limo cautiously, his ears searching the silence for any trace of a sound. Hearing nothing but the occasional rustle of wind in the trees, he climbed out into the dingy darkness of the garage.

He moved slowly towards the entrance, peering around the corner of the building. Scanning the grounds, the whole place seemed deserted. Turning his attention towards the chalet, he saw there were numerous lights throughout the building and noted another entrance with a ramp leading down to it at the side, as though leading underneath the structure of the building.

The ramp seemed wide enough to accommodate the largest of vehicles. He left the protection of the garage block, moving quickly into the shelter of some rhododendron bushes. There he crouched opposite the entry to the ramp. Taking a quick look back toward the garages he had just left, he noticed for the first time that there was another level above where the cars were kept.

Charles De Gaulle Airport, Paris

It seemed to Reilly one of the shortest flights that he had taken for some time. Much sooner than anticipated, the flight attendant announced their entry into Paris airspace as the plane began to descend. Reilly fastened his seat belt and the aircraft landed and taxied towards the airport. After the usual scramble to get belongings out of the overhead compartments, everyone stood during that interminable period whilst the doors were opened.

"May I have your attention please," came the message, and then once more, but louder: "May I have your attention, please. Will the passenger, Mr Kevin Reilly, please make himself known to the cabin staff."

The passengers began to move down the plane, but Kevin had stayed in his seat as he hated the mad rush, and could never see the sense in traditional bashing of hand baggage with the other passengers. He walked towards the exit, the last off the plane.

"Mr Reilly?" A pretty blonde attendant asked the agent.

"Yes, that's me." He looked beyond the girl into the exit tunnel and saw the face of a complete stranger.

"There are two gentlemen here to speak with you, sir," said the flight attendant. Two men dressed in the coveralls of airport staff entered the plane. Within seconds the agent was wearing the same apparel and was soon following the two men down the metal staircase that led to the underside of the aircraft. They led him towards a truck connected to a number of trolleys already filled with baggage from the flight. The three of them jumped into the front seat and moved off towards the main terminal and into the baggage handling area.

They stopped, and then climbed into a waiting car. So far not one word had been spoken, other than the instruction to put on the coveralls. The agent was not clear as to their allegiance so decided to wait and see.

The Chalet, Toulon

Hank Marlin stayed behind the shelter of the bushes for sometime. He had seen no more movement outside, but had observed various lighted windows in the upstairs of the chalet. He moved with caution and a certain amount of trepidation, as he went down the darker side of the ramp. At the bottom he came to a set of very strong metal doors, big enough to accept the largest of vehicles. Off to the side was a smaller door, which appeared equally strong, it too made of metal. Hank placed his ear to its surface, listening for any sounds. He could hear some kind of compressor running, maybe an air conditioning unit, he thought.

He decided to err on the side of caution. Slipping back into the shadows he climbed the side wall of the ramp and sat in the coarse bushes. As he did so the side door opened and a man came out followed by another. Hank recognised the second as the Arab, Ali.

"Kiev says that the Englishman is a tenacious little bugger. He won't talk," said the bigger man.

"He weel wen I am back in zere," said the Arab. Hank saw the whites of his eyes shine in the moonlight as he emphasised his words, his tombstone-like teeth showing as he grinned.

"Yeah, I bet 'e will mate," said the other man smiling as he lit a smoke. "I'm bloody sure 'e will, Ali. You're a vicious little bastard. I'm gonna take a walk round the grounds." He strode up the ramp.

"Hey an don't lock the bleed'n door, Ali, I ain't gotta key. I won't be more than a couple of minutes. I need some air." The Arab slipped back into the building, leaving the door ajar.

Seconds later, Hank came out of hiding. He squatted on the wall, then slid down to the ground, three or four feet from the sloping ramp. He was concerned about entering for two reasons. The obvious was the impending return of the big Englishman with the cockney accent. The second was the bright light from the moon. If anyone were to be watching from the inside, they would see his silhouette as he entered the door. He decided to throw caution to the wind and approached the door. It was hinged on the left; luckily the moon was shining from that direction. Pulling the door open no more than a foot, he moved quickly into the darkened interior, locking the door securely behind him.

He stood with his eyes tightly closed for a few seconds to accustom them to the darkness, and then moved further inside. The area was massive. It was actually a large underground warehouse, only a small part of it was under the chalet, but the bulk was obviously completely under the grounds.

Hank guessed from where he stood that there had to be at least a hundred thousand square feet, maybe much more. He went behind a number of large packing cases and taking the flashlight from his pocket he tried to get his bearings.

Over in the far corner he could see the glow from the window of what he assumed was an office. He began to make his way slowly in that direction. Feeling his way along, his foot hit solid metal. Looking down, he saw the track of a military tank. He moved round the other side. From the glow of his torch he saw armoured cars, tanks, rocket launchers, missiles — in fact what appeared to be enough equipment to obliterate a nation. The only things that were missing seemed to be jet fighter aircraft.

Hank continued stealthily towards the glow of the light. As he got closer, he heard the sounds of voices. "For the last time, and before I let Ali here loose on you, where is your friend, the English policeman?" It was the voice of Colonel Boris Kiev.

The City of Paris — that same evening

Kevin Reilly sat in the back seat of the car as it rushed across the suburbs and into the downtown area. Still the silence continued. The car entered through a wrought iron archway and was driven hastily past open gates, drawing up to a large door under a covered canopy. The car door was opened as he was pulled out of the car. Even though they were moving very quickly Reilly managed to catch a brief glance of a name on the wall of the building, it read: 'British Embassy' embossed on a solid brass plaque before he was hurried into the building.

The elevator stopped at the third floor. The two men and Reilly still wore their airport coveralls.

"Sit down Mr Reilly," said a distinguished straight-faced man sitting behind the big, shiny desk. The agent sat there feeling somewhat like a Fedex delivery, except that nobody had signed for him. The man behind the desk waved his hand in dismissal of the other two men as the door closed firmly behind the CIA agent. The ringing of the phone on the otherwise empty desk broke the silence in the room, as Reilly had held up his hands in a gesture of 'Will somebody for Christ's sake tell me what in the hell is going on around here?'

"Yes, hold the line will you." The man behind the desk passed the handset to Reilly. "A call for you old chap." he said pressing a green button on the side of the telephone receiver.

"Hello, is that you Kevin? Hello?" It was David Steel.

"Yes David, this is Kevin Reilly."

"Thank Christ you're still safe. I wondered what on earth had happened to you since we left Paris. You're on a safe phone; I'm on a payphone in Toulon. Come on, bring me up to date. There's a lot happening down here that I need to know about. Do you know where that bloody English cop and his sidekick are?"

"Hey slow down; take it easy," said the CIA man. "By the way, I suppose I have to thank someone for getting me out of this last mess. I reckon that goddamn Russian had it planned for me to retire permanently; retire from life that is!"

The man behind the desk shrugged his shoulders casually. The agent wasn't sure whether that was in respect of his gratitude or his early retirement. He started to bring Steel up to date. Steel's voice was also coming through a speaker on the desk phone, and no doubt being recorded, Reilly thought to himself.

At the end of the debriefing that took all of ten minutes, during which time Steel had asked innumerable questions, the man behind the desk had remained silent.

"What more do you need from me now?" the American agent asked.

"I'm not sure there's anything else that you can do, is there Kevin?" replied Steel rhetorically. The man behind the desk nodded in agreement, as he fiddled with a gold ring on his pinkie finger.

"It would be useful if you could remain available for a while, Kevin. We could put you up at the embassy here for a few days." The man behind the desk nodded in agreement.

"I think not, but thanks all the same. We too have an embassy here you know. If you need me, you can send a message there. I'll leave a contact number here." After Steel had cleared the line, Reilly got up to leave the room.

"Before you go, Mr Reilly, there are a couple more questions, and we'll need to know where you intend to stay in Paris."

"Again, I think not sir. Now if you'll excuse me, I'll be on my way. The last couple of days have not been the most restful. Have no fear, I will be in touch."

The man got up from the desk offering his hand to the agent. Reilly put two fingers to his right brow and gave a mock salute. He walked out of the room.

The two men stood outside the door bereft of their coveralls, wearing dark suits. They closed ranks as Reilly approached. The other man came out of the doorway.

"That's alright, Mr Reilly is leaving now. One of you please show him out of the embassy, the other come with me." They did as instructed. Back in the office the man returned to the tidy desk.

"I want Reilly tailed twenty four hours a day. I want to be kept up to date. The Russian will now know he is on the loose. He may try to terminate the American. It's your job to see that no harm comes to him right now, understand?"

"Yes, Sir Martin, I'll see to it," replied the agent leaving the room.

Sir Martin picked up the phone.

"Yes, get me Number 10 Downing Street. I want person to person with the Prime Minister. I want a sterile line, and I want the conversation scrambled, is that clear?"

"Yes, Sir Martin, we will connect you in approximately three minutes."

The Chalet at Toulon

The light became brighter and the voices more distinguishable. Hank neared the offices in the corner of the big warehouse. He slid behind a large packing case next to a trailer carrying what looked like a battery of surface to air missiles. The main lights in the office were extinguished; only a bright quartz-reading lamp was lit and was turned into the eyes of Michael Meadows.

Hank had a side view of his colleague's face. He looked pale and drawn; the bright light exaggerated the darkening blood on the side of his face. Both of his hands were tied behind his back.

Kiev stood to one side. The Arab was leaning over Michael and pushed the chair away from the desk. He was holding an electric cord with two alligator clips on the end. He had a sickly grin across his face as he clicked opened and closed the jagged metal teeth.

"Now col-o-nel, we weel see eef hooking hees manhood to eelectreecity weel loosen hees tongue." The Arab bent down to undo Michael's belt, his grin becoming wider. Michael was petrified.

Hank crouched down below the waist-high screen of the office wall and crawled along to the entrance. Suddenly the room was bathed in bright light as he switched on the lights.

"Don't either of you make one single move. I won't hesitate to kill you both. I have nothing to lose, you know that colonel, and nobody will hear a shot down here. Now get back into the corner there, both of you." Hank waved the Glock menacingly, and then looked at the handcuffs retaining his colleague's wrists. "Keys please Boris!" he said as he beckoned with his left hand. Kiev pointed to a key at the other side of the desk. "Slide it carefully over here big man."

Hank went behind Michael and he fished around with the key, not taking his eyes from the two men for a second. Eventually there was a click as one of the cuffs released.

"Thank God you found me." As Michael spoke he brought his hands to the front, massaging his wrists, moving them around to increase circulation.

At the same moment the Arab sprung over the desktop. Hank fired, the bullet hit him in the side of the neck, the shot throwing the man to the floor. Kiev dived towards Hank. The second shot hit the Russian high on the right shoulder, shattering his shoulder blade as he too fell to the floor writhing in agony.

"Look out, Hank!" yelled Michael, as the Arab sprang up from the corner, a vicious looking knife in his hand. The third shot hit him in the centre of the chest. He hit the wall from the force of the bullet and slid in slow motion down the partitioning to the floor leaving a scarlet trail as he fell. The Glock had done its job A final look of horror decorated the Arab's face; the black beady eyes no longer piercing, but glazed and dead like those on a fishmonger's slab.

Kiev was kneeling, silently holding his shoulder.

"On your feet, colonel. Let's have you out here where there's a bit more room," said Hank, waving the gun towards the warehouse.

"Put the cuffs on him Michael, hands in front and around that concrete pillar there." He led them to a pillar out in the warehouse behind the office, away from general view. Kiev stood hugging the pillar.

"You're a dead man, inspector. You won't leave here alive. Don't you understand that, you interfering English idiot?" the Russian snarled, as he pulled at the restraints, his face now tight against the support.Hank made certain that Kiev could not reach anything.

"Empty his pockets and search him thoroughly. Take off his belt and tie it firmly around and into his mouth. That'll keep him quiet for a while. Keep away from his feet. Here tie his ankles so he can't kick anything and make a sound," he added, throwing an adjacent roll of adhesive packaging tape across the floor.

While Michael completed his task, Hank took another quick look around the office. In the desk drawer he found another gun. Before leaving he pushed the diminutive body of the Arab under the desk, pulled a chair in front of the bloodstained wall, then turned out the lights, locked the door and removed the key.

"Let's take a quick look at that wound of yours," he said to Michael.

"It's OK at the moment. I think the bullet went straight through the soft part of my arm. The bleeding seems to have stopped though."

"Take your jacket off and stop trying to be the tough guy," said Hank, helping Michael as he spoke. The wound was a clean shot with no apparent bone damage. Hank had found a first aid kit in an adjacent washroom. He dressed the wound using some antiseptic cream and a bandage. "That'll have to do for the time being."

"Come on, let's get out of here," said Michael.

"Not so fast. Remember why we're here? There are just a couple more things I want to do first and there's another one of Kiev's goons outside trying to get in here. Follow me." Hank strode off across the warehouse. He stopped suddenly, turning to Michael. "Here you'd better have this, it may come in handy," he said, passing the other handgun to Michael.

They stood by the entrance door for a couple of minutes. There were no sounds from the outside, which concerned Hank.

"Come on, we don't have all night. Let's go up into the main building." Michael followed as they retraced their steps across the warehouse.

"Here it is," whispered Michael, pointing to the door of an elevator.

"We want the stairs though," Hank whispered back.

"Over here," whispered Michael again, pointing to the fire exit. Hank slowly opened the door into the stairwell and they both began their assent to the chalet.

The City of Paris

Kevin Reilly walked out of the British Embassy. He knew only too well that he would be followed. He paused on the sidewalk for a moment, then hailed a passing cab. He arrived at the American Embassy and after presenting his ID, was shown up to an office with the door bearing the euphemistic sign, Cultural Attaché.

"Kevin, how nice to see you! You've got half the department looking for you. Are you OK?" A man got up from behind the desk and walked across to greet his colleague.

"I'm fine, and how's life treating you, Mack?" He shook the hand of Alan McKenzie, the resident CIA boss in Paris, a man some ten years his junior; one of the newer breed — more an administrator than a man of action. After the expected reply, Reilly continued:

"I need a sterile phone and some privacy."

"Come this way. They seem keen to talk to you; the director himself has been on the horn earlier today. There's everything in there that you'll need. Come back to my office when you're done." McKenzie opened the door of a small unoccupied office as he spoke.

After a conversation with his boss in Langley, Virginia, Reilly left the embassy. He whistled for a cab and got into the rear of the first one that stopped.

"Monsieur?" said the driver in a questioning tone.

"Charles De Gaulle Airport and hurry will you," he said to the driver.

"Oui, Monsieur."

He had totally ignored the request of McKenzie, which he knew would irritate the man immensely. He also knew that the entourage behind him, consisting of MI6, CIA, Uncle Tom Cobley and all, were in for a disappointment as no doubt they tailed his cab towards the capital's busiest airport. He couldn't even be bothered to make the effort to look behind him.

The Chalet Toulon

Nearing the top of the stairs, with Hank leading the way, they saw a door off to the left. Another dozen steps further up was the main door, which they assumed led into the chalet itself. Pausing at the first door, Hank stood with his ears against its surface, but due to their heavy breathing from the climb they couldn't hear a sound.

"What's that smell?" whispered Michael.

"I don't smell anything. Wait a minute. There is a sort of clinical aroma here, bit like a hospital," replied Hank.

"Maybe it's some kind of a first aid room, though it seems a long way from the warehouse doesn't it?" suggested Michael.

Hank looked a little closer at the door. There was no handle but there was a metal flap at about waist height held by one screw. Hank pulled the flap with his finger. It swivelled to the side revealing a key entry. He crouched down peering through the orifice.

"Christ, take a look in here," he whispered. "There's a complete bloody hospital in there." Michael bent down towards the keyhole.

"I can't see a thing, just blank white." Hank went back to the keyhole. As Michael had said his view was blocked out by solid white, then it began to clear as he saw the back of a white coated attendant walking away from his direction. Eventually Hank saw that the man was pushing a wheel chair. As it turned to the right they could see that the passenger had heavily bandaged hands and also bandages to the face and head. Hank watched for a while, then a female nurse walked out of an adjoining room leading another patient by the arm, this time a woman.

She too seemed heavily bandaged. Her raven black hair hung down below the head bandages and her arms were strapped up to the elbows. She shuffled tentatively as though unable to see.

It was now totally dark outside. The other man, who had left the ware-house earlier for a breath of air, had returned to find the door locked. Assuming that Ali had not locked him out on purpose, he decided to re-enter by the main door, and then go back down by the elevator. On entering the chalet he was stopped by Mr Sahaed himself, who asked him to move some pieces of furniture into one of the guest suites. Having completed the task he now stood awaiting the arrival of the elevator.

"Come on, we have to get out of this stairwell before the other guy returns," said Hank. They climbed the remaining few steps. At the top Hank took a handkerchief from his pocket and removed the hot light bulb.

"I'm going to open the door slightly. If it looks clear, I'll go out there and take a look around. When the coast is completely clear I'll come back and get you," he said, peering through the crack he'd opened in the door. He looked out into the sumptuous hallway and saw the big Englishman standing next to the elevator doors, tapping his leg impatiently as he waited. Hank could see no other activity out there. He looked around for the inevitable cameras that he knew would be there somewhere. He watched the big man enter the elevator then slid through the doorway.

Meanwhile, Michael stood nervously in the absolute silence of the stairwell, wondering which would be the first door to open: the one next to him or the one at the bottom of the stairs.

The Londoner walked out of the elevator and strode across towards the warehouse office. The room was in complete darkness. The metal doors closed silently and at the same time the thermostat cut in as the air-conditioning unit roared into action breaking the silence across the warehouse once again, covering the muffled sounds made by the Russian as he tried in vain to shout past the strong leather belt that cut into his lips drawing blood. The handcuff chains rattled as he tore and pulled.

The force of his frustration coupled with his fierce temper and the pain from his shattered shoulder drained his energy with every move.

Charles De Gaulle Airport, Paris

The taxi carrying Kevin Reilly sped through the gates of the private jet area and on towards the top security sector. There sat the jets of the French and other governments, each with its own cloak of diplomatic immunity. After showing his ID, Reilly's cab was rushed through the gate. A security man jumped into the front with the driver.

The vehicle pulled up by the side of an unmarked Citation, its engines already running; its strobe lights flashing in the night air. The agent ran from the cab and up the steps, ducking his head as he entered the jet. The doors were closed and the engines roared as the plane moved off towards the runway.

As Reilly went to take a seat, he noticed that the seat next to his was occupied.

"Well, so we meet again, and so soon Mr Reilly." The agent looked into the face of the man he had met at the British Embassy earlier.

"Let me introduce myself. I'm Fields, Martin Fields, MI6." Reilly sat down and made no comment. Without turning towards the man he asked.

"Is this plane ours or yours?"

After receiving no reply, he turned and looked at an empty seat. Sir Martin was stooping at the rear of the plane with a telephone to his ear. He did not return to his seat, but sat down where he was.

The American found the answer to his question as one of the crew came off the flight deck wearing a New York Knick's baseball cap.

"Hey Kevin, Paris is a bit off your beaten track isn't it?" asked the pilot, pushing the cap to the back of his head.

"Why do we have the English contingent aboard?" asked the agent.

"Something big is going down. We were rushed over from Berlin this afternoon. They had us on instant standby until the smooth Limey and you got here a few minutes ago. So sit back and enjoy the flight. We'll be there soon — it's only a short hop."

"Where soon? What's only a short hop?"

"Chief's on the blower," said another face from the flight deck cutting short the conversation and pointing to the wall phone. The agent picked up the phone, and was soon fully apprised of the situation, the destination, and other requirements. It seemed only minutes before Reilly heard the familiar sound and sensation of engine tones dropping, the air pressure blocking up his ears and the undercarriage being locked in to place. Lights shot past the window and water bubbled along the glass as the night rains bounced off the Toulon runway.

"I have a car waiting at the plane," said Sir Martin Fields.

"You may want to go to the hotel first and touch base with Steel."

"You're not leaving the plane here then?" Reilly asked the English peer.

"Absolutely not, old chap. Why have a dog and bark yourself?" he said with an arrogance that made Reilly want to smack him right in the teeth. The agent left the plane, scurrying down the steps as the rains poured down. He fell into the rear seat of the waiting car and was whisked off towards downtown Toulon.

Back at the chalet, Hank moved quickly across the hallway, every nerve in his body tingling like a six-volt battery shock as he went towards an alcove by the side of the elevator shaft. He heard the sounds of opening doors echo in the shaft below. *I hope to Christ he doesn't find Kiev, or the shit will really hit the fan,* he thought to himself as an involuntary shudder coursed through his body, goose pimples bubbling up on his legs and arms.

The thought spurred him on. He looked both ways along the hallway, just as a servant came out of a door carrying a tray filled with sandwiches. Hank waited until the man had gone, then he made a quick check for cameras before he walked towards the door where the servant emerged.

Opening the door, he found himself in a scullery with a small kitchen leading off into a cleaning storeroom. Seeing numerous items of staff clothing, he put on a chef's jacket and apron. He took a disposable chef's hat from an open box then collected an extra jacket, apron and hat, putting them onto a tray along with two large cartons of milk. He left the room carrying the tray on his shoulder, covering his face.

Walking purposefully through the doorway, he retraced his steps to the entrance of the stairway. Inside, Michael looked pensive and scared.

"I thought something had gone wrong. I've been counting the seconds since you left."

"Put these on," said Hank, passing the jacket and apron to Michael, who winced at the pain as he took off his own jacket. Hank plonked the hat on his friend's head.

"Let me check that the coast is clear, then follow me," he added, opening the door a crack and closing it again very quickly. He saw the big bodyguard come out of the elevator.

"He's on his own and not unduly excited so obviously didn't find Kiev!" They waited for a few more minutes during which time they drank one carton of the milk between them.

An Ocean Front Hotel, Toulon

It was still raining heavily as the car pulled up outside the hotel. Reilly ran from the vehicle, his bag in one hand, the other holding a soddened newspaper over his head, as the torrential rains bounced up off the sidewalk over his shoes and up the bottom of his pants. He went into the reception area, wiping water from his eyes.

"At last! Are you OK?" David Steel stood in the centre of the hall holding out his hand. Reilly shook it.

"The least said the better," he said as he removed his raincoat, which was duly taken by a nearby porter.

"Come on, let's go up to your room. We need to talk and there's not a lot of time if we're to act quickly."

"What's with the 'we' crap?" asked Reilly.

"You know what I mean," replied Steel.

"No, I don't know what you mean. My instructions are crystal clear; give you what information I can. Pick up as much information as I can, then, as the good shepherd said: 'get the flock out of here!' This is a very delicate matter. The US of A cannot be seen to have any involvement in the affair. The eyes of the whole world are watching. It may become one of the biggest stories in history."

"Come on Kev, this is your old friend here, I need your help, I have to get into that bloody chalet, and I must do it now."

"Great, I'll tell you all I know, but don't expect any more from me. I already have a death threat from Kiev if he sees me around here again"

"Since when did that sort of thing bother you, Kevin?"

"Since right now. I want to live to enjoy my pension, and sticking my head in front of that Russian lunatic is not the best recipe for longevity. Come on then, let's talk. Incidentally, I just had the pleasure of the company of your revered boss. You have my deepest sympathy, old chap!" he said sarcastically.

"What did the DNA report say?"

"I can't remember the technical stuff, this new bio-technology is for boffins, but I can tell you there is something there that worries the Sahaed camp. It appears that the English cop knows more than anyone, but he seems to have disappeared off the face of the earth. Kiev is currently looking for him. By the way, I should have thanked your boss and his men."

"Why's that?"

"Well, I'm convinced that Kiev had ordered me killed. He just needed me away from here first; he didn't want the slightest attention drawn to this area for whatever reason. I reckon they would have had a bash in Paris, that's if your guys hadn't picked me up first — thanks to your timely phone call. He didn't reckon anyone would know I was arriving there. I owe you one!"

Reilly went on to tell Steel all that had happened since they last met. He covered every detail.

"That report must hold some really hot information because it's cost a number of lives already. You reckon that was the body of the taxi driver they dumped into the ocean, then for Kiev to actually kill one of his own men to cover up, it just shows they'll go to any lengths. The answers must be at the chalet. I'm going to need your help getting in there, and the sooner the better."

"I have told you once and I'll tell you again for the final time, I am not going back there. I am instructed to return to Cairo."

"They've taken the other agent off this job, he's gone back to Spain" said Steel.

"My heart bleeds for you, but I've told you where I stand. I'm out of here in the morning. You can kiss my ass goodbye, is that quite clear? Have you got the message?" Reilly stared the Englishman directly in the eyes as he spoke.

"You said it with your own lips a few minutes ago. You owe me one. Well I'm calling it in now!" said Steel, staring back at him. Reilly shrugged his shoulders in resignation.

Back at the Chalet

Hank and Michael came out of the stairwell and turned left down the hallway towards a door marked 'no admission.' Hank led the way through the door as they entered a clinical area. It was most certainly a well-equipped mini hospital. Hank spotted a small kitchen area. They walked purposefully into the room, placing the tray with the milk cartons on the centre table, then Hank turned off the lights.

"Where's the door that leads to the stairway?" he asked.

"Over there," said Michael pointing directly out of the door.

"Come on, follow me. Let's see if we can find it."

Leaving the room they walked along a corridor. They passed a door with round windows at eye level from where they could see that it was an operating theatre. Turning right at the end of the corridor, they saw two doors: one to a toilet and the other to the stairwell. There was a key in a small break glass case on the wall beside it.

Hank took out the knife from his pocket, flicked the switchblade and carefully forced the wooden rim around the break glass case. He unlocked the door then meticulously replaced the key. Suddenly all went dark as the lights were turned off in the medical area. They heard the swishing sound as two swing doors were released, then silence.

"Don't move for a minute. I'll be back," whispered Hank. He went back into the medical area. Minutes later Michael saw the glow from a flashlight coming down the corridor.

"The coast is clear. It looks like everyone's retired for the night. We need to find somewhere to hide until morning. There's no sense in charging blindly round the building; we're bound to be seen. Let's go back down to the warehouse, and find a cozy tank to rest in!" said Hank.

Michael shuddered at the thought of going into the same area as Kiev, but followed his colleague through the door, just as all hell let loose.

The lights came back on, doors banged, raised voices came along the corridor. Men were shouting, a woman's voice said,

"Sit him there. Put the other one in the operating room."

"Get off my arm, I'm not a cripple," snarled the voice of Kiev.

"Come on doctor, get this lot sorted out, I have things to do. Strap this shoulder up and let me get after those two interfering bastards. I take it Ali's dead? "

"I'm afraid so, colonel," said a voice with a strong Middle Eastern accent. "Now you sit there and let me take a look at that wound."

"Search every inch of this place, don't just stand there, get on with it!"

yelled Kiev. "They are somewhere in this building. I want them found! Get everybody onto it. Search the grounds while you are about it. I want these people now! This is personal."

"Let's get the hell out of here, I know the exact place to lay low for a while," whispered Hank. He opened the unlocked door into the stairwell. Hearing no sounds, he went through the door, followed by Michael. Searching his pockets, he found a small piece of notepaper, which he folded tightly forcing it under the door, keeping it closed.

At the bottom of the stairs, after making sure the coast was clear, they went into the warehouse, which was in total darkness. Making their way to the front door, Hank released the lock. They exited the building, leaving the door off the latch.

"Follow me," Hank whispered as he sprung up the three-foot side of the ramp and into the bushes. Within seconds they had entered the garage containing the taxi and the limo.

Hank found a wall ladder that led up to the staff quarters in the loft space above. They sat on an old bunk bed, breathless after their fast retreat from the chalet.

Though the glass was filthy, they could see through the dust and cobwebs to the front of the big house from the dormer window of the room.

"That was a bit too close for comfort," Michael said, almost stuttering.

"I think we've really pissed off the colonel now," replied Hank, a smirk on his face. "I still want to get into the rooms on the third floor."

Michael's expression was not exactly one of encouragement as he lifted his eyes heavenwards, in a gesture of total amazement. They continued to watch as almost every light came on in the chalet. The grounds were lit up like daylight and they saw men combing the bushes along the drive. Large dogs pulled and strained at leashes, barking and yelping with excited anticipation of the chase.

"Shhh, what's that?" asked Michael. They both heard the noise of movement in the garage below, then voices, followed by heavy canine panting, then squeaks, then the fearful sound of a large dog scratching and tearing at the foot of the loft ladder.

"Looks like there's somebody up there," muttered a voice.

"Sure does, me old mate," replied the unmistakable voice of the big cockney.

"Okay, we know you're up there lads. There's two ways ter cam darn, the easy wan an de uver. Please yerselves, we've got all night, but its nuffink a grenade won't speed up, get mi drift d'yer lads? On the uver 'and, we can always shoot a few bullets up frew the floor boards. What d'yer fink there lads eh?" Then there followed the unmistakable sounds of more than one automatic weapon being primed as spring loaded bolts were drawn, slamming lethal projectiles into barrels.

"Maybe we orta move the cars, the guv wut'nt wan 'em cavered in blad, nar would he?"

The last threat had the desired effect. Hank shrugged his shoulders.

"What do you think?" he whispered.

"Best do as he says," replied Michael, his face like chalk.

"Okay we're coming down, just keep hold of those bloody dogs," Hank shouted, as they walked towards the ladder.

Kevin Reilly sat in the front seat of the rental car, which was parked in a layby opposite the perimeter wall of the chalet. *Ever had the feeling you've been here before, Kev?* he thought, as he slid the window partially down and heard what he thought were the sounds of dogs barking and baying excitedly as though they were close on the scent of prey. Then he saw the shadowy figure come out of the bushes along the wall of the chalet, and cross the road.

"All hell seems to have let loose in there, the flood lights are on every-where, there are armed men all over the place, and unfriendly dogs covering the undergrowth."

"Let's get the hell out of here then," said Reilly, needing no more prompting

"I told you, once I'm in there, all you have to do is wait here and help me on the two way," the English agent said nonchalantly.

"I've got the rope ladder on the wall, just come and take a look, and see if you can make head or tail of what's happening in there. Come on! For the sake of old times, help me here will you?" said Steel.

"OK, but remember I'm not going in there. This is your, war not ours." The CIA man got out of the car, reluctantly crossing the road. He climbed the rope ladder and keeping his head below the lens of the invading camera he peered cautiously over the top of the wall. He could see no activity in the grounds as he scanned around through the night sights.

"Seems quiet enough to me," he whispered hoarsely. "Wait a minute, there seems to be a lot of activity around the garage block. Come and take a look." he went down the ladder as he muttered almost indistinguishably. Steel then took his place.

"The garages are the block to the left of the big house?" he asked. "Got it. Christ! It's the English cop and the princess's secretary. They have them cuffed and they're taking them into the main building," he whispered down to Reilly.

Steel watched as they took the two men through the main door, then he came down the ladder.

"Is there another entrance to the chalet?" he asked the American.

"Yes, if you look to the left of the main house and between the garages, there is a ramp leading down to an entrance there." Steel threw his leg across and sat atop the wall, timing the movement of the automatic cameras.

"I'm off then, Kev. Make sure you stand by on the radio. I may need some advice or assistance and stay up here will you? This wall could interfere with communications." He disappeared over the top into the darkness as the reluctant CIA man climbed back up the rope ladder.

Reilly looked along the wall towards the gates. Again he saw the glint of a camera lens in the distance. He ducked quickly behind the shelter of the greenery that grew along the surface of the wall. He could see no movement in the grounds and only a couple of lights coming from the chalet. He hung precariously from the ladder. *This looks like being a long night. What the hell am I doing back here? I must be out of my tiny mind,* he thought. The radio in his pocket crackled into life.

"You got a copy; you read me?" came the whispered voice of the MI6 man.

"Got you loud and clear. Where are you, you crazy son of a bitch?"

"Just coming up to the garages. You see anybody behind me in the grounds?"

"Negative on that."

"Good, I can see the ramp now. Doesn't seem to be anyone around, maybe they're not expecting company. I'm off now. Stand by where you are. Out." Reilly's radio went dead.

As he walked hesitantly across to the ladder in the roof of the garage Hank had slipped the flick knife down his sock. He took out the Semtex, which he pushed down the other sock. Taking the electronic sender and the detonators, he pushed them down the crotch of his underpants.

Rough hands grabbed at his legs as he descended from the loft. The gun and flashlight were taken from his pockets and handcuffs were painfully ratcheted onto his wrists.

As Michael came down, he was searched, but no gun was found. He too was handcuffed and then they were pushed roughly out of the garage and hurried towards the main building.

"I have both of them here, sir. I'm coming into the house now," said one of Kiev's staff. "Good. Are there any other signs of life out there?" growled an irritated Boris Kiev.

"None that I can see. sir," the bodyguard replied into the cell phone.

"Just the same, make sure the grounds are covered as usual."

"Will do, colonel," answered the man as he closed the phone and made off towards the side entrance of the building.

From his vantage point behind the bushes, Steel saw the man walk down the ramp, then pause to open the small door. Suddenly sensing a slight movement of air the man began to turn. He glimpsed Steel's figure from the corner of his eye, then his fingers clawed frantically at the piano wire tightening around his throat. He tried to yell, but like one of those unforgettable bad dreams, no sounds would come out of his mouth.

Steel dragged the limp body into the bushes. He took the phone and the man's firearm and silently entered the warehouse, locking the door behind him. The vibrator on his radio moved in his breast pocket, the speaker was off and the throat microphone and ear piece activated.

"There's quite a lot of activity in the grounds," came the voice of Kevin Reilly.

"That's OK, I'm inside. I'll be in touch," he whispered, pressing the microphone against his neck.

He moved swiftly through the vast warehouse, noting the varied armaments. He came up to the office, which was open, but in darkness. From the beam of his flashlight he saw the blood trail down the wall. He moved on, searching for means of getting up to the main house.

Hank and Michael were unceremoniously thrown into a small laundry room that had no windows or ceiling hatches. The only exit was the door by which they had entered. Expert training allowed instant cuff removal.

"Well things certainly don't get any better," said Michael.

"No, but they could be worse," replied the ever-positive Hank, as he felt around the door's hinges. Looking down at his watch he saw that it was now half an hour after midnight. "I wonder if we shall have the pleasure of Colonel Kiev's company tonight, or whether he will wait until the morning?" He picked away at the plaster around the doorframe with the point of the flick knife. He began to push the pin of the top hinge up from the bottom, slowly; the head came up at the top. He then took the knife and gently prised the head until the pin was almost free of the hinge, repeated the procedure on the bottom hinge, then popped both pins.

"So far so good. I don't think there is much time left. Kiev must be too annoyed to wait until the morning before he gets his hands on me," he said with a facial expression half way between a grin and a grimace.

Now he had the knife in between the door and the frame. Levering a fraction of an inch at a time from top to bottom, the door began to come out of the frame, slowly at first, then they could feel the air from the hallway. The hinges parted as the door dropped a half-inch, the locked side creaking slightly as the end of the dead bolt took the weight. Hank removed the door, checking that all was clear on the other side. They pulled the door back into the small room, and then re-hung the hinges replacing the pins.

Leaving the mortise of the dead bolt still protruding, they moved fast along the hallway and back through the door at the top of the fire stairs.

As soon as they entered the stairwell, they heard the unmistakable sound of the door at the bottom being opened, both hearing the hydraulic closer creak shut. Hank turned the doorhandle to the hospital, bent down and removed the temporary paper stop, praying a silent prayer as he pulled the keyhole cover towards him.

"I hope they didn't re-lock the door," he whispered. Michael had a look of almost overwhelming relief as the door came open and they both moved back into the medical area. Quickly, Hank removed the break glass key cover, and then carefully locked the door. He put his finger over the keyhole, only just in time, as he heard a gentle thud on the other side. He held his other forefinger to his lips; Michael had already heard the movement.

Hank moved swiftly along the corridor of the medical area. He peered through the doorway into the main hallway outside, and then closed it again, returning to where Michael stood.

"It's the British agent! It's the MI6 man, he's in the goddamned house!" he exclaimed, a look of total surprise across his face. "Shit, that could put the cat right among the pigeons," he added, punching the palm of his left hand. Quickly he walked the other way towards the sitting rooms.

"We really need to get up onto the next floor. We'll have to use the main stairs, but that could be a bit hairy. Maybe we can find another stairway." Hank said none too convincingly. "Let's take a look. We don't have a lot of time. My instincts tell me that this place will soon be vacated," he added.

Minutes earlier, Steel had moved up the fire exit stairway. At the top he spotted a door to the left. Pushing it gently at first he found the door was locked. He slid the keyhole cover aside, but could see nothing. He climbed the last few stairs up the fire exit to a door at the top, opening it just a crack. He could see no movement, so went out into the hallway, turning right. He passed an open door and thought it strange the dead bolt was sticking out in the locked position.

He could see the main entrance hall further along the hallway, and continued on cautiously. At that moment he saw Boris Kiev come out of a door at the bottom of the main staircase. His back was turned, as he spoke to someone. Steel ducked into the open doorway of a scullery room, closed the door, then peered through the crack and saw Kiev walking in his direction.

"Don't make the slightest move, or you're a dead man." Steel felt the hard stab of a firearm against the back of his neck; a big hand slammed his face against the door, flattening his nose and lips against the surface. He brought his elbow round, smashing it into the unseen man's neck. Hearing the grunt and the clatter of the automatic weapon hitting the tiled floor, he sprang around. At the same moment the door hit him full in the back, sending him sprawling on top of his first assailant, who lay still beneath him. He reached for the weapon.

"I wouldn't if I were you." A large boot landed on his hand, another kicked the weapon noisily across the tiled floor.

The agent looked up into the barrel of a Kalashnikov and then further up into the eyes of Colonel Boris Kiev.

"On your feet Mr Steel, and please, do try something stupid. You're going to die anyway and the mess will be easier to clean up from these tiles," the Russian said with a sneer. Steel needed no more convincing. He was led away, and out through the main entrance.

Hank had heard the two bangs from along the hallway. He peered out after the first one to see Kiev push the door of the kitchenette violently, then entered the room carrying an automatic weapon. Within seconds he saw the figure of the British agent come out of the room with his hands on his head; fingers interlocked. Kiev was close behind with the gun at his hip. Hank watched as they disappeared across the main reception.

He and Michael ran to the room that Kiev had just left. The door was open. There was the body of a man sprawled across the floor, another automatic rifle some feet away. Hank bent down to the man on the floor.

"Get the weapon Michael." He felt for the man's neck pulse.

"He won't be bothering anybody again," he said, taking the firearm from Michael.

"Come on let's move," he added, shoving his colleague who stared down transfixed at the corpse. Within seconds they were climbing the massive stairs, gold and crimson everywhere. Gold covered frames of portraits from the past hung on the towering walls amidst enormous, expensive handmade rugs. Glistening, sparkling chandeliers hung from the ceiling on great long chains like a myriad of crystalised rain drops suspended in time and the carpets on the floor were so thick they almost seemed bottomless.

Soon they were at the top of the stairs. Peering around the corner Hank saw no movements and beckoned Michael to follow. They had gone perhaps twenty feet along the hallway when they heard the noise of a door handle being turned. They dived into an alcove without hesitation, falling headlong onto a velvet couch.

Hank looked out and saw the rear of a man walking in the opposite direction. He wore a crimson silk dressing gown and had slippers on his feet. His blonde curly hair was damp as though he'd just stepped out of the shower. They heard him knock on a door. He entered and the door closed behind him.

"Come on let's move." said Hank.

"I don't think I can take much more of this; the pressure is killing me," said Michael.

"Come on, we're nearly there," was the curt reply as Hank took off down the hallway. He stopped at the door where the blonde man had come from and listened with his ear to the door for a few seconds, then slowly turned the handle and opened it. They went quickly into the darkened room, closing the door behind them.

Steel was taken into the warehouse via the side ramp and was firmly tied to the same pillar that had accommodated Kiev earlier.

"Now, Mr Steel, we have no time to waste, so start talking. I'm not even going to flatter you with interrogation. In your case, the days of pulling out fingernails, electric shock, or even truth injections are gone.

Either you talk, or you don't. If you don't, I'll kill you. Talk to my men. As you Brit's say, I have to 'see a man about a dog'; actually it's two men." He smirked as he walked out of the area. He turned about fifty feet away.

"Where's your old friend from the CIA? Is he around somewhere? If he has any sense he will be long gone." His footsteps echoed as he walked off into the distance.

"Well guv, you 'erd wot the man said, an' 'ee don't joke very often. If I was you mate I'd do wot 'ee arsked or 'ee'l blow yer away wivart a second fort. Oh, an' by the way, he said ter give yer this."

The man shot a round straight into the agent's left knee. Steel screamed in agony, then passed out, slumping against the concrete pillar. The big cockney then felt into Steel's waistcoat pocket, pulling out the two-way radio. He pulled out the earphone connector, saw that the radio was turned on and pressed the talk button

"You there, can you hear me?" he asked in a harsh low whisper. There was no reply. He repeated the same words; still there was no reply. The cockney heard static, but nothing else. He threw the radio down on top of a packing case.

"Get me some water," he said to his colleague. "This bastard has some talking to do."

Reilly stood on the ladder, his body perpendicular to the wall, his forehead and eyes protruding over the top, the radio in his left hand. It too rested on top of the wall. He had seen no movement since Steel had gone into the building. Then he got static on the two-way; the radio crackled again.

"Get on your feet Mr Steel." He couldn't make out the voice, but he had heard the words before the radio had begun to squelch again. He listened, turning up the volume as high as he dared. Then he heard more static. As the static stopped he thought he heard words, very faintly.

All of Kevin Reilly's instincts told him not to speak. He resisted the urge by taking his hand away from the radio. *Now what? That stupid SOB has gone and gotten into trouble. I damn well knew it.*

"Goddamn it, I knew I shouldn't have come back here," he whispered under his breath, his teeth clenched in anger. He came down the ladder quickly, walked further along the hedge way, and then stooped, crossing to the rental car.

Hank and Michael stood inside the darkened room in the living quarters of the chateau, their eyes slowly becoming accustomed to the blackness inside. They dare not turn on a light for fear of attracting attention. Hank cursed himself for not having hidden the flashlight.

"What do you think will happen next? Whose room do you think this is?" Michael whispered

"Wait here, I'll see if I can throw a little light on the subject." whispered Hank, moving off into the darkness. A dull light came on behind what looked like a bar to Michael. Gravitating towards both Hank and the welcome glow, he was soon starting to get his bearings. In a very short space of time they scouted the suite. It was very spacious with a large sitting room, two bedrooms, two bathrooms, a kitchen and a sauna. Hank tapped his forefinger across his lips and led Michael into the unused of the two bedrooms. He turned on the bedside light and proceeded to check the room for bugs.

"It's as clean as I can see without electronic sweeping." he whispered. "Now we wait." Turning out both the light behind the bar and that the one in the bedroom, they sat on the bed with the door ajar, and waited. Hank could hear heavier breathing as Michael began to nod off as he sat there. After what seemed an age, Hank's nerves rattled as he heard the click of metal when a ringed finger hit the door handle to the room. The door opened. He heard voices in the hallway, the sound of door to the suite closing and the bolt locked.

Hank put his hand over Michael's mouth as he awoke from his half sleep. The sitting room now flooded with light. They could hear the clink of glass and the sound of liquid being poured, the distinctive rattle and plop of ice, then silence.

Hank walked directly towards the light as it streamed through the partially opened door.

Boris Kiev had left the warehouse and was returning into the chateau by way of the main entrance. He wanted to check the grounds first before he attended to the interfering policeman and his friend. He stood for a while peering into the darkness of the garages, then turned as he heard the sounds of footsteps coming through the undergrowth, accompanied by the sounds of a panting dog. He waited until the man approached, and then shone his lamp unkindly into the face of the guard. The dog snarled, his yellow eyes reflected the bright light. The man reported to Kiev, and then went on his way.

The Russian stood at the edge of the undergrowth for some minutes, letting his eyes become used to the darkness, he moved towards the bushes as he thought he'd heard the snap of a twig underfoot. He took two tentative steps forward.

The next snapping sound he heard very loud and clear was the sound of his own neck breaking. Then there was nothing left for Colonel Boris Kiev but blackness. As his limp dead body crashed heavily into the thick undergrowth, two stiff fingers pressed into the side of his neck and felt no pulse.

"Well then, how do you like them apples, Boris? There's many a good tune played on an old fiddle, so I suppose one of us had to go sooner or later," said the voice of Kevin Reilly, the veins on the side of his neck straining as he dragged the heavy corpse further into the deep foliage.

"I seem to remember telling you before not to underestimate your opponent. You see what happens, when you ignore good advice, colonel!" The Russian stared up through unseeing eyes.

Reilly closed Boris Kiev's eyelids for the last time and chopped off a quick salute for old times' sake, and then disappeared into the darkness. In seconds he approached the door to the warehouse.

"Damn!" he hissed, pushing against the locked door. He heard voices from the inside, then footsteps running fast across the concrete floor of the warehouse. As he moved into the darkness at the corner of the ramp, the door burst open. He recognised the figure of the big cockney man as he rushed up the slope.

"'Ave you seen the guvnor?" the cockney asked the man with the dog.

"Yes, he was here just a minute ago," answered the guard. The big man ran up into the chateau and along the hallway, passing the room with the body on the floor and ran towards the laundry room. Finding the door ajar, he rushed inside the empty room, and then exited quickly, moving up the stairs and striding along the corridor.

He spoke to a blonde-haired man in a dressing gown coming in the opposite direction.

"'Ave you seen the colonel, sir? "

"No, not since much earlier this evening," replied the other man, opening the door to a room and entering as he spoke. The big man went to the security surveillance room. A man sat with his head resting on his arms, which were folded on the desk in front of him.

"Wake up, you stupid bastard!" he shook the man violently.

"'Ave you seen the guv?" The other man, still half asleep had no time to reply as the big man went to leave the room. He turned in the doorway.

"Keep your eyes on the job, you lazy git. If I catch yer kipping on the job agen I swear I'll soddin' well shoot yer miself." He slammed the door then went off down the hallway, an automatic weapon in his hand.

Reilly waited a few seconds, listening outside the door. He could hear a distant voice inside as he moved through the doorway. The darkness was almost total as he crept alongside the stored equipment. He was working purely on memory for the first few feet, and then as his eyes began to adjust, he saw the glow of light coming from the area of the office.

He decided to give the office a wide berth and approach it from behind. He heard the shrill tones of the telephone, followed by a man's voice. Coming up towards the petitioned walls he paused, trying to hear what the man inside was saying. His heart nearly came out of his chest. A few feet away from him there was sudden heavy breathing and agonising moans. In the darkness he saw the dim figure of someone tied to one of the roof supports.

"What about this one here?" he heard the man in the office say. "No, I can't get a bloody word out of him. He's a tough bugger this one. OK, I'll come right out. Where are you?... Be right with you, mate."

Reilly heard the man's footsteps heading towards the exit. He moved with caution as he approached the man whose moans were becoming louder.

The CIA man looked into the bloodied face of David Steel. His lips busted, one eye was completely closed and there was a large gash across his forehead. He seemed barely conscious. He had slid down the support, almost into a crouching position. The American moved closer, but in so doing, his right leg hit the left knee of the MI6 man.

His scream could have been heard in Paris.

"You stupid bastard, mind my leg. Where the bloody hell have you been anyway? I thought you were never going to get here," he hissed through clenched teeth. "Pull me upright and get these cuffs off my hands." He groaned in pain as Reilly pulled him up by the armpits.

"What happened to the leg?" Reilly asked.

"That cockney prick shot me in the knee cap, I think." Reilly went into the office and found an open first aid kit on the desk. Alongside were a pocket flashlight and a bunch of keys. He returned, selected the key of the cuffs, released Steel's wrists, and then bent down and tore the leg of Steel's pants. Steel winced in pain.

"Keep still. You're in luck. He didn't hit the knee cap; the wound is about an inch above," he added, binding a tight bandage around the leg.

"We need to get a move on. Kiev will be back soon," he said, speaking to the top of the American's head.

"Not in this lifetime he won't. Not this night or any night for that matter."

"How's that Kev, why not?"

"He's dead old buddy. The colonel is a gonner," replied Reilly, looking up from his task.

"Can't say that bothers me too much," muttered Steel. "You waste him Kev?"

"Come on let's get the hell out of here." Steel took Reilly's failure to answer as a yes.

"Hey, not so fast, there's unfinished work to be done," Steel replied as he limped off into the office.

"Goddamn it, I knew I should never have come back here," said Reilly.

"I never thought your face could look so good, you ugly old bugger," Steel whispered from the darkness.

"Come on, there isn't much time left."

Upstairs in the Suite

Just as Hank reached the bedroom doorway, he heard a loud knock on the door of the suite. The door was opened slowly.

"Sorry to bother you at this hour. You haven't heard any strange noises or had anyone at the door have you, Ma'am?" Hank couldn't hear the reply as the woman had her back to him. The door was closed. Next he heard the sound of liquid being poured. With the firearm in his left hand, he peered around the partly open door of the dimly lit room.

The dark-haired woman had her back to Hank and was still wearing her dressing gown. Hank walked silently across the plush carpet. As he did so, Michael appeared in the doorway of the darkened bedroom.

"Turn around slowly and don't make a sound. I have a gun trained on you and I won't hesitate to use it."

At first the woman didn't make a move then they both saw her bandaged hand lift a glass to her lips and her head tilted back as she drained the contents. The ice rattled around in the empty glass as she carefully placed it on the bar's surface then turned very slowly towards the two of them. She flicked the raven black curls that fell on her forehead, and then looked Hank directly in the eyes. Her dark brown eyes exuded defiance. There was something about her face, about her posture that made Hank pause; something about the eyes.

"Do you mind telling me who you are, and what you are doing here?" Hank asked her. By now Michael was standing next to him intrigued, staring quizzically at the stranger. The brunette turned back to the bar, poured another drink, then spun around on her heels so quickly that Hank had the Kalashnikov aimed directly at her head. A smile broke across her face.

"I might well ask you the same question, Hank, and you too, Michael." Instantly they both recognized the voice.

"Princess Anna? Ma'am! Is this really you? But how? It can't be! Ma'am you're dead!" blurted Michael.

"A pleasure to see you, Princess Anna, it really is!" said Hank holding out his hand, then looking down at her covered hands, drew back

"How on earth did you two manage to get here?" she asked. Now there was no mistaking the voice. Michael rushed across, taking the princess's right hand in both of his. There were tears in his eyes.

"But what about the accident and the deaths and the funeral in England?

"Whoa, whoa, one thing at a time," muttered Hank. Taking Michael firmly by the shoulder he led him into the bedroom and beckoned Princess Anna to follow.

"Where is Raffi, Ma'am?" Hank asked.

"He's in another suite along the hallway," Anna replied.

"You must have had a very hard time of it. What are your plans?" asked Hank.

"It's a long story Hank, but let it suffice to say that initially all of this was done without my blessing. We were drugged, and brought away from Paris, just after we left the restaurant at the Majestic Palace Hotel, before the accident. We've been kept virtual prisoners. Decoys were put in the car, and tragically, they died. As you can see there has been extensive plastic surgery carried out, even our fingerprints have been altered," she said, holding up the evidence.

"We both agreed to it all when it was obvious that the situation had gone too far to turn back and that it had been put together by powers greater than us. But now we're planning an escape and want to make a new start, as just two ordinary people. That, of course, does not figure in the plans of Raffi's father.

"God, I'm so pleased to see you two! I was told that you, Hank had been killed and that Michael had returned to England." Suddenly there was a loud and continued knocking at the door of the suite.

"You'd better see who that is Ma'am" Princess Anna quickly went across the room to open the door. The big cockney and another man rushed right past Anna, almost knocking her to the floor.

"I say, steady on there," she shouted after the two, as they separated, entering and searching both bedrooms then coming out quickly.

"Nufink in there," shouted the big man.

"Nor here," replied the other. They ran out into the hallway. The princess turned to the empty bedroom, a worried look on her face, as Hank and Michael came from behind the drapes.

"It's OK Ma'am, we were out on the balcony, and they didn't bother to look there!"

Back in the Warehouse

Steel had disappeared into the warehouse. In minutes he returned with two automatic rifles, and half a dozen ammo clips.

"There's enough gear out there to equip a whole bloody army," he said, passing a rifle to Reilly.

"Come on, let's get this job finished and get the hell out of here." He winced as he turned on his damaged leg, and then went off limping towards the fire stairs.

"Here we go again," Reilly muttered, following the British agent through the door and up the stairs.

"In for a penny, in for a pound."

"What did you say?" Steel asked, turning slightly.

"Nothing really. I was just thinking out loud."

"You can get taken away to the funny farm for talking to yourself," remarked the MI6 man, as he dragged his leg painfully up each step. They came out onto the hallway and moved along towards the main foyer, as automatic gunfire opened up behind them.

Reilly saw Steel fall to the floor, and threw himself into an open door landing on top of the body of a man. He crawled slowly back to the doorway, pushed the automatic around the door and sprayed the hallway.

He heard the gasp, he looked round the corner to see his assailant crash to the ground with half his face missing. He lay there twitching in the final throes. Across the hallway, the figure of Steel lay against the wall. Reilly checked the area first, and then went across to him. Steel lay in a twisted position, blood running from the corner of his mouth, his eyes already beginning to cloud over.

"Go get those bastards, Kevin," his voice croaked, as blood ran down his chin and into his ear. "Get 'em boy. Everybody in this building must be wiped out and that's an order. Everyone! Not one person must be left alive, you hear me?" Trying to get up as he spoke, he coughed and began to drown as his lungs filled with his own blood. His body went limp and his eyes finally settled into a fixed stare on Reilly's face.

"I don't really think so, my old buddy, slaughter's not my game. Bye. My debts are paid. Nice knowing you."

Reilly chopped off his second farewell salute in the space of minutes, checked the firearm in his hands then returned to the door of the fire stairs, quickly exiting the bloody scene.

Meanwhile, in the suite upstairs, they all looked startled as they heard the rattle of automatic gunfire somewhere below in the building. Hank noticed the rows of suitcases lined up in the foyer of the suite.

"Princess Anna, if you are to get out of here, it won't be easy. You will most certainly not be able to take this stuff with you Ma'am."

"They were planning to move us tomorrow, Hank. I think we were to spend time in Egypt until things had quietened down."

"Where were you planning to go, Ma'am?"

"We thought that maybe we would rent a small estate somewhere out in the country at first, then play it by ear."

"I really think you should get Raffi, and that we should be on our way Ma'am."

"We? Do you mean that you two will come along with us?" she said excitedly.

"That's if you don't mind having a dead man and a deserter along?"

"Hey, not so much of the deserter," Michael added. Princess Anna picked up the phone.

"I think you should go across there, Ma'am, and not use the phone. Michael will go with you; I'll keep a lookout," said Hank. He opened the door, peering out into the hallway.

"It's all clear, but be as quick as you can, Ma'am." Within minutes and after hasty whispered greetings to the blonde-haired blue-eyed Raffi from Hank and Michael, they followed Hank along the hallway then down the main staircase. They went towards the fire escape stairs, covering this part of the escape without incident. Standing in the stairwell at the top, they paused. Hank spoke quickly to the couple before they took off down the stairs.

"When we get to the bottom, I will go out first. If the way is clear I will come back and get you." They descended the stairs hastily. Hank turned, just before he opened the door at the bottom.

"Remember Michael, if anyone comes in here other than me, either behind you on the stairs or through this door, you shoot first, is that clear?"

"Yes Hank, quite clear," Michael answered hesitantly taking the weapon from Hank.

Reilly by now had found his way out of the building, and was taking stock of the situation from his hiding place in the bushes well beyond the garage block. A guard walked past some ten feet away holding the leash of a big and stocky rottweiler. *I hope I'm down wind of him*, he thought to himself, an involuntary attack of the shivers briefly covering his body. Then the man came running back from the undergrowth, shouting.

"The boss's dead, somebody's killed the colonel!" He ran towards the chalet, his big dog close at heel. After that, everything seemed to happen at once. Suddenly floodlights came on throughout the grounds. The big cockney stood at the top of the steps to the chateau, surrounded by five men, three with dogs. He waved his arms issuing instructions, realising that he was in charge now. He seemed to have adopted a different posture as he towered above the others.

"Yes, there are at least three of them on the loose, so you keep those gates locked. Don't open them for anyone and I mean anyone. That even includes Mr Sahaed himself. Turn on every sensor, make sure all firearms are loaded and shoot to kill," he screamed down the cell phone at the main gate. The group had now dispersed into the grounds.

Kevin Reilly knew that life was to become more difficult as he retrieved the infrared goggles from under the bushes, right where he had left them. He knew that without them he had little chance of reaching the perimeter undetected. He knew he still risked the chance of being rottweilered to death in the process. He set off through the undergrowth, keeping as close to the driveway as possible, without being seen.

Meanwhile, below in the warehouse, Hank had taken quick stock of the situation. Checking the escape route he'd opened the door to the outside, to hear the guard shouting the news of Kiev's death. *That's one problem less, but I wonder who killed him? Must have been the MI6 man,* he thought to himself; *all the more reason to get us all out of here quickly.*

He moved about the warehouse, climbing amongst the ammunition section then returned to the others. Tapping on the door before entering, he found them all standing white faced in the dull glow of the light bulb.

"Come quickly; follow me to the door." They did as he commanded. At the door, Hank turned to Michael.

"Now, this is what I want you to do Michael: you know where the garage is, so I want you to take Princess Anna and Raffi into the garage, but go behind into the undergrowth first. If it's clear, then take them inside the garage, then all of you get straight into the limo. Michael you are to drive. I found a spare key under the driver's floor mat earlier; it's still there. Keep out of sight, but be ready to leave immediately. I believe the vehicle is bulletproof. You will see and hear three explosions. As soon as you hear the first one, drive like a bat out of hell towards the main gate. Don't be alarmed by any other goings on, and Michael, don't stop for anything, or anyone. Drive at them if necessary. I should be at the gate when you get there. If I'm not, you must carry on. Your only concern now is to get these two to safety. If I'm not at the gate, go to the hotel and wait there." With that he slipped off quickly into the foliage.

Hank moved as quickly as he could. He knew that there would be heat sensors and having no infrared glasses, he was at their mercy. All that he could do was look in the places that he himself would have put sensors. He had got about half way when he heard snarling, growling and crashing through the undergrowth, then shots.

"Over here! I've got one of them, over here," shouted a voice, then more shots.

Kevin Reilly was making good progress. He could now see the perimeter wall in the distance, so he raised the night glasses to get a clearer view. Perspiring heavily, he raised his hand to wipe the stinging liquid from his eyes. One of the attack dogs saw the movement of his hand and in a flash it shot out of the bushes. With its teeth bared, all 120 pounds hit him full in the chest. At the same time a bright light hit him between the eyes as he disappeared backwards into the thick bushes. He shot directly into the savage dog's mouth, disintegrating its head. It never felt a thing.

Bullets peppered the ground around him as he rolled over and over. Then there was silence. *Where the hell is that son of a bitch?* the American thought to himself, *come on, show yourself.* Then the bright light came on again.

"I've got one of them over here," shouted the man just as Reilly sprayed bullets around the halo of light. He pulled down the night glasses over his eyes and moved off quickly into the darkness, as voices and lights converged on the area.

Hank seized the opportunity of the diversion with both hands. The distraction allowed him to come to the edge of the drive, away from alarm sensors and to run at top speed the remainder of the way to the gatehouse, where he arrived with lungs about to burst.

Moving behind the small building, he dropped to his knees. He placed Semtex strategically under the structure then listened with his ear placed to the wooden walls. There was only one man inside, who came out to see what all the commotion was, looking into the grounds with night sight covering one eye. Hank crept to the other side of the hut and began placing the explosive around the hinges of the big gate and then in the centre. After inserting the detonators he moved back into hiding.

Wisely or not, Reilly had decided to leave the rope ladder hanging down the inside of the wall.   He held his breath in anticipation as he approached the area. "If there is a God in heaven, please let it be there," he whispered aloud. He sighed with relief as he reached for the rope. He climbed the rungs as fast as he could go, chills coursing up and down his spine, waiting for the sound of gunfire from behind, or the inevitable thud of a bullet in the back, but it never came.

Michael looked at his watch as he sat in the driver's seat of the limo. It had been eight minutes since Hank had left; it seemed more like an hour. His two passengers had not spoken a word and now there was gunfire going off everywhere. He had almost started the engine after the first shots.

"Come on, Hank, come on, for God's sake," he whispered through clenched teeth. He ducked down behind the dash as a man ran across the front of the open garage, rifle in hand.

The night sky lit the grounds as the first big explosion shook the still air.

"Here we go, hold tight," he shouted through the open divider. A silent prayer was followed by a twist of the key, then a roar of the engine. Tyres screamed as the big car leapt out into the mad night. Burning rubber hung in the air in the wake of the limousine. Another almighty explosion shattered the air, this time behind them. Princess Anna looked out to see that most of the chalet had gone. The car was being hammered by flying debris, which was landing all over the lawns and drive. It was like a scene from a World War II bombing raid — a picture of absolute devastation.

The third massive explosion was by the gates as the limo headed that way. A man ran across the drive in front of the speeding vehicle, which was travelling too fast to stop. He was hit by the front bumper and went cart-wheeling through the air like a rag doll, right over the back of the limousine. Michael still did not waver from his task.

The scene at the gate was that of more carnage. Not only was the gate gone, but so was the guardhouse, along with a good length of the boundary wall. With headlights blazing, the big car bumped and crashed over large pieces of stone and debris.

"Look, he's there, over there on the other side of the road!" the princess yelled at the top of her voice. They all saw Hank in the glare of the limo's headlamps. He was waving them on frantically.

The car lurched and screeched out of the entrance, dragging along a large piece of masonry in front of the rear wheel, which fell away as Michael pulled up to collect Hank.

"Go, go!" yelled Hank as he landed heavily onto the front passenger seat.

Not a word was spoken as they drove down the hill. Michael kept an eye on the rear view mirror as the long clumsy vehicle veered and screeched hideously round the bends in the narrow road. Nobody followed. The road behind was completely deserted.

"I think you can slow down a little my friend, the worst is over now," Hank said as he placed his hand on Michael's shoulder. He looked round into the shaken, but grateful, new faces of the princess and Raffi.

Two days later, Kevin Reilly sat in the first class section of the Continental Airlines 767 bound for New York. He had a connecting flight to Arlington. He could see nothing but cloud below. He sighed and took an extra deep slug of the large Johnny Walker Black Label that sat on the table in front of him. He pulled out the leg rest and settled back into the sumptuous leather seat. His newspaper lay across the unoccupied seat next to him. **Billionaire Arms Dealer's Home Totally Destroyed,** was the front-page heading.

The article went on to say that a series of unexplained and mysterious explosions had totally destroyed one of the homes of a well known international arms dealer. A number of bodies had been found, but no-one was able to give an explanation. International terrorism was most certainly suspected.

"Mind if I join you, Mr Reilly?" the agent looked up to see the face of Sir Martin Fields.

"I most certainly do mind, and anyway, can't you see the seat is occupied.

"You're going to have to talk to me sooner or later," said the Englishman.

"As it happens there is nothing that I can tell you, other than a lot of people are dead, including your man, Steel. As for me, I'm just about to write my letter of resignation."

"I'm afraid I don't believe you, sir," replied the MI6 chief, arrogantly.

"I don't give a goddamn what you believe or think, your sirship. Now get out of my face before I have you reported to the captain for the harassment of an American citizen. You are on American territory whilst on this aircraft you know!"

The agency chief leaned over the empty seat, clinked a miniature bottle of Johnny Walker Black Label against Reilly's empty whisky tumbler.

"Cheers, dear boy. Do have this one on me. It's the least we can offer you." he said with a sarcastic smirk on his face, shaking his head from side to side as he spun round and returned to his seat at the rear of the section.

The flow of traffic had ground to a complete standstill. Police strobe lights were exaggerated by the heavy rains as they flashed, piercing the dark evening sky, making any movements reminiscent of an old silent film. The fire truck and paramedics' ambulance had blasted their sirens, forcing their way doggedly through the heavy traffic toward their target; a solitary taxi cab.

It stood alone and isolated in the outskirts of Langley, Virginia, with both rear doors wide open as though it had been evacuated in a hurry. People milled around silently, nosily and ghoulishly watching as only sightseers do, now from beneath the shelter of their umbrellas as the rains poured down relentlessly. The rescue vehicles were now silenced; an inquisitive by-stander broke the eerie quiet as he shouted across to a cabbie standing there, looking irritated and impatient.

"What happened here then, buddy?"

"I picked the guy up at the airport. He never spoke after he gave me his destination. Later I did the usual check in the mirror, couldn't see him, and then saw he was slumped across the back seat. I stopped and went to see if he was alright. Luckily there was a doctor in the car next to mine. I don't know why I say luckily, for when he came to help he said the guy had died instantly."

The paramedics slowly strapped the body bag to the gurney then began closing up the long zipper as large raindrops formed into globules trickling continually down the still, white face of CIA agent, Kevin Reilly.

Epilogue

Two Years Later, Somewhere on the French-Italian Border

The late afternoon sun reflected from the thick white walls of the old villa. Farm buildings and cottages spread over the lush green pastures while cattle grazed lazily in the distance as two fine examples of thoroughbred horseflesh cropped the short grass in the meadow, their tails swishing rhythmically at the pestilent summer flies.

Some dust hung temporarily in the air as the Range Rover pulled up to the front of the big house. A tanned and healthy-looking blonde man climbed out and walked round to the passenger side door. He stood and assisted a beautiful dark-haired woman out of the car. She appeared to be about six months pregnant.

They walked slowly towards the house with his arm around her shoulder, just as a twin-engine plane flew so low overhead it nearly took the chimney pots along with it.

The couple stopped, looking skywards waving and smiling happily. The plane landed in the distance then taxied up to a building outside the back of the villa. The dark-haired woman walked across to the plane and pulled the steps down as Michael Meadows climbed out into the bright sunlight.

"Did you have good trip, Michael?"

"Splendid thanks, Anna. Where's Hank?"

"Oh, he's just done a deal with that big dairy. We're increasing the herd ten-fold," Anna said, smiling as they walked towards the house together, with Anna's arm placed lightly around Michael's shoulder supporting herself.

"How was England?" asked the princess.

"Pretty much the same as ever, Anna. Little has changed — just the same really."

"I miss it a lot, Michael. I miss my boys terribly. But I don't miss the publicity and the pressure. I have to resign myself to the fact that my sons George and Edward, were born to be royals and I never was. At least I get to see them on television regularly. I'm so proud of them."

"What's in the news?" she asked as Michael passed her copies of the British papers.

"Well, you're still quite dead, though they can't say whether it was an accident or not. Your charity funds are worth multi-millions and all of your causes are being kept up."

Anna put her other arm around the neck of a smiling blond-haired Raffi as he joined the couple.

"Here, have a commemorative mug of yourself, Anna."

The princess roared with laughter, as Michael passed a Wedgewood mug bearing Anna's image. Looking at the effigy she said:

"I think maybe I prefer the blonde hair. How about you, darling?" she said to Raffi.

"It's good to be alive and to be surrounded by friends and loved ones," he smiled, kissing Anna lovingly on her cheek.

Michael watched them walk slowly towards the villa, Anna's head on Raffi's shoulder. He patted the fuselage of the Navajo, picked up his bag and then followed them into the villa.

It was a far cry from the pomp and ceremony of Buckingham Palace. Hank pulled up in the open truck, high above the estate. He'd watched the scene through high-powered binoculars

At least they are happy and safe from harm and treachery. Free from the paparazzi and publicity, he thought as he climbed back into the cab of the truck.

But were they? And if so, for how long?

Enjoy other mystery novels written by Mike Rollin.

Black Gold
Mayhem in Paradise
Vengeance

Read a synopsis of each of these thrillers on the web site.
mrlproductions.net